Where Are the Victors?

Where Are the Victors?

Where Are the Victors?

A Novel by
Donald Richie

Charles E. Tuttle Co.: Publishers
Rutland, Vermont & Tokyo, Japan

Representatives

For Continental Europe:
Boxerbooks, Inc., Zurich

For the British Isles:
Prentice-Hall International, Inc., London

For Australasia:
Bookwise International
1 Jeanes Street, Beverley 5009, South Australia

Published by the Charles E. Tuttle Company, Inc.
of Rutland, Vermont & Tokyo, Japan
with editorial offices at
Suido 1-chome, 2-6, Bunkyo-ku, Tokyo

Library of Congress Catalog Card No. 55-10624
International Standard Book No. 0-8048-1512-7

Originally published in 1956
under the title This Scorching Earth
First printing, 1986

Printed in Japan

Preface

IN THIS YEAR OF THE FORTIETH ANNIVERSARY OF THE END
of World War II, and of the beginning of the Allied
Occupation of Japan, I am pleased that my 1956 novel
about this latter event is being reissued—and is appearing for the first time under its original title.

Back then it was perhaps felt that *Where Are the
Victors?* was too provocative a title, since it seemed to
suggest that the losers were not entirely vanquished. Also
there was the implication that the winner of a war is also
in some measure the loser.

Now, forty years later, one often hears people wondering just who won the Pacific War anyway. What I had thought to be a paradox has become a commonplace. Japan's winning of major postwar economic battles has made many forget its wartime military defeats.

Perhaps this is the reason that interest in the Occupation period continues. People wonder what happened and why. This is also perhaps why my novel, originally written as novelistic journalism, is now read as history.

It is reliable, as far as it goes. It is a connected series of portraits of people and places during those few years which saw the greatest head-on cultural collision of modern times. I happened to be there and I sketched what I saw. But I did not see everything. The bias of the journalist and the inclination of the novelist left lots out.

Strange—this world was so alive when I was writing of it in 1948. And the Occupation was still going on when I was finishing this book in 1953. There are histories, to be sure, and artifacts in archives, but this book is perhaps all that remains to describe the texture of life during this Occupation, what it "felt" like.

And so I now see, though I did not know it at the time, that I was really writing history, that I was in a way—a biased, partial way—preserving this strange, infuriating, admirable Allied Occupation of Japan.

Donald Richie
1985

Where Are the Victors?

The cities in ruin,
The land made waste,
Foxes and badgers now
Where armies once fought.

Where are the vanquished?
Where are the victors?

—*Early Chinese Poem*

part 1

TOKYO LAY DEEP UNDER A BANK OF CLOUDS WHICH
moved slowly out to sea as the sun rose higher.
Between the moving clouds were sections of the
city: the raw gray of whole burned blocks spotted
with the yellow surfaces of new-cut wood and the
shining, felt-like tile of recently constructed roofs,
the reds and browns of sections unburnt, the dusty
green of scarcely damaged parks, and the shallow blue
of occasional ornamental lakes. In the middle was
the Palace, moated and rectangular, gray outlined with

green, the city stretching to the horizons all around it.

The smokes of household fires, of newly renovated factories, of the waiting, charcoal-burning taxis rose into the air, and in the nostril-stinging freshness of early autumn the bitter-yellow smell of burning cedar shavings blended with the odor of roasting chestnuts. In the houses bedding was folded into closets, and the mats were swept. Beneath the hanging pillars of the early-rising smoke there was the morning sound of night-shutters thrust back into the houses' narrow walls.

Behind the banging of the shutters was the sound of wooden geta—the faint percussive sound of walking—and the distant bronze booming of a temple bell. Jeeps exploded into motion, and the tinny clang of streetcars sounded above the bleatings of the nearby fishing boats. A phonograph was running down — Josephine Baker went from contralto to baritone—and a radio militantly delivered the Japanese news of the day.

A few MP's in pairs still strode the partly empty streets, and a single geisha, modest in bright red and rustling silk, hurried, knees together, to her waiting morning-tea. Greer Garson luxuriated, her paper face half in the morning sun, and a man dressed like Charlie Chaplin, a placard on his shoulders, began his daily advertising.

In the alleys the pedicabs all stood motionless, and around the dying alley fires the all-night drivers yawned and warmed their hands both in the fires and in the morning sun. The early farmers led their horses through the city.

An empty Occupation bus, with "Dallas" stenciled neatly on both sides, made its customary stops—the PX, the Commissary, the Motor Pool—but no one rode. The driver, in cast-off fatigues, smoked one of the longer butts from the several packets he had. An Occupation lady, very early or else very late, tried unsuccessfully to hail a passing jeep.

The blank windows of the taller buildings now caught the rising morning sun and cast reflections—a silver flash of spectacles, a passing golden tooth, or the dead white of a mouth-mask. The food shops opened, and the spicy bitterness of pickled radish mingled with the soft and delicate putrescence of fish, mingled with the odors of the passing night-soil carrier, his oxen, and his cart.

The rolled metal shutters of the smaller shops were locked, but before the open entrances of larger buildings MP's stood and waited, their white-gloved hands behind their backs, their white helmets above their white faces. They stood before the main Occupation buildings, opposite the Palace, across the street and moat—the gray Dai Ichi Building, the square Meiji Building, the tall and pale Taisho Building, and the squat Yusen. To the south rose the box-like Radio Tokyo and, in all directions, the billets of the Occupation. The American flag floated high above them all.

The clouds had drifted out to sea, and the city lay beneath the sun. The pedicab drivers went home, and the carpenters began their work; the geisha sleepily sipped their tea, and the housewives served the morning soup. The railroads, holding the city in their net, brought more and more people into the stations and then returned to bring yet more. The sun and smoke rose into the air, and the radios shouted into the sky, while the streetcars rattled, and the auto horns honked, and the fishing boats cried, and the railroads filled up the city.

■

The Saturday-morning train for Tokyo on the Yokosuka line left Yokohama Station precisely at six-thirty. At every station passengers had crowded on, and past Yokohama there was never any room. This did not bother Sonoko. She lived at Zushi, and the train, leaving precisely at six, was always half-empty. She could always sit next to a window, either studying her *Basic GI English in 12 Simple Steps* or just thinking. Her preference was for the latter, and as a consequence her English was not too advanced. This morning both pleasures were denied her, because Mrs. Odawara, from the house across the street, had taken the seat beside her. For half an hour they had talked of nothing but the party.

"My, how lovely it will be," said Mrs. Odawara for the twelfth time. Sonoko had unwillingly invited both her and her family after the second time. Now Mrs. Odawara felt a proprietary interest and kept adding little touches here and there. "I'll bring some sushi, and we have some saké left—oh, no, it's no imposition at all."

"My parents and I shall remain forever grateful," said Sonoko formally, wishing she had never breathed a word about the party to Mrs. Odawara. The thought of its finally occurring had made her talkative, had made her forget that people like Mrs. Odawara are always waiting to pounce upon extraordinary social occasions and make them their own. Since this was going to be so very extraordinary an occasion, she'd had no choice but to invite her.

"But are there enough guests to do the American proper honor?"

Any more and there wouldn't be room in the house. All of Sonoko's relatives—and now the Odawaras! This party wasn't going to be at all what she'd originally planned. It was to have been something intimate, comfortable, democratic, with only a few speeches by her father and a well-organized schedule of parlor games. Now she would rather not have the party at all. But it was too late. The invitation had been accepted; her father had bought an extra saké ration; her mother was assembling the ingredients for "mother-and-child"—a lovely dish which used both the egg and the chicken, to say nothing of frightening quantities of black-market rice—and her brother was cleaning the entire house.

"Yes, there are enough people, I think," said Sonoko.

"But you must remember your position with the Americans, dear Sonoko. This is an important occasion. This may well further your Career!"

Mrs. Odawara knew all about careers, for she had had several. She had been an Emancipated Woman in the Taisho Era, and during early Showa had been one of the first suffragettes in the country. She wore lipstick and silk stockings right through the great Kanto earthquake, and often said so. Then she'd been married twice. She'd even had a divorce, of which she was intensely proud, even though it turned out later not to be legal. At present she was campaigning for birth control.

Sonoko smiled and nodded politely. It might indeed help her career. Ever since she had begun to work for the Americans she had dreamed of becoming a career girl, American-style. In fact, the dream was already becoming true. Since getting the job with the Occupation she had begun to enjoy privileges at home which had never been hers as a schoolgirl. She was, to be sure, supplementing the family income, but that was not the real reason. It was that she was working for the Americans. There were a few Zushi girls who were employed by the nearby Military Government unit, but it was Sonoko alone who made the daily one-hour train trip to the city, and it was she who came back with stories of American kindness, generosity, and nobility which far surpassed those her high-school friends working for the MG could contribute.

And that wasn't all. She had come back one day, for example, with the blouse and skirt, both brand-new from the PX, that Miss Gramboult had given her. The family had been highly gratified by this typically American bit of prodigality and could not admire the blouse enough nor too often finger the luxurious texture of the skirt. Her mother had clasped her hands in admiration, both of the clothing and of her child, and her father had spent far too much in obtaining a basket of ruddy apples to take to the kind American in return. The lovely Miss Gramboult had been so touched that she had actually kissed Sonoko, who thereafter did not wash that cheek for three days.

"One never knows the results of such things," Sonoko answered politely. "It might well assist my career, or it might not."

"Well, it certainly won't unless you put sufficient thought into it," said Mrs. Odawara. Her tone was not nearly so domineering as usual. She was thinking. Sonoko guessed that she was working at further party details, anxious to extract the last morsel of instruction and enjoyment from the American's visit.

Everyone thoroughly misunderstood Sonoko's real purpose in inviting the American lady to her house. They all took for granted that she herself would derive eventual benefit from the visit. But to Sonoko that aspect made no difference whatever. It might have done so if the invited guest had been Miss Gramboult, who had already proved herself generous to an almost idiotic degree, or any other of the ladies in the hotel. But this guest was very special—it was *Miss Wilson*.

Miss Wilson was more than her employer—she was her friend. Though Sonoko loved all the American ladies dearly, it was Miss Wilson whom she loved the most, even though, oddly enough, it was Miss Wilson alone who had given her no presents beyond the usual Saturday-morning candy bars. It was something much stronger than gifts that bound them together. It was their Souls.

Like Sonoko, Miss Wilson could not be called pretty. Though she did not wear steel-rimmed glasses and did not have to hide her teeth with her hand when she smiled, as did Sonoko, her mouth was too large, even by American standards, and her eyes stuck out a bit far. She had what was called a good shape, however, and her legs were very long. Sonoko admired both these attributes, which she unfortunately did not possess herself, but not to the extent of feeling any the less affection for their happy owner.

But perhaps the strongest of Miss Wilson's many attractions was that she was worldly. Sonoko knew that she was the secretary of a colonel, that she went to parties at the French Mission, that she went often to the American Club, that she belonged to some very exclusive literary organization called the Book-of-the-Month Club, and that her parents were actually Baptists. Also—and this was Romantic—many times over she had been seen escorted by handsome and gentlemanly men. All of them were, naturally, officers. Sonoko could not imagine her going out with an enlisted man, and that just proved how superior Miss Wilson was. If General MacArthur went with women—other than Mrs. MacArthur of course—he would probably choose to go with Miss Wilson. Sonoko was sure of that!

Then, Miss Wilson always dressed like the ladies in those fashion magazines of which she owned so many and over which the plump Sonoko pored hopelessly every afternoon when her work was finally done. And she had seven pairs of shoes—Sonoko had counted them—all of them high-heeled, with not a sensible pair in the lot. And that proved how really sophisticated Miss Wilson was. She was, in fact, everything Sonoko ever hoped to be, and that was the reason they were soul-mates, and *that* was the reason Sonoko loved her so much.

"There are no men," said Mrs. Odawara suddenly.

Sonoko, caught with tears of emotion in her eyes, looked at her lap and said: "Well, there's your husband and my father and brother—"

"No unattached men," Mrs. Odawara explained impatiently.

Mrs. Odawara knew all about the desirability of unattached men, just as she knew all about a career for the emancipated woman. This naturally gave her an enormous amount of prestige and an enviable reputation for being progressive. Of course, during the war her reputation had counted against her, but she had overcome that obstacle by working in a factory and staging anti-American demonstrations. She had aroused the admiration of the countryside by systematically breaking every piece of American manufactured goods which she owned. But that was in 1942. Now, over half a decade later, when just everyone smoked and wore lipstick and was progressive, Mrs. Odawara hoarded American goods and kept her reputation alive by acting as adviser on matters Western, particularly on fine points of American etiquette. Thus it was that she knew that all parties with American ladies should have as many unattached males as possible.

"Well, perhaps my brother's school friends could—"

"No good! No, someone about this lady's age. How old *is* she?"

Sonoko never could guess the age of Americans. They always looked older than they were, just as, to them, the Japanese always appeared younger. "Perhaps thirty," she suggested.

"Well, that's nice. Now, I have a nephew, my sister's boy—she was killed in the air raids, you know—and he's just twenty-eight—that's American counting—and a very well-mannered young man. Of course, he's married, but we won't invite his wife. After all, I've sort of protected him ever since dear Michiko's death."

This was just like Mrs. Odawara—no false nonsense about not mentioning death. She even made a point of standing her chopsticks up in the rice, though it was the worst kind of luck to do so. She was very advanced.

"Oh, do you really think—" began Sonoko.

"Of course I do. I'm calling on his wife today and I'll ask him. It will be quite wonderful—you'll see. The lady Wilson and my nephew will become the best of friends. Won't that be nice?"

"Very nice," said Sonoko, miserably. "I'm forever indebted for your kindness."

Mrs. Odawara took the acknowledgment with a complacent nod. She was so emancipated that she always purposely neglected making the little negative signs of self-disparagement with which anyone else would have received the thanks.

Sonoko did not want this married twenty-eight-year-old at her party. More than ever she regretted the whole business. The party seemed headed for disaster, but now it was too late to do anything about it.

The party meant nothing to her. Far more important were her delightful and personal relations with Miss Wilson. If she could only speak English well enough, she felt sure that she could tell the American lady anything, everything, and that the lady, like a wiser older sister, would understand, would console. Then Sonoko, too, might have become Miss Wilson's secret confidante, holding the doubtless many secrets of the American lady's life and guarding them with her own.

Their relations, Sonoko had finally decided at the peak of her enthusiasm, were truly democratic. Sonoko thought democracy was wonderful. Yet as she thought of the coming party, she felt a certain chill. For one thing, despite her almost daily readings in *GI English*, which she had purchased after a great amount of deliberation, her command of the language was not precisely secure. For another, the responsibilities of the party were so great that she was actually fearful for their friendship. Miss Wilson was still as lovably democratic as ever, but Sonoko felt herself becoming hopelessly feudal.

"Does he speak English?" she asked, trying to conceal her curiosity under her customary politeness. If he did, this might help the party a bit. At least Miss Wilson would have someone to talk with.

"Oh, I suppose," said Mrs. Odawara, who didn't speak English herself. She smiled patronizingly. "He too works for the Americans."

"May I ask in what capacity?"

"Yes."

"What capacity is it, please?"

"Something to do with transportation, I think."

Sonoko was relieved. If he was with Transportation and also spoke English, he could really be of help. He might be able to do Miss Wilson some favors, and she him, and they would all be friends together.

"Oh, please do invite him, Mrs. Odawara," she said, turning around in her seat.

Her companion looked at her, slightly startled. "I intended to."

Contented, Sonoko looked at the other passengers. A large farm woman with fat red hands sat opposite her, leaning forward, a large bundle of vegetables on her back. Mixed in with the vegetables was a child who, from time to time, peered through the radishes at Sonoko. Beside the seat there stood a disabled soldier, all in white, wearing his field cap and holding a crutch, his other hand on the luggage rack. His long hair was beautifully parted, and from where she sat Sonoko could smell the pomade. Near him stood several businessmen, briefcases in hand. They were noisily discussing some contract or other. They were not arguing, but were only engaged in a typical business conversation, banging their briefcases emphatically on the other passengers. Beyond them Sonoko could see yet more passengers, standing and sitting. There was room for no more. She occasionally glimpsed the car behind, the Allied Forces car, completely empty.

Sonoko did not question this fact any more than did the rest of the passengers or, for that matter, the rest of Japan. It was well and fitting that the Allied car should remain empty if there were no Allied soldiers or civilians to ride in it. The Japanese, after all, should not expect to ride in the Allied car—except the girls with the Allied soldiers, but then they really didn't count. Just as it was perfectly natural that the sidewalk snack-bar of the PX in the Hattori Building at Tokyo's busiest crossing should sell Coca-Cola and popcorn and hot dogs to the soldiers and that the little street children clustering round should get none. This was as it was and as it should be.

It never failed to delight and amuse Sonoko that truly democratic people, like Miss Wilson, should think differently. It was admirable of them, but also very amusing. Quixotic was the word she wanted, but she'd not read far in Western literature. If Sonoko had ever consciously thought about it, she would have freely admitted to herself that, had the war ended differently and were she a colonel's secretary in New York, she would think nothing of the Japanese Army's eating sushi and tempura in front of Macy's while the little children from the Bronx and Brooklyn got none. But Miss Wilson had been much upset and called the Hattori snack-bar an atrocity. When Sonoko had finally understood the word—it was the same word the Occupation-controlled papers used in speaking of the rape of Nanking—it had seemed so irresistably funny, applied as Miss Wilson applied it, that she'd giggled about it all day long. Miss Wilson was just like that proverbial American she'd heard of who possessed a heart of pure gold.

Her reveries were interrupted by Mrs. Odawara, who had also been thinking.

"We must have a Bible reading," Mrs. Odawara said suddenly but resolutely.

Sonoko closed her eyes, stricken. Mrs. Odawara was progressive and therefore Christian.

"Of course we must," continued Mrs. Odawara reasonably. "It's Sunday, isn't it?"

"Yes, but..."

"You're not suggesting that the American lady isn't Christian?" She made it sound rather horrible. "And she *is* coming out early, isn't she?"

"Well, in the morning."

"Just so. She won't have had time to go to church, and so we can hold a reading. Perhaps even a little prayer meeting too. Oh, she'll like it. It will be just like home—Sunday morning and so forth. I know their ways, these Americans.... Let me see—why, I believe I have a large colored picture of our Lord and Saviour Jesus Christ, and we can put it up in the tokonoma."

"But—she's the guest of honor," said Sonoko faintly. As such she would have her back to the tokonoma—the small alcove which had already been most carefully arranged with their finest scroll-picture and the most subtle arrangement of autumnal flowers—and would consequently hold the un-Christian position of having her back to the Lord and Saviour.

Mrs. Odawara gave her a long, hard look. She had her own opinion of outdated and reactionary Japanese customs and superstitions. "But, my dear Sonoko, she *is* American," she hissed.

There was no denying the logic of her argument and, perhaps, a small prayer wouldn't hurt anything. Her own parents were sort of Shinto, and her brother had just recovered from a passing enthusiasm for Zen Buddhism—brought about by his judo practice and his Chinese-ink drawing lessons—but these feelings would certainly not preclude polite participation in a short, a very short prayer meeting. If only Mrs. Odawara didn't start on birth control. She couldn't stand that.

It would be most rude, for after all, where would Miss Wilson have been if her parents had practiced birth control?

"Yes," said her neighbor, for it seemed all settled now. "We will read a part of the Book of Exodus—Israel in Egypt, you know. It will have a contemporary flavor, quite befitting the presence of a member of the Advancing Forces." Unorthodox though she was, Mrs. Odawara had adopted the standard Japanese euphemism for "occupying army."

"It will make her feel her position and will, in a way, be a subtle compliment," continued Mrs. Odawara. "You see—we are Egypt, and she is the visiting Israelite. It is very fitting and will furthermore lend a good moral tone to the party."

"But what about the plague of locusts and the darkness over the land?" asked Sonoko. As part of her education she had attended Mrs. Odawara's Bible school. The objection also occurred to her that the Israelites had been brought to Egypt as slaves. "I doubt that Miss Wilson would too much appreciate the—"

"Obviously," Mrs. Odawara interrupted savagely, "we're not going to read *that* part. Besides, since I'm reading it will be in Japanese." She fixed a stern eye on Sonoko, just in case there might be a desperate last-moment refusal.

Sonoko turned her head toward the window, determined to be rude if she possibly could. As she well remembered, Mrs. Odawara read slowly—very slowly—and with maddening emphasis. But her neighbor didn't even notice and went on about the virtues of Christianity and birth control, the iniquities of Shinto and Buddhism.

The girl scarcely listened. She looked out on Tokyo and saw how much it had changed since she'd first begun these early-morning rides. It was like maple trees in autumn: one didn't notice the leaves gradually turning ed and yellow until, one day, the mountain was afire with them. So with Tokyo, she had not noticed the new buildings, the new streets, the new people, until now when she looked from the window and suddenly realized that the entire bombed-out stretch of Kawasaki, which she remembered as a plain of ruins, had been completely rebuilt.

At Tokyo Station Mrs. Odawara was still fairly budding with suggestions, but Sonoko with a low bow put some distance between them, and even Mrs. Odawara had to respond to a bow. Thus, each bowing to the other, they moved farther and farther apart, and Sonoko, hidden by the morning crowd, left her companion shouting into the recesses of the station.

Once in the billet she punched the time clock, pleased as always that she was five minutes early, and walked up several flights to Miss Wilson's room. It never occurred to Sonoko to resent the fact that Japanese employees were not allowed to use the elevators, and the signs "Off Limits to all Indigenous Personnel" remained for her but delightful examples of military English at its sonorous and incomprehensible best. The great delicacy with which the signs avoided the nasty word "Japanese" was unfortunately completely lost on her.

At Miss Wilson's door she hesitated and finally decided not to go in. The dear American must have her sleep. Sonoko could just picture her there, so innocent and childlike in her little pajamas, like a large and expensive doll, her eyes shut, sweet dreams painting a smile of cherubic peace on her generous mouth. Almost in tears, Sonoko turned away from the door.

■

Just on the other side of the door an extremely vivid Bengal tiger crept through the bamboo, its eyes shining yellow-ochre, about to pounce on a half-used box of Kleenex and a hastily tossed brassiere. Against the other wall was a large glass case containing an equally large doll holding a spray of paper wisteria. Around its neck had been hung a sign reading "Off Limits to Allied Personnel." Beside it was a plaster miniature of Mount Fuji, the crater of which was hollowed out for an ashtray. On the wall was a Nikko travel poster in full—too full—color. Hanging above it was a paper dragon, and beneath it a silk slip. Against the other wall hung a large Japanese flag, scribbled all over in ink, the brushed characters faded into the silk. Everyone who'd signed the flag was probably now dead.

In the bed was a long, sheeted figure which coughed miserably and hoarsely. Its long brown hair was half covered by the sheet and the pillow. At the other end a foot was sticking from under the Army blanket. The foot had red toenails. Beside the bed the alarm clock clicked once and, in half a minute, rang. The figure, its head muffled in the sheet, put out an arm and turned it off, then sighed.

Gloria sat up painfully, her eyes still closed, and covered her face with both hands. She got unsteadily to her feet, licked her lips, and walked to the mirror. Her roommate was gone for the weekend, so she didn't bother with her robe. She always slept naked. Now she had a hangover.

At the washstand she took a long drink of cold water and opened her eyes. It was after some effort that she remembered today was Saturday. But where was she? She glanced covertly around the room and realized she was in Japan and not in Indiana. For years she had had an early-morning fear of opening her eyes and seeing the tiny doilied bedroom that was hers in Muncie. She had opened her eyes in all sorts of beds and on all kinds of bedrooms, but still the fear remained.

This morning even the bedroom didn't reassure her. Something was the matter. She began to brush her hair, fifty strokes every morning like *Charm* said, first thing. On the fiftieth stroke she remembered what it was: she couldn't remember what she'd done last night. Dropping the brush, she looked into the mirror and tried hard to remember. Actually she knew, from experience, what it was she'd probably done. She just couldn't remember with whom.

It had been like this every morning for years now. The alarm would drag her safely away from vaguely terrifying dreams about God and Father and Mother and Indiana. Then, washing her face or brushing her teeth or combing her hair, she would suddenly come to realize the extent of her sin. The pattern was dreadfully familiar, having been repeated so many times, but the reality of sin was always naked and new and startling.

Every morning at seven she was at her most vulnerable. Naked and alone, she stood before the mirror, hiding her face in her hands, her guilt lively as a child within her. The bedroom, despite Fuji and the painted tiger, seemed in Indiana, and soon she would force herself downstairs, to her parents, to the poached egg on soggy toast—knowing she was a sinner.

Later, after she had put on her clothes and her face, she would also put on her attitude. Her parents were narrow-minded bigots. If they thought her spawn of the devil, she returned the compliment. After all, she would think, it was just a matter of which Satan you chose.

But now she was still cringing before them as before a whip, and hungry guilt gnawed. It was worse than usual this morning because she couldn't remember her partner in sin of the night before. If she could only identify him, then some of the early-morning shame would rub off on him, but this way... it might be just anyone.

Well, someday it would be too late. There was always the chance that some day precautions would be forgotten and that she would pay, in that humiliating female way, for what she laughingly called, in the bright light of full noon, her very own "American way of life." And perhaps this was the day. Frantically she began gathering up her clothes and, just as frantically, began searching through her memory.

She remembered going to bed, sort of. She also remembered kissing someone—perhaps good-by, she hoped —in a sedan. Before that it had been either the Officers' Club or the American Club, but she couldn't remember which. And whom could it have been with?

Shivering, she put on her robe, then began brushing her hair again, feeling better each time the brush hurt her. She brushed harder and harder, until the hair started coming out. Then she stopped, thinking that one really mustn't carry masochism too far. She looked into the mirror, particularly at her mouth and eyes.

"Well, you'll never be a pretty girl," she said softly, and at once felt better. "But you do have such lovely hair." She always felt better when she could make a joke.

There was a soft knock at the door, but Gloria paid no attention, knowing it would immediately open. It did, and Sonoko, smiling, walked in with clean towels over her arm.

"Good morning, Sonoko," said Gloria brightly, hoping to sound a good deal brighter than she felt.

"Ohayo gozaimasu," said Sonoko. Then: "Hi, there." She always gave a bilingual morning-greeting, the first to show respect for herself and the next a genuflection to all great Americans. Walking to the opposite bed, still made-up, she pointed questioningly to its undisturbed covers.

"Weekend trip. Far, far away," said Gloria, making vaguely distant gestures with her hands.

"So desu ka?" said Sonoko and put the towels on the chair.

Gloria was examining her eyebrows, which she thought

looked as though they'd been trampled on. "Sonoko, be a perfect lamb and run out and see if one of the girls can spare me an aspirin. I've got a little headache." Little, my god! Her head was coming off.

Sonoko looked at her and smiled, as though Miss Wilson had recited a poem, then went back to making up the bed.

"Sonoko—asupirin."

"Ah, so," hissed Sonoko, her eyes blank behind her glasses, "asupirin—I catch quick—I hubba-hubba."

She clattered out of the room, leaving Gloria wincing first at the clatter, second at Sonoko's GI English. It always unnerved her when these people used it—which was often. It was as though the Great Buddha at Kamakura had come out with Brooklynese. She slipped her feet into sandals and went down the hall to the shower.

In the shower she suddenly remembered whom it was she'd been out with. It had been Major Calloway, of course. From her own office. Imagine having forgotten! A gentleman of the old school. No passes, only comfortable, cozy talk of the just-you-and-me variety. Much explanation of power politics behind the command, climaxed by the revelation of who really ran the office —the Major himself. All of this interlarded with compliments to Gloria about her dress, her personality, and her soul—in that order. They talked shop for a while; then he told her how lonely he was and what a nice homebody she was. She'd used her little-girl smile and folded her hands. Receiving homage from the peasants was always fun.

The warm water was reviving her memory more and more. They'd had steak and apple pie at the American Club, and in the sedan coming home she'd gotten kittenish and wanted to wade in the Palace moat until he told her it was eight feet deep. In front of the hotel they had kissed good-night, very decorously, using only the lips, and she'd come in and gone to bed. As simple as that! She hadn't done anything at all. Because no one had asked her. Heavens, the Major probably had honorable intentions!

Gloria put her face under the shower. She was awake and clean. Her early-morning fears were already down the drain. She'd scrubbed her long legs and her flat stomach until they were red, and she felt much better for it. Muncie seemed just as far away as it actually was. She was in the Glamorous Orient and was one of the most glamorous things in it. The hot water gave out and put an end to further reflections for the time being.

As she dried, she said to herself very softly: "No, not really beautiful, you know, but interesting looking, awfully interesting." She had no doubt that this was what they—the men—said about her, and she also had a fairly accurate idea of what the women said. Holding the towel, she thought of the hundreds of days she'd been in Japan. Each had begun with a shower, and almost every one had ended with a man. She couldn't even remember them all.

"This is a rare and sober moment, Gloria," she told herself, and tried to remember all the men she'd ever known in her entire life.

In such moments as this she'd often thought of compiling a little history. Nothing too elaborate—just the man's name, the date, and the place, if she could remember it. Single spaced. About a dozen sheets should do it. Then she could subdivide the total and cross-reference it according to the different nationalities. There was the attaché at the French Mission, the nice British sergeant at the Union Jack Club, that lovely Italian correspondent.... Then, after she had divided them, she could take percentages. Of course the Americans would win, but it would be interesting to find out by how much.

But it was hopeless. She had forgotten too many. As she tied her robe she decided that the only immoral thing was her forgetting. This comforted her. That was her only sin, to have forgotten anyone with whom she had shared what one very earnest second lieutenant had once called "the holy happiness." He was Southern and had religion, she remembered; afterwards he'd tried to baptize her with what was left of the whisky.

Well, she'd start a diary soon. That should help her memory. Each entry burned and the ashes stomped on and eaten as soon as written. No lurid details—just the name and her thoughts for the day. What names would not grace its pages! Who would be next?

This was a favorite game, but the odds were hopelessly against her. It never turned out the way she hoped. That gorgeous Depot sergeant was virtuous; the dark correspondent at the War Crime Trials had gone completely Japanese; and the cute little dancer with the USO hadn't liked girls very much. Alas, one always remembered the failures best.

The next just might be Private Richardson, also from her own office. The only trouble was that they'd built up a kidding relationship which rather well precluded their ever getting within five feet of each other. Besides, she'd heard he had a Japanese girl. Really, it was sinful the way they had become such competition. (Wonder what our brave boys would say if we started running around with Japanese men?) Oh, well, she'd just have to wait and see about Private Richardson.

Back in her room she carefully turned her back to Sonoko and put on her pants, brassiere, and slip. The girl was plumping up the same pillow for the tenth time that morning.

"You have a boy friend, Sonoko?" she asked.

Sonoko giggled, covered her mouth with her hand, and said: "Nebah hoppen."

"Oh, some day it will," said Gloria airily, zipping her dress up the side. "A nice . . . farmer."

Sonoko giggled from across the room.

A farmer! Gloria had never even met a farmer, not the kind with dirt under his fingernails and sweat in his armpits, that is. That was another way she could cross-file her little history: occupations. Except that it wouldn't be quite fair. Her wishes hadn't always been observed in the matter. It was the white-collar boys, the lieutenants and up that she always got tangled with. They were somehow so much easier. They spoke her own language, and they were always available, being as neurotic as she.

How, she wondered, did one go about meeting a farmer, a truck driver, a boxer? The lower classes were always so damned suspicious. Enlisted men the same way. And, at least, you could trust an officer to keep his mouth shut, which was more than you could expect from sergeant on down. Except, perhaps, Private Richardson.

She wondered if part of his attraction didn't come from his being *Private* Richardson. She tried to think of him as Major Richardson—General Richardson. Sure enough, some of the brightness faded. A part of the attraction? It was apparently the whole thing. Well, she'd just have to see. Now, when could she snare him? Tonight perhaps?

Oh, no! She sat down on the bed, one foot in high-heels. No, not tonight. All morning long she had felt that all was not well with the world, and now she remembered why. Carried away the night before, she had said yes when Major Calloway had suggested dinner and the opera this evening. He had seemed such a dear after their dozen-odd Scotches. Now, in the merciless light of day, she saw him in his true form.

"Not a deer, but a boar," she said to herself. But even this reminder of ready wit didn't cheer her. Here she'd gone and ruined a perfectly good Saturday night, just to be brought home and pecked on the lips. Much too late to do anything about it. After all she *was* the Colonel's secretary, and he *was* the Colonel's executive officer.

"Well, we're obviously made for each other," said Gloria, wriggling into the other shoe. "The Fates are against us."

She stood up and put on the last finishing touches before the mirror. Sonoko, looking as though she was about to start fluffing the pillow again, peered shyly over her shoulder. The pancake make-up, the mascara, powder, and lipstick were all understood by Sonoko. It was in the last-minute attentions that mystery lay. She watched while Gloria deftly unclotted two eyelashes, cleaned a tiny speck of lipstick off one of her front teeth, and gave herself a final spray of scent. If she ever wore make-up, Sonoko often thought, she would do just as Miss Wilson did, even if she had to put lipstick on her teeth in order to take it off. It was in these final intuitive touches that all true art lay.

Gloria saw the steel-rimmed spectacles over her shoulder and handed Sonoko the atomizer. "Go on," she said, "only don't waste it. It's Sin Incarnate or some such thing, and I'd never be able to afford it if the PX didn't mark it down ninety percent. Go on. Dozo."

Sonoko giggled, holding her hand in front of her teeth, and carefully put the atomizer back on the table. Gloria waved good-by and started for the door. The giggle suddenly stopped, and the dark eyes behind the steel-rimmed spectacles grew wider.

Gloria smiled politely, one hand on the doorknob: "What is it, Sonoko?"

Her room girl swallowed, then said: "You no forget —o-pahti tomorrow?" It was midway between a declaration and a question.

Suddenly Gloria understood. Oh, god! She *had* forgotten—but completely! So, as was usual with her under these circumstances, she shook her head, smiled in a special way that wrinkled her nose, and said: "You bet your life I didn't forget, little old Blue Sonoko. I can hardly wait." And for Sonoko's more immediate comprehension she added a bit of pantomime.

They parted with bobbing on one side and nose-wrinkling smiles on the other.

Waiting for the elevator, Gloria felt like kicking herself. Now she perfectly remembered accepting an invitation which at the time seemed to be for some vague, indefinite future. She'd been half-asleep, still in bed, defenseless. Now she was trapped. Oh, well, so she was trapped—so what? She could always learn something. And if tonight was going to be wasted with the Major anyway, she might as well have something to look forward to when she woke up Sunday morning.

Her own nature never failed to delight her. So philosophic. She always said there was so much to be learned from the little things in life—then laughed herself sick; but, nevertheless, it was true—there was. Now, a lot of other American girls under like circumstances would have pleaded off—sick headache or the like. Not Gloria—true blue, she stuck to her word, and what's more, damn it, she'd enjoy herself even if it killed her.

Not that it was likely to. In fact it might be fun—afterwards. She could tell about the quaint little paper house; how meekly she took off her shoes; the good, good soup—like Mother used to make—and the squealy little dishes that Gloria, good sport that she was, ate right along with Papa Sonoko—octopus, seaweed, fish heads, and the like. And then they'd sit around the family koto, and she'd lead them in "Home on the Range" or something like that. Pure strawberry-festival—Japanese style—but it would make a great story Monday morning at the office. And Private Richardson—he'd be thinking a little about the strange home-life of his Japanese biddy before her tale was done.

Already flushed with success, she smiled at the elevator boy and was carried down to the basement dining room. Under the mockery, the laughter, and the attitude, she was dimly aware of a real curiosity and a real pleasure at being invited. But, what the hell, if one wore one's heart on one's sleeve and one's feelings on one's shoulder, one could well expect to end up with neither sleeves nor shoulder, and she, for one, needed hers. So, when she walked into the dining room, she felt her usual cynical self.

At the same time she remembered she'd forgotten to put out the candy bars she usually gave Sonoko to take home to the countless brothers and sisters she doubtless had. Oh, well, she gave the girl enough of a treat just being around. She suspected Sonoko had a crush on her, and this made her feel quite good. Tonight she'd put out the candy and, after the sleep of the innocent, lug it out to this god-forsaken place called Zushi or Fushi or Mushi. She was such a good kid, Gloria was. A real heart of gold—just like the proverbial whore.

It was still early. The tables didn't fill up until just before nine. At nine everyone was supposed to be at work. Today was Saturday and most of the tables would remain empty: many of the female members of the Occupation found it convenient to take sick leave on Saturday mornings—it gave them such an early start for their weekend dates by the sea or in the mountains.

Gloria saw Dorothy Ainsley sitting alone, and before she could turn away Dorothy had seen her and was making frantic motions with one hand, the other holding a piece of toast.

"Oh, darling, *am* I glad to see you!" Dorothy shouted halfway across the room. "I feel just like an interloper or something." She smiled and moved her chair further around the table, patting the other with one hand.

Gloria sat down.

"I was up quite early—shopping, you know, at the Commissary. Us wives! If you don't get there early, all the lettuce is gone, or something. And you know Dave! He loves his lettuce so. Well, I was passing by in our car and I thought: I'm hungry, that's what I am. So I told the girl on duty I'd forgotten my purse because, natch, I don't have any meal chits, and then sat down over here, out of harm's way, and was feeling *so* guilty. That is, until I saw you."

"I'm so happy for you, dear," said Gloria, while she thought: You lie in your teeth, you slut. You just want one good witness who'll say she saw you here and who'll believe your silly Commissary story. Little me, however—I know what you're doing, though maybe not who with. One of the few good things about our little colonial society is that people know what other people do. So just don't give me any of this marriage crap. I wonder what you told your husband.

"Of course, Dave will be just furious. He doesn't like me to get up early. It's bad for a singer he says. Imagine! Besides—he's so silly—he says he likes to watch me asleep." She giggled self-consciously, one finger extended away from her toast.

Gloria could just picture this. She didn't know Dave Ainsley very well, but she'd seen that faithful-dog look following his beautiful, talented wife around, his smile half-apologizing for her, his eyes shining with devotion. Jealous too. Tried to thrash a sergeant once who made eyes at her. And the poor soldier was probably only acting on advice given him by a lieutenant who'd gotten it from a major. Dorothy was such a snob. No one below field grade. Poor Dave. Gloria could imagine him tiptoeing around their apartment—complete with artificial Ming vases made into lamps—casting loving glances on his sleeping wife. On the nights she sleeps at home, that is.

What would he say if he saw her now, she wondered. Sitting there fat as a grub and almost purring with contentment. Her face was still pink. Gloria guessed that he had never seen her this satisfied. Dorothy would walk in on him at work about an hour from now, still rosy, having been home, washed, and depilated, with some whopping story about a cousin or an aunt in town and that she just couldn't get away and it was too late to call because she "didn't want to disturb your rest, Davie-boy." Or maybe she'd use that one about furthering her career.

Or else she'd turn up with what Davie-boy always called "one of Dorothy's"—a real stunner involving a sedan breakdown and how she partook of Japanese hospitality and how nice they were to her and sat her in the place of honor and how she could scarcely gag down a breakfast of seaweed, fish, and tea, but how low she bowed afterwards—right there on the tatami—and what really exceptional people they were, too. Not at all usual, you know. Nothing run-of-the-mill ever happens to our Dorothy. And all of this would be told in her low, modest, little-girl voice, the one that doubtless sent her husband into ecstasies....

Dorothy broke into Gloria's thoughts, saying: "You know, dear, we're rather alike. I mean, we really do seem a bit similar. Don't you think?"

Gloria looked at her, noticing with some satisfaction that Dorothy was getting a bit saggy. If she was a singer, her diaphragm looked pretty unprofessional. She always kept her profile high too. That was so the extra chin wouldn't show. But, there was no doubt about it, she was quite beautiful in that brittle, china-doll way that men unaccountably seem to find so attractive.

Gloria decided they weren't at all alike and, as coldly as possible, said: "In what way?"

"Oh, I don't know. We seem to have found ourselves out here—in Japan, I mean."

"What have you found?" asked Gloria, whose head was beginning to ache again. Sonoko hadn't brought the aspirin, and eight-o'clock solemnities with Dottie Ainsley were just too much.

"Well, for one thing, a husband," said Dorothy seriously. "They're necessary, you know. All girls should be married." She suddenly smiled, as though what she was saying could not possibly have any personal reference. Nor did she try to explain the illogical sequence of her thoughts from their being alike to husbands.

Gloria stared at her in mild disbelief. Just what did she think she was doing? Gratuitous insults were a bit coarse, even for Dottie.

"Well, Mrs. Ainsley," she finally said, "we can't all be as fortunate in our choice of husbands as you were."

"Don't misunderstand me, dear. I mean, if a girl has a chance of marrying these days, she ought—no if's, and's, or but's about it. She really should. What she does is her own business, but she ought to have a husband, first."

"Your meaning is awfully subtle," said Gloria, "but I think I'm catching on."

Dorothy began sipping her coffee daintily, and Gloria's oatmeal arrived to fill the gap in their conversation. As she ate it she decided that Dorothy's meaning actually was rather subtle. Either Dorothy guessed that other people knew about her, and hence the girls-will-be-girls kind of talk, or else . . . or else she wanted Gloria to get married for reasons best known to herself. At any rate, she had looked uncommonly honest when she spoke, just as now, sipping her cold coffee with a pinkie in the air, she looked uncommonly uncomfortable.

The silence after their orgy of intimacy was getting a bit heavy, Gloria thought. She was about to ask whether the plates' willow pattern was Chinese or Japanese when Dorothy, apparently feeling the same, gave a little scream and bent under the table.

"Oh, my, what pretty shoes! Where *did* you get them?"

Gloria stretched out her legs so Dorothy could see the shoes without disappearing completely under the table. "The PX," she said.

"Don't tell me you get your clothes *there!* Why, I haven't been near the place for years. Not since I was what they call a 'vocalist'—whatever that is—with the USO and all that, you know. And that—well, just between us, it's been ages ago. No, after I met Dave (he made me over, you know) I started buying from New York—by mail, natch (and it takes just forever getting here!) and then, of course, there's that wonderful little tailor in Hong Kong. But those shoes you have there—they rather interest me. Any other sizes?"

Now, this is our old Dorothy, thought Gloria. It feels good to be back in a mutual understanding again —the understanding that we loathe each other. "I don't think so," she said. "If they do, they're larger."

"Larger? Oh, not really!" Dorothy sipped her coffee and tried again to pretend, somewhat less succesfully, that she had meant nothing personal. "Why, my little feet couldn't begin to fill those up."

You're asking for it, thought Gloria. She'd known girls like Dottie before. Real bitches. Just couldn't stand not tearing in with their little claws. Anything that would hold still was fair game, no matter what. Her poor husband must be just a mass of tangled ribbons by this time. She was the kind of healthy American girl who would write a four-letter word on the upturned lid of the ladies' john in lipstick—backwards. Then stick around and watch the fun when the next occupant, in a cool white blouse, walked out. She'd heard men's cans were all scribbled up. They should see the ladies'—after a crowd of Dottie's type had gotten through with them.

Gloria looked at her shoes. "Well, they're comfortable."

Dottie had apparently expected to get clawed back.

She looked disappointed. "Oh, I can see. They're just lovely—exquisite." She sighed shortly. "I only wish I could get things like that." She smiled, her just-between-us smile, which wrinkled up her nose and never failed to infuriate Gloria.

"Oh, you might be able to," said Gloria smoothly. "Perhaps one of the officers you know is in the Quartermaster Corps, or Procurement, or even the PX for all I know. If you really can't bear to go near the PX's yourself, perhaps you could get one of them to scout for you. Yokohama, Kobe, Nagoya—you know."

"Well . . . but I really don't know any officers that well," said Dottie after hesitating just a second too long.

She was such a bad liar. Goodness knows it was difficult enough to be a good one. Gloria was a good one, but even she forgot her lies eventually and got into trouble. So she decided to be charitable and say nothing more.

Dottie gave her a hard little glance, disagreeable over her cup. She put it down with a tiny clatter, then softened almost at once and became again feather-brained and flighty:

"Well, I must run. Dave will be furious. You coming?"

"Yes, I'm off to work."

"You're lucky, you know," she said, turning her head whimsically. "I wish I was a career girl again. But I'm not. Just a drudge—a regular Hausfrau type. I bet I couldn't even hit a high C any more. And, you know, my range used to be four octaves. I forget who it was called me the Lily Pons of the Occupation. Silly, but fun." She laughed. "Know what Dave used to say about my range? No? He used to say that I was composed of a bass, a tenor, and a small boy who got pinched. Cute, huh?"

Gloria gave a sick smile, and Dottie rattled on: "Oh, hell, I just remembered—tomorrow's a big Japanese party. They're picking us up. That means I've got to get the servants busy cleaning the house—four of them and not a brain in the lot."

"Real Japanese party—or just Japanese-style American?"

"Oh, the real thing. Ex-zaibatsu or the Imperial family or something. Dave's business. On the paper, you know. Tatami, hashi, the works—all-night deal."

"Well, that might be pleasant."

"Pleasant? You ever had a Jap breakfast?"

"Often," lied Gloria.

"Well, you're a better woman than I am then."

Gloria wisely said nothing to this.

"Oh, by the way, did you hear what happened to Lady Briton last night?" asked Dottie, somehow seeming to want to delay the moment of parting they both wanted so badly.

Gloria groaned. Not Lady Briton again! Gloria bet that at any given moment of Tokyo's social life the antics of Lady Briton would be on a dozen tongues. She was the wife of one of the Australian Mission people, a big horsy woman who was attempting to establish a Society for the Protection of Our Dumb Friends—SPODF she called it, but to the rest of Tokyo it was SPOOF. It was to rival the Tokyo chapter of the SPCA, of which the British ambassadress was patron.

Dottie continued: "Well, you know, a couple of weeks ago she saw some trained dogs in Asakusa or some such place, and she decided they were being cruelly treated—they juggled or sat up or something. Of course, she cares about animals just about as much as I do. But she just can't stand seeing that English woman in the newspapers all the time. And so she confiscated the whole troupe, dismissed the owner out of hand—the Australians are like that, you know—and decided to play Lady Bountiful to all the animals. She thought they'd be good entertainment at her parties, juggling and all. But they wouldn't do a thing—

just moped. They were nasty too; got into some of Randolph's—that's Lord Briton—old ambassadorial papers or something and chewed them all up. Well, last night was the payoff. They'd been just darling little nuisances before, but last night one of them bit Mrs. Colonel Butternut on the thigh when she was down on the floor being the the head of John the Baptist during charades." She smiled. "Isn't that a scream!"

"What happened to the dogs?"

"Well, this was one time, believe you me, when our dumb friends got short shrift. She probably had them drowned."

"All of them?"

Dottie shrugged her shoulders—this wasn't the point of the story. "And Mrs. Colonel Butternut is in St. Luke's under watch—she might have rabies. Can't you just imagine her frothing at the mouth? She's done it all her life, but until now no one thought anything of it. Oh, it's a panic!" She stood up.

Together they walked past the girl who took tickets, and the headwaiter at the door bowed to them.

"Why don't their clothes ever fit, I wonder?" asked Dottie, looking vaguely at the small man in the dress suit too large for him.

"Their Japanese clothes do," said Gloria.

"Oh, those!..."

They were silent as they walked through the revolving door into the already dusty sunlight.

"Well, that was a nice breakfast," said Dottie, "but tomorrow's won't be."

"What I like best about spending the night with the Japanese," said Gloria, who had at least spent nights with Americans in Japanese on-limits hotels, "is that no one says good-morning to me until I'm presentable. They have a tacit agreement that you're not even visible until you get your face on and are ready to meet the world." She'd read this in a book somewhere.

"Yes, I know," said Dottie. "They do act that way, don't they?" She was anxious lest it seem she didn't know as much about the Japanese as Gloria, and was at the added disadvantage of not having read a book through since finishing high school.

Directly at the billet entrance was an Army sedan, the young Japanese driver leaning against its shining fender. He stood away from the car as they came out and made a tentative motion toward the handle of the rear door, his black hair shining in the sun.

Gloria wondered whom the sedan was for. You never saw them waiting in front of the billet except very late, when the field-grade officers were saying good-night to their girls. The hotel was for lower-rated civilian girls, who never got to use anything better than a jeep. Only the upper grades rated sedans. She found herself wondering about Dottie, who could get a sedan on the strength of her husband's high civilian rank. So, then, whose transportation could this be but Dottie's? But she'd said she'd come in her own car. Then Gloria remembered that the Ainsleys didn't own a car.

Gloria glanced at Dottie, who was squinting in the early-morning sun. Such a poor liar. This was certainly her transportation, ready and waiting, yet she couldn't take it because she'd already told Gloria about the car. And she needn't have lied either. Lots of wives used sedans to go to the Commissary.

While Dottie hesitated on the hotel steps, Gloria swiftly reconstructed the events of the night before. Dorothy had probably left her husband rather late, pleading relatives or something. Then the adulterous meeting, perhaps at his billet. She'd probably sneaked out in the cold, dark morning when it was too early to go home. Perhaps she'd tried to hail a passing jeep. Then the sudden determination to have breakfast. It was probably a combination of hunger and the perverse desire to expose her own position. Now the finale—

home in the sedan which she had probably called just before going in to breakfast. But Gloria's presence had spoiled this last touch.

"Well," said Dottie briskly, "I parked the car around the corner—past the station as a matter of fact. Thought I'd just walk to the Commissary. Exercise, you know," she concluded brightly.

"Yes, it's only halfway across town."

"What? Oh, yes. Well, one can't get too much exercise." Then, anxious not to seem to be avoiding the obvious, she said: "These poor drivers!"

"Why poor?"

"Oh, I don't know. It's in their eyes—that lovely melted-chocolate color, you know. And then, Japanese men are always sad looking anyway, like dogs left in the rain. Breaks your heart." Dottie was not without her sensitive side.

"The women look comparatively dry," said Gloria.

"Oh, them! Isn't it strange—the men look just like dogs, and the women look just like cats. You know— cute little triangle faces, button noses, and those lovely slanting eyes. It's really the animal kingdom."

"Maybe that's why Lady Briton likes it so much over here."

"Yes," giggled Dorothy, "someone should start a Society for the Prevention of Cruelty to Japanese."

Someone really ought, thought Gloria. It wasn't that the glorious Occupiers were cruel. They were merely thoughtless. There was something about having plenty in the midst of famine that made people thoughtlessly cruel. When she was good and drunk Gloria always felt like apologizing to beggars. So far she had restrained herself. She didn't like Dottie's saying what had so often occurred to her; so she asked if Dottie was going to the opera.

"Well, if you call it an opera, yes. It's good business, you know."

"You don't like *Madame Butterfly?*" asked Gloria.

"Oh, adore it! Simply adore it! But that soprano! Know the girl. A nice voice, though a shade overly cultivated—that is, when you realize that she had nothing to cultivate in the first place. Can't hear her except in the first three rows. Bad breathing, that's what Mme. Schmidt says. You know her, dear? My old sensei—that means teacher, you know. From Vienna and just the sweetest old lady ever. Poor thing—half-starving now. Whenever I take my lesson I go to the PX and just load up—crackers, cheese, sardines, that sort of thing, you know. I suppose they have a banquet after I go. Awfully odd position she's in—white, natch, and yet can't use the PX or, well, any of the Army things. Can't even ride Army busses, or the Allied cars on the railroad. Doesn't go out much—no shoes! Of course, she was here all during the war, and I suppose that's why. And the CIC is always investigating her—as though she cared about Hitler or Mussolini or anything but music. She'll be at the opera tonight probably—I'll bet she's off borrowing a pair of shoes right now. That soprano is another pupil of hers."

"I guess I'll be going," said Gloria. "Some major or other from the office asked me."

Dorothy looked at her intently for just a second, the look of a person who is trying to decide whether or not to tell a woman that her lipstick is smeared, that an eyelash has fallen to her cheek, that her nose needs blowing. Finally she said: "Oh, really? What's his name?"

"Calloway. Why?"

"Oh, nothing. Just thought Davie or I might know him. We know scads of people in Special Services—I used to be USO, you know, and of course Davie is on the paper. Guess we don't."

"Guess not," said Gloria, wishing that Americans had a custom like bowing. It made difficult things like parting between two people who didn't like each other so much easier.

"Well, dear, I must run," said Dorothy, her eyes still intent on Gloria. "Perhaps I'll see you there tonight." She smiled briefly.

"Hope so," said Gloria and turned quickly away. She rather wanted to know just who Dorothy's officer was. In all likelihood someone she herself had known, would know, or was knowing. There were only so many officers. Well, bless the grapevine. She probably would know before the day was over. Really, Tokyo was Muncie all over again—such a small world after all. Muncie all over again, but different.

She drew a deep breath of the cool autumnal morning air and, for no reason, felt better. She breathed and smiled, realizing that, absurdly enough, she felt happy.

It was being in Japan that did it, she guessed. Here she seemed to weigh less, her body had a suppleness and dexterity that surprised her. The sun shone directly into her face, and she felt tall, beautiful, and altogether different from what she knew herself to be.

Often she had seen other Americans here smile for no apparent reason as they walked in the sunlight. Was it because they were conquerors? She doubted it. It was because they were free. Free from their families, their homes, their culture—free even from themselves. They had left one way of living behind them and did not find it necessary to learn another. Nothing they'd ever been taught could be used in understanding the Japanese, and most of them didn't want to anyway. It was too much fun being away from home, in a country famed for exoticism, in a city where every day was an adventure and you never knew what was going to happen tomorrow.

Actually, thought Gloria, there was something paradoxically reassuring about being in this country where the ground might shake at any moment, where the distant, snow-covered mountain might, for all one knew, blow the whole island to pieces. You could almost feel yourself living. At any moment the ground might crack beneath your feet and you'd find yourself face to face with eternity. It was quite different from safe, dull Muncie where habit very soon cut you from life, and Gloria was inclined to prefer Japan.

The gold-spotted leaves fell at her feet, and the cool air brushed her ankles. There was a clarity here—so different from the foggy, rainy island she had expected —a dryness, a precision in the atmosphere which made the most ordinary occurrence—a walk to the station for example—something joyous, as though a carnival were just around the corner.

There was another kind of clarity too. She felt herself a part of something larger, something benevolent, like god, engaged in kind works and noble edifices. And she could see enormous distances. Her own country— the United States, Indiana, Muncie—like an arranged vista, fell perfectly into place. She understood it; she understood her place in it and even that of her parents. It was as adorable as an illuminated Easter egg.

And here, all around her, was freedom, even license. The ruins were one huge playground where everything forbidden was now allowed and clandestine meetings were held under the noonday sun. The destruction, evident everywhere she looked, contributed to or perhaps caused this. She felt like a looter, outside society. Society no longer existed.

Here she was free, here in this destructive country where autos collided as though by clockwork, where sudden death was always a possibility, and where dogs went mad in the sun, casting their long, barking shadows behind them. More than at any other place she had been in her life, Gloria felt alive in Japan.

Two university students, black in their caps and high-collared uniforms, were walking toward her. They stopped talking to stare. When she passed them they both stood respectfully to one side of the sidewalk, their eyes never leaving her. As she walked beyond them she heard their conversation, suddenly animated, bright with words she would never understand. They were talking about her.

She turned to look behind her. Both of the students were walking backwards, gazing after her. Gloria read only appreciation in their faces. They saw her looking, blushed, and turned around.

Japan was like that. You could walk down the street and be admired. A visiting deity, deigning to step upon the common pavements. All the men would look at a white woman as though she were some rare, incalculably expensive and probably breakable object. At least, so Gloria believed.

She turned around again, but the students were gone. If she had smiled at them she might have assured for herself a kind of immortality. The handsome youngsters would reckon time from the day the American lady smiled at them. They would excitedly recall to each other just what she looked like; they would vie with each other in flattering descriptions. At least, so Gloria believed.

The next two men were middle-aged businessmen, and they didn't look at her at all. This did not disturb Gloria's illusion, however, for she considered them quite ugly. A man whom Gloria could not imagine as a bed companion simply didn't exist for her. But, in the next moment, a young carpenter on a bicycle turned to gaze so long that he almost ran into a taxi. Gloria turned around to look. Just to make sure he hadn't hurt himself. He was very handsome.

She realized she was smiling. Just before she passed through the Allied free entrance to the trains, she turned to look at the plaza before her, at the great city spreading beyond it. She saw the sedan and the driver still waiting back at the hotel, small and distant in the morning sun. He seemed to be looking at her. She couldn't remember whether he was good looking or not. Oh, well, it didn't make any difference. He seemed to touch his hat, but she couldn't be sure. It was this typical gesture which reminded her that he was Japanese. Really, Gloria, she giggled to herself, your standards are getting lower—or higher, as the case may be.

Still smiling, she nodded at the boy taking tickets at the wicket for Japanese and, feeling delightfully like Babylon herself, swept through the free Allied entrance to the trains.

■

When Tadashi first saw the tall American coming toward him in the fur coat he thought she must be his passenger. But then she and the shorter lady with her walked on toward Tokyo Station. Tadashi shifted his weight to the other leg and went on waiting. Straightening his cap, he watched the MP on duty at the billet entrance. The uniform was nice—sharp creases, boots like mirrors, immaculate gloves.

Tadashi remembered his own war-time uniform with something approaching nostalgia, then turned his own cap over one ear, slouched against the fender of the sedan, and deliberately scuffed his already broken and dusty boots on the tire. The military now sickened him as much as it had once attracted him.

He remembered when he had been a lieutenant. It had been the same then. Affection and loathing. He had both loved and despised the Army. Now that Japan had vowed never to fight again this was one responsibility that was no longer his.

But one less among so many didn't make much difference. There was his wife, his child, and the uncle who now lived with them. There was his job, so precious and so coveted by others that he had to fight daily for it. And there was his poverty—so extreme it seemed almost like a joke. He had never been poor before the war and now, after it, could scarcely remember being anything else.

He smiled reflectively. This was far different from the war days, when his sole responsibilities were toward Emperor and country. Those times had been holidays. Even in the face of certain destruction—perhaps because of it—he had felt it was eternally New Year's, a joyous time filled with gifts and pleasures, extraordinary occurrences and freedom.

Pulling a crushed Lucky Strike from his jacket pocket, he lighted it. It had been given him by his last passenger. Now he was dependent even for his few pleasures—and he saluted privates and corporals. At the Motor Pool he bowed to the lieutenant in charge.

He looked again at the trip ticket. His departure from the Pool was penciled in one corner, and when his passenger released him he was supposed to pencil in the hour and the minute. There was not supposed to be too much of an interval between the two.

Tadashi saw that the time of departure was seven-thirty, half an hour ago. If the lady didn't come soon, he would be in danger of a delinquency report. But if he went away without her and she made a complaint, that too might mean a report. Under the new officer a driver was discharged who accumulated three reports. He'd already gotten one, on the first day, because he'd stopped to watch a baseball game.

That was very typical of the military of any land. There was no consideration for the individual. He found it ironic that the American Army, enforcing democracy, should be so undemocratic. On the surface, of course, it made a great show of democracy, which had amazed the Japanese—the non-coms didn't slap their men around, and officers were actually seen talking affably with their subordinates—but basically it too was undemocratic. Any army was like this of course, but he had felt somehow that the American Army would be different. But it wasn't. Except that it would say that it would do one thing, for one reason, and would then do something entirely different, for another reason, whereas the Japanese Army had been almost monomaniacal in its adherence to established ways. But, whatever the difference in approach, all armies were alike in being convinced that the way they did things was absolutely the right way.

Such thoughts no longer disturbed Tadashi, for he was through with armies—forever. He might be forced to work for one, but he would not obey its rules. He would be a person and would triumph over it. His friends called this sentimentality, but that was what he believed.

He was nodding his head shortly and sagely in complete agreement with himself when he happened to see the fur-coated lady standing in front of the large entrance of Tokyo Station, outlined against the white sign of the Allied entrance. She appeared to be smiling at him—he couldn't be certain. But, just in case, he smiled and, standing up straight, touched his cap, though they were blocks from each other. There was nothing servile in his gesture, it was more a thank-you for the smile she'd given him earlier. She hesitated, then disappeared.

Perhaps she had been smiling at him, and perhaps she hadn't. At any rate, with the Americans there was always the possibility that they would, and this made him feel good. Americans were actually notoriously friendly when they let themselves be. Perhaps she was simply more friendly than most. It would be so nice being around them were it not for the military.

It wasn't specifically the American military that Tadashi hated; it was the military of all nations. He even had a theory about it. It was the Army, the Navy, the Marine Corps of any nation that was responsible for that nation's difficulties. And they were so lethal that even owning one guaranteed trouble. If a country had an army, it was going to use it and could always find some excuse to do so. Japan was a perfect example.

Since the war Tadashi had become what his friends called a militant pacifist. This was very important to him, as important even as his job as sedan driver, for, in a way, his new ideas insured his dignity, his individuality—the latter concept was none the less precious to him because 'it was new—and made it possible for him to give a sort of allegiance to his job, if not to his uniformed bosses.

How ironically appropriate it had been that Japan should be destroyed by the forces she herself had used. The punishment had been terrible—and just. He was happy that there would never be another Japanese Army. The new Constitution had forbidden it. Maybe it *was* all General MacArthur's idea as they said, but it was the *Japanese* Constitution. And he—as valiant a crusader for peace as he had ever been for war—would never comply with the wishes of any army—American or otherwise.

Of course, this was all after the fact. For Japan had been destroyed—destroyed in that particularly terrifying, physical way that armies always choose. Perhaps it was the memory of the destruction that made his hatred of all armies burn as fiercely as had the fires of Tokyo. He could never forget it, and even now, years later, he relived it nightly.

He looked at the MP, at his own torn uniform, threw away the Lucky Strike butt, and again remembered what he could never forget—the destruction of Tokyo.

■

He remembered the day perfectly. It was in a cool, sunny, and unseasonably windy March. The children who had them still wore their furs. His two sisters, dressed alike in little fur hoods with cat's heads embroidered on them, were sent off to school, and his father went off to work next door at his lumberyard. His younger brother left for his classes at Chuo University, across the city, and he was left alone with his mother.

It was the third day of a leave from the Army. He had a new lieutenant's uniform. His mother wanted him to stay near home and call on the neighbors. He wanted to walk around the city and show off his new uniform. As she began the housework his mother smiled, told him to do what he wanted, and asked only that he come home early because his uncle was calling on them that evening. He told her he would, gave her a mock salute at the door, and went into the street.

Their home was in Fukagawa, which was like no place else in Tokyo. It had its own atmosphere, even as Ueno and Asakusa had theirs, but Fukagawa's was nicer, perhaps because it was not purely an amusement district. It hummed with industry; it was as though a carnival were continually in the streets. The carpenters pulled their saws, and the logs floated in the canals. The factories blew smoke to the sky, and the dye from the chemical plants made the canals green as leaves. The Chinese owned prosperous restaurants, and even the poor Koreans happily opened oysters all day long. It was the nicest part of the city.

He walked briskly, and by noon had been through all the main streets of his district. Now, having eaten three dishes of shaved ice, strawberry syrup on top, during the morning, he was ready for Tokyo's glittering center across the river, Ginza. It was time for lunch when he crossed the bridge to Nihombashi. He ate noodles at a little restaurant in the Shirokiya Department Store. Wanting to bring his mother a present, he selected a bolt of cloth—one of the more expensive cloths from under the counter, for the stock was small and consisted almost entirely of the war-time synthetics —and arranged to have it delivered to their home on the following day.

Then he went to see a movie. It was a war movie. Afterwards he walked past the Imperial Palace and took off his cap. Inside the outer moat it was cool under the pine trees, and he stood stiffly at the base of one, hoping a girl would sit nearby and think him handsome and soldierly in his cap and boots. But none did. Everyone was so busy. He'd never seen Tokyo so busy, and was pleased with the war which had given everyone his own higher duty.

After that he ate supper—he forgot where—and drank saké. Eventually he did find a woman, fashionably dressed but none the less available. They drank at a private table, and it was not until he heard the watchman making his rounds near Shimbashi Station that he realized it was ten o'clock and that he should have been home hours before.

But even then he did not leave. He could be home before eleven, and his uncle would be there at least until midnight. His father would be at one of the joro houses in the Susaki district and probably wouldn't be home until morning. So he decided to stay half an hour more, talking with the woman and enjoying her interest.

Later he was to think of the woman, whose name he could not remember having heard and whose face he had forgotten. She was dressed Western style, a rare thing during the war years, and was beautiful. And, had it not been for her, he would have been home, where he should have been and where, for many years afterward, he wished he had remained.

Some of Tokyo had already been bombed, but those few districts were far away, and the people in the rest of the city were not afraid. The radio said that the Americans dropped bombs indiscriminately and that there was no need to fear a mass attack, as the radar would detect the intruders and give ample time for escape. Just a year before, Fukagawa had been bombed, but the damage had been negligible. The bombs fell mostly into the country, and most people decided that the Americans were not very skilled in this important matter of bomb dropping. Fukagawa, near the country, had seemed as safe as Shimbashi, in the center of town.

Tadashi heard the watchman at eleven and was regretfully taking leave of the woman when the call of the watch was interrupted by the air-raid sirens. Earlier in the afternoon, while he had been in the movie, there had been an alert, but the all-clear had sounded immediately after.

Now Tadashi walked swiftly through the exit stiles of Shimbashi Station—secretly rejoicing that his uniform allowed it—and ran through the standing passengers, past the halted trains, to the top level of the building. He didn't really expect to see anything; he only wanted to be soldierly. This would impress the lovely lady.

He arrived at the top level just in time to see the sudden flair of massed incendiary bombs. It was Fukagawa. The planes were apparently traveling in a great circle. It was impossible to say how many there were, but it seemed hundreds. A great ring of fire was spreading. The planes were so low he couldn't see them and could tell where they had been only by the fires that sprang from the earth behind them. There was an enormous explosion, like August fireworks on the Sumida River, and a great ball of fire fell back on the district. A chemical plant had been hit. Minutes later, Tadashi felt the warm gust of air from the blast, miles away.

Later he heard that the planes had come in so low

that they escaped the radar. The anti-aircraft could do nothing against planes that near and that swift. The stiff March wind helped spread the flames. Tadashi remembered thinking, at the time, of the canals that cut through the section, and he realized that the people could at least find safety in the water. There would be water enough for all.

He didn't know how long he stood on the top platform of Shimbashi Station watching the destruction of Fukagawa, Honjo, Asakusa, Ueno. It must have been for a very long time, and he wondered why they were so selective—why not the Ginza, why not Shimbashi Station, why not him, Tadashi? He remembered walking up the deserted streets past the closed motion-picture house where he had been that afternoon. It was near dawn when he reached Shirokiya Department Store again. The last pink of the fires had been replaced by the first pink of dawn.

At that corner he first saw those coming over from Fukagawa. Most of them were burned. They carried scorched bedding on their backs, or trundled bicycles with a few possessions strapped to them. They walked slowly and didn't look at him as they passed. He wondered where they were all going. Finally he stopped one old man, who told him that everything had been burned and that everyone had been killed, and his tone of voice seemed to include himself in the death list.

It was at the bridge across the Sumida that he first saw Fukagawa. He couldn't believe it. There was nothing. Nothing but black and smoking ruins, as far as he could see in all directions. He had never known that so much could be destroyed in one night.

On the bridge he found a bicycle that belonged to no one, and on it he started toward his home. Nothing looked the same. There were scarcely streets any more. In cleared places were piles of burned bodies, as though a family had huddled beneath a roof that had now disappeared. They seemed very small and looked like charcoal.

He peddled slowly along the street. Long lines of quiet, burned people, all looking the same, came toward him. He didn't know where to turn north to go to his father's lumberyard. Nothing was familiar. He leaned the bicycle against a smoking factory wall and looked toward where his home should have been but wasn't. The lines of the burned moved slowly by, and suddenly, for the first time in years, he began to cry.

After he had cried he looked at the people again and saw his younger brother coming toward him. They were both amazed. It was fantastic that such a thing had happened. The slowly moving lines parted around them in the middle of what had been a street.

His brother had spent the night at school because he had to finish a war-work project of some kind, and he hadn't heard about the raid until he awoke. He had just arrived and didn't know where their house was either. So they began walking.

Troops had already been brought in and were clearing the streets, or where they supposed the streets had been. They shifted the bodies with large hooks and loaded them, one after the other, onto trucks. Often the burned flesh pulled apart, making their work difficult.

They walked on, past mothers holding burned infants to their breasts, past little children, boys and girls, all dead, crouched together as for warmth. Once they passed an air-raid shelter and looked in. It was full of bodies, most of them still smouldering.

The next bridge was destroyed, so they decided to separate. His brother would go north, and he south. It was the first time they had used the words north and south to each other. They usually spoke of "up by the elementary school" or "down by the chemical plant" or "where we saw the big dog fight that day."

His brother started crying and walked away rubbing his eyes. They were to meet at their uncle's house in Shinagawa.

Tadashi walked south to the factory section. The chemical works had exploded and what little remained was too hot to get near. Some of the walls were standing, burned a bright green from the dye, the color of leaves. In a locomotive yard the engines were smoking as though ready for a journey, the cars jammed together as in a railway accident. There were some in the ruins still alive, burned or wounded. Those who couldn't walk were patiently waiting for help by the side of the road. There was no sound but the moaning of an old woman. It sounded like a lullaby.

He saw only two ambulances. They were full of wounded, lying there as though dead. Farther on, prisoners-of-war were clearing the smoking ruins. They wore red uniforms and carried blankets for the removal of the dead.

Eventually he recognized the Susaki district. Yesterday it had been a pleasure center, with gayly-colored decorations, sidewalk stalls, girls peeping from behind lattice-work screens, and music. Now there was nothing. The houses, like the decorations, had been made only of wood and paper and had burned almost at once. Now in the early morning the district was very quiet, and no one moved.

He turned back. The small bridges across the canals had been burned. He had to stay on the large island connected to Nihombashi by the bridge across the Sumida. He looked across the canals and saw people still alive on the little, smoking islands. They shouted and waved, but there was nothing he could do, so he went on. Some were swimming across to the large island. They had to push aside others who floated there face down.

In a burned primary school he saw the bodies of

children who had run there, to their teachers, for protection.   Later he learned there had been two thousand dead children in that school alone.   They lay face down on the scorched concrete floor, as though asleep.   The kimonos of some still smoked.   The teachers to whom they had fled lay among them.

It was past noon when, suddenly very tired, he walked back across the bridge, back past Shirokiya where only twenty-four hours before he had been eating noodles, buying his mother a present, stealing a look at his uniform in a mirror.   He took a trolley to Shinagawa. It was almost night before he reached his uncle's house. The trolley stopped continually.   It was filled with wounded, and others, less wounded, hung from the roof and the sides.   He could have arrived sooner by walking, but there was a fascination in the macabre ride from which he could not tear himself away.

At his uncle's house he found his brother and, surprisingly, his uncle.   The latter's arm was badly burned, and he was wounded about the face and head.   He had come home that afternoon, walking the entire distance. He told them about their family.

They had been sitting around the table drinking beer, his sister and himself.   The younger girls had already gone to bed, and his brother-in-law was at Susaki.   He said that first the planes bombed the outskirts of Fukagawa and Honjo, then closed the circle, making it smaller and smaller.   It was difficult to escape because it happened so swiftly.   Almost instantly there was fire on all sides.

By the time the air-raid sirens had begun they heard the explosions, and flames were leaping up in the distance.   The airplanes wheeled over them, and the circle of fire was much nearer.   They got the little girls up, but by the time they were dressed the fire was only a block away.   They tried to escape from the lumberyard, but the little bridge which led to the Tokyo road was burning. So they climbed into the canal in back of the house.

Sticks of bombs were dropping constantly, and finally one of them hit the house. The heat was terrible. Even the logs in the canal began to smoke. They watched the fire spread, in just a few seconds, to the storehouses and then to the entire island. Tadashi's mother and sisters held on to a log and began crying.

Their uncle found a pan and dipped water over their heads and shoulders. The little fur hoods with cats embroidered on them helped protect the children for a while, but when the fur began smoking he tore off the hoods and poured water directly on their hair. The portion of the log above water cracked in the heat, but he kept on pouring water.

There he remained until early morning. About one, the fires burning around them just as fiercely as before, he became very tired. He tried to get a better grip on the log but found his arm so burned that it stuck to the wood. He was unable both to hold up his sister and nieces and at the same time continue to pour water over them. They were very quiet and, he was sure, unconscious. His arm was so tired that he too must have lost consciousness. The pain of his arm's slipping across the the burning log woke him. The mother and two little girls were gone.

The next day Tadashi and his brother went again to Fukagawa. It was now filled with rescue workers. They found their canal and the ruins of their home. Everything was gone. Only the earth and a few stones remained. They identified the house from its unburned foundation stones. Near where the house had been they were removing bodies. He tried to find some of his neighbors but couldn't. Everyone there was a stranger. No one knew where his father's workers were either. They had lived above the warehouse where the finished lumber had been stored.

Later he learned that thirty thousand people had been killed that evening. Some said it was the unseasonable wind that had done the most damage. It spread the fire and the heat. The explosions caused more wind until, about one in the morning, it flew through the flames at a mile a minute.

It was almost a week before the Emperor inspected the ruins. By this time the bodies had all been removed. Already the streets were being re-mapped, and bright wooden bridges connected the islands. The people Tadashi talked to all felt that the Army had delayed the Emperor's arrival. They didn't want him to see how terrible the fire had been. If he had, he would have stopped the war at once. But now, with a new week's fighting begun, he naturally could do nothing about it. It was the fault of the Army.

For the rest of the summer Tadashi's brother went to live with his uncle. Lieutenant Tadashi was sent to Tachikawa Air Base. Then soon it was August, and the war was over. About the same time, Shirokiya sent the bolt of cloth he'd ordered for his mother. There was no house at the address, and they sent him a card about it.

When he saw Fukagawa again he was surprised. People were living there once more. The main business was still lumber. Before the fire there had been over two thousand lumber dealers, but now there were only slightly over a hundred. There were no chemical industries, but the dye-works were open and the canals were green again. The Chinese restaurants were thriving as usual, and even small Korean centers had sprung up. But now their old occupation—opening oysters— had been taken over by Japanese. It was about the only way of making a living.

He no longer liked Fukagawa. Its atmosphere was gone, as was Asakusa's. It was now only the poorest section of the city. Whole families lived in four-

and-a-half mat rooms; some lived in U. S. Army
packing cases or former air-raid shelters. It was no
longer a unique district. It was being rebuilt, like
every place else, only it was uglier than most. He
hated going there and very rarely had occasion to do
so since few Americans ever went there. He never
went back to where his house had been, nor to the
green canal behind it.

But sometimes, after work, he would take the slow
and noisy trolley past Fukagawa to the old Susaki district. It alone remained black and empty, a barren
field, with no ruins, no trace of life. Sometimes he
stood there for fifteen minutes or so, his head bowed.

■

The MP walked over.

"Looky, Joe," he said, "you been standing here staring
for the last fifteen minutes. Gimme your stub. Trip
ticket. That's right."

The soldier took the ticket. "O. K., Joe, she no
come. You go." He made waving motions with his
hands. "Go on now—hayaku. Your lady-friend's not
gonna turn up."

As Tadashi was climbing into the sedan the MP felt
in his breast pocket and brought out some cigarettes.
He handed half a dozen to Tadashi.

"Here, Jackson, for your trouble," he said and smiled.

That was the second smile he'd received. Tadashi
touched his hat gratefully, took the cigarettes and the
trip ticket, and smiled back. The MP winked, went
back to the entrance, took a parade-rest stance, and held
both it and the wink. Tadashi laughed and started
his motor.

Just as he was backing out a soldier ran up to him
and, in Japanese, said: "Can you please take me to
Shinjuku?"

Tadashi was both surprised and embarrassed. If it

had been English, he wouldn't have understood or, at least, could have pretended not to. But the soldier's Japanese was remarkably good. So Tadashi could only shake his head.

"Please," said the soldier. "I'm late for work."

Tadashi put his foot on the accelerator and released the brake. It was against the rules. One must have a trip ticket. An Occupation driver could not drive just anyone who asked him. Those were the rules.

"I sorry," Tadashi said, in English.

The soldier reluctantly pulled out a full pack of Chesterfields. "Please," he said.

Tadashi became frightened. Any infraction of the rules still frightened him. "No," he said shortly, "I sorry." And the car rolled backward.

The soldier took the cigarettes from the window and put them into his pocket.

The MP stepped forward and said: "Hey, what's going on here?"

The soldier turned, looked at him, said: "None of your god-damned business," and began running as fast as he could toward Tokyo Station.

The MP was about to run after him, but then decided he couldn't leave his post to go chase the soldier.

Tadashi by this time had backed the car out and was starting down the street. He passed the soldier in the next block, but he was not thinking of him, nor of the American lady, nor of his own ideals. He was thinking that he was forty-five minutes late and would receive another delinquency report.

■

The sedan passed the running soldier and was far away by the time he reached the Allied entrance to the trains. He glanced behind him, but the MP was not pursuing. Overhead a train rolled in, and he ran up the steps two at a time, down the length of the waiting train to the last car, which had a broad white line painted along its side.

"Chuo?" he shouted at the train boy, who nodded. As he stepped into the train, the doors slammed shut.

A dozen soldiers were in the car and a couple of civilians. In one corner three Nisei soldiers were pointing out the sights to each other, and in another two very young buck privates were lost in dozens of comic books. He shoved his bag into an overhead rack and sat down beside an older soldier who was looking out the window. The train curved out of the station, above the buildings, toward Kanda.

The older soldier looked at him. He had a large bulbous nose, pitted like a raspberry. "Boy, you just made it, didn't you? One more minute and you'd have been real left out."

"I ran all the way." He looked out the window at the receding platform, still thinking of the MP.

The older soldier laughed indulgently. "Do it all the time myself, out after a shack-up job and run like hell to get in. You got to be in by noon?"

"I'm supposed to be now. I work this morning." He looked at his wrinkled uniform and felt his day-old beard.

The soldier with the big nose nodded sympathetically, then asked: "You going to Shinjuku?"

He was answered with a nod.

"You with the Engineers out there?"

The younger soldier shook his head no. He turned away and looked out of the window. He wanted to think, not talk with some old Regular Army gasser. You could tell them a mile away. It seemed he hadn't thought for weeks, and he had lots to think about. One never seemed to have time to think in the Army, or in any event it certainly wasn't encouraged. And he must think now. In a week he might be married. Or well on his way toward it. But there was no reason to feel so continually surprised. He might have seen it coming a year ago.

Even his first letters home had shown some indication of what might happen. Those letters must have sounded pretty enthusiastic, all filled with discoveries he took for granted now. That the people weren't yellow after all, that their eyes didn't slant, that it wasn't a small country, and that the Japanese weren't midgets.

The letters from his parents said they were glad that he liked it over there and that he was enjoying himself. He must remember to dress warmly enough because his mother had heard on the radio that it was a cold winter. And his father hoped he was enjoying himself and wasn't letting his enjoying himself interfere with being a good soldier which was, after all, the reason he was there. They'd apparently thought Japan was like a new bicycle or an electric train.

Half a year later he'd tried to tell them how he felt. He'd used phrases such as "I feel I really belong here ..." This had inspired letters, by return mail, in which his mother asked about his health and was he sure he was dressing warmly enough, and his father seriously asked if he were learning Japanese and, jokingly, if he had a Japanese girl.

As a matter of fact, he *was* learning Japanese, in the Army school, but he hadn't met the girl yet. It wasn't until three months later that he met her. He'd gotten tired of wandering around Tokyo on a rainy Saturday afternoon and had gone to the Servicemen's Center for a free cup of coffee. In the next room a flower-arrangement lesson was going on. He stood in back of the officers' wives and WAC's and saw her for the first time. She was bending an iris so deftly that it seemed to have grown around the pine branch.

Afterwards he'd elbowed his way through the WAC's and used his best Japanese to ask questions about flower arranging. She'd answered, her eyes lowered, one hand holding a spray of wisteria, for all the world like one of the girls in the old prints he'd seen and liked. After the others had left he asked if she would give him lessons, and she, pleased and flattered, said she would. She was very pretty.

In Haruko he had found personified what he liked about Japan. He watched her cut a camellia and put it near a rock, and the rock became beautiful. It was like those farm houses he had seen which were built around a tree or a boulder. The farmers, unwilling to sacrifice the natural surroundings, had fitted the houses to the landscape.

When he tried to learn to do the same thing and, disillusioned, stood back regarding the sprays of iris all going one way, the magnolias the other, she complimented him on supposed beauties of construction which he knew did not exist in his arrangement but which she created with deft touches, apparently mere caresses of admiration, until, after the last admiring pat, the arrangement was just right. It was never necessary to admit he was clumsy and unskilful, just as it was never made apparent that he could be wrong. One week they had changed the time of the lessons, and he had forgotten. She came an hour later and, when she saw him, understood at once and could not often enough remind him of her tardiness.

And just as she was sensitive to flowers, so was she sensitive to all beautiful things. Occasionally she recited Japanese poetry to him and taught him how the haiku and the tanka were constructed. One day she looked at him for a long time, then wrote a haiku. She lived naturally with beauty, he liked to think, and used it daily as other women use the mirror....

"Pretty hot place, Shinjuku?" It was the old soldier with the nose. He moved closer and said: "Wouldn't know myself. I'm out Tachikawa way."

"Then you're on the wrong train."

"Aw, hell, I got the whole day. I'm not on my way back. Ginza's dead. I'm gonna go over Shinjuku way and try it out. Hell, I'm gonna have myself a real time today."

"Oh, you'll probably find Shinjuku pretty dead too then. It all depends on what you want to do."

The old soldier shrugged his shoulders. "You know —usual stuff—get a few souvenirs, get laid. Can't get drunk around here—that saké rots your guts right out of you. Go to the EM Club and you blow your dough in five minutes. Jesus, prices are high here, you know."

The younger soldier turned back toward the window and said shortly: "I don't know about Shinjuku. I don't spend much time there."

"Well, guess I'll just have to find out for myself then. I hear tell the gook girls'll lay faster there than any place else though." He paused and the asked: "What do you think?"

The younger soldier didn't answer. He was allergic to the word "gook."

"Course," the old soldier continued, "I always say that any gook girl'll spread her legs if you ask her the right way—and get her away from mama." He laughed heartily and blew his raspberry nose before continuing: "Hell, man, why I don't know when I had so much fun as with some of these little gook girls. Why, I know one..."

He continued on and on, talking into the younger soldier's ear while train boy carefully swept the cigarette butts from between the passenger's feet and entered the small compartment at the end of the car with his dust pan.

Past the door at the opposite end of the car was the next coach. There was no glass in the door, and the people were pressed tightly against each other. A student, in his high-collared uniform and cap, was pressed against one corner of the door-frame. Beside him was a short little man with a bow tie and a derby hat. The student seemed to be staring at the younger soldier, who looked back once and then turned toward the window again. Since he'd met her he didn't much like institutions like the Allied car.

Beside him the old soldier talked on. The Army was full of men like him. That was what armies were for apparently, to provide homes for otherwise homeless men like this one. The younger soldier wondered what would happen if he were to turn around and hit him. Nothing probably. Yet it was strange that while he himself wouldn't hesitate to talk back to an MP just doing his duty, still he wouldn't—couldn't—push around men like this one.

His barracks were full of them. He had to live with them. His flower-arranging lessons had been their delight once they had discovered them. But, come to think of it, they had been more approving than otherwise. They sanctioned any method which worked toward the given, the approved end, no matter how devious. But when they discovered that this wasn't what he was after, their attitude changed.

They no longer kidded him, and if he mentioned her, there was a depressing silence. They could somehow detect the difference between lust and love, and they behaved accordingly. And when they saw him being friendly to their Japanese janitor, they found a name for him.

Eventually the lessons were held at her house. He was surprised to find that hers was a wealthy family and that she had been sent to the Servicemen's Center, not to earn money, but to overcome a natural shyness which her parents thought excessive. They were quite delighted when she brought home an American. He usually bought presents at the PX for them, and they insisted he spend Saturdays and Sundays with them. She acted as an occasional interpreter or helped him

with his Japanese lessons or just sat beside him while
he, his shoes off, lying on his stomach on the tatami,
looked through her photograph albums and decided
he had never been happier. It seemed inevitable that
he fall love with her.

When he wrote his parents about his feelings, his
mother hadn't even answered, and his father, refusing
to believe his son was serious, attempted a joke, asking
if it really went sidewise. He'd written back angrily,
and there had been no more letters for a time. In the
barracks for several months now he'd been known as
a gook-lover.

This disapproval of his parents and the soldiers he
lived with had only made him the more determined in
his belief in her and his love. Last night her parents
had gone to Atami, and after the servants had gone to
bed, he had scratched at the shoji, and she had let
him in.

" . . . and so I went to the PX and I got the prettiest
little dress you ever saw." The older soldier was still
talking, leaning confidentially toward the other. "And,
boy, you ought to seen those eyes light up like Christmas trees when I give it to her. I said, 'Baby, you
done earned this,' and laughed my fool head off. And
then, you know, first day she wore it outside, one of
these god-damn snoopy Jap policemen stopped her and
took her to the station. Thought she stole it, you
know. Made her give up the dress and sent her home
with just her coat over her underwear. Told her she
wouldn't get it back until whoever gave her the dress
showed up and said he had. So she came to me, all
tears, you know." He stopped and blew his nose.

"What did you do? asked the younger soldier,
interested.

"Me? Why, I never went near the little bitch again,
of course. She knew where I was though and used to
ride those damn crowded gook trains out Tachikawa

way every day. I never let her see me after the first time, though. Jesus, you'll get into trouble, you know. You're not supposed to let PX stuff get to the Japs— black market. I don't mind the black market, of course, but you got to watch it and make clean business—this messing around with the Jap police could put me right in the stockade. So, if I hadn't been smart and tossed her on her big fat can, I'd of wound up with all sorts of trouble on the deal. See what I mean?"

"Yeah, I see what you mean."

This poor girl probably loved that raspberry-nosed bastard too. Japanese girls all seemed anxious to love and to trust. He closed his eyes and turned his back on the older soldier. The very thought of something like this happening to Haruko made him cold all over.

He remembered how she'd looked last night when he'd scratched on the shoji and she'd opened it. She'd been sleeping in a light-blue summer yukata dyed with a pattern of cranes. Her face was pink, and she rubbed her eyes as though she could not believe it possible that he was there.

"Why?" she asked softly, in English, looking over her shoulder, afraid the old servant might hear. "Go back. Do not do this," she continued in Japanese. She didn't seem afraid, merely concerned for his sake. "When they discover you, you'll be punished."

She was so sincere, and looked so much like a little girl as she knelt by the shoji with one hand delicately on its frame, that he could not help smiling as he said:

"I came to ask you to marry me."

"Marry you?" she asked, and her hand dropped into her lap as she knelt by the shoji. She had apparently never thought of this. "Do you want to be married. To me?"

He nodded.

The moon came from behind a willow, and her face was white.

He stood in the shadow, black, unable to speak.

Somewhere behind her a clock struck one. "Come in," she said softly.

He sat on the edge of the sill and took off his shoes, then swung his feet around and sat inside. She pulled the shoji closed behind him. He looked around him. It was the first time he had ever been in her room.

It was perfectly plain and rather small—six tatami in size. During the day the doors were opened and it became a part of the house. He had often seen it from the main room. This was where her mother knelt, sewing, during his visits—near enough to be seen, far enough away not to appear to be chaperoning them. At night, however, the doors were slid to and it became Haruko's room.

In the tokonoma, below the scroll picture, were some chrysanthemums, arranged in a flat, square bowl, their stems cut very short. There were chrysanthemums in the garden too. House and garden flowed one into the other, separated only by the paper doors, doors so insubstantial that they seemed to Michael more symbolic than actual, symbolizing a barrier that he had just crossed.

She knelt before him. "I could bring you tea. But it might wake the servant. Her room is very near."

He shook his head and looked at the futon where she had been sleeping. Her pallet was very narrow and looked small lying there on the tatami, reminding him of a child's bed. The pillow was small, round, and probably hard. It was still slightly dented from where her neck had laid against it. He put his hand under the padded coverings on the bed. It was warm inside.

"Are you cold? I could bring in the hibachi, but it might wake her. And in the morning too she would wonder. It is too early in the year for me to want a hibachi. Shall I bring it?"

He shook his head again. There was nothing in the room that showed it was hers except the high chest that held her clothes, and her few possessions on top of it. There was a tiny wristwatch and a small statue of Beethoven. Next to them was a small plastic wallet containing her identification card, some pictures taken on a school picnic almost five years before, and her monthly train pass. There was also a rather large French doll in the shape of a brown-satin negress with golden hair. Beside it there was a child's bank, which was made to resemble a Swiss chalet with painted snow on the roof. These, and the clothes in the closet, and a few books—mostly translated German and French novels —were her only belongings. They looked so fragile, these few possessions—one swing of the arm could break them all. Michael, thinking he had never seen anything so lovable, so unbearably sad as the top of that chest, turned quickly away.

"Are you hungry?" she began again. "I could—"

"No, I'm not hungry. Nor thirsty. Nor cold. I came to ask you to marry me."

She was silent for a moment. Then, suddenly, in English: "No, me promised."

He had noticed before that whenever he wanted to say anything serious, to say anything that mattered to either of them, she always insisted on English, as though it put what they were talking of farther away from her—and as though that was what she wanted.

"Let's speak Japanese," said Michael. "My Japanese is better than your English."

"All right, we'll speak Japanese. English is so difficult. I've studied since I was a little girl and I'll never be able to speak well. The words are so long and so hard to pronounce and each one has so many meanings. When I was in high school—"

"Haruko! I came to ask you to marry me."

"Oh."

"Will you marry me?"

"Me promised," she said in English.

"All right, we'll talk in English if you want. In English, now: Will—you—marry—me?"

"I understand. I good understand. Me promised."

"I am promised," he corrected. "Is that what you mean—engaged?"

"Yes, I engaged," she repeated. Then she continued: "Young man, same age."

Michael had known this for some time. On his first visit her father, with great delicacy, had hinted until there could be no doubt that he was understood. She was to marry the son of an important man in one of Japan's largest entertainment combines. It was really a merger of the two families and would supposedly benefit both.

"Tomorrow I see," said Haruko. "At opera—at, how you say ...?"

"At the theater," said Michael. For some weeks he had also known that the official meeting would take place at the Imperial Theatre. Both Haruko and the boy had known each other almost all their lives, but tradition must be observed, and everyone would pretend that this formal, ceremonial meeting was the first time they'd ever seen each other. Michael had seen these meetings before, at the Kabuki, in the cherry groves at Ueno during the spring, in fashionable restaurants. Both the boy and the girl would avoid each other so far as possible. She would exclaim constantly upon the beauty of the blossoms, while he would examine his shoes or his hat. Up until this very moment Michael he had always thought such meetings both ludicrous and amusing.

"That's why I came, Haruko. I want you to marry *me*. I love you." It sounded strange in English, and then he realized that he'd always thought these words in Japanese.

She looked away. There was no light, and the moon shone through the paper, filling the room with an almost luminous glow. She reflectively ran her finger along the pattern cast by the shoji.

"I love you," she said, but it was only the repetition of an unfamiliar phrase. Then she looked up and said: "I love you too—I think."

"You think? Don't you know?

She laughed. "How I know? Japanese girl no know anything. I know Papa-san and Mama-san no want I love you much. They know you love me. But I love you? I no know." She smiled, as though it were a joke between them....

The train jerked to a stop and the doors opened. An old lady, looking straight ahead, tried to board the car while the train boy, pushing her away, kept pointing in the direction of the Japanese cars. Understanding at last, she was still running awkwardly along the train when the doors slammed to and the train pulled past her and out of the station.

The older soldier was still talking: "Yessir, lot's of trouble if you're not smart enough to watch out for it. You got to understand these folks, got to understand their psychology. And, course, they ain't got good sense and that makes things more difficult. Now just look at them, like a bunch of animals."

He jerked his thumb over his shoulder at the next coach, and the student stared at the younger soldier, whose eyes had inadvertently followed the other soldier's thumb. The old soldier stuck out his underlip, then suddenly smiled expansively and dug the other in the ribs with his elbow.

"But—we should worry, huh? We never had it so good." He laughed good-naturedly and blew his nose.

Michael did not turn away this time. He looked steadily at the nose and the good-natured eyes for a second. For some time he had known that just as he had come to love Haruko as a personification of Japan, so had he come to despise representatives of America like this soldier. What happened to Americans abroad? They changed somehow. This fellow in the fields of Arkansas or the hills of Tennessee would have been a nice guy. But here he became a kind of monster. Was this what came from being a native of the richest, most powerful country in the world? Or was this what came from being a conqueror? Or was it both?

He didn't know, but he did know that one either went the way of this bastard or else went the way he himself had gone. No one ever felt lukewarm about Japan—you either loved it or hated it. It brought out a strong emotion in any case. The only difficulty was that either way it also changed your opinion of your own country. It made men like this think America was best because it was richest. And it made men like himself critical of America, just because it was the richest, most powerful, and because it could create sons of bitches like this one. He shook his head and turned away.

The soldier leaned forward and touched Michael's shoulder.

Michael moved his shoulder quickly. She had touched his shoulder last night. She had bent forward and said: "If I love, I love Michael." He shook his head, wondering how it was possible not to be certain whether one loved or not. You either did or you didn't.

He had looked so unhappy that she had laughed again, the way Japanese always laugh when they are about to tell you something particularly sad.

"Michael," she said, "come sit. More close." She pointed to her narrow futon. "We talk."

They talked until the moon had long faded and the first sunshine turned the panes of the paper shoji a faint pink. She argued that marriage was impossible. She could not leave home. She could not disappoint her parents. He said that if she loved him as much as he loved her she wouldn't even think of reasons like those. Surprisingly, she agreed with him and seemed to feel sad that it was so. Frightened, he explained to her that she did indeed love him very much. She appeared to believe it and was happy again. He told her how he would take her home and how his parents would love her as though she were their own daughter and how happy they would all be. She said nothing, merely sighed.

Later on, he kissed her, and she turned her head shyly and laughed.

"What's so funny?" he asked.

"Nothing," she said, still laughing. "This is my first time to be kissed. It is strange."

He leaned over her, holding her by the shoulders. "Does it seem nice?"

She wrinkled her forehead, thinking, then said: "If we do it again, we will know, won't we?"

He kissed her several more times.

"Yes," she said finally, "it very nice. Now it is morning. I'll get tea for you—at last."

She made him sit in the corner so that anyone opening the doors would not at once see him. The Japanese house had absolutely no privacy. There were no locks on the doors, no doorknobs—actually no doors in the usual meaning of the word. He had always vaguely approved of this until now.

So he had sat and watched the new sunlight creep slowly across the tatami. . . .

He opened his eyes. The train was going through a large park. In the distance was a dome. Near the track were a number of small new houses and beside them a stretch of burned ground with a single tall chimney in the middle. Children were playing in roads, and beyond them a fleet of kites rose from behind a clump of dusty trees.

The Nisei soldiers pointed the kites out to each other. The very young soldiers were still deep in their comic books.

"Where are we?" asked the older soldier.

Michael looked out of the window. "Shinano-machi."

"Boy, that's a mouthful," said the other.

Michael didn't answer.

"Boy, I bet you get tired of the same old route. I know just what you mean. There's a little old street-car out of Tachikawa and, Jesus, do I get tired of that thing—take it to. see my girl. The new one, that is."

"I usually take the subway," said Michael. It made him feel a bit noble, being polite to someone he hated so.

"Do you now?" He had at last sensed the formality of Michael's manner and, in turn, spoke a bit stiffly and politely himself. "I always wanted to do that, but it's kind of unsafe, isn't it? Hell, I wouldn't want no DR." He laughed self-indulgently. "I got enough of them as is."

Michael rubbed his eyes and felt the beard on his chin. "Never saw any MP's on it. It used to be on-limits, you know."

"Don't I know!" said the older soldier, drawing himself up. He had been offended. "Hell, man, I was one of the first GI's on Jap soil. I came in with the Bataan boys. Why, we used to have the run of this place. Nothing chicken like now." He smiled in re-miniscence. "Sure, subway and all. Boy, used to get right in among 'em. And the smell! Damned if I see how the gooks stand it. I never could. Hell, how you stand it, man?" This was a joke but, now unsure of Michael, he laughed to show it was.

Michael didn't see the laugh though. He was looking out the window, and the train had started again.

The older soldier scratched his head, then turned around and looked covetously at the comic books.

The park flashed past, and Michael realized he was hungry. The tea, soup, and pickled vegetables that Haruko had finally brought him wasn't very much for breakfast.

"I thought you could eat some miso-shiru," she said, uncovering the soup.

"You've been gone an hour," he said accusingly.

"Yes," she said. "But no one hear—talk quiet." She was speaking English again.

The tray she put before him was a work of art. She'd had to clean a whole daikon in order to make a single slice, like a full moon on one side of the plate; she'd gathered and cut scallions so that a touch of green balanced it; she'd made a fish-cake flower, all pink and white in the middle, and had balanced this with a carefully grated mound of red radish. This alone must have taken the hour.

He drank the soup, wondering if she would ever realize other things were sometimes more important than etiquette, than the art of graceful serving, than the conferring of favors like the exquisite plate before him.

"I'd rather have had you with me during that hour," he said softly.

"If we be married, you have me many, many hours. Too many, I think maybe."

"No, not too many. You mean a great many."

"Yes," she laughed, "I always mistake. Many, many."

She had already started to ask him about a fine point of English grammar when he suddenly realized what she'd said. "You said—if we are to be married!"

"Yes. If."

"But then, you *will* marry me?"

"Oh, yes. I would. Happy, many happy."

"Then you will?"

"Will? Oh, no. I don't know about that. I must think much."

They talked until almost seven. Their voices grew more and more soft, and they held their breath when the old servant passed along the corridor outside the door, separated from them only by paper. Fortunately she was hard of hearing.

Haruko had wedged a small table against the fusuma opening into the corridor, but it wouldn't hold if anyone used a bit of force. Like most Japanese things, it too was intensely fragile. If you moved too swiftly in a Japanese house, you broke something.

It was full morning and he was sleepy. "Please," he said.

She smiled and then said he must go. They would be discovered if he remained. And he must not allow the neighbors, who almost always saw everything anyway, to view his departure. He must be very swift and very silent.

He said he wouldn't go until she said either that she would marry him or that she wouldn't.

Quite suddenly she kissed him and said: "Yes, yes, I will marry. Now go."

She pushed him from the shoji into the garden and then, kneeling, waved good-by, though they were only a few feet apart.

He let himself out the gate and took the crowded subway downtown. So now he was going to get married. And the sooner the better....

"Shinjuku," said the older soldier, looking out of the window. Ahead, a group of higher buildings rose above the small houses, above the maze of small streets—four or five high buildings, all white in the sun.

"I know; I live there," said Michael.

"You live there? What d'ya know." He was starting another conversation, but the train was slowing down, so he stood up. He laughed and carefully laid his half-smoked cigarette on the floor. "Boy, you can't say I'm not good to these gooks. Hell, I never step on my butts." With exaggerated care he stepped over it. "When Junior comes by and takes his dust pan into that closet again to count over the butts, he's gonna have a real nice surprise."

He swayed slightly. The car came to a sudden stop

and threw him off balance. He had stepped on the cigarette and swore, then laughed and turned to Michael: "Well, here we are!"

"I know," said Michael shortly.

The other looked at Michael over his large, pitted nose. "Hey, how's about showing me around a little? I don't know this place, you know. You could just steer me a bit. Hell, I got money. I'm gonna have me one hell of a good time."

"I told you I had to be in. I'm supposed to be at work now."

"That's right," said the other. He seemed dimly aware that he had antagonized Michael, and it disturbed him. "Just a drink maybe—some good ole Shinjuku saké."

They were all alike. Show them you didn't like them and they came fawning like puppies. Any number of Americans he knew just couldn't stand not being liked. They liked being conquerors, but they wanted the conquered to like it too. He remembered overhearing an American woman's dismissing the entire population of Japan by saying: "They really don't act like they're glad we won the war." This craving for being liked—it was the American's soft spot, and it was a yard wide. And they could never understand why sometimes people didn't like them—they all got childish hurt eyebrows such as this one had now.

The coach door was thrown open and the train boy called the station in the typical high chanting voice that all train boys in Japan have used, apparently, ever since there have been trains. The two soldiers were thrown together, surrounded by those pouring from the other coaches. Women with children on their backs, old men, girls going to school, young businessmen, all pushing each other unmercifully, safe in their anonymity.

"Jesus!" said the older soldier.

Down the stairway, on the street level, the crowd was less dense. Both soldiers passed through the Allied entrance, and Michael started down the street.

"Hey, Mac," called the older one, "come on. Let's have ourselves a real time. Come on!"

Michael did not not turn around until he reached the street corner. By then the old soldier with the red nose was standing there, stupidly looking around him.

Shinjuku was where the farmers came, and Michael was glad he was stationed there. Around the station, street stalls lined the gutters, and opposite them stood small open shops. Sides of red beef hung from the ceilings on hooks; whole fish, brittle and dusty, fastened through the gills, lay against the walls; and the floors were covered with barrels and boxes. In the stores were country people carrying large bundles carefully wrapped in pieces of cloth. The bright colors of other parts of town were missing. Instead there were the somber blues and browns and grays, the slight checks and stripes of country people's clothing.

Whole families loaded with bundles struggled through the crowds, calling to each other at times. Cocks in wicker cages crowed, and pigs in baskets squealed. Some little children, playing a game like hide-and-seek, ran skilfully between the passing legs.

Further along the street the stalls disappeared. There was no more room for them on the sidewalks. The buildings were taller now and the busy intersection was the center of Shinjuku. There were small hardware-shops, teashops, small theatres, and geta-shops where rows of wooden clogs and sandals stretched in lines of yellow unfinished wood, white in the sunlight.

Michael smelled the clean rice smell of the Japanese. In close quarters it tended to grow musty, but in the open air the smell was exhilarating. He smelled something else, and it reminded him of Haruko—as did everything Japanese. He finally located it. A Japanese war veteran, with one leg and one arm gone, was standing on the corner in his clean white robe and field cap. His long hair was beautifully parted, and Michael could smell the same rich odor of pomade that he had associated up until now only with Haruko.

Further on was an antique store. There were English signs in the window as well as a suit of ancient Japanese armour, a hand-wound phonograph, and a Petty-girl calendar. An elderly American couple, man and wife apparently, and a young lieutenant were looking in the window.

"Oh, but it can't be. It just *can't*. Not here, not right out in the open," said the woman in little screams, her white hair upswept and held in place by several lacquered geisha combs. She was uncommonly white.

"Well, my dear, as they say in New York, step in and try it on," said the elderly gentleman, also quite white.

"But not here, not here where we've combed every alley for years. Not a real piece of celadon. I simply can't believe it."

"That's what it looks like, ma'am," said the lieutenant. "Let's go in and see."

"But you know it couldn't be. You just don't *find* things like that—except in Korea, of course."

The lieutenant took off his cap and ran his fingers boyishly through his brown, curly hair. "Well, I don't know much about stuff like pottery, ma'am. But you never can tell." He put one hand rakishly on his hip and with a bow, like an Oriental shopkeeper—or his idea of one—indicated the door.

Michael purposely chose this moment to salute. The lieutenant, with a glance of alarm, put on his hat and saluted in return. By that time, however, Michael was past.

The lady laughed merrily. "Oh, Lieutenant, your hat's on sidewise. You look just like Napoleon."

Her husband laughed too, gruffly, like an old campaigner. As Michael turned the next corner he could still hear her, even above the noise of the traffic:

"Oh, but—it simply couldn't be! Not celadon, not in Shin-jew-kew."

Outside the office building where Michael worked and lived two soldiers were leaning against the wall, gazing at all the prettier girls that passed. One of them ostentatiously carried two Hershey bars, and the other had a package sealed with PX tape. First one would whistle and the other would howl; then they would exchange comments. Thus far no girls had stopped nor, apparently, been even interested. The sun shone on both, and thin lines of perspiration had appeared at their temples and over their lips.

At the main entrance to the building was an MP; inside were two more. To all of them Michael showed his pass.

"Look, Private, I know you live here and have it real cushy, but if you keep on shacking up outside every night I'm going to report you."

"What you talking about?" said Michael innocently. "I just went out half a hour ago to run an errand for Colonel Ashcroft."

The MP rolled both eyes high under his eyebrows. "Oh, these kids," he said to the other MP, who sighed mockingly.

"All right, Private Richardson," said the first, "you run on in. But next time"—he waved a forefinger— "Papa will spank."

Michael smiled wanly at the MP. They had what was called a kidding relationship.

The first MP turned to the other. "My, these recruits aren't what they used to be. Remember a year ago? Things are much too soft for them now. Can't even get a rise calling them recruit any more."

"Oh, well," said the other, "things are soft all over."

He nodded down the corridor to where the private had stopped and was talking with a rather tall girl in a long fur coat.

"Darling boy," she was saying, "where on earth have you been?" She shook her finger at him. "The Major has been simply furious. And the only reason I came to work on this festive morning—imagine, working on Saturday—only peasants work on Saturday—the only reason was to see you. And then you weren't even here. Where *do* you spend your nights anyway?"

He turned toward the two MP's who were listening.

She waved her hand airily. "Michael, dear, don't you know they don't do anything but stand there—they're supposed to be guardians of the peace, and goodness knows we're peaceful enough. Or, at least, *I* am. Anyway, no soldier of this great Occupation could conceivably return to his quarters to sleep. It would be like admitting defeat. So, now, tell me All. What —or, more likely, whom—have you been doing."

"If I told you, I probably couldn't go there again. You'd edge me out," said Michael. Here was another kidding relationship.

"You don't trust me! And that's the thanks I get for coming down here of a morning when I could have been sleeping."

She screamed slightly: "But you're so *dirty!*" She walked slowly around him and shook her head. "My, is this a neat soldier?"

"No, Miss Wilson."

"Oh, call me Gloria. We know each other's faults *so* well by now. Being named Gloria is one of mine. I hate it. Makes me think of sunrises and other revolting things."

She continued walking around him. Gloria now had her face—and her personality—on.

She suddenly stopped and clasped her brow. "Now I've gone and gotten quite dizzy. Look, why don't you go to bed or something? You look as if you didn't go to bed at all, or at least didn't sleep, or at least didn't take your clothes off."

"We're both supposed to be at our desks now. Why are you marching around here in furs?"

"Ladies' room, dear. And it's simply icy this morning."

A major came out of a doorway, stood looking at them for a second, and then disappeared.

"There he is, spying on us again," said Gloria. "An investigation is doubtless coming up. For all he knows I have half the Communist Party hidden under here."

"He'll keep," said Michael, who was feeling sleepy, hungry, and very tired of Miss Wilson.

"You think so? I have my doubts. But you're lucky. At noon you get shet of him, as you say out Indiana way. With me it's just beginning. Yes, I have what they call a date. But just one of these over—and under—the desk romances. Nothing like yours and mine. Still, I'll be happy, if only for the liquor I'll get out of it. I could stand a drink, and thank god he does."

"Does he?"

"Oh, heavens, yes. That's my only stipulation—that they drink. But, then, you don't, do you?"

"Not to excess."

"Oh, but you should sometime. With me. Just lots and lots of excess."

Michael looked down the hall and tried to stifle a yawn. "Aren't you hot in that fur coat?"

"Smothering, but one must have the proper effect upon majors. I couldn't run out in a sunsuit, particularly since I don't know where we're going for lunch. There're really only a couple of places, and I hope it's the American Club. You can get more liquor there somehow.... But, darling, you're fidgeting, and I know that's a bad sign. So come on, back to the mines and another glorious three hours for the greater glory of Mac, our Lord and Saviour."

The major stepped out of the doorway again and looked at them.

"There's Simon Legree Calloway, darling," said Gloria. "Come, let's cross the ice together."

■

Major Calloway had a mistress. He was also in love —though not with the mistress. The position in which he now found himself was a usual one for the Major. Not content with what he had—the mistress—he wanted something he strongly suspected he couldn't have —Gloria. He always wanted more than he had. Consequently he was very ambitious. He wanted to be a lieutenant colonel, he wanted to run the office, and he wanted Gloria.

The first two wishes he felt relatively certain of being able to realize in time. Gloria was another matter. He had suspected for some time that she might be willing to sleep with him, and this cheered him up. He'd reached this conclusion after hearing an unusual amount of talk about her and after noticing that whenever she was with him she looked rather attentively at other men. This did not make him jealous. It merely pointed out to him her probable availability. This, however, was not at all what he wanted. He wanted her to love him as he loved her. He loved her for her soul.

He never said this and but rarely thought it, for he was from Texas and consequently believed that any talk of the soul was either unhealthy and fanatical or, worse, effeminate. A soul was something like a truss— doubtless useful if you were so unfortunate as to need one, but the least you could do was to keep it decently out of sight. He had never once entertained the idea of harboring one—a soul, not a truss—until he met Gloria.

But Gloria had not wrought this miracle all by herself. Japan had helped. Until the Major left America he never felt a soul to be particularly necessary—Dallas was substitute enough. There were girls to date and friends to meet and big deals to put over. Here everything was different. Few girls, no friends, and making money the way he made it back home was illegal. So he was lonely, and with loneliness had come self-scrutiny.

After giving himself a long steady look, he decided that he must affiliate himself with some successful organization, some growing venture, if he were to get the things he wanted. After looking around, he decided that the most successful organization he could find, and one of which he already happened to be a member, was the Occupation. So he ceased thinking of his daily work as merely a job and began to think of it as a mission. He began saying that his duty was toward America. Therefore his real duty in Japan was not so much making Special Services bigger and better as it was explaining America and Democracy to the Japanese.

This was the first conscious thought completely unconnected with tangibles that he had ever had. He was proud of himself. Abstract thoughts were difficult, and he'd managed to have one. He now thought of himself as something of an educator, a mature if stern taskmaster who, in complete possession of all the necessary know-how, was going to make the world, or at least this part of it, a better place. He said as much in his letters back home, and his paragraphs were filled with talk of higher purposes and further meanings. His friends were very surprised, perhaps even a bit embarrassed.

The Major, at thirty-five, considered himself a man. Japan had matured him. But a man cannot succeed all at once, no matter how great his ambition, and so the Major viewed his own retreats and failures with kindly indulgence. This was where Gloria came in. She was comforting; the very personification of home and family;

worldly enough to smile at his misgivings and fallings from grace, yet doubtless innocent enough to believe, with him, that the world—particularly his own private one—could become ever so much nicer than it was now.

To be sure, he was aware that Gloria had never done anything but laugh at him. Still, this was better than nothing. It proved that she had a sense of humor, and he had long believed that this quality was very precious and very American—almost exclusively so. In fact, having one was practically a patriotic duty. He was rather proud of his own.

Gloria also had for him another and a higher meaning. He had selected her to help him achieve his ambitions. Together they would rise or together they would fall, though he never for a second believed that anything but success would crown his patriotic endeavors.

Already he was insuring success by making a bit of money on the side, for how could one be truly successful without money? It couldn't be done. Therefore, for the sake of his soul and Gloria, for the good of Japan and America, for a more complete identification of himself with the glorious ideals of the Occupation, the Major was neck-deep in the black market—and this was the reason he was staring at Michael and Gloria. He was merely waiting for her to leave before bringing up a little business matter with Private Richardson.

No sooner had they squeezed past him into the office than he barked out: "Private Richardson, I want to see you."

Gloria, already at her desk, raised her eyes, grimaced a smile of commiseration at the Private, and began the day's typing.

In the hall Michael found the Major striding up and down.

"Private Richardson," he said, "you didn't come in last night."

"No, sir, I didn't."

"Private, you're given quarters in these here offices as a convenience to the Army. If you're not here at nights, then there's no use you living here at all. Next time this happens I'm gonna personally send you back to barracks. Just like anyone else. Understand?"

"Yes, sir," said Michael. He purposely refused to stand at attention. Resting one foot behind him, he folded his arms across his chest.

"You think I won't, buddy, but I would. Just like that! You wouldn't want that, would you?"

"No," said Michael, "but, then, you wouldn't either, would you? Who'd run your errands then?"

Major Calloway turned slightly pale, his freckles bleaching to a light orange. He glanced up and down the hall and then said: "No, naturally I wouldn't." He grew slightly red and added: "But you don't need to think you can walk all over me, Private. Sure, we're both in this, but you're gettin' yours. So don't think you can get snotty."

Michael shrugged his shoulders and waited.

This, as was intended, irritated the Major: "And I got news for you, Private. After tonight we part company."

The soldier looked mildly interested. "That so, sir?"

"And I wish it was tomorrow already," said the Major.

"So do I, sir," said Michael.

Here, thought Michael, is the kind that could be very dangerous. The kind that doesn't feel he's doing wrong, the kind that can talk himself into being self-righteous about breaking the law. Around the office he was the clown, the regular cutup, half-purposely, half-unintentionally. But all of his practical jokes, his cute sayings, his sunny smiles were false. He could be vicious.

The Major's mouth relaxed and he smiled. Their enmity was becoming too apparent. "After all," he said, "this is the last time. I'd think you'd be glad to get rid of the responsibility and all."

"It's as much yours as it is mine, sir," Michael reminded him.

"Aw, look at you," said the Major, laughing. "Here you act as though you think we're sinners or something. It's just a fast buck—no harm in that. And I bet you can use it too. What we acting so doggone guilty about?" He rolled his eyes, licked his lips, and his accent became broader and broader.

Michael watched, slightly ill. He was always surprised at how phony the Major could be.

Michael was acting guilty because he, unlike the Major, felt guilty. He had ever since he first started running those innocent-looking errands for the Major, delivering packages to Japanese office buildings or rich homes, drinking tea in damp waiting rooms, being bowed out of invariably overcrowded Western-style parlors, each complete with plum-colored easy-chairs and an upright piano. At first he'd thought the errands a part of his duties, but it was soon made clear that the Colonel was to know nothing of them. When he confronted the Major and refused to run any more errands, the latter grew red and threatened a great deal, but ended by giving him a percentage of the profits.

The Major was a big-time operator and consequently dealt only in money changing—dollars to yen or yen to dollars, but always at an enormous profit, and if occasionally he had to use his official position to put the screws on, well, that's why he kept those golden oak leaves so brightly polished. Michael didn't mind the illegality of the transactions so much as he hated being involved with the Major. He felt guilty because, hating the Major as he did, he still worked for him, still shared the ever-present danger of discovery.

The Major was saying: "This morning O'Hara's coming in." (It was definitely the Irish name on the Major's

lips—not the softly spoken Japanese "small field" at all.)
"I already got him almost talked into it. Hell, you'd
think these people'd know a good thing when they see
it. But they got no business sense, no get-up-and-go.
Cautious. Real cautious. That's what they are. How
they ever expect to get ahead in the business way beats
me. But maybe you think I don't have a way to light
a fire under O'Hara's tail! Just watch him this morning."

"What am I supposed to do?"

"The usual. He's taking dollars for the yen payment,
or my name's not Calloway. It's for that opera tonight,
you know. You'll deliver. Gonna buy that little girl
of yours something nice out of the proceeds?" He
smiled broadly.

This was the usual finale to business arrangements
between the Major and the Private.

"After all, Richardson, it isn't as though it was just
us doing things like this. Hell, half the Army's selling
cigarettes or sugar or something. That's the way things
are. I don't think it's up to us to go around trying to
change them, do you?" He smiled again and said:
"Besides, some changes are gonna be made in this here
little old office before very long, and I think it'd be
real nice if you stayed on—and as something a bit more
important. Sergeant or something like that."

The Major stepped back to see what effect this had.

Michael looked at the floor. He'd suspected this was
coming. Poor Colonel Ashcroft. Only someone like
Major Calloway could possibly do something like this.
And he was right. He could make a private a sergeant,
simply through pull in the proper direction, a little
juggling of the Table of Operations, a little interview
with the proper colonel, then the proper general. Major
Calloway was an operator.

Michael turned to go back to the office, and the
Major almost ran the few steps between them: "So—
you got it straight about tonight? Got it?"

Michael couldn't decide which aspect of the Major was the worst—the phony commander, leader of men, head of the office; or this ingratiating puppy-like little man, all buddy-buddy with the privates, the good Joe. He simply nodded to show he had in fact "got it."

Instantly the Major became extremely affectionate. He threw his arm around Michael's shoulder, and they walked back into the office. The Major always overdid everything, and now he no more thought of the advisability of a major's throwing his arm over a private's shoulder than he thought of the Articles of War or the meaning of morality. He winked, and for an awful moment Michael thought he was going to nuzzle his cheek. But, instead, he sat down at his desk and became very busy.

Gloria, on the telephone, looked up, amused, mock-despair in her eyes. "... No, sir," she was saying, "you have the wrong number. This is the Liaison Office of Special Services.... Not at all." She hung up with a bang.

"Isn't the telephone wonderful," she said. "You can commit any number of atrocities, like wrong numbers, over it and never get caught. I think I'll call up the Provost Marshal and tell him that the Bank of Japan has just been robbed and a perfectly reliable witness— namely me—saw little Arthur MacArthur MacArthur scooting away with the loot in his kiddy-car. They'd believe it, you know."

The telephone rang again. "... Oh, you wanted Major Calloway.... I see.... Very sorry," said Gloria, then turned to the Major. "Same party again. Turns out she thought I'd said it was the Imperial Household or some such thing. At any rate, she's waiting."

The Major picked up the telephone. "Hello," he said, and then was silent for a long time. "But you got me all wrong—I never ... Oh, that's just one of those things." Another long pause, and then: "No, of course it's nothing serious, dear.... Well, I can't.... No, I can't explain right now.... All right, I'll see you this afternoon. But listen— Hello, hello."

He handed the phone back to Gloria. She gazed at Michael with slightly widened eyes.

The Major looked at both of them and then said: "Must have got cut off."

Gloria put the phone back on the hook; then, with a satisfied grimace in Michael's direction, she began typing again. The hush of industry finally—at ten— settled over the office.

■

In the next room Colonel Ashcroft was looking out of the window. He heard the click of typewriters, the rustle of papers, and the self-important squeaks of Major Calloway's swivel chair. He looked at his gold watch, then shook his head.

Perhaps he was just old-fashioned, yet it did seem to him that when the working day began at nine the work itself should begin at the same time. The work, after all, was important: that was why they were all here. It was for that reason he'd forbidden coffee-hour in his offices and had thus earned the reputation of being a martinet—a reputation he felt he didn't deserve.

He watched the other officers he knew and saw their refusal to take obligations seriously. They consequently enjoyed the reputation of being what the soldiers called good Joes. The Colonel would never be a good Joe, and he knew it. It was the price that conscience and duty exacted of him. But then this, as the Colonel saw it, was life itself.

Long ago he had learned that if you did not take yourself seriously, no one else was likely to. To be sure, it was not the way to become popular. Becoming popular was easy: all one needed was a fairly destructive sense of humor and a complete lack of dignity.

The Colonel had often longed for popularity, but eventually he always believed that it was better to take himself seriously—to refuse to see himself as others saw him, in the perspective which would have revealed to himself his smallness and his misery; to refuse to turn against himself the damaging glance of humor; to refuse to make fun of himself. This would have made him popular, but it would also have deprived him of all dignity in his own eyes. For the Colonel there was no choice at all—popularity was as fragile and ephemeral as most things in life; only human dignity was enduring. Only through dignity were you allowed the privilege of a motive and a goal in life.

The Colonel stroked his silver moustaches. As always, this action calmed him. It had also always calmed his father and his father's father, both of whom had also worn silver moustaches.

On his desk the Colonel always kept his grandfather's letter opener, solid silver and marked "Colonel Randolph Ashcroft," and his father's pen holder, marked "J. D. A." for John Delancy Ashcroft. He had his own date pad, given him by his father, but had never had his own initials engraved upon it. He had not felt they should be. His grandfather had been a great leader in the Civil War—or, rather, the War between the States— and his father had commanded with distinction in the first World War. He himself was in charge of a subsection of entertainment for the troops—Special Services.

Calmed, he took his hand from his moustaches and felt in his pocket. There he carried his father's gold watch. On its chain was the State Seal of Virginia in gold. This too had belonged to his grandfather. The sound of industry in the next room made him feel important, a bit at least. His forces—all the forces he now commanded—did their duty well. Responsibility, industry—this was all that really mattered.

He looked out of the window and saw the street full

of Japanese. The Japanese were industrious, and the Colonel liked them for it. The first day he'd come into this little office he'd stood and looked out and seen the blackened ruins stretching away to the horizon. Now, only a few years later, a new city had been built upon the ruins. It was a jerry-built city of frame buildings and colored stucco fronts to be sure, but a city none the less. And Atlanta had been longer reconstructing than Tokyo. He was pleased to see that now some of the earlier buildings had been destroyed to make way for new concrete office buildings. There was one near him. It was up halfway and seemed to be held together entirely by bamboo and straw rope. The workmen in their Army hats and straw sandals swarmed over the structure carrying miscellaneous loads in haphazard ways, adding bit by bit as though they were building a sand castle.

Like ants, Major Calloway had said one morning, looking out this same window. Like everyone else, he had been surprised at their industry. The Colonel knew better. It wasn't ant-like necessity; it was hunger and need. At other times they were bored and listless. The Colonel had seen this state often enough in his own men, brought back from combat during the war. They were too tired to turn the pages of *Life* or to drink Coca-Cola. The Japanese were suffering from the same old-fashioned complaint—shell shock. Realizing this, the Colonel thought even more highly of their industry.

Of course, Major Calloway had been surprised that they would work at all. He'd been expecting snipers, sabotage, the undergound. Like most other Americans, he'd been surprised at the complete lack of resistance and, like most, had been distrustful because of its absence.

Yet, from their point of view they were behaving very sensibly. The Colonel could even reconstruct their attitude. They were only a hundred years old as a

Westernized nation and were anxious for respect, anxious not to do anything laughable. Having given up their familiar kimonos, they still felt a bit uneasy in pants and sack coats. Wanting to make certain their pants fit like everyone else's, they had looked about them and had seen not only that the wearers of pants always swaggered a bit, but also that aggression was profitable —Britain in China, America in the Philippines, the grab-bag of Africa. So they tried it, just as they might have tried a washing machine or an automobile, just as they discarded the kimono for plus fours.

Now they had discovered that their studies, though thorough, had been built on false premises. America had been protecting the Philippines; Britain had been engaging in free trade with China. The Japanese had had the right spirit but had used the wrong methods. They had made a mistake. So, with an astonishing amount of good will, they became friendly. On the day after the Emperor's rescript ending the war, any American could have traveled anywhere in the islands with perfect safety. More than that, the children at the roadside would have waved his own flag at him. At the time some of the conquerors said that you'd have thought the Japanese won the war, rather than lost it, the way they carried on.

And, privately, the Colonel wasn't too sure they hadn't. What did one do with a people who, after a fierce and brutal four-year battle, suddenly waved the enemy's flag? Even Hiroshima had not antagonized them. It was just another natural calamity, like an earthquake. They were quite used to accepting the calamities of nature.

They could even accept an army of occupation, accept it with serenity, if not enthusiasm. They did what it told them to and thus transformed the conqueror into an instructor. And all this time they did not seem to resent the presence of the recent enemy, although, to be sure, there were some small antagonisms. The slight anti-American feeling that the Colonel detected from time to time was, he thought, first, a very natural feeling of revolt which, in a healthy nation, would have occurred long before, and second, yet another of Russia's machinations. (The Colonel felt very strongly about Soviet Russia.) All of which did not alter the fact that the Japanese, while not particularly contrite, were now just as anxious to work with the Americans as they had been to fight against them.

He had known their Army well. It was a paper army, a textbook army, and once it lost the advantage, an appallingly bad army. The Colonel, when he had been a major, had seen the Japanese Army coming wave after wave between the palm trees, or skulking about in some antiquated fashion copied from a 19th-century textbook on tactics by Herr Someone-or-other. The line of advancing soldiers would run toward them, shouting banzai's, waving their flags, and all the opposing army had to do was sight and turn on the machine guns, the bazookas, the flame throwers. It was a bit like an old-fashioned shooting gallery, with a choice of weapons. Of course it was frightening also, the way they kept coming, the way the blood kept spilling. And, too, there was something glorious about it, something uselessly gallant in the old Heidelberg tradition—something the Colonel had to respect.

And now, just as this most industrious of peoples had learned tactics and maneuvers by rote, never once believing that a European book could be wrong or that the knowledge in it had to be applied intelligently rather than literally, so they were now learning the principles of democracy by heart, not understanding that democracy was more than a simple method, more than a technique.

Still, what could one expect from this strange country which excelled in techniques and nothing else? The

Japanese could not tolerate the amorphous, the ambiguous: they, in fact, lacked the kind of faith, mystical if you liked, that made democracy what it was, that made the ideals of Jefferson—so impractical, so idealistic, so impossible and yet so true—a living reality. Instead they insisted upon definition, upon the hierarchy, upon the letter and not the spirit. Illogical though their Oriental thought-processes often were, still they insisted upon strict logic when it came to anything Western.

This, after all, was the country where one adopted a different code of behavior toward each of the many different strata of society; where there were he didn't know how many terms for the simple word *you*, each to be dealt out according to the just deserts of both the speaker and the person spoken to, these usages in turn being based upon complicated formulas involving age, money, family relationships, a careful accounting of past favors given and received, and social position. The social order was the most important way, the only way, through which millions could live together on these few acres. Any fool could see it was absolutely necessary.

And it was for this reason that the Colonel took a rather dim view of the Occupation's self-appointed task of democratizing Japan. He believed it useless and saw, instead of a new democracy in the making, only a scrubby little country which, with infallible instinct, insisted upon importing and making its own those elements of American culture which were most superficial, that dross which seemed almost to be a by-product of true democracy in action—chewing gum, modern plumbing, advertising, the movies. To be sure, these things were important to democracy, but in Japan they became simply ugly objects, large and formidable once they lost their place and their purpose.

However, thought the Colonel, this democratization did have one good effect. It was much more attractive to the Japanese people than the only alternative they were offered—communism. He could imagine, centuries from now, a democratic Japanese nation, but he could not imagine a communistic one. At least capitalism allowed social distinctions of a sort, but communism insisted upon there being—ostensibly—none. Japan without social distinctions was a patent impossibility. For one thing, their economy would never stand it, and with this many people, their economy would not change. Order—that was what they needed and wanted —order above all else, and in a nicely antiquated pattern, just as though Perry and then MacArthur had never set foot on their shores.

Order, in a nicely archaic pattern, this was what the Colonel wanted too. This was one of the reasons he thought so well of the Japanese, the reason he so wanted to help them, and the reason he felt himself able to. He now thought of Special Services as a kind of retreat from his real purpose in the country. He should be in Government, on policy-making levels, and though he realized his views would be thought both idealistic and suspect by his commanders, still he might benefit the Japanese nation, and this, after all, was his duty.

But he must be content with this small part of the potential duty which he now performed—and after all, he told himself, it was not negligible. And perhaps, in time, he would rise to the position where he might fulfill his entire obligation.

The Colonel stroked his moustaches and looked out of the window at the bamboo skyscraper. Wood and bamboo—almost everything in Japan is made of wood or bamboo. There are no pyramids. The closest thing to them is the Imperial Hotel, but that is scarcely the fault of the Japanese. The Ise Shrine—the most important in Japan—is made of straw and wood. Every twenty years it is dismantled and an exact replica is built. Then that is taken apart in its turn and another constructed. This was what impressed the Colonel about Japan. Time has been conquered. It is conquered by allowing it to have its own way. When the pyramids crumble and the Imperial Hotel has long been swallowed up, the Ise Shrine will remain—as new as ever.

The Colonel turned away from the window and looked at his desk. It was filled with the check-sheets, the memos, the endless paper paraphernalia of official endeavor. Soon Ohara would appear, late as usual, and he would find himself in the position of having to defend himself and, tacitly, the Occupation. And a man like Ohara was Japan's worst enemy. The Colonel sighed. Some mornings he just didn't feel up to it.

He straightened the letter opener, pushed the pen holder a bit to one side, and heard Miss Wilson's voice in the next room.

"Mr. Ohara and his son are here, Mike," she said.

There was a slight pause for which the Colonel could not account. Actually, it was caused by a moment's hesitation on Private Richardson's part when he looked up to find the eyes of the son fixed on him, as though they knew and hated him. There was somehow something quite familiar about the son. But he shook it off, and then the Colonel heard the smoothly oiled machine of office procedure begin to function again as the Private turned to Major Calloway and said: "The Oharas are here, sir." He gave the name its proper Japanese pronunciation.

The Major said: "Boy, you sure got a way with that lingo—how you ever get that word spit out right?"

The Colonel guessed the visitors would be standing there, understanding every word. He must sometime attempt to do something about Major Calloway.

Finally the swivel chair creaked protestingly, and the Major appeared in the doorway. Mr. Ohara always sent his card in, and the Colonel always winced when he read it—"Taro Johnnie O'Hara."

The Major was still standing there. "Them Japanese nationals are here, sir."

"Will you please show Mr. Ohara and his guest in, Major Calloway."

■

Taro Ohara, Cornell, 1924, stood in the doorway, beaming. He thought a big smile was the best way to meet Americans. This was often difficult, because he always got all dressed up before meeting Americans, and his collar choked him, his coat and pants bound him, and his shoes hurt him. He never felt like smiling then. In Western clothes he was always hot, uncomfortable, and determined. Beside him was his son, a student. The celluloid collar of his uniform was wet with sweat, and his hat was in his hand.

Ohara held the big smile until the Colonel nodded and indicated two chairs beside his desk. He'd tried to get his son, Ichiro, to give the big smile too, but Ichiro had refused, just as he refused everything modern and progressive.

"Well, Colonel," said Mr. Ohara, leaning forward, both elbows on the desk, "how's the thing cooking?"

The Colonel smiled a bit wanly. "Just fine, Mr. Ohara. How are things with you?"

"I can't complain," Ohara said, laughing loudly and leaning back in his chair, anxious to appear at home in the office of a colonel, his friend, Colonel Ashcroft, U. S. Army. "Everything's just hunky-dory."

The Colonel cringed. Why was it that Cornell 1924 or Princeton 1926 or Harvard 1929 always thought slang remained frozen from its time of origin, like forms of court address?

"Everything ready for this evening?" he asked, determinedly pleasant.

Mr. Ohara looked up warily. This was getting down to business a bit too soon. He thought he ought to chew the rag just a little longer, if only for the sake of appearances. Making the best of his friend's rudeness, he leaned forward, smiling in anticipation, rubbing his hands together. "That's what I like, Colonel. A businessman—an A-Number-One businessman."

The Colonel knew he liked nothing of the sort. Yet, as he watched Mr. Ohara dissemble, rubbing his hands together and professing a delight he didn't feel, he again thought how very Jewish the Japanese were. He remembered a very funny, pseudo-scholarly and self-congratulatory article in the *Japan Times* called "Are the Japanese the Lost Tribe?" He was inclined to agree with the article—they were. Or were these only the mannerisms of any minority, the manifestations of any intensely self-conscious people? He tried to remember the Virginia Negroes of his childhood but couldn't recall their rubbing their hands and leaning over with unctuous familiarity. The Colonel, to be sure, liked the Japanese better than the Jews and the Negroes, but, like them, they obviously had their place, and the Colonel thought that Mr. Ohara was out of his.

Suddenly Mr. Ohara stopped smiling. One didn't smile during business. Only before and after. "Yep, you bet. Everything's under control, as they say," and he laughed.

He also pulled out a package of cigarettes and offered one to the Colonel, stealing a glance to make sure he'd not brought out his black-market American cigarettes. "These are Peace, you know. Like what we are celebrating."

The Colonel knew the next move. "Why don't you have one of these?" He offered Lucky Strikes.

Mr. Ohara laid his pack of Peace on the desk and took a cigarette from the Colonel's. Before he put it in his mouth he raised it toward his forehead. That was the only thing Cornell hadn't taken from him. He still bowed—in his own way—whenever he received anything.

He no longer insisted upon the absurdly literal translation of the Japanese form—"I am sorry"—but he still gave it deference with a little twinkle of despair.

The Colonel took one of his own cigarettes, trying not to look at the package of Peace lying before him.

Well, even if he won't take one, he's been asked, thought Mr. Ohara. He resolved to leave the cigarettes in full view throughout the interview. It wasn't as though he hadn't offered. He had. There they were— the proof of it!

"You understand that the money will be paid, as usual, some little time after the performance. With the usual amount of red tape involved, the money should come through in about a week, at the most. No need to worry." The Colonel stopped, realizing he always had an absurd inclination to reassure Mr. Ohara as though the gentleman were a child. Actually, a company as large as that Mr. Ohara represented, one of the big three of Japan's amusement world, had no need of such paltry sums. But then this visit *was* rather childish. There was no reason for it. A telephone message that everything was ready for the evening would have been much more efficient.

Mr. Ohara looked sad. All the business at hand had been discussed and disposed of with typical American efficiency. Money had been discussed without so much as green tea as a preamble, making his own position seem more like that of an errand boy than that of the representative of one of Japan's most important corporations. There had been no circumspection, no concern for his own feelings, no politeness. The visit was actually over.

Anxious to put a good face on it, he turned toward the Colonel and said confidentially: "It will be a Number One performance. The boys will like it."

The Colonel could not imagine the boys liking *Madame Butterfly*, but he knew that most of the boys would not be there anyway. It was Saturday night and they'd be out drinking and running after girls. The only boys there would wear glasses and carry books to read at intermission. Actually this was a treat for the officers and the civilians. It was a big social occasion.

"I'm sure it will be, Mr. Ohara," said the Colonel, rising. He smiled as he did so. From his father he had tried to learn this trick of handling men. When you wanted them to go you stood up, rising slowly, smiling all the time, and continued the conversation. Just as naturally they too would rise and be out of the office before they even realized they had been dismissed. But, like so many of his father's ways, this one refused to accomodate itself to his son. It merely appeared rude. He looked at the father and son before him. They hadn't risen. The son wasn't even looking at him.

Mr. Ohara saw the Colonel looking at his son. "Don't believe you know the young sprout here. Name's Ichiro—eldest, naturally." This was the card up the sleeve. Ohara had kept it in reserve. He hated to use it now but was forced to. At least it would make his friend, the Colonel, sit down again, and they could continue the visit in seemly fashion. "Ichiro here is the prize pitcher on his college team, but"—he leaned forward confidentially, just between men—"but his English she is not so hot."

His son stood up and bowed. The Colonel bowed back. Then he offered the boy a cigarette. The younger Ohara smiled, made a little negative sign with his hand in front of his face, and sat down. His father looked around the office and crossed his legs.

"You know, this office reminds me of the dean's at Cornell," he began.

Colonel Ashcroft was still standing. If he sat down, the Oharas would stay half an hour. So he pretended not to have heard. "Well, that takes care of that, I guess," he said, smiled, and heartily held out his hand.

Mr. Ohara sprang from his chair as though shot, his smile still there but tight. "Yes, sir. It does. Well, I want to thank you very, very much. We all appreciate this. The troupe, the committee, and not least, myself. It is the most gracious of you and we shall endeavor to do our most very best to give before the great American Military Forces audience one of the finest performances of that immortal classic of song, *Madame Butterfly*, that they have perhaps ever been privileged to see before in their lives." Scarcely pausing for breath, he hurried on: "And not only will they ..."

As he went on and on the Colonel stood with a frozen smile. Why, he wondered, did they always have to give speeches? Formal, rigid little people, they could never let anything, be it a pine tree or a good-by, go its own natural way. They were always fussing with it, making it what it wasn't, perverting it into something they thought it should be. It was so typical of Ohara, first the needless visit—completely ritual, no logical reason for it—and now this flowery and pathetically absurd good-by speech.

The Colonel had heard a hundred good-by speeches just like this one. He was enduring it with a stretched smile and an interested look when Gloria came in and said that someone was waiting to see him—a Mrs. Schmidt. While he was wondering who she was and why she had come, he held out his hand again and said: "Forgot that I had a visitor coming. You will excuse me, won't you?"

Mr. Ohara broke off in the middle of a sentence. "Sure, sure, you're a mighty busy man, Colonel, anyone can see that. I'll just stop and say a few words with my friend Major Calloway, if it's all right with you, sir."

The Colonel detected the sarcasm and smiled right through it. "Naturally, Mr. Ohara, please make yourself at home." Then to the boy: "Pleased to have met you, Ichiro."

The boy shook hands limply, shuffled his feet, and didn't look up. His father clasped the Colonel's hand with some emotion and then, with waves and backward glances, left the room.

Gloria brought in Mrs. Schmidt. That she was poor was the first thing that impressed the Colonel. She was poor the way he had always thought of Warsaw or Prague or Berlin as being poor. Having been to none of these cities, he usually thought of the inhabitants as being rather spectacularly impoverished, somewhat like the pictures he used to see of immigrants at Ellis Island, bundles of shawls and old shoes, held together with safety pins.

Mrs. Schmidt wore a shawl, a long, gray one which looked Jewish to the Colonel because he thought it looked as though it should be worn over the head and he'd seen pictures of Jewesses wearing shawls over their heads. It was secured around her shoulders with a plastic five-and-ten-cent-store brooch showing a Walt Disney fawn. There were tortoise-shell combs in her gray hair, and her shoes were cracked, the heels badly run over.

"I am Lotte Schmidt, the voice teacher," she said. Her voice was rather high, but the Colonel thought it melodious. In spite of the accent and the faint quaver of age, it made him think she may at one time have been a great beauty. It was the kind of voice one might have heard, years before, in ballrooms, under elaborate chandeliers.

"I would guess you are Viennese, Mrs. Schmidt," he said, offering her the chair recently vacated by Mr. Ohara.

She smiled, showing tiny, fragile-looking teeth, and the soft skin around her light-blue eyes wrinkled with pleasure. "You are quite correct, Colonel. I lived in Vienna until—well, until the war. Then I was living here."

"It must seem rather different from Vienna," said the Colonel.

She raised one small hand into the air. "Oh, Colonel, the difference is extraordinary. Tokyo and Vienna..." She laughed as though she had often been amused by the absurdity of the idea. "They are on opposite sides of the earth—I mean figuratively as well as literally." She paused. "But, you, Colonel. I would guess that you are from the South—perhaps Virginia."

"Well, how did you guess that?" asked the Colonel, pleased and aware that he was sitting too straight in his chair. Soon he'd have to make her state her business. But in the meantime the conversation was a pleasant antidote to Mr. Ohara.

"Your accent, of course, but, besides that, you are kind to me, whom you have never heard of, have never once met. You are a gentleman. You are—what is the word? Oh, yes—you are chivalrous."

Seeing that this embarrassed the Colonel, she laughed again, patted the folds of her shawl, pretended to examine her brooch for a second, and then, raising her light-blue eyes, said: "But you are probably a busy, though gallant, gentleman, so I will tell you why I have come."

The Colonel had begun to protest, but she held up her hand in a small negative gesture, the kind of gesture he himself might have used to a child.

"No, Colonel, chivalry and business do not mix. You Americans, even when you happen to be gallant, are really businessmen. Why, you even appreciate the American businesswoman." She looked at him and didn't smile until he did.

"I'm afraid I'm old-fashioned," said the Colonel. "I don't much like the new American businesswoman."

"No more do I," laughed Mrs. Schmidt, adjusting her shawl.

The Colonel thought the quaver in her voice more

pronounced, yet she was no older than he certainly. She was still in her fifties. He also noticed that her hands shook very slightly. At first he thought it might be that she was cold. Then he realized that she was afraid.

In the next office Major Calloway had drawn a chair next to his and both he and Mr. Ohara were deep in conversation. Ichiro stood stiffly at one side. He had been offered a chair but had refused.

"It's this way, O'Hara," said the Major. "Like I was saying last time, if you have to mess around with the department of this and the sub-section of that, you'll just never get any place. The Japanese government is one big snarl of red tape. It's real feudal-like. Now the democratic way would be—"

"But just now the Colonel himself was talking about the Army red tape. Is the American Army feudal? Could that be?" asked Mr. Ohara brightly, pleased at being able to show the Major that he was up on his toes too.

"The Army's different," said the Major flatly. "Besides, I'm talking about the Japanese government, not the American Army. Two different things. So, like I was saying, the American way of doing things is to go right to the person in charge and just say your piece and get it over with. None of this behind-the-scenes business. All open and honest as the day is long. You don't need any of this old-fashioned third-party business. If you want to do something, you just go do it—that's Democracy."

"But if it is a real complicated business," began Mr. Ohara, "then you take all the responsibility on your own shoulders, as they say. What if, well, what if something went wrong—what then? I'd really be in the soup then, wouldn't I?" and he laughed somewhat feebly.

Michael looked up from his filing. From what he

had overheard, it seemed to be yet another of the Major's reforming lectures. He had thought it was some sort of theoretical argument. Apparently it wasn't.

". . . so, you see, I really came to ask a favor," Mrs. Schmidt was saying. She attempted to smile again, but her hands still shook slightly. She felt she could no longer avoid an explanation. "I've never been in one of your offices before. I am a timid, a very timid, person. As you know, I cannot go to your PX nor your Commissary nor your theaters nor even come into your buildings without a pass, and since I am so timid, I thought for a long time before deciding to come. But this morning I thought to myself: No, I really must. It is important."

The Colonel reached for a cigarette. "I very much wish it were in my power to do what you want, Mrs. Schmidt, but you are asking for the impossible. I'm only a colonel. I can't allocate money for something like this. I suggest you try the Army Educational Center. They have funds for this sort of thing."

She started to speak, her lips half-open, then sank back into the chair, half in despair, half in amusement. "It's so odd to find myself in this position, Colonel. As you have already seen, I am no businesswoman. I can't even keep our little grocery account straight. I'm of no use in the world except as a voice teacher. I had thought I would try to be a businesswoman this morning, but I cannot be. And this is my second attempt. I've already been to that Army school. They are not interested. I"—she began to smile—"I really don't know what I'll do."

The Colonel restrained an impulse to touch her hand, to reassure her. She seemed so pitifully alone. His own wife, equally well-bred, equally cultured, equally helpless, could very well have been sitting before him, her humility growing through every minute of silence. There were tears in his eyes.

The Colonel had already invented a history to fit her. Born in Vienna, she had been beautiful and beloved. The toast of Vienna, young men pulling her carriage, no champagne baths only because she would never want anything like that. Then marriage, her husband persecuted by the Nazis, flight to Japan. Here among an alien people, unknown, uncared for, she lived through the horror of the war, and now that the war was over she was no less alien. Surrounded by wealth, by food, by warm clothing, she could have none. Like the other Europeans who had survived the war while in Japan, she lived on the edge of existence. Her condition was much worse than that of the Japanese, thought the Colonel, because she had been used to more. The ridiculously small amount which satisfied their needs could not satisfy her. She had come, politely, with dignity, to beg.

"I'm only asking to give a recital, and to be paid for it," she said. "I would sing Schubert and Schumann and maybe some Hugo Wolf. And then, for encores, some of the songs that were so popular before the war, long before. From operettas, you know, like Richard Tauber used to sing. That kind of program. Surely your soldiers must have heard of Vienna. At one time or another they must have listened to some Schubert lieder. It is impossible that they couldn't have."

"I'm sure they have. I am certain they'd love dearly to hear you, Mrs. Schmidt, but you are asking for what I cannot give you. The money at my disposal is solely for engaging Japanese artists. And you..." He sensed he was on dangerously emotional ground, and quickly continued: "Besides, I cannot on my own responsibility schedule a Special Services program. We receive our schedules, and I only expedite them."

"Expedite," said Mrs. Schmidt with a trace of bitterness, "that is an Army word, is it not? I don't remember hearing it before. My English is quite old-fashioned, I fear. I never found it necessary to speak the Army language. Before the war—" She stopped, then said: "Well, before the war it was quite different here in Japan."

Yes, thought the Colonel, before the war perhaps she was a member of what must have been called the international set. She had been younger then. He could imagine her then, exclaiming with pleasure over the quaintness of the hibachi, the shoji, the tatami, but continuing to live in a world of Schubert and Strauss, hot chocolate for breakfast and gossip from Austria. One now saw little of the foreigners who had lived in Japan before and during the war. Occasionally in passing streetcars, entering the subway or coming out of a theater, one saw, amid the Japanese faces which the Colonel found identical, the blue eyes and brown hair of an Occidental. You could always recognize a member of the once-flourishing Continental society—he would be wearing an overcoat ripping at the seams, a too short and too tight belted coat, shoes which were cracked and glued; she would be wearing a hat with a mended veil, and her shoes would be the Japanese imitation of high heels. One could recognize them by their white look of poverty, by the furtive look of expired passports in their eyes. They were like another race, existing in the purgatory between the Japanese and the new army of—the Colonel's thoughts came to a sudden stop, for he had been just about to think "the new army of barbarians."

"What you folks don't seem to understand," said Major Calloway not unkindly, "is that us Americans are doing our damndest to give you all a decent way of life. We want to raise your standard of living. You know—a washing machine in every home, that sort of thing. Now that sort of life is worth working for, don't you think, and that's why all of us are out here working up a sweat over you."

The Major's evident willingness to go on forever mouthing such generalities was the soul of politeness, so much so that Mr. Ohara hated to bring up the mundane business at hand. But even exquisite politeness must have its end, especially when Mr. Ohara suspected the other didn't want to give him a chance to speak. "True, true, Major, absolutely and one-hundred-percent correct. But in reference to what you were suggesting before, I don't see how we could possibly explain, if anything happened, what we were really trying to do."

Since Mr. Ohara himself didn't understand too well what they were trying to do, he felt doubly inept, first in attempting to connect what the Major wanted with what he said he wanted and, second, in insisting upon a discussion of business matters which, he felt sure, could be so much better handled by someone else, by the middle-man procedure that the Major so disliked. That, after all, was the civilized way to do business—not this way.

"Looky, O'Hara, I thought we had all this settled. But I'll spell it out for you once more." The Major glanced at the others in the office and lowered his voice. "Your corporation could use dollars, couldn't it?"

"Yes, but—"

"And we could use yen. Now if we go through the banks there would be endless red tape, wouldn't there?"

"Yes, from my government and," he hastily added, "from your Army."

"O.K., I'll agree. So what we're doing is the smart thing, isn't it? We're going directly to the top, not fooling around with any of those in-between guys. You bring the yen, we supply the dollars. It's as simple as that."

It really was simple when you understood it, Mr. Ohara decided. Quite simple. To be sure there was a rigidly enforced directive against any illegal yen-dollar exchange, but Mr. Ohara was cosmopolitan enough to realize this law was simply for the soldiers, for the lower-ranking civilians. It didn't touch the more important. Japan had lots of laws like that. He began to feel a certain warmth toward democracy. Here it was on terms he could understand.

"I get you," he said, and smiled knowingly.

"It's about time," said the Major.

Mrs. Schmidt was fingering her brooch again, looking at the Colonel. He looked at her fingers, busy with the plastic fawn, and realized that she found it exotic, perhaps even thought it fashionable, having no way of knowing it had been designed for children and that more selective little girls would never have worn one. This made her seem more completely different from him than anything else. Here she was, a woman of obvious culture and talent, tact and kindness and sorrow, fondling a five-and-ten plastic fawn. The saddest thing of all was that it was perhaps the only gift she had ever received from the Americans.

"I suppose you find us—what shall I say?—" He hesitated, and then continued: "...find us a bit barbaric."

She looked at her shawl for a second, then raised her bright blue eyes. They were surprised. "Whatever would make you say that? We—we older Europeans —find you young and brash and splendidly active. Barbaric, no. It is curious for you to ask."

"I suppose it is. We do have our culture and—"

"No, I meant you personally. I don't understand America now. I cannot connect, oh, what shall I say? —well, posters of Rita Hayworth and the laws against adultery.... Oh, now I've shocked you, I'm afraid."

The Colonel pulled his moustaches. "No, of course not, of course not."

"What I meant was that, though I don't understand America now, I think I understand you," she smiled, "as well as two people can after only fifteen minutes of conversation. But I understand your society—yours, Colonel. It is so much like my own. So much like my own was."

"I'm afraid my idea of yours is rather false," said the Colonel. "I'm always apt to think of crystal chandeliers, Strauss waltzes, and drinking champagne from slippers."

She laughed, almost like a young girl. "Oh, Colonel," she said, "it's far from the truth. As far, let us say, as my idea—since girlhood I've had it—that someone like you lived only in a great Parthenon-style house with nothing but magnolias to look at and nothing but some kind of cold gin to drink, surrounded by white-haired Negroes."

"We're both wrong, it seems," said the Colonel, tapping his cigarette in the ashtray. "Tell me, how did you happen to come to Japan?"

"My husband's business," she said at once—a bit too readily, thought the Colonel, as though she had said it often before. "He was in the export business—everyone was you know—and he was sent here, so naturally I came too. That was, well, let me see—that was ten years ago, in 1939."

"And, if I may ask, when did he die?" asked the Colonel.

She was startled. "He didn't die, Colonel. Did I say he did? No, he is alive."

"I'm sorry," said the Colonel, "I don't know what I could have been thinking of. I—"

"You were thinking of me as a widow, Colonel?" she asked.

"No . . . that is . . ." He didn't finish.

She sighed and rearranged her shawl. "It is truly amazing that so many people think of me as a widow. Isn't that curious? My husband is quite well so far as I know." She stopped suddenly.

"So far as you know?" asked the Colonel.

The Major and Mr. Ohara both sat back in their chairs. They had reached an equitable yen-to-dollar exchange rate, a bit different from the legal one.

"Well, it's a pleasure to do business with you, Major," said Mr. Ohara. "You're quite certain that nothing unpleasant will come of this, however?"

"How could it?" asked the Major.

"Well, I hope my bottom dollar not. I also hope there's no reason for the Colonel to know of our little arrangement. Is there?"

"Look, just between you and me, Mr. O'Hara, I wouldn't worry about what the Colonel thinks or says. I don't think he'll be with our outfit much longer."

"Oh, I'm sorry. Very sorry," said Mr. Ohara.

"Yeah, you know, he's getting on. He'll get his pension soon and go on back. Must be about over the age limit now, I'd guess."

"I am so sorry."

The Major, having made his point, could not resist adding: "And, besides, you know, he's a little old-fashioned. Doesn't know the score any more. Times have changed, and all that. Still thinks in terms of the gentleman's army, and all that."

"Gentleman's army," repeated Mr. Ohara. The phrase obviously appealed to him.

"For example, you know who he's talking to in there?"

"A lady."

"If you want to call her that—it's Frau Schmidt."

"Commander Schmidt's wife?"

"Ex-commander."

"Ah," said Mr. Ohara.

"You see," said the Major smiling, "the Colonel, he don't know these things. He'll listen to just anybody. Now I say forgive and forget along with the best of them, but you got to draw the line some place, and the wife of a former Nazi chief is the right place to draw it. Particularly since he's in jail right now."

Mr. Ohara didn't reply. He merely tried to look intelligent. He couldn't very well explain that, a decade before, he and her husband had been the best of friends and had together drawn up plans for the future.

"So," continued the Major, drawling more than usual, "you see what I mean. Getting on, the Colonel is. Fine man, of course, but this is a young man's army. So, as I say, I wouldn't be at all surprised if he got his pension before too long now."

Mr. Ohara straightened his glasses, then smiled brilliantly at the Major. "Are congratulations in order?" he asked loudly.

The Major cringed and looked around apprehensively, smiling all the while so Mr. Ohara would know a joke when he saw one. "Not yet," he whispered. "You know how it is...."

"Yes, yes, I know how it is. Cornell was the same way. Why, I remember..."

Mrs. Schmidt stood up. "I've taken much of your time, Colonel, but you've been most kind. I know that you would help me if you could. I know the Army well, believe me. I know what men like you must do, whether you want to or not. And I know what you cannot do. So I know that you would like to help and are sorry that you cannot."

"I am truly sorry, Mrs. Schmidt. But perhaps we might see more of you—my wife and I. We should be delighted to help in some, let us say, unofficial way. Why don't you call on us sometime. My wife would be charmed." In the next room he could hear Mr. Ohara, making another farewell speech.

Mrs. Schmidt turned to him, her eyes bright. "I would love to, Colonel. But only to meet and talk with you. No unofficial help, please. I am not begging. Not yet."

"I didn't mean—"

"You are a good man, Colonel. You mean very well. I do appreciate your intentions." She stopped and then, as though talking to herself, added: "I don't know what happens to people over here. My husband found himself in the same position. Perhaps"—she paused cautiously, then continued—"perhaps it has something to do with being on the winning side. Wasn't it your Oscar Wilde who wisely corrected the saying to read: Nothing fails like success? But, I'm being indiscreet. Here I am in the very heart of what is only too obviously a highly successful military operation, as my husband used to say. Again, thank you, Colonel."

Rising, she turned swiftly and walked into the outer office. Mr. Ohara was bowing and smiling at the Major, who was now standing beside his desk. The Colonel started to follow her—he'd forgotten to ask her to give her husband his regards when next she visited the tuberculosis sanitarium. But she had already left the outer office, and Mr. Ohara and his son, the former still bowing and smiling, were backing out the door. The Colonel knew he could not get past them without another speech from the father and another of those even more disturbing glances from the boy.

Colonel Ashcroft walked swiftly to the window, hoping to see Mrs. Schmidt as she crossed the street. There was something very young about her, and he liked that. She must have taken another way, however, for he only saw Mr. Ohara and his son. The father walked about five steps in front of the boy but talked constantly. The Colonel suddenly had a horrible vision of Japan democratized—a hundred million Taro Oharas, clustering worshipfully about five-starred emblems.

He closed his eyes and stroked his moustaches.

■

In the street, Mr. Ohara wasn't talking to his son as he strode ahead. He was furiously talking to himself. Finally, near Isetan Department Store, he stopped and allowed his son to catch up.

"Perhaps it would have been better had you taken the chair the Major offered you," he said in Japanese, "and also the cigarette offered you by the Colonel. They offered. You could have sat down. You could have taken the cigarette, though offending the Colonel was not so bad as possibly offending the Major. But you didn't!"

"I didn't want to."

He didn't want to! That was just like him. Mr. Ohara turned and walked swiftly for a time. As though in this life one did nothing but what one wanted. Ichiro was eighteen and should have known better. Life was a series of responsibilities, not a series of evasions. Whether one were American or Japanese, this was true—and this was the cornerstone of Mr. Ohara's life.

He looked back at his son, who was plodding along behind him, his face turned to the sidewalk. The father shook his head and walked yet more briskly, placing his feet squarely before him, turning his head and smiling in all directions—this was his American walk.

Most fathers and sons had their little difficulties these days. Mr. Ohara knew this because he was usually on the side of the sons. One could understand their positions only too well. After all, if Japan were to take a leading place in the world, especially after the defeat, one would have to forget the old ways of doing things and become in reality the New Japan. The sons had the right ideas. Even if they took to running around the streets and going with ladies of the night and speaking GI slang in the home, it was, in Mr. Ohara's eyes, a good beginning.

But Ichiro was different. In this regard the Ohara family was ironically twisted, for it was the father who was forward-looking and the son who was the reactionary. Ichiro wouldn't even talk with American soldiers, members of the Gentleman's Army. If one came up asking for directions or some simple aid—where could he find a girl, for example—Ichiro would not help him, though his English was good enough for that. If he were forced to answer, he would give purposely detailed and inaccurate directions, or say that many ladies of the night were found in the Dai Ichi Building. That was no way to behave!

Mr. Ohara prided himself upon the fact that he could meet, on their own grounds, any of the representatives of the U. S. Army or Navy and trade stories about Cornell with them. They would leave with a better impression of Japan than they had had before, he was sure. Ichiro contributed nothing to this. Just now, for example, during that delightful call upon his friend the Major, it was he alone who had put everyone at ease in the American way, and it was his son who with his black scowling had almost ruined everything.

"Do not lag behind!" he turned and shouted at his son, regardless of the stares his rudness brought him from the passers-by. "This is *not* a feudal country. You are *not* a retainer. I am *not* a daimyo. Walk here with me."

But still Ichiro would not hurry, and his father had to wait on the sidewalk until they were side by side.

"What did you learn from this morning's interview?" he asked, determinedly pleasant. The catechism was a favorite form of conversation with him. Through it both learned, one how to ask questions, the other how to answer them. Thus a pleasant walk could be made profitable to both parties, even be they father and son.

"I learned that one should take cigarettes when they are offered by Americans though one does not smoke oneself."

This was a pleasant answer. It showed that a mistake had been acknowledged, and this in itself was pleasant, for it meant that the mistake was now dead and could be forgotten. "That is very true," said Mr. Ohara sagely. "But, more generally, in the most important sense, what is it that you learned?"

"I learned that it is politic to forget that we are Japanese when in the company of important foreigners. I learned it is important to imitate them."

This was less satisfactory, because even Mr. Ohara began to suspect sarcasm. Still, what the boy was saying was perfectly true, and perhaps in his own way—a way now fortunately as obsolete as the way of his own grandfather—he himself was right.

"Anything else?" he added pleasantly. On the third question the compliment usually appeared, and though he admitted it was childish and unworthy of him, he did love to receive compliments—no matter how empty he knew them to be. They were so reassuring.

"I learned my father is more foreign than Japanese."

Mr. Ohara turned and looked at the expressionless face of his son. Though this was meant as no compliment, he might, if he tried, interpret it as such. But his shoes pinched him, his coat was binding his arms, his hat hurt his head. He lost his temper.

"I too learned something. I discovered that my son is not intelligent."

It had escaped before he had thought to stop it. Though he began smiling at once, he saw it was too late. Never would Ichiro understand that it was an innocent phrase. It was used all the time at Cornell.

It was, to Ichiro, a direct insult, and the color slowly left the boy's unsmiling face.

■

It had come to this. A public insult on the street! Ichiro looked at his father, took off his cap, and bowed very low. Then he turned quickly and walked away, leaving his father speechless, furious, and remorseful in the street.

He was the eldest son and, though still young, carried

already the air of responsibility which is so striking in the first child of a Japanese family. He was a model —industrious, devoted, dedicated. That was why the insult had reached him. Many other sons these days would have giggled and begged pardon instantly. To Ichiro the insult was also a falsehood. He could not believe he had merited it and would not forgive his father. Ichiro had no small opinion of himself.

To be sure, everything that he was he owed to his father. This was true of all sons. It had been true of his father before him. Yet, recognizing this, he could not imagine his father reacting to a direct insult as he himself had just done. His father would have begun stamping his tight Western shoes, would have shouted, and finally, would have trampled his dignity under his own feet. His father was by now a man without dignity.

Just in front of Ichiro there walked a mendicant priest, wearing the inverted-bowl-shaped hat, the dark, oddly formal kimono, the straw sandals. In one hand he held a Buddhist bead-string and a shallow pan for offerings; in the other, a tiny tinkling bell in the shape of a cat's head. He walked slowly, the crowd pressing around and past him.

Ichiro, behind, smiled. There was something reassuring about this priest, here on the crowded, modern streets of Shinjuku. Wandering priests were no rare sight, yet they were more than an anachronism—they were a reminder. They were a kind of symbol of Japan's integrity.

At the street corner Ichiro already had his hand in his pocket, feeling for small bills, when the light changed. Rather than cross in front of the priest—on principle Ichiro paid no attention to traffic lights—he waited behind him. The priest, however, seemed deep in meditation. His head down, his eyes covered by the hat, he continued walking against the traffic.

A charcoal-burning taxi, trailing a great cloud of

yellow smoke like a battle banner, came around the corner at great speed and knocked the priest down.

Ichiro's first impulse was to run to the fallen priest. The hat had fallen from his head and was rolling in the intersection. His face was quite old and his eyes were closed. The pan was caught under one of the worn tires of the taxi and the bead-string was broken. The cat-faced bell had disappeared.

A crowd was gathering around the stopped taxi, and Ichiro successfully suppressed his first impulse. This was, after all, the responsibility of the driver who had struck the priest, and, now, Ichiro no more thought of going to the old man's aid than did anyone else gathered around, silent and looking. If Ichiro, or anyone else, interfered and performed any service, no matter how small, the priest, his abbot, his entire sect would be forever in debt, in theory at any rate, and there was always the possibility that this would in turn complicate the donor's life no end. It would therefore be cruel to the priest if he were still alive, and useless if he were dead.

Now he lay quite peacefully, his arms outstretched, his legs curled under him, as though he were the main figure in some Chinese assumption scene. The terrified driver had not yet climbed from his smoking cab. The crowd looking at the now feebly bleeding body was growing larger. When the driver, frightened and pale, opened the door, more and more curious passers-by stopped.

Ichiro stayed longer and watched the pale driver bend over the old man. The taxi smoked, and the cars, piled up behind it, honked incessantly. Suddenly Ichiro felt very sad and very angry. He turned abruptly and started down the street.

By the time he reached Shinjuku Station he was almost running, accidentally bumping against others, who turned, marveling at his rudeness. He bought a ticket to Ochanomizu and walked to the platform for the Chuo Line.

He had thought perhaps to go to Asakusa and walk through the park and the amusement district, feeling his spirit recoil with disgust at the naked girlie shows, the American gangster movies, the black-market cigarettes and whiskey, the hunger and sadness and poverty that was Japan. That would be punishment enough for his shocking behavior toward his father.

But then he realized that it would also be self-indulgence. It was better to carry one's shame within, until it was entirely expiated. As he waited, he solemnly pinched first one thigh, then the other. After that he cruelly twisted all of his fingers.

It was past the rush hour and the trains were less crowded. All the seats were taken, naturally, but it was possible to stand without danger of being crushed. He stood, one hand on the rail above, the other in his pocket, still wickedly tweaking his already bruised thigh.

Before him sat a young girl, and as he watched her Ichiro felt a great and satisfying wave of disgust. From head to toe she was everything a Japanese girl should not be. Her feet were forced into high-heeled shoes which he recognized as PX. Her stockings, though not the luxurious American nylon, were the Japanese substitute and wrinkled around the heel. (He decided that Japanese girls should never show their legs—not that it was immoral, it was just that their legs were not adapted to Western clothes. He'd heard GI's call them "piano legs" and that seemed most apt.) Her dress was too short, either through choice or necessity; it failed to hide the roll of her stockings above the knee. Under her coat she wore a Japanese imitation-silk blouse torn at the neckline. She had tried to hide the tear by fastening it with a pin—a Chuo University pin. Her hair was frizzed in the current "cannibal" fashion and stood straight out from her head.

The face beneath was pretty, however, for it was the classical moon-face, always so beautiful in Japan. But the cheeks were rouged so heavily and the lips painted such a thick red that the face itself was all but hidden. The rice-powder on her nose was caked and cracked, and the mascara on her eyebrows was greasy with perspiration.

He watched her, positively enjoying his disgust. And, too, how symbolic of Japan she seemed. If he remembered, he would write a waka or perhaps, to limit himself still more severely, a haiku about her. The moonfaced beauty so reminiscent of Japan's past, the loveliness of Kyoto in the autumn, the full moon rising above Edo—then all of this mutilated and disfigured by the paste for the lips, the powder for the nose, and the American permanent wave. If he could cut it down, it would make a good haiku.

The girl looked up from her movie magazine, and he glanced rudely away, hoping to offend her as she deserved. But she was not offended, for she was not interested. She had eyes only for the next car, which she could see through the end windows. Several American soldiers were sprawling in it. Ichiro closed his eyes. This was much better punishment than Asakusa would have been. As his eyes closed he bit his underlip. This before him could have been his own Haruko.

And Haruko might yet become like this shameless creature sitting before him. For a time he allowed himself the indulgence of imagining a meeting years from now between Haruko and himself. She would be a prostitute and he an internationally famous lawyer, devoted to his task of showing the way to Japan. It would be in Shinjuku Station. He would have come from an important meeting with the Prime Minister during which he had changed the destiny of his people several times.

Ordinarily he would be in his own car, being driven

home, perhaps to Denenchofu, where they had the latest plumbing, and where his wife, a beautiful, meek, and very rich girl from the country, would be bowing low at the portal. But tonight, for some reason, he would be in Shinjuku Station, like a samurai in disguise. And this little prostitute would timidly approach him, somehow aware that she was in the presence of a great man. She would lay a tiny hand upon his arm, and he, smiling at the folly he was seeking to correct, would begin to turn away. But before he did—the Recognition Scene!

It was Haruko, her teeth blackened, her hair frizzed in the still-popular "cannibal" style, her eyes dropping mascara-like tears. Ah—she knew him also. Their eyes would meet, and the Truth would lie between them.

It would be enough that they both knew. Then he, sadder but wiser, would turn away, and she, with no backward glance, would go and fling herself under the next train.... The only thing spoiling this otherwise enjoyable vision was Ichiro's feeling that he'd seen it all someplace before.

The train stopped at Ochanomizu, and both Ichiro and the girl got off. She sauntered close to the window of the Allied car, peering in, and Ichiro suddenly remembered how he himself had peered into the Allied car that morning at the soldier from the Colonel's office—his rival. He would go see Haruko now and confront her with his evidence. Despite the fact that they were not supposed to meet until tonight, they had been seeing each other off and on since they were children, and this meeting at the opera was simply a public way of announcing an engagement. If he saw her this afternoon, he could throw her off guard. Eventually, weak and womanly, she would creep to him for forgiveness, which he would magnanimously give. It would get their marriage off on the proper footing—himself as master. The only thing the matter with Haruko was that she had big ideas about the equal importance of women and so forth. Well, she wouldn't have them long!

Meanwhile the train pulled out, and the prostitute—what else could she be?—continued her stroll along the station. Ochanomizu was a respectable district, and it seemed decidedly bad business that she should be here even at night, not to speak of noon. She was approaching a rather dirty student, and Ichiro, despite his disgust, turned to watch. He had hoped to see her rebuffed, but instead, the student smiled and bowed. After a few words she turned and strolled away. Ichiro saw that the boy was Yamaguchi, a schoolmate of his.

Just then Yamaguchi saw Ichiro and waved. He was a short boy with enormous glasses, long uncut hair, and a vast amount of dirt. Even though it was no longer in the height of fashion, he still affected the traditional filth of students, and his bare feet were thrust into high wooden geta which clattered along the station floor as he ran, his cape flying behind him.

"Hello, Ohara," he shouted.

"Good afternoon, Mr. Yamaguchi," said Ichiro, knowing he now liked to be called Comrade Yamaguchi since his recently acquired enthusiasm for communism. Before that it had been the French films and, before that, stamp collecting. Ichiro, on principle, disliked the idea of calling anyone comrade and so always declined. He nodded toward the distant swaying girl and said: "You were speaking of Marxian dialectic?"

Yamaguchi turned brusquely, head over his shoulder, and looked after the girl. His actions always seemed parodies of themselves. When he shook hands with a comradely enthusiasm, it was as though he were pumping water; when asked an opinion, he would screw up his eyes and visibly think; when told a joke, his braying laugh could be heard for blocks. Now he turned and stared back along the station as though he had been told that Marx himself had suddenly appeared there.

He looks like an ugly, dirty little bird, thought Ichiro, like the latest metamorphosis of the imperial phoenix.

"As a matter of fact, yes," said Yamaguchi, turning his head with a quick motion which threatened to dislocate it.

Ichiro laughed, but the other looked so hurt that he turned it into a polite cough and said earnestly: "Is she of the underground also?"

Yamaguchi looked innocent. "We are not to say, but as a matter of fact, yes."

Ichiro had never been able to determine exactly how much of a communist his acquaintance was. He attacked each new enthusiasm with such vigor and militancy that it became impossible to gauge accurately how implicated he was in any of his interests.

Now he bent forward, his cape around him, and, in a conspiratorial voice, dramatically lowered, said: "I can say no more, but it has to do with a great demonstration which we are at present engineering. You will doubtless hear of it in all the papers and on the radio by tomorrow at the latest. It will be a great blow given for Truth and Freedom."

"Is one to know the nature of the disturbance?"

"No," Yamaguchi said shortly. But then, unable to forego the pure pleasure of sharing, he lowered his voice still further and whispered: "It is aimed at the heart of the American Invasion, the infamous GHQ."

It was always difficult to know how seriously to take Yamaguchi's pronouncements. It was quite possible that there was actually to be a demonstration of some kind, though it would probably be an all-student one, and hence rather inoffensive. But Yamaguchi's enthusiasms often bordered on mania. His intensity had made possible the finest stamp collection at Chuo University, and even now he probably knew more about the private life of Viviane Romance than anyone else in Japan. On the other hand, it was equally possible that he wasn't even a Party member and was simply one of those many students whom the real organization used from time to time.

Yamaguchi saw the unexpressed doubt on Ichiro's face. "Well, you remember the May Day demonstration when so much good was done."

"Or so much damage, as you like. What about it?"

Comrade Yamaguchi tapped his chest complacently.

"All of it? asked Ichiro.

Yamaguchi held up a modest hand. "No, Comrade Ohara, not all—but," and he lowered his voice tenderly, "a little."

Ichiro knew all about this and felt like smiling. Five students had been implicated, all of them innocently. They had enjoyed the riot for its own exciting sake; it was only afterwards that they realized it had been anything but spontaneous, realized it had been engineered. All, including Comrade Yamaguchi here, had been quite contrite, and all had been punished by a public reprimand from the president of the university. At the time Yamaguchi was making a scrapbook devoted to Odette Joyeux and almost failed to attend his punishment.

"Well," said Ichiro, "it was a stroke of genius to use the Imperial Plaza."

Yamaguchi smiled, touched. "We thought so," he said quietly.

"By the way, are you a member of the Party?"

"It's no crime," said Yamaguchi, instantly defensive —or perhaps avoiding a direct answer. "Not like in some countries I could name. Japan's still a free country."

"Oh, no, it's not either—it's a colony."

Comrade Yamaguchi could very easily turn any comment to his own advantage: "Yes, of a vicious and corrupt capitalistic system which, in the end, can only defeat its own purpose. This we true Japanese will wish for and will encourage. Then will come—among other nice things—the Worker's Paradise."

Ichiro didn't laugh, knowing Yamaguchi had no sense of humor, but the idea of Japan's being a worker's paradise strongly tempted him to. A dictatorship of the proletariat was impossible, and as for anarchy, the ultimate goal of communism—well, Japan was simply too tidy a country. But, then, Yamaguchi didn't know what he was saying—he always parroting phrases he'd picked up here and there.

"You don't seriously believe that, do you?" asked Ichiro, still amused.

The amusement stung Yamaguchi, who stuck out his lower lip. As a matter of fact, he didn't but was scarcely in the position to admit it. It was an attitude, like many others, and self-respect must be maintained at any cost. Actually, he had long before begun to have doubts.

His first doubts had occurred when, at his own expense, he had gone to see the prisoners returned from Russia. He, and almost everyone else, had been profoundly shocked by the behavior of the indoctrinated soldiers toward their own families. He'd seen a young ex-soldier nod only slightly to a weeping father whom he had not seen in years, in the meantime shouting and carrying around the placards used in what was called their spontaneous demonstration. He'd seen another, about his own age or a bit older—he must have entered the Army from grammar school—standing undecided between his weeping mother and his jeering comrades. It was a most dramatic scene, illustrating the theme of conflicting loyalties which fills all Japanese literature, and yet the resolution of the conflict in this case was one which any Japanese would have found repugnant. Thus is was that Comrade Yamaguchi began to have his doubts.

And with his doubting came a tendency to find flaws

in the Communist world-pattern, just as he eventually always found flaws in his hobbies. Thus he had finally decided that Arletty was the epitome of the bourgeois. And now he slowly turned from Marx, saying, first, that Stalinism was not true communism at all and, finally, that true Marxism was no real answer in itself—it answered the body, he was fond of whispering to himself, but what of the soul?

This might have led him to Buddhism or to Christianity, but instead, following the obscure pattern of his enthusiasms, it led him to American literature. He had already been reading much of it, in translation, under the guise of "getting to know the enemy." But after reading Emerson and Whitman and *Moby Dick* he had been stirred into curiosity. What, indeed, of the soul? So, being commendably thorough, he attempted to find the answer where he had found the question—in American literature.

He read Hemingway, but received small comfort. Scott Fitzgerald was no better. Miss Louisa May Alcott seemed to him to have a somewhat superficial view of the subject of the soul, while the solution of Longfellow's, though probably more practical than that of William Faulkner's, was, perhaps, a bit optimistic. Thus he waded through American literature, receiving much pleasure but little instruction.

His doubts concerning the Communists had begun to be considerable, but it was not yet time for him to change his attitude publicly. He would wear it a while longer, deriving whatever solace it gave while he searched for a substitute. His heart, however, was no longer in it. He never went to French movies now and had sold his stamp collection so he could buy the collected works of O. Henry. His gradual political apostasy, however, dissemble it as he might, had not gone unnoticed.

So when Ichiro smiled and said "You don't seriously believe that, now do you?" Yamaguchi was stung: he was the first to realize that, of course, he didn't. But he couldn't simply admit it—there was his position to think of.

"Yes I do !" he shouted. "But I can see that you don't. You and your capitalistic, war-mongering, fraternizing father ! You're just like him—an opportunist, a non-altruistic Philistine !" He was spluttering with rage and, being unable to think of anything more damning, turned and ran quickly—bird-like—along the station, his clogs clattering on the concrete

These were very harsh words for Ichiro, but then Yamaguchi always used very harsh words. Sometimes he got himself slapped because of them, but he never learned. Ichiro merely sighed and refused to take the words seriously. Besides the words didn't bother him, though their application did.

Why was it, he wondered, that one was always expected to be one thing or another ! His own father occasionally indulged in towering rages, during which he would accuse Ichiro of being radical, anti-social, probably a Communist, and certainly an ingrate. Just now Comrade Yamaguchi had accused him of precisely the opposite—of being a reactionary, a capitalist, probably a fraternizer, and certainly an opportunist.

The saddest part, thought Ichiro, was that he was none of these things. His sympathies, if they had to be some place, were with the Americans; it was only natural for a Japanese that they would be—after all, Comrade Yamaguchi was an exception—but that did not necessarily mean that he approved of everything they did or stood for. That was one thing people like his own father and Yamaguchi—the world seemed to be full of such—could never understand: that a divided loyalty was a natural thing and one to be desired. Ichiro's view of the world, whatever its limitations, did not confine itself to merely black and white. There was more than this to life. But, at times like this, Ichiro strongly doubted that he was particularly fitted for his future career. He was in law school.

He walked to the street, past the Julien Sorel Men's Wear, the New Kleine Fujigetsudo Patissiere, and the Monster Atom Bar. At the corner he caught a crowded streetcar and, hanging on the outside, the wind whipping his face, wondered how he ought to act toward Haruko after all.

In the ordinary course of events he would have been calling merely to instruct her how she should act that evening at their official meeting. But now that he knew about the soldier, this was obviously impossible. Yet he could not confront her with his knowledge. This was not permitted. If she were as high-minded as Ichiro would have her, she would have no other recourse than suicide, and he had to admit he didn't want that. So he decided to be stern, to allow her to suspect that he knew. He would watch her torments in silence and then, finally, relieve her of them by announcing he was bowing to his father's wishes. He would coldly ask her if she would do him the honor of becoming his wife. She, covered with shame, would kneel low before him, beg forgiveness, and promise to be the model wife.

By the time he rang the bell he had all the details worked out.

The old female servant opened the door and at once prostrated herself. She knew in which direction the wind lay. It was she who had telephoned his father's servant—her dearest friend—and told about the soldier's having finally stayed the night. She had heard him come and heard him go—with almost four hours intervening between those two shocking occurences. She had also heard laughter—and suspicious silences. But she resisted the impulse to elaborate upon these significant details, finding it more pleasant to allow her friend to fill in the probabilities with her own lively imagination. Now she lowered herself before the wrathful lord.

He nodded brusquely, anxious to get on with the interview, and allowed himself to be led into the main room, where he was seated before the small red-lacquer table and given tea. The old servant, all unspoken condolence, bowed again and disappeared. He waited for Haruko, contrite, frightened as a kitten, to appear.

When the fusuma at the far end of the room opened it was not pushed by the gentle hand, graceful as a falling petal, of a well-trained Japanese maiden who would thus have revealed herself, dramatically, in a pose of silent contrition, as though her hand, now falling equally gracefully into her lap, had not even touched the door. It was pushed by Haruko's foot as she, bending over a mass of chrysanthemums from the garden, backed into the room.

She didn't see him until she was well into the room. "Good morning," she said, bowing clumsily over the load of flowers.

"Good day," he said shortly, a bit aware that his formal pose—one fist around the teacup, the other at his side as though upon a sword hilt, a combination of the samurai and David Lloyd George—was none too effective.

"I've been out in the garden," she said and gracefully piled the flowers at one side of the tokonoma beside him.

"Yes," he said, and waited.

She knelt beside him, her legs folded under her, her hands in her lap, and successfully resisted an impulse to laugh. He looked so pompous sitting there glaring down at her. They had known each other from childhood, far too long for her to take his pretensions seriously now that he was of a marriageable age. Then she sighed, for, even if it was rather amusing, it was also rather sad. She had seen so many of the boys with whom she had played as a child become pompous bores. It seemed, in fact, a national pattern.

When he'd been young he'd been charming. They had played together every day, as though they were both boys, and he'd taught her to fly kites, and she'd always had him as a special guest on the festival day for girls. It was he who had always been allowed to touch the dolls.

Then, quite suddenly, he had been removed into some other world, put into a boys' school, and their meetings had been frowned upon. Soon she had gone to a girls' school and had never again known any boys her age until Michael. Perhaps when she and Ichiro were very old they might play together again, but certainly not before that. In the same way she had put her bright-colored kimono away upon going to school, and could not again wear the brilliant reds until long after her children were married.

So it was sad to be sitting like this with him now. He had apparently forgotten every one of their childhood confidences. She was going to be a celebrated airplane pilot, and he was to explore Mongolia and become extremely famous. But it had all changed. She was simply a Japanese girl, and that in itself was a lifetime of labor. He would become a bank clerk or a shipping official and, after years of labor, would remain a manager or a president or a something. And already he was more successfully facing his future than she. Only a future Japanese magnate of industry could sit there as he was doing now, glaring at her.

She doubted that she could make him a satisfactory wife. It was not that she didn't like him—quite the contrary. When she'd first learned she was to marry him she had been ecstatic, but that had been years ago and her romantic devotion to the handsome student whom she occasionally saw on the street or in the homes of mutual friends had long since become something more sober and enduring. They had shared a life in common, and that was the most important thing. For that reason alone she could be his wife. But then, of course, she no longer knew him—she only remembered him as he had been. It was best to pretend he was a stranger and treat him accordingly.

Tentatively, she said: "The chrysanthemums are very full this year."

"So I have seen for myself."

"Might one bring you hot tea?"

"As one may notice, it has already been brought."

"May one inquire after the health of one's future parents?"

"One may. They are well."

"And of one's future husband."

"He also is well."

After a pause, he continued: "It is concerning the marriage that he comes to speak with you." He leaned back slightly, waiting for this pronouncement to have its full effect upon her. He had hoped for blushes and a lowered head.

Instead, she leaned forward on her elbows and said: "Good. I've been wanting to talk to you about it too."

"It is the husband's prerogative to speak with the wife. Not the other way about."

"I know. That's why I've been waiting." She folded her hands and waited.

Ichiro didn't like the turn the interview was taking. As always, she was aggressive. If he'd thought of it, he could have sent his mother, and she could have found out all he wanted to know through the female combination of maternal petting and quite objective poking and pulling. But he hadn't thought of this until now.

"The marriage is what our honored parents wish."

"Isn't that so, though?"

"And, upon proper consideration, I believe it neither possible nor good that we attempt to run counter to their wishes."

"Oh, I don't know about that. After all, it's not they who are getting married. It's us.... How do you really feel about it, Ichiro? Not too good, judging from the way you're acting."

Ichiro swallowed, then finished the rest of his tea. She was quite impossible, positively unladylike. It was because she was so Western. In spite of the servants' gossip he still believed her pure of body—but of mind, no. Her mind was corrupted. He was certain of that.

"My feeling in this matter, which you so kindly consider, is not entirely based upon personal considerations. I, not unnaturally, am also motivated by considerations for the future, the fact that our parents will come more and more to depend upon us, that our children will find in us that which we have found in our parents."

"Oh, I hope not," said Haruko, without thinking. "If you're anything like your father—"

A stern though scandalized glance from Ichiro stopped her.

"As I was saying, all of these considerations conspire to create within me a condition which you quite accurately noticed as troubled. I do not feel that a marriage between our houses is feasible until a certain obstacle is removed and until we ascertain precisely how much damage this obstacle has already occasioned." That, thought Ichiro, was very well put. Now at last he would be rewarded with a few tears and probably a blush as well.

"You mean the American?" asked Haruko. "Well, to be sure, he must be considered. For he, too, has asked for me as his wife, and, frankly, I don't know quite what to do. You must help me, Ichiro, because I'm just a girl and I can't decide things like this—important things, you know. And you can."

Her flattery did not even reach him. Ichiro was shocked, much in the way his father had been shocked by the Colonel's dragging business so indecently into the open and then heartlessly dispensing with it. The son had expected modesty and contrition. Perhaps, after several hours of conversation, the existence of the soldier might have been casually mentioned, there might have been more subtle references, so slight that if the other did not wish to acknowledge them, he—or she—need not do so. But this indelicate blatancy, and the further insult of asking for aid in a problem so uniquely her own—he was rendered quite speechless.

Haruko toyed with the insignia of his cap. "I suppose you think me impolite, but, really, Ichiro, this is far too important for both of us not to discuss it in full. I don't really mean to be impolite, but I am forced to be since you will not do me the justice of speaking about it openly."

"The fact that I am here proclaims that I am ready to do so," said Ichiro, feeling his honor at stake.

"It proclaims nothing of the sort. It merely indicates you are suspicious. You are here because you know the soldier was here last night. I suppose you want to know what happened. Nothing happened—that's what happened. Nothing but that he asked me to marry him. And he kissed me, which is, or so I hear, an old American custom meaning no more than shaking hands or bowing." She broke into tears.

Ichiro had indeed been hoping for tears—but these were born of anger and rebellion. Since they were not at all of the variety he expected, he was at a loss as to what to do in such bizarre circumstances. Frantically he searched for a model. In the Kabuki he would probably have dismissed the creature with strong words advising suicide. In the Noh he could have come back as a ghost and made life miserable for her. Or perhaps she would have come back and made life miserable for *him*—you could never tell about the Noh. What would Yoshitsune—one of his heroes—have done in the unlikely event he'd ever faced such circumstances?

Failing to find a model among Japanese sources, he thought abroad. Now what would Emma Bovary's husband have done? But, finding he could remember nothing whatever about Mr. Emma and very little about Emma herself, he decided, like Daruma, to put stones from the garden in his mouth, that he might never speak again. But at that moment he remembered Demosthenes had put pebbles from the beach into his mouth that he might speak the better. Momentarily torn between the rigid opposites of East and West, Ichiro did something he practically never did, something indeed which he virtuously fought against ever doing—he acted as he felt, said what he thought:

"There is nothing wrong in kissing, I'm sure. You should feel no shame. I feel no humiliation. You are, however, presented with a choice between us. It is otherwise of no importance, and you merely waste your tears."

Haruko raised her head, tears clinging to her lashes. "You are not angry with me, then?"

Ichiro decided he had gone too far. This is what always happened when you spoke as you felt—you were taken advantage of. "I don't say that," he said, attempting to regain some of the dignity he had so foolishly cast away, "but I will say that if you have done nothing that wrongs either your honor or mine, or that of our families, then the problem is simplified rather than complicated."

"But what of tonight?" asked Haruko, her underlip trembling.

"What of it?"

"We're to be meeting for the first time. The go-between will be there to introduce us. The fact that we meet proves that we have intentions, that our parents approve. It is all but an announcement to the world."

"Oh, not at all. Why, many times parents take their

sons or daughters to the theater, or to view the cherry blossoms at Ueno, or to Enoshima, simply to meet someone eligible who will be there too. And if the boy isn't interested, he simply doesn't make any further move, makes no attempt to see her again; then their go-between says the boy has pneumonia or has gone to Kyushu or something of the sort. You know all this as well as I do."

"But they know better—these girls and their families —about Kyushu?"

"To be sure, but they aren't going to have a public disagreement. And, when next they see each other on the street, the son and daughter simply pretend the other doesn't exist. It's very simple. In the same way this meeting tonight need have no great meaning."

This information irritated Haruko: she had been quite certain of Ichiro's affections. Besides, how could he treat so lightly this meeting which was to be the turning point of her life? Their lives had been so designed that it was mathematically impossible for them not to meet tonight, and if nothing came of it, it would be she who had disturbed the pattern, not he.

"Well," she said, "if the meeting makes so little difference to you, perhaps we could well dispense with it entirely. I could get pneumonia and you could go to Kyushu, or the other way about if you happen to have a preference."

Ichiro looked at her with real annoyance. Her refusal to play her traditional role, the one already indicated for her, the one exemplified in all of her female relatives and friends, wounded him considerably. But, at the same time, he seemed to detect in her a disinclination for the meeting, the success of which he had for years taken for granted. And as soon as he realized that it might be possible that she did not wish the marriage, he began to want it more than he ever had before.

"My statement, if you will remember, was not that it made little difference to me, but that it did not necessarily compromise either of us. I think our parents would be most upset if we didn't meet this evening. Besides it's the opera about Madame Butterfly, and you like that."

Haruko smiled. So he remembered that, after all these years. She had had a phonograph record of the part about the one fine day, and had played it over and over again until poor Chocho-san sank, struggling, beneath the needle scratch. "Yes, I still like it," she said.

"Well, then," said Ichiro, "it's all settled. We'll meet this evening as planned and be introduced, which will be amusing, and then—about the other—we shall see."

"Yes," she said, smiling through her tears, "it's all settled."

He then realized that, indeed, it was. This was the ostensible reason he had come to see her—to arrange the evening. It was now all arranged, and he had no further excuse for prolonging the interrogation. There was no recourse but to stand and go. He began to understand how his father must have felt with the Colonel.

As he opened the fusuma, Haruko bowing low beside him in a sudden return to Japanese etiquette, he almost caught the old servant with her ear pressed to the door. She instantly began dusting the floor with her handkerchief, but not before he realized she had heard everything, had seen him come like a samurai and depart like a ronin. She would doubtless lose no time in running to the telephone and pouring out the news to the servant at his house.

The old woman bowed, but not so low as before. She was no longer so certain how the wind blew. If the soldier came back, thought Ichiro, he'd probably receive a bow equally low.

"Until tonight," said Haruko from the tatami.

"Until tonight," said Ichiro, bowing stiffly from the waist.

Then there was nothing left for him to do but leave the house, in a much different frame of mind from that in which he had entered it. He saw the husks of his determination scattered about his departing feet, and could only wonder, in chastened awe, at the inconsistency of life and the appalling fact that it was now he himself who was contrite.

A single leaf fell artistically from the maple tree. This was too much. A large tear rolled down his cheek.

■

After Ichiro left, Haruko remained alone, kneeling in the center of the room before the red-lacquer table. The cup, half-filled with cold tea, was on one corner, and in the alcove beyond, the untended chrysanthemums were gracefully dying, their leaves curling, their petals falling away from the closely packed heart of the flower.

She was presented with a dilemma. Her problem was so classically correct, so very Japanese that—had she not been so unhappy—she might have smiled. Since no one was watching, she slid sidewise from her knees and stretched her legs before her, the bottom of her kimono falling open. If her mother had entered at that moment and found her daughter sprawled on the floor, her legs open, she would have believed her quite demented. She would have thought Haruko had been very poorly trained.

But, of course, that was part of the problem. Haruko knew just what she ought to do, just as she knew, from years of training, that the well-bred Japanese girl did not sit otherwise than securely upon her feet. A good girl would not question her parents' wishes in the matter of marriage, but would willingly comply, would bow before her husband and be the perfect wife with unquestioning devotion and unswerving loyalty. In this many girls had succeeded before her and many would after her.

But, for Haruko, this was not enough. She had been to girls' school and had learned Civics and Home Economics and Biology. She spoke English a little and read it rather considerably better. No, she was plainly an individual, and must treat herself as one, particularly since no one else seemed likely to.

She did wish, however, that her problem were a bit more unique. To have achieved a problem was in itself no small triumph—lots of girls didn't even do that. But it was insulting to realize that the problem was the same old dilemma that had faced every Japanese girl from Townsend Harris's Okichi to the war brides she'd been hearing so much about. It was the classic choice between the Japanese way—self-abnegating, compliant, serene—and the new way—adventuresome, bold, romantic, the very selfish and quite American way.

She had often seen this problem in the movies and been moved to tears. In the Kabuki the problem was actually the same, though abstracted, and the unfortunate lady nearly always killed herself. In Western novels it was the same, and if the girl didn't end like Madame Bovary, she ended like Sister Carrie, and to Haruko there didn't seem much choice between the two.

What one didn't read about or see in the films was what eventually happened to the many young Japanese ladies who had chosen the romantic way. Presumably nothing too violent occurred, or else the papers would carry it. Lacking information, Haruko had no clear idea of what to expect if she married the soldier. The only hint she could think of from literature was that she would be relatively unhappy—as in *Madame Butterfly*, that most beautiful of all operas, through which she was sure to weep tonight, seeing herself on the stage, feeling the dagger in her own vitals. The thought thrilled her most pleasantly. Still, whatever the fate of the expatriated Japanese maidens, nothing could be as bad as what she saw occurring to them in Japan.

All this thought had inspired her. She decided to write in her diary. Like all her friends, Haruko too kept a diary, very elaborately locked up and filled with her most precious thoughts. She often stole away to the corner of her room to read it, for it was better than a novel—which it greatly resembled.

She could always cry at the entries she'd written upon receiving word that her elder brother had been killed at Saipan, and there was one beautiful page devoted to the death of their old cat. She shed tears indiscrimately over both—not the events but the extreme beauty of her style caused her to weep. Her diary was in English, and that was what helped make it so beautiful

She stood up, for now she had enough material for a long and beautifully pathetic entry. Quickly she went to her room, opened the bottom drawer of the chest, and after feeling through her folded summer kimono, discovered the volume. Fountain pen in hand, she composed herself; then, one hand shading her eyes, she began to write, giving voice to all the beautiful thoughts which were welling up from within her.

"O, horrid dillema of Japanese girl," she wrote. "O, immortal confrict of will and idea. My head grows numm at thought. Can I choice wise between my true Japanese way and new American way? Yes. I can wisely choice. But. How? When He (Private Michael Richardson, US Army at Shinjuku, Tokyo) kiss my heart burn with love and admiration. My breast pulpitate. My blood rush in mighty river and my sense grow dumm."

She stopped and reread the paragraph. Of course that last part was not quite true, but it was not truth that made her diary so interesting. Now she must have a contrast to that.

"But, when the Other (Ichiro Ohara, student only)

touch my hand nothing happen my heart, my breast, my blood, my sense. I do not reaction to him. Therefore I have fatal love—like Romeo and Juliet, like Tristan and Isolde, like Miss Greer Garson in Dusty Blossoms. Soon I must decide my mind. If not I die. I fade away."

'She decided the latter was not becoming and crossed out "fade away," substituting "linger slow like autumnal flower, perish like Japan's lovely clisanthemum." That was very poetic—and also very true. In the next room the flowers were slowly dying.

"But action is expected from heroine (Myself) and soon comes time for eternal and important choose. Which shall I be? O, horrid dillema of Japanese girl. O, that I was ever born to suffer sharp tooth of sorrow so much."

Haruko quickly placed a blotter on the words lest her falling tears blur them. Then, shielding the diary from the falling drops with her hand, she read the entire entry. It was very beautiful.

At the end she suddenly jotted down, in hurried Japanese, a poem which had just occurred to her:

> Tokyo's windy sky
> Bears the aspect of winter
> And the radio
> Is intermittently heard
> Through the noises of the wind.

To be sure, this was not nearly so beautiful, just a perfectly traditional waka. The Japanese characters looked all crabbed when compared with the easy-flowing, open, and friendly English letters. Besides, her American thought was so much more satisfying than her Japanese.

She was about to cross out the waka, when it occurred to her that the idea of a radio in a waka was nicely anomalous—and very modern sounding. She closed the book, put it away, stood up, and then realized that in the distance she actually could hear a radio. Smiling, she began to change her clothes.

At least she had made up her mind and knew what she was going to do. She was going to Shinjuku and see Private Richardson—that was something she must do. She must also hurry because, for one thing, the chrysanthemums needed water, and for another, it was almost afternoon.

Part 2

part 2

THE OFFICE CLOSED AT NOON ON SATURDAYS, AND Gloria occupied herself with a copy of *Vogue* she had in the desk until time for the Major, who had returned to his quarters to change, to pick her up. After half an hour Gloria looked at the clock, examined her teeth in the mirror, combed her hair, pulled on her coat, and walked down the corridor.

At the bottom of the stairs she turned to the MP's and said appealingly: "Look, you both know me. Do I *have* to dig out that stupid pass?"

"I'm sorry, lady—we got to see it."

With a gesture of exaggerated impatience she opened a large suede purse and began pushing about the contents. From time to time she threw objects onto the floor—half a stick of gum, a name card, an empty book of matches, and, inadvertently, two hairpins. These last she picked up. Eventually she found the pass, ran it under the MP's noses, and flounced through the doors.

One MP turned to the other: "And who the hell was that?"

"Her name's Gloria and she works in one of the offices here for some colonel or other. She's a secretary —a sexatary, if you get me."

"Christ, I thought she was the Queen of Sheba. What ya mean—sexatary?"

"Well, she's the Queen of Special Services—distributes her favors right royally."

"And how do *you* know—she ever distribute in your direction?"

"Nah—she's the officer type. Nothing lower than looies."

"Is there anything lower?"

They both looked out of the window at Gloria, who was standing by the curb gazing affectionately at a small child playing on the sidewalk. She picked it up, tickled it under the chin, and set it against the building, out of harm's way. A sedan drove up, the driver in front; the rear door opened.

"Hop right in, Miss Wilson. Hope I didn't keep you waiting long."

"Not long, Major—just waiting." She climbed in, carrying the end of her coat over one arm, then waved to the child before closing the door.

"O. K., Joe—American Club."

The driver turned around and looked inquiring.

"American Club! American Club!" shouted the Major, loudly.

The driver frowned apologetically.

"Tokyo Kaikan," said Gloria quickly and pleasantly.

"Gee," said the Major, shaking his head with admiration. "I didn't know you could talk Jap."

"Why, Major, I talked Jap since but a child."

"Well, is that so, Miss Wilson? What d'ya know! And here I thought you were just another DAC. Born here, I guess?"

"Yes, I'm part Formosan, you know."

"No, I didn't."

"Oh, heavens, yes. You see, my father was from Tierra del Fuego and my mother was Laplandish, but they settled in the Pacific. Both so disliked the cold, of course."

"I guess I can understand that, being from Texas and all. Why, we—"

"Oh, no, it's not the same at all. You can never realize the intense cold of a good old Lapland winter. Even the Laplanders have difficulty believing it. So a Texan . . ."

"I guess that's so . . . . Gee, I never knew that. Makes me think I'm out with somebody real important."

"What an extraordinarily sweet thing to say."

She turned and looked at the approaching park, green in the distance. The Major, always cordial in the office, became positively overpowering on their "dates." On each one he behaved precisely as though he had never met her before.

This was what he called "not letting the office get in the way." In this way he was able to forget how Gloria often glared at him and always took Private Richardson's side during any of their many arguments. The Major had his eye on Gloria. He was constantly on what he called his "good behavior" with her, even when he sometimes half-suspected she was making fun of him.

Now he said: "Well, it's Saturday again. What'd you do last Saturday night? Really live it up?"

"Me? Heavens, what on earth makes you think that? I hope I don't appear to be *that* kind of girl, Major. Why, I stayed in my room and wrote my dear old mother, and then I washed my hair, and then I went to bed."

"It's a shame more people don't follow your example, Miss Wilson," the Major said seriously.

"I suppose there's always a great deal of drinking and such—Saturday and all."

"Altogether uncalled for, I must say." He paused, then quickly added: "But I was out Tachikawa way last Saturday—business, you know. Us PIO's got to keep good contacts with all the boys . . . and, well, I won't sully your ears, Miss Wilson, but the things I saw weren't fit for no American woman to see."

"I can just imagine. . . . Were many there?"

"Women? Oh, lots."

"And . . . the others?"

"Men? Oh, yeah, lots of men, all drunk and lying around, just not caring what happened to them. Like Babylon in the movies. I bet I saw a regiment stretched out."

Gloria turned and looked out of the window. "Well, it's doubtless not loyal of me," she went on after a minute, "but I've noticed that the morals of some Americans over here seem rather low."

The Major turned to her and leaned forward. "You know, Miss Wilson, I feel exactly the same way. You and I agree on that."

Gloria skilfully slid her hand across the seat, out of reach of the Major's.

"Isn't it beautiful?" said the Major, indicating the park, though at the moment they were again in the midst of blackened ruins.

"Gorgeous," murmured Gloria. She waved her hand toward the window. "Particularly that portion." A woman had come from one of the board huts nearby and was squatting on the ground, her bagging trousers around her ankles.

The Major quickly averted his eyes, then caught a glimpse of distant green. "Oh, yes, the trees you mean. Isn't that a nice shade of green though? You know, I just love nature. Nature in everything."

The Major was edging closer.

"Look, isn't the sky lovely—so blue—for November, that is."

Just as his hand touched hers she reached for her purse, drew forth her handkerchief, and daintily blew her nose. Then she put both hands securely in her lap.

She looked at the neck of the driver. His hair had been recently cut and lay short on the back of his head. His ears, nicely shaped, were flat on either side of his head. Whenever he turned his head, his profile, seen against the moving background of traffic, was of a wonderful regularity, his nose meeting his forehead with complete lack of bridge, his mouth firm, and his chin square. He was quite handsome, and just in time Gloria realized she had been about to lay her hand upon the newly cut hair at the back of his neck.

The Major followed her gaze. "These Japanese are good drivers, aren't they?"

"Extremely good. Good at most mechanical things."

"But not quite good enough, eh, Miss Wilson?" and the Major laughed heavily.

Gloria smiled and turned to him. "Not quite, Major.... Tell me, what did you do during the war?"

He smiled ruefully and dug his fist into the car seat. "Aw, I was one of those poor guys that got stuck in the States. Boy, I tried everything and just couldn't get into the game. They really had me stuck there—responsible position, you know—couldn't replace me. Got a game leg, you know, playing basketball in my high-school days."

"How unfortunate."

"Don't hurt none but can't go in much for athletics, you know. Course, I'm a bit out of that age group now." He shrugged his shoulders, laughed, and slapped his thigh, then winced painfully. "It's nothing, nothing," he murmured, but Gloria was paying no attention.

"Boy, I was sure hopping mad," said the Major. "Had to fill some old executive position over there when I wanted to be out with the boys giving these Japs—" He laughed uneasily and went on: "—these Japanese the licking they deserved."

The driver skilfully turned the corner, and Gloria was thrown against the Major.

"Very good at mechanical things," said Gloria.

The Major laughed indulgently and made an attempt to put his arm around her. This she avoided, and the Major, a bit put out, said: "For whatever that's worth. I must say I've gotten along well enough without knowing much about machinery. Mechanics always bother me."

I wish they'd bother me, thought Gloria and continued looking out the window. The back of the driver's neck and the stretched-out regiment at Tachikawa occurred to Gloria simultaneously. What was that story she'd heard about some WAC's and a jeep driver?

The crisp, straight black hair lay straight against the very lightly colored skin. The driver opened the window and held out his hand. The rush of air brought to Gloria the smell of polished rice and hair pomade. The driver turned his head, and the long, beautifully formed tendons in his neck stood in relief for a second. His eyes were completely black and reminded Gloria of the eyes of children, the eyes of a little boy who does not yet know the meaning of the word Sin. And his face was somehow vaguely familiar, as though they'd once met.... Oh, to hell with it. She closed her eyes, and suddenly the car stopped.

"Well, here we are. Hope you got a big appetite,

Miss Wilson." They were under the marquee of the American Club.

"Famished," she said pleasantly.

With officious help from the Major she climbed from the sedan and stood waiting by the curb. Leaning back inside, the Major was talking with the driver, signing the trip ticket. The driver had turned his head toward the Major, and his throat rose cleanly above his open collar.

Gloria looked away, then impulsively said: "Oh, can I borrow that pencil a moment, Major? I want to jot something down before I forget." She opened her purse and found an envelope containing a letter from her parents. On the back of it she wrote the car's number and the driver's number. To ascertain the latter she peered in at the identification badge he wore. She glanced up to see him looking at her. He was smiling, but looking a bit puzzled as though he were afraid he had done something wrong, as though he was afraid of having his number taken. She smiled reassuringly, felt faint, and handed back the pencil.

"What time is it, Miss Wilson?" asked the Major, still leaning into the sedan.

"About one."

"I got to know exactly, I'm afraid—it's for this damn ticket."

Her watch showed exactly one. "It's precisely ten minutes after one, Major." She felt like a goddess, dispensing the supreme gift of time to her worshippers.

"Thank you," he called, preoccupied, the important man—not too important, however, to pause over those little details he was so far above—trip tickets for example. Then he fumbled at his jacket pocket and finally drew out two bent cigarettes. These he gave to the driver, who touched his cap. Gloria smiled at him, and he, at first surprised, smiled back, reassured, and touched his cap again. The Major turned away from the car, and with a backward half-smile the driver drove off.

The Major glared after the car. "What's he grinning so about? You know him, or was he being fresh? If he was, I'll get his number right now, and believe you me—"

"Oh, shut up."

"Well, maybe I'm just being silly, Miss Gloria, but when a man, even a Jap— I mean, Japanese, looks at a lady like that, my blood boils. Particularly about you ... somehow."

"You've been in Texas too long, Major. Besides, he's my brother."

He gazed at her for a long second, then laughed heartily. "Oh, you're joshing me, Miss Wilson. You're pulling my leg."

"Oh, no—not that. Not now that I know about your poor leg. It might come off."

He laughed even more heartily and guided her, by the elbow, across the drive and up the steps. Suddenly he looked at her watch. "Why, it's only one. You said ten after one."

"That's so my brother will have time to get back to the Motor Pool and smoke one of those cigarettes before they send him out again."

The Major looked at her suspiciously and then, deciding it was yet another joke, laughed. "You're really a card, you are, Miss Wilson—really a good Joe."

She looked at him coldly and took off her fur coat, throwing it over his arm. "Check this, will you? I'll be in the bar."

As he followed her up the steps, he looked puzzled, scratched his head, and smiled at the two small uniformed boys who opened the doors and bowed. Then he crossed the carpet to the checkroom, where he threw the coat at the girl and turned to look after the tall Miss Wilson as she disappeared between the swinging doors of the bar.

Inside the bar Gloria found a stool, ordered Scotch, and looked around. The room was nearly full—all the imitation-rustic booths were in use and, all the over-stuffed divans and armchairs in the next room were full of people eating, laughing, talking, and drinking. At the other end of the bar a young lady dressed in extreme fashion was talking with four captains. They all had their arms around her.

The Major came in, laughing as he walked toward her. "My, you really sailed in here. Thought you'd run away from me, didn't you?"

She looked at him and tried to veil her distaste under an alluring glance. It wasn't that he wasn't good-looking—in a bucolic kind of way—it was simply that he was such an ass. Actually, he was sort of interesting looking, like any number of Angus bulls she'd seen in Indiana. The same wide-apart eyes, the same surly set of the mouth. All he needed was horns and bangs—she presumed he had the other necessary appurtenances.

"Oh, no," she said, "nothing like that. I just thought I'd save us seats."

"Lucky you did. Really crowded.... By the way, you a member here?"

"Why, no. I took it for granted you'd borrowed someone's card to get us in."

"Well, that's just what I did," said the Major, both embarrassed and pleased. "Thought I might blow us to a little treat, you know. Just wondered if you were a member."

"No, I've avoided that ever since the place opened, but of course I make full use of it." She smiled at the Major's knowing wink and drank her Scotch.

"What you drinking?"

"Scotch is its name. It's good, but sort of tickles my nose."

"Guess I'll get that too—sounds good." He ordered two more.

There was no opportunity—since both were seated on separate stools—for further advances, so the Major put his elbow on the bar and lay his head, little-boy fashion, against his fist.

"Be careful, Major," said Gloria. "You remember what happened at the officers' bar in Kyoto."

"But I've never been there."

"No, not you, dear. Those others, in Kyoto, who used it."

"What about it?"

"Well, it seems the lacquering wasn't too well done or something, or else in Kyoto they lean more. At any rate, three days after it opened, in the heat of summer, everyone—every member—was down with lacquer poisoning, which is a bit like poison ivy only worse. There was one young lady who contracted it in the most intimate place—like under her arms, you know—and no one has ever been able to figure out how she got it." She smiled.

The Major smiled, then glowered like that Angus bull again. "Do you think they did it on purpose? Sort of a last-ditch stand, like?"

"The Japanese you mean? Sabotage, you think?"

"Something like that," said the Major vaguely as he took his arm off the bar. But he kept his fist against his cheek, which looked a bit odd now that his elbow was unsupported.

"You know, you look fresher than any dame here," he said, and removed his fist.

Gloria now realized that the cheek in fist was simply to enhance the little-boy aspect. She understood the Major's game at any rate. "That's what comes of clean living." It was really a riot—his taking her for the motherly type!

"Wish I'd lived clean last night. You were swell, but me, I drank too much. I got a little headache, you know."

"Um poor widdle boy," said Gloria. "But I rather imagine a drink or two will fix that up."

He turned bashful. "You know, I still feel funny about drinking before supper."

"So do I, but only after the first five. In fact *I* usually feel funny about drinking *after* supper."

He slapped his leg but forgot to wince. "You really are a card, Miss Wilson. I didn't know you were so much fun."

She smiled wanly. "People never do."

". . . and so I said to him: 'You leave my breasts out of this,'" said the young lady at the end of the bar, and all four captains broke into simultaneous guffaws.

The Major, embarrassed, looked into his Scotch. "Wonder what kind it is?"

"Oh, probably flown from the Orkneys or someplace —they do things on a big scale here."

"Wonder what they got to eat?"

"Everything."

"Yes, sir, home was never like this."

She looked around the bar. "I supposed that's why most people are here. I doubt you could make them go home."

"Well, here's one boy you wouldn't have any trouble making go back to God's country."

"Major—I bet you're from Texas!"

"Aw, you've known that all along, Miss Gloria." He looked down modestly.

"Well, that's so. But today you're even more inimitably Texan than usual."

"Boy, you sure do take the cake, Miss Wilson." He looked at her appreciatively. "You know, you're one swell egg—kind of hard to understand—deep, you know —but still a real good kid—"

"—at heart," concluded Gloria, and the Major slapped his thigh.

"What say we get more of this stuff?" said the Major.

"And get to know each other? Why, I feel I scarcely know you at all."

"You do." And she pushed her glass toward the boy behind the bar. "This is our first real date, you know. Last night we didn't know each other at all." She wrinkled her nose, and he leaned forward on the stool.

". . . and then, of course, there was nothing for me to do but gather my clothes as best I could, and go home," continued the young lady at the end of the bar, and again the four captains bent forward, choking with simultaneous laughter. She was a thin, blonde girl, wearing an extremely low-cut dress of green felt.

The Major turned his head. "Her kind is a disgrace to American womanhood."

"It certainly is."

"You know her?"

"Really, Major, what do you take me for? Naturally not. She's probably another secretary though. They all get delusions of grandeur out here."

"Know what I like about you? You're the real home type somehow."

"So are you, Major."

"There—see? We *do* have something in common. You know, I get kind of lonely out here, far away from home and those I love—my family, my Mama. Surrounded by hostile strangers, in a strange land where there is nothing familiar and where I'm cut off in this lonely outpost. . . ."

"You mean Special Services?"

"No, I mean Japan."

"There's nothing very lonely nor very strange about the part of Japan we see. Look around you."

"I thought you might be sympathetic, Miss Wilson."

"Oh, but I *am*. At the proper times."

"And this isn't one of them?" He looked hurt, like a sick Hereford, and withdrew his hand the distance it had advanced toward hers.

"Really—you sound like your own copy, Major. Remember—it's little me that types for you."

"And what's the matter with my copy? I bet it wrings their hearts back home."

"That it undoubtedly does. But, just between us, we both happen to know how true it is—which isn't very."

"Miss Wilson, that hurts." The Major adopted a puzzled expression and put his face in both hands, resting his elbows on the bar again.

She became grimly pleasant. "All right, Major. Didn't mean to hurt you. Let's be friends again."

He at once held out a hand and, after shaking hers, did not again release it. "Hungry, Miss Wilson?"

"Not yet. But I'm rather thirsty."

"So am I. Hey, boy. Fill 'em up—pronto! hackoo!"

The bar was more full than when they had first come. Others were standing, glasses in hand. A female voice called past Gloria's ear: "Gimme a Bloody Mary, Jack."

"What's that?" asked the Major. "What it sounds like?"

"I trust not," said Gloria.

"Haven't you ever had one, honey?" asked the female voice. "They're divine. You take half vodka, half tomato juice, and half Worcestershire—I think—sauce. They're divine. Can't taste the tomato juice at all."

"Wanna try one?" the Major asked Gloria.

"I think not. I'll stick to this." Gloria looked around the crowded room and then opened her purse. "You know, Major, around this time the bar actually begins to look interesting. When anyone in it begins to look good, then I go home." She lit herself a cigarette and saw the envelope in her purse. Closing her purse impatiently, she bit her underlip—really, I am such a fool.

The Major leaned forward, thrusting his face into hers. "Doesn't anyone look good, Miss Wilson?"

"No one, Major, just no one."

"Well," he said, narrowing his eyes craftily, "that one

at the end looks kind of good to me." He stared at the young lady at the end of the bar, who was now deep in whispered conversation with three of the captains. The other captain was building matches on top of a beer bottle.

"Well, if I wore my dress slashed to the navel, you might like me too," said Gloria.

"But I do like you," said the Major, then laughed. "Anyway."

"Well, I hope she doesn't lean over," said Gloria. "It will be a second Hindenberg disaster if she does. All those matches."

But the Major didn't hear. He was too busy trying to look down the green-felt front—a bit difficult at thirty feet.

Gloria looked around her. The bar was full of people who, like herself, had never had it so good. We're a nation of nouveaux riches, thought Gloria, now nicely muddled, as she looked at her Orkney Scotch, as she fingered her Mikimoto genuine cultured pearls.

Had it not been for the Occupation of Japan, when could all these people, herself included, have enjoyed the benefit of servants, of an inflated social position, of tax-free liquor and unobstructed use of the Sears Roebuck catalog? They'd still be home in Kokomo and Tacoma and Muncie, still going to bed early, still dreading the dull expanse of Sunday. But the Occupation had taken care of all that. Here everything, including love, was free to an American citizen, here where there was a continuous air of the simply extraordinary, as though the end of the world were just around the corner and they'd rediscovered the calf of gold.

It was also a bit like being on stage before the final curtain, when the comedy of manners was reaching its height and the husband was about to burst into the plywood and chenille drawing room. One felt continually on display, and the groundlings all had slanted eyes and would have worn pigtails if they hadn't been white enough to cut them off. There was no doubt about it—those of the Occupation were sitting on top of the world.

Except, felt Gloria, that they were sitting on top of an enormous bubble, a balloon which was going to be pricked at any moment. It didn't much matter who did the pricking—the Russians, the Japanese, or the loyal American taxpayers—the important thing was that it was going to happen. The mushroom couldn't get any larger, and Gloria felt as though she were in Sodom before the sword fell, the tiptop of the tower of Babel before the revolution, the Garden of Eden before the Fall.

And so it was with a feeling of enormous self-satisfaction that Gloria looked around her and, in so doing, saw the Ainsleys.

■

Dave and Dot Ainsley were a pair and, like book ends, did not look well separated. Had Dave had his way they would never have been. He never called her Dorothy or even Dot; instead, it was always "Hey, Beautiful," or "What you say, Good-lookin'?" She was beautiful; she had the face of an expensive doll and the body of an aging athlete. She never called him anything except Dave.

He was Irish and cultivated the appearance of a newspaperman. Half the time he was sloppy in an open collar and dirty cuffs. The other half he was a meticulous dandy in Cuban-heeled shoes. When they had first met, the glamorous war was still on. She was a singer for the USO, and he was a correspondent for U.P. They married as soon as possible in Tokyo. It had been a case of love at first sight, for he had adored her instantly.

But they were often separated, despite Dave. He had his job, and she had her work. His job was that of an editor on *Stars and Stripes* and a stringer for *Field and Stream*. He had once been on the Washington *Post*. Her work was the opera. She was the premiere diva of her own group, "The Cocktail Hour Singers," and founder of the not-too-flourishing Dorothy Ecole du Voix. She was from Wyoming, and he was from Chicago.

At the moment they were separated as usual, sitting back to back on two of the love seats and not talking to each other. They had come together and would go together, and Dorothy would have resented any implication that she was not giving her husband sufficient attention.

She had just come from the Dispensary and was giving Mrs. Swenson, the other occupant of her love seat, a display of her fine temper: "... and then the fool told me that this breaking out—if that's what it is—god knows, he didn't—is just nervous trouble. Me! Nervous trouble!" She was furious and slapped the furniture in her irritation. "And as though that wasn't bad enough, I had to wait hours on a sedan—I spent the night, you know, out with those orphans. Such charming children—all Negro and Japanese and White—sort of dappled, you know. And, then, come time to go home to my old one and faithful here and—no sedan. Well, you can just believe me that that driver got a nice fat DR out of the thing. There he was back at the Motor Pool, had gone to the Naka Hotel—by mistake as he said it. And then—this damned itching. Oh!"

Dave Ainsley turned to Mr. Swenson, an old-Japan-hand, former society editor of the *Japan Times* before the war and at present connected with the *New York Tribune*. "Funny isn't it," said Dave, wrinkling his Irish nose, "how all beautiful women hate to see themselves marred." He slid over the word "beautiful" carefully, as though the loveliness of his wife were taken for granted. Then he turned and looked at her. She was pouting. He was intensely proud of her, proud to be seen with her, proud sometimes to have her in the same house, proud to be her husband. "No matter how unimportant the flaw," he finished softly, as though to himself.

Dottie, as usual, had caught just one word. "Unimportant?" she called over her shoulder. "Well, I'd like to see just how you'd react, David Ainsley, when you're all covered with some loathsome tropical disease."

He laughed easily, from long practice. At the same time, above the grin, his eyes wrinkled as though he expected to be hit. "Well, not every place, beautiful," he said and turned to Mr. Swenson again, this time man-to-man: "It's not been like sleeping with an elephant—not yet."

Mr. Swenson opened his mouth and laughed shortly.

Dottie had turned back to Mrs. Swenson, who likewise sat with her back toward her husband. "Oh, god, what stupid jackasses those colonels are. Nervous troubles!" She could no longer contain herself and, standing up, made a circle through the love seats, elbowing her way through the crowd. As always, her stride was a bit absurd because she was so small. "Four hours—four whole hours, from eleven to now. Just waiting, and then he tells me to stay in bed, fold my hands and—" She could think of nothing dreadful enough. "...and twiddle my thumbs!"

"There are so many incompetents over here nowadays," said Mrs. Swenson sadly, shaking her head. Whenever it became necessary to sympathize she usually retreated into generalities.

"Did it just appear?" asked Mr. Swenson turning around.

"About nine or so," said Dorothy, miserable.

"And where might it be?" asked Mrs. Swenson, now being motherly.

"It might be on my twat, but it's not. It's on my tummy."

Dave laughed loudly, so loudly that several passing people turned and looked. "Give it time," he shouted, and Dottie giggled. Any reference to the privates usually reduced her to helpless merriment.

"You're going to the opera tonight, I suppose," said Mrs. Swenson quickly.

Dottie groaned. "Oh, god, I suppose so. I do owe it to the public. But, believe me, I'm not looking forward to it."

Mrs. Swenson was bewildered. "But—*Madame Butterfly* and all, and you with the opera."

"Well, Mrs. Swenson," said Dave patiently, as though all the words were of one syllable, "that's a kind of opera, to be sure. But I'm afraid my wife has what we must call advanced tastes. It's a bit too—well, shall we say old-fashioned for her." He didn't mention that Dottie always wept from sheer nostalgia whenever she heard any part of *Cavalleria Rusticana*. "Besides," he continued, "Puccini, you know. It isn't as though Beautiful here weren't musical, after all."

This was a cue, and Dottie, standing up, performed what she called a parody of "One Grand Day." She clasped her hands: "Oh, one grand day, he'll come along . . ."

Dave laughed very loudly. "It will be just as fine as that *Swan Lake* we were permitted to view last month. Boy, that's one lake that needs dredging."

The Swensons laughed politely at the performances of both the Ainsleys.

Dave himself had reached the last Beethoven quartets and *Wozzeck* through a very real appreciation of good jazz and saw no reason why Beautiful should not reach Bartok through Mascagni. He was doing his best to detour her past Puccini, had in fact carefully formed her musical tastes until now she thought that late Stravinsky was cute and found that bit in the Prokofieff piano concerto just darling—meanwhile humming Franck to show the part she meant.

"Well, I for one like *Madame Butterfly*," said Mr. Swenson suddenly and positively.

As a matter of fact, Dave did too. But whenever anyone obviously enthusiastic asked him how he liked something, he at once answered with disagreements. If this enthusiasm was stated positively enough, however, he would at once change his mind and find just as many things about it to praise as he had formerly found to condemn.

"Well, of course," he said, smiling, "I think the second act is about the best thing of its kind ever written by anybody, be it Bach or Beiderbecke."

This satisfied both of them, for Mr. Swenson had been thinking of a 1918 performance, and Dave, though he refused anything pure admiration on principle, could very easily revive dead enthusiasm for times gone by, whether represented by Puccini or by Glenn Miller.

"Of course, the performance won't be like the one I saw a few years back with the ever-lovely Galli-Curci," said Mr. Swenson laughing.

Dottie, taking this for a cue, stood up again and resumed her parody. But Dave interrupted her, saying: "After all, it is rather a shame the Japanese try to sing. For naniwa-bushi they have the finest vocal equipment in the world—but just imagine a Mozart opera here at the Imperial Theatre!"

Mr. Swenson was unconcerned. For him Mozart was never opera, but a kind of vaudeville, like that hectic and trivial *Don Giovanni*. The real opera was Verdi, Mascagni, Wagner, Gounod, and of course, the late lamented Richard Strauss.

Dottie, seeing that she wasn't going to get to perform, sat down again and pouted. She sighed and then, to irritate her husband, said: "You're so right, dear. Oh, these Japs!"

The Swensons sat up straight, as though they had just heard a four-letter word, and Dave glared at her. Here he was without pity. Through the years of their marriage he had corrected her when she made the social mistake of disliking Kikes, Niggers, queers, Japs. And he knew well how to correct these little backward slippings.

"Honey, I think you got a run," he said leaning backward to speak to her in a half-whisper.

She did. He'd spotted it before they'd sat down and had been saving it for just such an emergency.

"Oh, my sakes," she said, reverting to Wyoming, as she always did under stress. "I go to stop it. 'Scuse me." And she hobbled quickly from the room.

Dave, very experienced, at once began repairing the damage. He shook his head lovingly. "Poor kid—all wrought up," he said. Then he added: "She works so much with the Japanese, you know, that I expect her to come home and bend right down on the floor to me any day. Of course, learning anything new—like opera —they're naturally a little slow—just as you and I would be if we tried to learn the Kabuki, say—if, indeed, we could at all. But she has the patience of a saint, I will say that." He smiled fondly in reminiscence. "And, then, there are days when she just comes home radiant. When she's been able to give a part of herself. Like last night."

"Poor orphans," said Mrs. Swenson, mollified. "Well, giving is what counts."

Mr. Swenson, however, was anxious to prove that he was completely open-minded on the burning topic of the Japanese. "No, in her way she is correct," he said. "They *are* slow. There is just no denying that. But they are thorough—I'll say that for them. They *are* thorough!"

"That's right—thorough," said Mrs. Swenson.

"You know that newspaperman you're staring at?" asked the Major, leaning toward Gloria.

"Of course. His name is Pygmalion."

"It's not either, begging your pardon, Miss Wilson. It's Dave Ainsley."

"Wrong again. And he's talking to Lafcadio Hearn."

The Major smiled slowly. "Oh, that name's familiar. What outfit's he with?"

Mr. Swenson took a deep breath. That meant he was going to explain something. "The differences between the two races, theirs and ours, are almost as profound as the similarities are startling."

Mr. Swenson's life was devoted to the Japanese, and he was the Authority speaking. Dave involuntarily yawned, but changed it into a cough, then into a monosyllable of interest.

"Now," continued Mr. Swenson, coughing professionally, "take this curious matter. We are proud to say that we owe no man nothing—"

"Anything," corrected Mrs. Swenson.

"But they are proud to owe everyone something," he continued, ignoring his wife completely. "Emperor, father, on and on."

"Yeah, ancestor worship," said Dave.

The baby-blue eyes of Mr. Swenson looked offended and he bent over Dave with a mixture of pity and gentleness. "Oh, no. That's Chinese."

"Sorry," said Dave.

"No, with the Japanese it is different. It is nothing that localized, shall we say? Rather, the entire people have a national debt to the past. Look around you." He indicated the flower shop, which displayed orchids flown from Brazil; the bar, its chromium from Pittsburg; the Harris tweed and Dior-fashioned clothing standing near the windows or sitting in the chairs. "You see, for them there is no present and little future. That is why the country is a living museum, why we can see a man using a 12th-century hammer and a woman wearing an obi which has not changed its style since the late Tokugawa. That is why a battle cry of one of the Yorimitsu clans of the eighth century is still used as a common salutation on the street. Why, even the lowly peasant in his field pens the most exquisite haiku, just as did the sages in days gone past."

Dave had never seen one of these peasant-penned poems and doubted there were any. At any rate, he must remember a cute remark he'd just thought up: "For old man Swenson the Noble Savage turns out to have a yellow streak up his back." No, that wouldn't do. He'd have to work on it a while before it could become "one of Dave's."

"A debt to the past," said Mr. Swenson, looking into the Coca-Cola machine as though it were a roaring fireplace. He was bemused for a moment, then recovered himself and added, with a smile: "Consequently, they are more bowed under their obligations than we are under, say, the idea of Original Sin. We feel guilty, it is true. But they—they feel ashamed. It is the same thing. In this way we are alike."

Mrs. Swenson, used to this, nodded sagely, gratefully basking in the rays of wisdom.

He went on: "Except, of course, they don't have sin!" This was a favorite thesis of his. The sinless nation, like Sparta, or better, like Athens under Socrates. "At least," he continued, anxious to give the devil his due, "not as *we* know it. Every man is pure —as in Heraclitus—and all his emotions, be they e'er so base, are good! You see the difference in conception. Now, we feel that every man is sinful—"

"Like in Milton," interrupted Dave.

"Precisely. And that we can obtain the state of grace only by a virtuous life and, shall I say, a propitious death, for which we are suitably rewarded. Now, I think it quite significant that there is no Japanese afterlife." He paused significantly, a half-smile on his lips.

"Ghosts!" said his wife suddenly.

"Nonsense! Poppycock! Peasant superstition!" shouted Mr. Swenson, furious, the shattered remains of a very carefully contrived Golden Age lying at his feet. In despair he began at once reassembling it and even retraced the conversation that he might get a better grip. "Look you. The Japanese condemns nothing he finds within himself, that is, he find all things good. But at the same time he has an obligation. Obligation? What am I saying! He has a million of them. And he must live up to them. Self-indulgence, as such, is unknown."

He smiled in reminiscence. Cold baths under waterfalls at two in the morning, when the gods are bathing; beautiful young priests kept awake for a week; golden youths wrestling nude for honor in the palestra...the scourging of the flesh!

"I suppose," he continued, more mildly, "you've noticed the prevalence of the suicide theme in their literature."

"Sure," said Dave. "Hara-kiri."

Mr. Swenson pursed his handsome lips. "Oh, no, do forgive an obvious pedantry, but the word, like jujitsu, is just not Japanese. They themselves never use it."

"I know," said Dave angrily. "Judo!"

"Well, my dear fellow," said Mr. Swenson, attempting to mollify and correct at the same time, "in the same way, not hara-kiri, but seppuku."

Dave made a show of shrugging his shoulders. Actually he tucked the thought carefully away, just as he had previously carefully folded up the idea that it was permissible to like Puccini. Thus did he change his opinions and add new thoughts.

"Well, as I was saying, the suicide theme is very common in Japanese literature. In literature, I say, because it has come to my attention that the rate of actual self-destruction is much higher in Scandinavia, of all places, than it is here and, for all I know, always has been."

Dorothy returned and sat down again. She had heard the last sentence and, after turning it over a moment in her mind, said: "That sounds like something I read in a book not long ago."

"I'm not surprised that someone wrote it up—finally," said Mr. Swenson.

"What book, I wonder?" She turned a petulant profile toward Dave. "You must remember, Dave. It was that one all about the Jap-an-ese. Could it have been *The Rose and the Sword* or something like that?"

Dave looked at his wife, unable to decide whether she was being witty or had just forgotten. He decided the latter. It didn't make any difference, for the Swensons hadn't read a word on Japan—except their own articles—since they'd come out, twenty years ago.

"*The Ring and the Book?*" asked Mrs. Swenson anxiously.

"My wife's such a Browning addict," said Mr. Swenson, and Dave went into private convulsions.

"But no, my dear," continued Mr. Swenson, smiling at Dorothy. "We were just discussing suicide."

"Oh? Whose?"

"No, my dear—the institution, or rather, the ideal, since in Japan no one ever really commits it."

"But lots of times, in the newspapers—" Dorothy began.

"Oh, those!" he said, with scorn, then, suddenly disconcerted, looked at Dave and thought of their respective newspapers. He managed to turn his stare into a wink of connivance.

"I guess you're both right," said Dave easily. "After all, to ego-centered people suicide, either the act or the idea, seems attractive."

"Well, if you're going to talk Freud..." said Mr. Swenson smiling, anxious to show himself right up with the times, yet equally anxious to communicate the fact that he didn't for an instant subscribe to these ridiculous notions. Ego-centered. His Japanese. Indeed!

"Yes," said Dottie eagerly, "they're just as ego-centered as anything—like children."

There was a slight pause, then Mrs. Swenson, measuring her words, said slowly: "I suppose that their immaturity is what makes them so appealing. I'm sure that is why so many Americans, for example, like them. It's a—a sort of feeling of kinship."

There was another pause, this one longer. Mrs. Swenson had hit all too close for comfort. "Well, my dear," said Mr. Swenson, "after all, you're a woman."

Mrs. Swenson wisely let this lie, and Dottie, examining her run, hadn't heard.

"Get it fixed?" asked Dave pleasantly. "Took you long enough to get lots of things fixed."

"Yup! Borrowed some nail polish from the girl on duty. Turns out she knew one of my pupils and recognized me. So we chewed the rag for a while. Showed her my tummy, but she doesn't know what it is either. Can't see anything anyway."

Dave laughed uneasily. "My wife's such a tomboy—always running her socks. Keeps me up to my ears in bills. This nylon's expensive."

Mrs. Swenson, who was wearing service-weight, hid her legs as best she could under the love seat.

Mr. Swenson was anxious to reassert his authority on the Subject. "A strange and wonderful people—" he began.

Dave disliked sentimentality. It was part of being a newspaperman: take the bitter with the sweet, and be damned for personal feelings. "A strange and wonderful war they waged too."

"Yes, an oddly warlike race. Primitive, yes. Barbaric in their own way too, I'll agree. Even brutal ... for I don't pretend that some of those atrocity stories aren't true. But what we tend to forget of course is that they treated their own men just as badly. But, then, with all of that, a sensitivity that is rare in history, in the history of the world, and which is absolutely fantastic in modern times." He liked the sound of the word and bit it out a few more times: "Fantastic, utterly fantastic."

He continued: "And perhaps it is that sensitivity which allows them, when they turn to things Western, to grow impatient. They want to hurry through. They are too swift, too fast. Fast, but not thorough. Not at all."

It was enough to make one hate the Japanese for life, thought David Ainsley, their innocently having a spokesman like Swenson. Then he indulged in a gambit which usually extricated him from his difficulties. "Well," he said, sounding homespun and scratching his Irish nose, "of course I don't pretend to be a literary man—I'm just an old newspaper hack. In fact you might even say I'm a prostitute, because in my work I'm forced to be a lot more whorish than any of the pom-poms at Yuraku-cho."

Mrs. Swenson smiled to indicate that she too was up with the times as well as her husband, that she knew what Yuraku-cho was famous for.

Dave smiled, having discharged half his battery, because he knew himself to be a damn good newspaperman, filled with his own kind of integrity and far more cultured than most. After all, he'd read *Finnegans Wake*, mostly in the bathroom it was true, and he could tell Debussy from Ravel, which was something damn few other people could do.

"But," he continued, "even if I am a hack, still I think that we're not so different in this world. We're all just a bit alike. We're all, as they say," and he laughed hesitantly, "one world, as they say."

"You are so right," said Mrs. Swenson. "One world

—I put that in my column every day. One world."
And she sighed.

"Basically, yes," said Mr. Swenson, disconcerted at
feeling the conversation slip away from him. "But—"

He was interrupted by Dottie, who, ever since "ego-
centered," had been engaged in thoughts of her own.
"*And* bullheaded!" she said, dimpling. "They'll just
never once admit that they're wrong. Never. So, so—
defensive. That's what they are—defensive. They get
real mad at you too if you tell them they're wrong—
which they are." She turned brightly to her husband
for approval.

Mr. Swenson smiled briefly. The little silly had played
directly into his hands. He looked tolerantly down
upon Dorothy and then, sadly, gazed into the distance.
"In Japan," he began, very simply, "this 'defensive'
quality"—he handled the word at the tips of his fingers,
his nose slightly puckered, his lips pursed—"is a virtue."
That was a statement of fact, and he stopped long
enough for them to become aware of it.

"Likewise, it is a virtue not to inform a person that
he or she has committed an error. This is their etiquette but, unlike our Emily-Postian variety, it has a
social function. They must, after all, live together."
And he spread his arms hopelessly. "They must live
together, thousands to the square mile, with no undue
friction. And"—his voice became more loud and more
sharp—"I say they do it pretty damn well!" This surprise conclusion—it surprised no one more than himself
—was barked out, and he looked violently at the other
three, as though expecting contradiction.

Dave was again anxious to repair Dottie's damage.
"Hence the famous middleman," he said heartily.

"Yes," said Mr. Swenson, feeling bereft of the next
link in the forged chain of his argument. "The 'middle-
man' as you call him. He approaches both parties in
case one desires the services of the other or in case

they've had an argument. Thus the faces of both are saved, and neither has cause for offense. A nice institution. There is no direct competition."

The others nodded, all except Dottie, who, without a thought in her pretty head, agreed even more enthusiastically. "Exactly. No competition. Why, if I'd stayed back in the States I bet I'd still be just another girl in the chorus."

Conversation stopped abruptly, and even Dottie realized she had scored a direct hit. They sat and looked at each other. She was quite right. There was no direct competition. And that was why Mr. Swenson was an authority on the Japanese, as well as a poet and a famous philosopher, why Mrs. Swenson was a well-known lady columnist, why Dave Ainsley was the very model of a crackerjack newspaperman, and why his wife was the prima donna of the Occupation.

■

Just then one of the pageboys approached and said that a lady wished to see Mrs. Ainsley. Even though the boy spoke good English, Mr. Swenson made him repeat the message in Japanese, then corrected his grammar and patted him on the head. Dave raised his eyebrows quizzically, and Dottie made big, wondering eyes.

"Whoever do you suppose?" she asked. Then she followed the boy through the swinging doors into the main lobby.

"Oh, Sensei, Sensei," screamed Dorothy and ran as swiftly across the deep rug as her heels would permit, dropping breathless beside Mrs. Schmidt. "What a *nice* surprise!"

Dottie looked at the fawn breast-pin and wished her teacher wouldn't wear it. She also wished she could afford American stockings to show off her still shapely legs. Too, she would have liked it had Mrs. Schmidt not insisted upon a shawl—at least not that one. It looked dreadfully Old World to Dottie—not the old world of cathedrals and the La Scala that she'd read about, but the real old world, the world of poverty and wailing walls, of persecution and hungry children. To be sure, Dorothy had only read about this world, but the morning headlines every day seemed to her much more real than, say, a guide book to Chartres. Sometimes she spoke to Mrs. Schmidt about her clothes, about how much better she ought to dress, and then her teacher would look at her sadly, as she might have looked at a brutally uncomprehending child, and remind her that she had no others. Today, however, Dottie was careful to say nothing. She had been saving for some time to buy Mrs. Schmidt a new winter coat from the PX and didn't even want to hint about the surprise until it was all ready. (In her mind she'd already buried the fact that the last time she had enough money saved she'd sent away for two ridiculously expensive pairs of shoes for herself.)

"I suppose it is rather a surprise, isn't it?" said Mrs. Schmidt. "You'd never expect to see me against this kind of background, would you?" As she spoke she indicated the high ceilings and decorated pillars of the lobby. "But I've been here before, years ago, often. This used to be a favorite meeting place for foreigners in Tokyo. It was expensive in those days and very elegant. Naturally, in Vienna it would have been third-class, but here, in Tokyo, in those days it was the most popular of places to go."

"Has it changed much?" asked Dottie. Whenever Mrs. Schmidt talked about the days before the war, which was rather often, Dorothy always felt as though she were listening to a kind of fairy tale, an unlikely story of something which occurred when she was a little girl thousands of miles away. Now she imagined the tired and familiar American Club with crystal chandeliers and hundreds of candles; she heard the sound of taffeta and the strains of a string ensemble playing Strauss; and there she was, on the arm of a handsome cavalier wearing a kind of Regency costume —Dottie's nearest approximation to the period.

"Oh, not so very changed," said Mrs. Schmidt, looking around. "The people look much the same, except now they have what we call the frank and open American look and they're in uniform, many of them. Not really changed at all."

"Oh, really," said Dottie, a bit disappointed. "But tell me, Sensei, how did you know I was here?"

"I didn't know, really. But I called your house and found you had left with Mr. Ainsley, and so I decided to go various places until I found you. I was fortunate, for this is the first place I went."

"You find everyone here eventually. There's no place else to go—all the Japanese things are off limits and all. You're lucky—you can still go to the theaters and restaurants. Everything like that."

"But you, dear," said Mrs. Schmidt, "can come to places like this where, alas, in these days I can't."

"It isn't fair," said Dottie, pouting, "it isn't fair at all. After all, it isn't as though you're Japanese."

Mrs. Schmidt hid her smile by adjusting her pin. "But," she said, looking up, "here I am keeping you, and you must be rather curious to learn why I've come to hunt the fox within his lair, as Schiller says."

"No," said Dottie casually, "but I am pleased. I'm always pleased to see you." This was said with the simplicity of truth, for Dottie had long ago decided that if there was anyone whom she really liked in the whole wide world it was Mrs. Schmidt. This didn't prevent her from making fun behind her teacher's back, nor from slandering her when the occasion seemed appropriate, but her affection was genuine. Mrs. Schmidt was one of the things that Dottie lived by.

"Strange person you are, Mrs. Ainsley. You know,

I actually believe you. Why? I wonder." Indeed, she had often wondered why. That Dorothy was unintelligent had to be agreed before one could begin to understand her. That she was selfish and excessively self-indulgent was manifest. Yet, somewhere within her, Mrs. Schmidt saw a childish kind of trust, not entirely free of the awe which children sometimes show toward very tall or very fat people.

This was, in fact, the kind of trust which Dottie had for her teacher. Mrs. Schmidt, though neither fat nor tall, was old and, in her student's eyes, wise.

Dottie giggled. Mrs. Schmidt was always quite direct when it came to speaking of emotions, and any talk of emotion always affected Dorothy. She became embarrassed and pleased, as though they were schoolgirls together discussing forbidden subjects. When she'd stopped giggling, she said: "I don't know. Dave says I have a mother complex on you."

"Is he jealous at all?"

"Him? If I pet a dog too much, he gets jealous."

They were both silent for a time, but it was the silence of mutual consideration, the silence that can only occur when two friends, secure in each other's company, part for a time, their thoughts going separate ways.

Dottie's thoughts didn't go very far, for she soon asked: "Have you ever had a lover, Madame Schmidt?"

"What an extraordinary question!"

"No, really, I mean."

"Now, my dear, one woman doesn't ask another that question."

"I'd ask my mother, Madame Schmidt, and I'm young enough to be your daughter."

Mrs. Schmidt smiled. Remarks like this were what made Dorothy so universally disliked, yet it was quite obvious that she had had no intention of wounding, did not even comprehend the idea that an older woman might like to receive the lie of being thought young.

"Well, then, all right," said Mrs. Schmidt. "Let us—what do you say?—oh, yes, let us blackmail each other. Are you asking because you have one or because you want one?"

"Oh, I've had them, if that's what you mean," said Dottie. "That's the only reason I'm asking. How does one manage them? Mine is here right now and with another woman. Hasn't so much as looked at me. I thought with lovers you were supposed to exchange hidden glances and notes and that sort of thing."

Mrs. Schmidt didn't attempt to hide her smile. "You are so exquisitely naive, my dear. Just what sort of romantic literature did you read when young? Besides, I've alway thought that the American way was rather to flaunt the attachment, perhaps tell the husband even."

"My husband? Oh, no, he's the type that would want to fight a duel or something."

"That's quite old-fashioned now," said Mrs. Schmidt.

"But you must have had duels fought over you, I guess."

"How old do you think I am?" asked Mrs. Schmidt, laughing. "I once heard of this kind of duel when I was very young, and that has remained my closest contact, I assure you."

Dottie was disappointed. In her mind, Mrs. Schmidt's existence in Vienna had been punctuated with duels, the intervals between being consumed by illicit trysts in vacant summer pavilions.

Mrs. Schmidt continued: "However, if Mr. Ainsley would fight a duel for you—which I don't for a moment doubt—then you should be very proud, very happy, and should stop entertaining a lover. A man who loves one that much is worth some consideration."

"Oh, I love him all right," said Dottie half resentfully. "He used to be a lot of fun, before he got this job. Big-wheel newspaperman and all. But since then

—I don't know—he thinks he's so damned much and . . . You know, at home—in the States, I mean—he was nothing, just nothing, and he must have been a real lamb. But here, well, he's successful now, and god knows we could never afford to do the things we do— the money we spend is simply scandalous—if it weren't that we are here in the Occupation. I mean, but really, none of us ever had it so good. No one wants to go home and no one will until they make us. We were all just nobodies before. You know, I lie awake at night and think about that. In fact, just before you came we were talking about that very thing. I don't know, but it seems to me that just coming over here has changed us all. It's changed me a lot, I know. I don't know if it's Japan or the Occupation or the weather or what."

She turned briefly but sincerely to Mrs. Schmidt and said: "Do you know what I'm talking about?"

"I know very well. No one has a better view than those on the outside. I've wondered myself sometimes. Everyone knows that Americans are kind and friendly and open-hearted and often amazingly thoughtful. All of us here were very happy when the Americans came four years ago. We didn't expect them to be the way they are now. I don't know what you'd call it— what they are. They certainly mean no harm. It is the other way about. And they do no harm, because evil, you know, is a positive kind of thing. But they do nothing good. They err continually, but always through omission. My own people in these circumstances might have been evil—and again they might not have been—but your people, my dear, are not even that— they are lax, have no discipline, no guiding ideals. They think only of their own comforts and, if they remember in time, they share them."

Dottie had attempted to follow this, but had rapidly become lost. "I didn't mean Americans," she said mildly. "I meant me—me and Dave. You always talk so political all the time."

"That, I suppose, is the limitation of the outside view. After all, I well know how the Germans behaved here and how the Japanese themselves were during the war. The Americans are to be preferred, believe me. My only point is that it takes a very strong person to be able to handle unlimited power and not let it—that power, I mean—handle him. But—" She broke off in a laugh. "My English will become hopelessly confused if I attempt to explain that, and I must admit that in German I could do no better. Women are not supposed to think of these things. You are right. Better to think of yourself and your anonymous lover than to trouble yourself with these weighty problems. Let the men squabble among themselves."

"Squabble! That's all Dave and I seem to do these days. He'll never come right out and fight. Just follows me around with that dying-spaniel look until I think I'll scream. It isn't that I like the Major so terrifically; it's just that he's different—that's all. ... But here I run on and on, and you probably had something to ask me about."

"I do," said Mrs. Schmidt. "I have a request. I don't even know if you can help me or not. But it is this. This morning I went to see a charming colonel in Special Services, as I believe you call it. I need money, you know. And I had heard that this organization puts on entertainments—like the opera tonight."

"You're going, of course. What's-her-name—your student, you know—is singing."

"I wish I were going. As you know, it is an Allied performance."

"Oh."

"And so, I thought maybe this organization would sponsor a recital. My pupils and myself. But the colonel said that he could not. I wonder if you could ask someone, could explain to them for me, could tell them how necessary—"

She broke off and looked at her hands. When she raised her head there were tears in her bright blue eyes. "Dorothy, may you never know how terrible a thing it is to beg like this."

Dottie's face softened until she was near tears herself. "Poor Sensei," she said several times. Then her face grew hard again. "Well, I know just what I'll do. And I know just the person I'll go to. And we'll have this recital if we have to turn the Occupation inside out to do it," she said fiercely.

"Do you think you *could* do something?"

Dottie's black eyes were glittering, both with unshed tears and determination. "You bet I can! And I know just how to go about it, too."

"Oh, if you could, I would be—" Mrs. Schmidt began.

But Dorothy brushed aside her thanks, already planning her strategy. "We'll need help," she said. "Do you know the Swensons?"

"Before the war we were friends. I know them, but we haven't seen each other for years."

"They'll help," said Dorothy. "They'll have to. I know enough to hang them both. And Dave'll help, naturally.... Look, you come back here around supper time, and I'll have talked to them, and then we'll see.... Now, don't cry—there's nothing to cry about."

They both stood up, and Dottie patted the older woman on the cheek. "Now, cheer up, for goodness sake," she said. "The people around here'll think I've ruined you or something. Go some place and drink tea until time for supper."

"You're so nice, Dorothy," said Mrs. Schmidt, tears standing in her eyes. "And you're so American." Her underlip quivered slightly. "You even ... you even call dinner supper."

As they stood, Dorothy began to feel the inequality

of their positions. It made her uncomfortable. "I'm awfully sorry I can't ask you into the bar. I think the rules are just too stupid.... But you know how it is."

Mrs. Schmidt nodded. She knew how it was. Dorothy, so well-intentioned, like so many Americans could only tolerate exposure to emotion so long. Sooner or later they all were forced to retreat behind empty phrases, behind the polite conventionalities which they had been taught were useful. And useful they were, for Dorothy, having been very near compassion, was now placing herself behind the hollow mockery of apology, ironic in that the words themselves carried the connotations of concern but were empty of it, while only seconds before real concern had come naked and alone and touched her as it passed.

But it *had* passed, and so had tears, and now Dorothy, perfectly dry-eyed, was bobbing and smiling and saying: "These rules are tiresome, aren't they? But what can one do? Now, you just run along and come back before supper—I mean, dinner."

Mrs. Schmidt adjusted her shawl and watched the doors swing shut behind her pupil.

■

Gloria watched Dorothy as she marched with tiny, defiant steps toward her husband and the Swensons. She was still curious and would like to know just whom Dorothy had been out exchanging billets-doux with. Not for a second did Gloria doubt that it was an officer.

The Major swallowed his Scotch. "Hungry?"

"Frightfully early, but we might as well get it over with," said Gloria and carefully slid from the stool.

There were some small furtive movements behind her as several people tried to sit on the vacated stools at the same time. A stout man won one of the prizes and turned to the ladies around him. "Sorry, dears," he said, "but I really couldn't support all this bulk much longer. Now, all gather round, for I've the most splendid and juicy story of all—and it's about Our Lord himself."

Always talking about MacArthur, thought Gloria. How terrible to be in charge of something like an Occupation.

"Don't get lost in the carpet," she called, taking her hand from the Major's.

In the elevator he said: "Which floor's the restaurant?"

"I don't know. Ask the boy."

But the boy had already stopped at the third floor; opening the door, he stood waiting.

"Officious little bastard," said the Major, then begged Gloria's pardon.

"Watch out for the carpet," called Gloria.

They walked slowly down the wide hall, looking into various rooms.

"What do these signs mean? asked the Major, reading: "*Miss Gramboult. Lt. and Mrs. Schwartz.* And look at that one over there: *Mary Patsy Snied, daughter of Colonel and Captain Snied.* What goes on there?"

"Maybe they're brothers."

"Let's go see," said the Major and peered past the door into the room.

There were a number of children, not yet of school age, sitting on chairs talking with each other. Two or three regarded the Major and then turned back to their companions.

"Hi, kids!" called the Major.

None of the children answered. They all turned to stare, and then resumed their conversations. The youngest rose and shut the door.

"Officious little bastards," said the Major. But Gloria was no longer there. "Miss Wilson! Where are you, Miss Wilson?" he shouted.

Then he caught sight of her, just entering the room marked *Miss Gramboult.*

"Oh, there you are," she called to the Major. "Well, don't just stand there. Heavens, you'd think you weren't invited."

Cautiously, he entered the room, passed the small portable bar, behind which two boys were working, and looked around. Dozens of people were standing or sitting, all with drinks in their hands. The air was blue with smoke.

"Darling," said Gloria to the lady with whom she was talking, "this is Major—. What *was* your name, dear? Oh, yes—Major Cowhand. And Major Cowhand, Miss Gramboult. Pudding, Alice. Alice, Pudding.... Well, darling, as I was saying, I thought we'd never make it at all, and then suddenly I decided, headache or no headache, Berle Gramboult is one of my oldest friends. And *so* I just dropped everything." She lowered her voice: "Though one thing I couldn't drop was this Texas idiot, but I trust you'll understand."

Miss Gramboult steadied herself at the bar. "Of course, dear. Though actually this"—she helplessly indicated the room—"was just going to be a little intimate gathering." She make some attempt to pull herself together. "But I understand perfectly, and I'm thrilled to death you could come, for after all" —she looked at Gloria and wrinkled her brow— "there's just no one I'd rather see—I think."

"A drink!" cried Gloria and moved to the bar.

The Major followed her. "You know my name isn't Cowhand."

"It is now. Don't fight life. Make the best of it!"

"Do you know that woman?"

"Never saw her before in my life and hope I never do again—as soon, that is, as we've made an appreciable dent in her liquor supply."

"I don't think all of this is quite right. And it's only afternoon. Isn't it sort of early for a cocktail party?"

"Oh, we civilians live dangerously. This has become

the fashionable hour. Besides, would you like to be spending your—ha-ha—hard-earned money?"

"What do you mean?" said the Major brutally.

"I simply mean: What would you like to drink?" Gloria pointed to the almost empty remaining bottle of Scotch, and the boy emptied it for her. "Besides Scotch, that is," she added.

Glass in hand, not waiting for the Major, she turned to see if she knew anyone at the party. She didn't, but the Major did.

"Why, Sam, how the hell are you? Billy! I sure didn't expect to see you here. Why, Frankie, you old son-of-a-gun. Hey, there's Willy!"

Gloria moved slowly away.

"Hello there, Colonel Watkins, sir, nice seeing you," continued the Major. "And, for Christ's sake, there's Phil. Sure didn't expect to see you this morning—or is it afternoon?"

Gloria moved further away.

"Well, here's Bobby. What do you know?" the Major shouted.

And Gloria moved completely away. She looked out of the window. The sun was surprisingly low; it was, somehow, late afternoon. The moat, the Palace, and the streets were gray. Beneath her were patches of color as crowds passed the plaza; further away, they became a uniform gray themselves, like the street. In the distance the Diet Building was white.

"Look at Fuji," said someone behind her, and a finger was pointed past her face.

"It's the Diet," said Gloria, not turning around.

"Oh, you old spoil sport, and I was so anxious to see Fuji just now."

Gloria turned around and confronted a familiar look-ing elderly lady who held a long cigarette holder in one hand and a dark-brown drink in the other.

"As I said in my column the other day, Fuji is never

so beautiful as when half-hidden by rains. And now you tell me you can't even see Fuji."

"In any event," said Gloria, "you can't see Fuji from here on any day."

"But, honey, this is where I do all my writing." She pursed her mouth with annoyance and almost turned her back; then suddenly she swung again in Gloria's direction. "But we don't know each other, do we? I'm Mrs. Swenson—Hilda Swenson. You know!"

"I thought your face was familiar, but how did you get up here so fast?"

"I beg your pardon?"

"I said: I read your stuff in the *Japan Times*."

"Oh, not really." She seemed genuinely delighted. "How most interesting to find one who knows one. Did you read yesterday's?"

"Unfortunately not."

"Oh, it was quite fine," Mrs. Swenson said, with an attempt at impartiality. "It was all about birth control. Both my husband—*New York Tribune*, you know—and myself are all for it."

"Need you be?"

"I beg your pardon?"

"Nothing. I was just saying that I'm one of your most devoted followers. I'm the one called 'Just an Observer'."

"Really?" she gasped. "Why, only last week I printed a simply extraordinary letter of yours. Only I thought it was from a Japanese—most of them are, you know."

"Yes, I read it."

"All about temple reconstruction. It is *so* needed, don't you think?"

"No, it was about the pedestrian problem."

"Oh, you're so right. And what you said just echoed my own views so. I just printed it as was with just a few teeny changes—grammar and things, you know.

But, oh, the Japanese feeling was there, my dear, it was there! You obviously have the Gift."

"What's that?" asked Gloria.

But Mrs. Swenson was motioning toward a crowd of men in another corner. "Dearest, dearest," she called. "I've found the most amazing person I didn't even know —or rather, I knew but actually didn't. Come here." She paused, and then shouted: "Come here!"

Mr. Swenson moved toward them, holding himself and his drink erect, his classic profile toward them as he addressed amenities to those he passed.

"Darling," said his wife, "this is 'Just an Observer.'"

"I'm delighted to meet you," said Mr. Swenson, extending a hand to Gloria, who curtsied.

"Isn't this a divine party! One meets such fabulous people. And, dear, she has the Gift. She writes just like a Japanese."

"Yes," said Gloria shyly, "me pray for the General's coming erection."

Mrs. Swenson giggled nervously. "Yes, I saw the sign too. You know, dear," she said to her husband, "that sign written by some Japanese—that billboard, you know." And since he still seemed thoroughly confused: "The age-old difficulty Our Friends have with the l's and r's and their differences."

"Oh, I see," said Mr. Swenson. "Election—oh, quite good! Very amusing. Keen sense of humor, these Japanese."

Mrs. Swenson forgot herself to the extent of throwing a hopeless shrug of the shoulders to Gloria before she ran across the room and threw herself into the arms of another elderly lady who had just entered.

"Lady Briton. Darling!" she cried.

Mr. Swenson turned to Gloria. "I suppose you're a great fan, shall we say, of my wife's?"

"Let's be daring and say it. Yes, I wouldn't miss an installment."

He nodded his head and pursed his lips. "Yes, that girl has talent. Real Talent. I was afraid for a time that it might be dulled by the newspaper grind."

"I'm sure it's not been."

He looked at her with appreciation. "You know—I don't think it *has* been. There's always some talk around the house as to which is the best" —he paused and laughed— "she or I. But then a comparison would be quite invidious. After all, she explains the West to the Japanese, and I explain the Japanese to the West. It's a nice arrangement."

"I understand."

"You know," said Mr. Swenson as he was pulled away by his wife, who had unexpectedly returned, "I think you do."

"Darling, it's Lady Briton," said Mrs. Swenson, sweeping her husband grandly into the great lady's presence.

"Dear Lady Briton," said Mr. Swenson and kissed the tips of the fingers which were extended to him. "Dear Sacred Protector, as says Tennyson, of Our Dumb Friends."

"Our 'dumb friends' had just better toe the mark or it will be jolly well up with them," snarled Lady Briton. She was Australian and most outspoken.

"No, no, no," tittered Mrs. Swenson, hovering between Lady Briton and her husband. "My husband means the animals, not the Japanese."

"Oh, well, whyn't you say so? Awfully sorry. But really, Swenson, if you'd just been through what I have, you'd be a bit upset yourself."

"Whatever?" asked Mrs. Swenson, her eyes round. What indeed could so upset the Lady Briton who was, after all, Royalty. Or almost.

"Well," the Lady began with a sigh, "we were motoring with General Hughes and his wife. And we were in the midst of this really divine countryside when, all of a sudden, coming around a bend, what did we see but one of these—these people most inhumanely beating his animal. Which, by the by, wasn't much to look at. But still, it *was* a horse." She stopped and with glittering eyes surveyed her almost entirely American court.

Actually she wasn't too strong for horses. Dogs were her strong point. She always felt slightly ill when she realized that hundreds of big, virile but gentle-eyed dogs were being starved, beaten, and maimed every day of the week around her. To be sure, she had never seen any of this, but she knew it occurred with frightening regularity. Dogs, after all—unlike people—were the same the world over. She remembered those fine, upstanding, military-looking Australian dogs and, as always, felt a little tug at her heartstrings. Randolph—that was Lord Briton—liked dogs too, and that helped.

To be sure, even the dog kingdom had its slackers—like those utterly nasty little beasts which had bitten Mrs. Colonel Butternut on the thigh when she was being the head of John the Baptist during charades. But then —and this was telling—they had *not* been Australian animals. They were some mongrel Japanese variety.... But her audience was waiting.

"Well, the reason this poor animal was being punished was because he had stopped in the middle of the road, and the reason he had stopped was obvious to everyone but the little man who owned him. He was overburdened. Dreadfully so. That little cart was piled to the skies, and that little man was standing there using a long, cruel switch on the animal. Just in the manner of these appalling night-soil collectors—how do you call them? Honey carts? Yes, that's it—most amusing— honey carts it is!"

She continued: "Naturally, it made my blood simply boil. We stopped the car. The chauffeur's native too, of course, so you'd expect him to side with his countryman, which is just what he did. And I walked over to that little man, all dressed up in his own fashion—

a rag here, a rag there, actually rather picturesque, but filthy, of course. Well, I told the little blighter to stop. He didn't; he merely took off a rag from his head, as though it were a fedora, and went right on beating the animal with the other hand. So, with a self-possession which I must say Randolph later admired—dear Randolph—I stepped right up to him and took his switch away. Then I deliberately broke it over one knee." She glanced down at her beaded cocktail dress. "And it wasn't too easy in this dress which, after all, is just about as comfortable as a straightjacket."

"No, no, Lady Briton, it is lovely," came several voices at once. "So smart. So chic. Just a dream."

She held up a hand. "But I was successful. The whip broke!"

She paused to reap her reward of compliments and smiles, and then went on: "So, using our native as interpreter, we discovered that this fellow thought it was important for him to get somewhere or other with a funny name before nightfall. I asked, through the native, if it were important at the expense of the horse's life. And, after a great show of thought and much smiling, the little beggar said that yes, he thought it was."

In the general consternation that followed, Lady Briton had to use both hands to reestablish her authority. "Well, infuriated, and with jolly good reason, I—with these two hands, and at the risk of this silly little gown I have on, which came, by the way from Melbourne, so you can see we 'Aussies' aren't quite so far behind you 'Yanks' as some would like to think— well, so at its risk (though, as a matter of fact, it didn't hurt it at all) I began unloading that despicable little cart, while Mrs. General Hughes tried to comfort the poor animal. To be sure, it is a bit unfortunate that the good woman doesn't know much about horses. She put her fingers in his nostrils, and, naturally, he bit her."

Wasting no time over the plight of Mrs. General

Hughes, she went on immediately she had taken breath:
"Well, when the load was down to a decent weight, we
told the man to go on. But the beggar wouldn't. He
just kept pointing to his stuff on the road and the rest
of it in the cart, and finally he started crying. Well,
that *was* too much. These people never show much grit
and determination as it is—but tears! Well, as I say, it
was just utterly too much. One can only tolerate so
much, and I picked up that broken switch, and I swung
it back with such purpose that that little blighter was
only too happy to pull the horse away and start off down
the road."

There was general laughter and some scattered applause, but she silenced it again with a held-up hand
and an impassive face. "Well, we naturally all enjoyed
a merry laugh, and Randolph, I must say, who is not
usually particularly emotional, rather surprised me by
putting his arm around the back of my seat—that is,
the seat in which I was sitting. And so, all in all, as
they say, it ended happily ever after and was responsible
for my seeing that, indeed, Tokyo is not the only place
in Japan that has need of our Society. Now, I think
that traveling stations of workers, visiting farms and
the like, could ..."

But the majority of her audience had melted away.
She always put in a plug for her organization. Only
Mrs. Swenson, Miss Gramboult, and a few other ladies
remained faithful and looked up at her, their eyes
shining. They had known of Joan on the walls of
Orleans—or was it Arc?—the queen of Naples defending
her ramparts, Barbara Fritchie and her old gray head,
and Queen Elizabeth, or somebody, with her arm through
the door sockets. But the spectacle of Lady Briton at
bay in the Japanese countryside surpassed them all.

"My god," said Gloria to herself, "she makes Major
Calloway look like Albert Schweitzer."

"Talking about me?" said the Major, unexpectedly

circling around with another drink in his hand. "Say, you're right up there."

"Up where?"

"You know what I mean—up there with the VIP's. Lady Briton, Swenson of the *Tribune*—just had him pointed out to me. I didn't know you knew *him*."

"He was Papa's best friend—stood at his wedding and became my very own godfather at my christening. I wore the most adorable little white—"

"Well, what do you know? Say, suppose you introduce me. They say he's a good man to know."

"What man isn't? But, no, you'd have to ask Mrs. Swenson about that.... No, on second thought, don't."

"Liquor's running out. Liquor's running out," cried Miss Gramboult, running from one guest to the other.

"Go get another," said Gloria, and the Major slowly moved in the direction of the bar. Sipping her drink, she again looked from the window. It had begun to rain, and now the streets and sidewalks were spotted with large, yellow, oiled-paper umbrellas.

Two women were talking behind her. "Well, I'm Berle's roommate, and I should know. Listen. She gets up every morning and walks around the room stark naked, and believe you me, that's no treat. Scares the poor room girls half to death—big naked American, all hair, parading around. Then she starts washing. Says she's too shy to use the big bathroom. Shy, my foot! And so she has this poor girl—Sococoa or Sonoco or something like that—get her a big pan of hot water right in the middle of our only table. Then she washes her armpits and her crotch—believe me, this is quite true. Then, since she never takes off her make-up, she just dabs her face here and there—afterwards, mind you. Then she brushes her teeth—she's so proud of them—and slobbers in the big pan. She must brush those teeth of hers five minutes, dipping her toothbrush back in the water and everything. Then—and only then

—she combs her hair. That hideous upsweep, you know —never wears anything else. And—would you believe it—she dips her comb in the same water, all gummy with toothpaste and god knows what else, and puts up her upsweep—literally sticks it there. Then she dips her little fingers in the mess and smooths her eyebrows. Then, still naked as a jaybird, she looks at herself in the big mirror and hollers for the girl to come and take away the pan. Every day—it's simply revolting!"

"I didn't know Berle was that way," said the other.

"Listen, you should live with her," said the first. "I can hardly eat breakfast after that exhibition. Hair! I never saw a woman with so much—like a fur coat— and that's not all—"

"Here she comes!"

"And that's not all," continued the first. "She has the most divine shoes. And as for taste—well, just no one has the really good taste our Berle does in clothes. Now, that wonderful black—Oh, Berle darling, I didn't know you were there. My, I bet your ears were burning. But, after all, they should have burned nice."

"Nice," said Miss Gramboult, who, at this point, would not have noticed had her ears been burned entirely off her head. "So—nice. Such a nice party. Such lovely people. My friends." And she began to weep. But soon she forgot about that too and wheeled slowly among the guests, saying: "Sorry the drinks are all gone. Awful sorry." She paused from time to time, delivering a smile of exceptional whiteness, one hand smoothing her upsweep.

Unable to find another drink, the Major returned to Gloria. "We'd better go," he said. "They just wheeled the bar out."

"Go?" said Gloria. "Go where?"

"What you need is some fresh air," said the Major heartily. "Let's you and me go for a little spin, huh?"

"Why, it's perfectly lovely here. More room now."

She looked around the smoke and the furniture. "Look —all those drinks going to waste. We could just finish them—every one." She motioned vaguely toward a large brown tumbler before her.

The Major was called away by more departing friends, and Gloria, still enjoying the doubtless quite accurate description of Berle she had overheard, reached for the drink—then stopped. The same two were still talking.

". . . but take some of the others. They just hog the whole field."

"I know just who you mean."

"Sure, little Miss High-and-Mighty herself, Queen of the Naka. And the killing thing is that, to see her at meals for example, so modest, so sure of herself, you'd think she believed she was getting away with it."

"Don't they always though?"

"At least, being fast is a private affair, but being nympho is about as private as carrying on in Grand Central. And I must say that nothing turns my stomach quite so quickly as an out-and-out bug-eyed nympho like our Gloria."

"So public too. Why, a girl with her rep gets her dates for just one reason."

"That kind never cares about her reputation—you can always count on it."

"And she's absolutely brazen too."

"Well, that type always gets her due—and alway in the same good old-fashioned way. So, just watch out Queenie Wilson."

They both laughed.

Gloria reached for the drink and downed it all. It had been left by Lady Briton and was almost straight Southern Comfort.

"Think I'd gone and left you?" It was the Major, back again.

"No, nothing like that," said Gloria.

"Hey, you look pale."

"It's the alcohol."

"And you sound sober."

"It's the alcohol." She stood up. "Shall we go?"

"Boy, you sure can hold it!" said the Major, admiringly.

She held it halfway across the room, and then was suddenly hit by the Southern Comfort. By the time she had reached the door everything, including herself, was hysterically funny.

Gloria stumbled and steadied herself against Miss Gramboult, who said thickly to both Gloria and the Major: "It was lovely having you. Do come back." She in turn steadied herself against Gloria, whom the Major was pulling from the room.

"Good-by, you old bear rug," shouted Gloria to her hostess, as the Major finally drew her out the door.

At that moment the Major collided with a soldier and shouted: "Who you lookin' for, Mac?"

The soldier was rather old. "Nobody, sir. I was just walkin' around. I just been on this here ole town, and I thought I'd—"

"Don't you know this club is off-limits for enlisted men?"

"No, sir, I didn't. I just walked in, to sit down, you know. I been walking most of the day, sir. Then I thought I'd just look around, and I saw a party was goin' on here, sir, and—"

"Well, you know it now. Get out."

"But, sir, I didn't—"

"You want an MP, soldier?"

"No, sir, I don't."

Gloria was surprised to see that the soldier had tears in his eyes, caused either by emotion or alcohol, or both. It was touching but would have been considerably more so had the soldier, one, been young, and two, not possessed such a nose. It fascinated her. It was long, and pitted like a raspberry.

"I just wanted to have a good time, that's all. I'm having a real good time today, sir. I just—"

"Get out of here, soldier, or you're going to the Provost Marshal's."

The soldier saluted, his nose quivering, then turned and ran down the marble staircase.

"This place isn't off-limits to enlisted men," said Gloria, "not if a member invites them."

"Well, it should be," said the Major.

"Stop pulling me!"

The Major decided to placate her as he drew her toward the elevators. "My, it certainly hit you in a hurry, didn't it, Miss Wilson? Just like a knock on the old bean. Well, that's Scotch for you. Never you mind though. What you need is a nice little ride in the open air. Yes, sir!" He pulled on Gloria's wrist.

"I don't want to go with you, Major Cowhand."

"Oh, you don't, eh? Who will you go with then?"

"With whom will you go," corrected Gloria.

"What?" said the Major with some irritation.

"Nothing. But stop clutching me."

"Well, then, let's eat."

"All right, then," Gloria shouted, "let's eat."

In the elevator a pregnant young woman was talking to a man with steel-rimmed glasses: "Now, of course, I know all about the servant problem, but when one of your own girls dishes up the mashed potatoes cold—stone-cold straight from the icebox, mind you—well, that's just too much. So I sent her back to the agency —it's not my business what she tells them. . . . Really? You blame me? After all, one has to put up some kind of resistance, if you don't want to end up with Climalene on your crêpe suzettes, that is. After all, I'm not like our neighbor—oh, you know her: Mrs. Colonel Ashcroft—who eats her ham-hock sherbert, dresses her maids to match the drapes, and then sits back and thinks everything's lovely."

The Major raised an eyebrow at Gloria. She was staring at the elevator boy. They'd changed boys; this one was older.

"Well, won't have to stand too much more from old Ashcroft," the Major said softly.

"What are you mumbling about?" asked Gloria.

"Nothing—just a little something a bird told me."

"Well, stop simpering."

They got off at the second floor, and the Major walked to the dining-room door and looked at the menu. "Yes, they're really having a feed tonight. Want some guinea hen under glass?"

"No, we might get splintered," said Gloria. "You don't have to smile at my little jokes. They're almost entirely nervous reflex."

"What's truffles?"

"What I have on my underskirt."

"They good to eat?"

"Why, Major, you never told me!"

"I'd like a big, thick steak. Doesn't that sound good, Miss Wilson?"

"I'll take an egg in a glass, or something." She didn't feel well and walked over to the window. It was much darker, and the Palace was blue against the late sky. It made her feel sad. "And here all the time I thought it was lunch," she said helplessly, several tears rolling down her cheeks.

"Hell, no, Miss Wilson, we done miss lunch. This here am supper. We got a couple hours before that opera affair begin, so we can take our time, real nice, you know."

"How much am those truffles?"

"Jesus, five bucks the serving."

"Good. I'll eat an all-truffle dinner. Truffle soup, truffle steak, mashed truffles with gravy, truffle salad with Miracle Whip, and good old American ice-cream banana-split with truffles."

"Feeling better, huh?" asked the Major uncertainly.

"I could eat a horse."

"Not necessary. We gonna eat high on the hog to-night, Miss Wilson."

"Well, that's better than eating low, though I've heard of folks eating those things."

The Major looked back to the menu.

"But what about the starving urchins in front of the PX?" she suddenly cried.

"What about them?" Then he looked pained. "Come on, you don't mean to tell me that you fall for that too. Why those fat little rascals get fed better than we do."

"But—maybe they don't like truffles."

"Look, they get enough to feed an army. The GI's are always feeding them. Popcorn, hot dogs, Coke..."

"Such a well-balanced diet too," murmured Gloria.

"Look, no one's starving here except me," said the Major.

A woman with her hair piled in a ball on top of her head, miniature silver honey-buckets swinging from her ears, strolled from the dining room with a distinguished-looking civilian, speaking in a shrill voice: "And so this girl went to the Japanese bakery here—really, these people are *so* darling—and ordered a birthday cake for her husband. He's in Forestry or something—no, maybe it's Labor—well, it doesn't make any difference. And so she thought it would be real quaint if under the 'Happy Birthday' part was the same thing in Japanese. So, on her little order blank, she put down: 'Happy Birthday, Frank,' and then added: 'Japanese character.' When the cake was ready she picked it up, and that's just what she'd gotten: 'Happy Birthday, Frank Japanese character.' Isn't that priceless?"

"Well, go on and starve," said Gloria.

"You feel all right, Miss Wilson?"

"Yes, and take your hand off me. That's not the

place that's bothering me. It's my stomach—I think. No, don't touch that either."

"Miss Wilson, please sit down. I want to talk to you."

"Major, what can we possibly have to say to each other?" asked Gloria, recklessly hopeless.

"Will you sit down!"

Catching hold of the table to steady herself, she very carefully lowered herself into the chair. "There, I did it!" she said. And at once she felt better. She must always remember to sit down whenever she possibly could. Lying down was even nicer, but the table didn't look big enough.

She examined the table and noticed that the cloth had been expertly darned in several places and that the napkins were quite new. The coat of the passing waiter was a brocade of darns and patches. A fork prong was bent, and the silver plating on her butter knife was peeling. All of this excited her very much. She sat very still, thinking: "I must sit very still or else I'll never understand." For it seemed to her that she was very near comprehending the secret of life. It had something to do with butter knives.

"Miss Wilson," said the Major solemnly, and Gloria looked up irritably. Now she would never understand.

He swallowed some water and then said : "I wouldn't be saying this if I hadn't had a little to drink—"

"And I wouldn't be listening if I weren't too plastered to stand up."

"But I've been thinking about it for a long time, and, well, I just wanted to tell you how swell I think you are."

Gloria stifled a yawn. Why, she wondered, was she always going out with men of such limited imagination. The Major here had only one approach. He only knew one way to make a pass and that was to be soulful about it. He really was a pig. This, she decided, was their last date. Never again!

"I can guess you probably don't think too much of me, Miss Wilson. I'm sort of dumb, but I'm not *that* dumb. And you're right—we sure don't have much to talk about. But I guess that's the reason I like you. I never met anyone like you before. And I like you. And that's why I'm so stupid around you. I don't know if you've ever had the experience, but around people I like I get just twice as dumb as I ordinarily am.... But you probably don't know what I'm talking about."

Gloria had begun to listen. She knew exactly what he was talking about. She remembered trying to be interesting, trying to force another to like her. And she remembered the failures—the times when the sentence that would make the other look at her and smile died upon her lips, when the remark designed to convey her regard emerged monstrously shaped, devoid of meaning, so hopelessly different from what she'd intended that she was forced to follow it with the cheapest sort of joke, the easiest kind of wit, very often the precise opposite in meaning of what she had intended.

"Talk away," she said. "You have an audience." At once she hated herself for the remark. The Major was too vulnerable.

"Please try and take me serious for a few minutes, Miss Wilson. This is hard for me to say." He paused for a second or two. "I mean that I think of you different from other girls. I think—"

Gloria had been rearranging her silverware. Now suddenly she looked up, her mouth a long line of exasperation. "You can stop any time, Major. I know all the approaches to the particular stronghold you're storming, and, believe me, the one you've chosen is the least likely to get there."

The Major looked at the tablecloth, and, suddenly sorry, Gloria cast about for something to say. "I didn't think Japan was going to look like this."

He was still looking at the tablecloth. "Nothing in

Tokyo does. Looks just like a bad copy of Chicago."

"Oh, come, Major—Beaumont, surely."

"Avenue A looks like Michigan Boulevard."

"Particularly with the Palace along one side of it."

"If you ignore the Palace, you'll see what I mean."

"Ignore the Palace—" Gloria began, but the Major suddenly pounded the table, making the silverware jump.

"No, damn it!" he said. "I'm gonna say this if it kills me. Now you listen here! I don't care what you've done or what you haven't done. Oh, I've heard all the talk that goes on. I know what people say about other people. I know what they say about *you*, Miss Wilson. I know they only say it because they're jealous or something and that it's always the least sinful that gets the most mud thrown on her. Well, I want to tell you that I don't care. That's what—I don't care. Not even if it's true!"

Gloria was staring at him in amazement. He knew too! Did anyone not know? Did the waiters know? Did Sonoko know? Did even Michael know? Those two waitresses whispering in the corner—were they talking about her? Ever since she had overheard the conversation, Gloria had fought against believing it. Now she believed it. She believed that everyone she met on the street knew. Everyone knew!

She glanced quickly around. The Major was still talking, but she couldn't hear him. His mouth moved, but she couldn't understand a word. At one of the tables a girl in a low-cut, green felt dress, surrounded by four captains, was rapidly becoming ill. They were pushing back their chairs.

Gloria closed her eyes and felt her chair move slightly. She'd just had too much to drink, that was all. She opened her eyes and looked around her. Then she recognized it. It was the end of the world, the fall of Babylon, the destruction of Sodom, the flaming sword dripping fire, purifying fire, over her head. The four trumpets and the seven plagues, the breaking of the seals and the opening of the graves. She heard the two hundred thousand horsemen, and on her forehead was written "Mystery, Babylon the Great, the Mother of Harlots and Abominations of the Earth." The Apocalypse!

Very ill, Gloria tried to stand. The girl in green felt was lying back in her chair, and waiters were fanning her with napkins. One of the officers was cleaning his uniform. There was a discreet murmur from the tables around them.

The grapevine is growing, thought Gloria, her mind working more and more slowly. It is growing. She found that she had the napkin at her mouth, and she bit it again and again. The Major's hand was on her arm, like the green tendril of a vine, groping forward, blindly, seeking, entering.

She stood up so suddenly that her chair fell backward. From the distance she heard the voice of the Major saying: "But, Miss Wilson, I'm asking you to marry me—to marry me!"

Biting the napkin, she turned and ran across the crowded room, tears blinding her, feeling more and more ill. Far away she heard the Major's voice, sounding like that of a child lost in the woods.

"Miss Wilson!" the voice called. "Miss Wilson!"

She ran into the darkness.

■

At a nearby table a stout gentleman was talking to two very pretty and very young ladies. "But, my dears," he was saying, "Japan is a divine place to be. Take culture, for example, the heritage of the ages. Why, in Kyoto—"

"Kyoto?" asked one of the girls. "That sounds familiar. Where is that?"

"It's a large city," said the stout man reprovingly. "The ancient capital. It's where the finest—"

"Kyoto, Kyoto," she said reflectively. "I don't think I know—"

"It's near Osaka," said the man. "Really the cultural center of the—"

"Kyoto . . ." said the girl.

"Yes," said the man, "it's—"

"Sure, Kyoto!" said the other girl. "You remember —we were there. Sure, you remember. That's the place that had the French perfume in the PX."

part 3

COLONEL ASHCROFT LEFT GENERAL KEAN'S OFFICES IN the Dai Ichi Building, motioned for his sedan, closed the door behind him, and told the driver to go to Washington Heights. The General and he had talked from one to five, and this talk had changed Colonel Ashcroft's life. He had been relieved of his post in Special Services, had been told that travel orders would shortly be cut for him, and had been informed that the Army, in honor of his long and faithful services—particularly considering the fact that he had but five years before retirement—would be pleased to place him in a less responsible position in the States. This, however, was but the barest skeleton of their actual conversation.

General Kean, as his friend—they had been in the States, Hawaii, and the Philippines together—was much kinder than the occasion demanded, filling out the few facts he imparted with the most solicitous kind of verbiage. In deference to their long-standing friendship, he intimated rather than stated that the Colonel was being pastured out for possibly subversive opinions— which, just between the two of them, they both knew to be one vast joke, but still one couldn't buck public opinion—and that it was only through deference to his long and even brilliant Army career that reports of these opinions were being killed within the Dai Ichi Building itself and would hence cause him no further difficulty just in case, say, he ever cared to visit Washington.

The Colonel also learned, through this joking, familiar, and indirect manner, that it was a major in his own office who had reported most of the so-called subversive opinions, and that, had it reached the General through non-official channels, it would have ended right there, because, of course, he knew his old friend Rand Ashcroft was constitutionally incapable of anything of the sort. But, as it was, the news was known to many and its approach had been most official. The agency designed for ferreting this sort of thing out had been alerted, and the most the General would be able to do would be to consign the entire case to his closed files.

There were also relatively unimportant side issues: neglect of duty, the uttering of disparaging remarks about the splendid achievements of Special Services, and a general tendency toward playing the martinet— thus earning no little unpopularity with the men.

There was also the personal criticism that the Colonel was of a definitely anti-social nature.

Now, of course his old friend Kean knew better than this, but, alas, others did not, and consequently he really thought it the better part of valor to bow to their mistaken conclusions because, after all, the States *were* home, and incidentally, Mrs. Ashcroft might welcome the change.

The Colonel, in the automobile, now thought of all this. He had tried, unsuccessfully, to adapt his own line of reasoning to that of the General's. But, instead of becoming resigned, he, with enormous impracticality considering the number and power of his adversaries, could think only of revenge. And, with still greater impracticality, he privately considered that this natural and healthy emotion was worse than a disgrace—was, indeed, a sin.

The temptation to revenge was very insidious, for it was so easy to rationalize it. The Colonel might, for example, given a bit of time, convince himself that it was not for the sake of revenge that he was exposing Major Calloway and his accomplices. After all, it was his duty as a military man to apprehend any variety of misdemeanor within his command. It would be for the good of the Occupation, which, naturally, did not approve of such activities as the Major's.

Yet, while knowing this, the Colonel also knew that this would not be his true reason. His reason would be revenge, petty, sinful revenge, through which he would be at once reduced to the moral level of his enemy. He would have sold out, through weakness, and would voluntarily have given the enemy that which it could never have taken from him by force.

The Colonel took off his cap, smoothed his gray hair, looked from the window, and stroked his silver moustaches. His moral code, long held rigid by training both in the Army and through the ever-present example of his father and his father's father, was slowly disintegrating. He himself felt it and realized it daily in the small concessions which he made—a bit less small every day—to others and to himself. Formerly the code had been strong but not inflexible, for it was more like a religion than a philosophy, and his precepts of humanity and justice and liberty had been entirely personal, as he believed they should be for every man.

Now, however, the code had lost its elasticity; it had become brittle, and it cracked under any strain. The Colonel need only look about him to discover that these self-imposed rules by which he lived were antiquated; that he could have been no more anachronistic had he worn the tall plush hat and gaitered trousers of his grandfather. He was silent as to his beliefs and, as yet, listened patiently to the brainless creatures about him who brayed as their own discovery his own most personal principles.

Major Calloway, for example, spoke of democracy as though it were a newly acquired uniform, his own private jet-plane, the lucky prize for the sixty-four dollar question. Yet, had it not been for the wars, and the resultant public reaffirmation, the Major would doubtless have gone through life quite ignorant of the quality in his country and its government in which he now took so personal yet so cursory an interest. He didn't know too well who Jefferson was, but he spoke with authority of the Founding Fathers, among whom he included Sam Houston as the possible framer of the Constitution. His idea of democracy as a government was somewhat like the parvenu's idea of the high society in which he now happily found himself. Lacking any understanding or sympathy for its actual meaning, its real idea, the Major, under the Germans, would have been a perfect Nazi and, under the Japanese of ten years before, would doubtless have been shouting

,'Banzai!" with the best of them. These were the Colonel's thoughts.

And, Colonel Ashcroft was certain, the Major's thoughts—or feelings—on this subject of democracy were those of the majority. For them democracy had become a possession which added somewhat to the wealth of the country. And to their minds the richest and most powerful became indistinguishable from the best. They patriotically believed that America was the best country in the world. So did the Colonel, but for entirely different reasons.

Come to think of it, their reconstruction of democracy was a bit like the reconstruction of Williamsburg, a city the Colonel had seen once and loathed. It was an empty shell, devoid of life, a travesty on what it had once been, a tourist attraction which was generally advertised as something quite noble and special, something to which one might make an occasional pilgrimage. To the Colonel's way of thinking, their America was like this false Williamsburg. One block from the democratic highroad one saw that the house fronts were false facades, that the backyards were no less filthy than anywhere else, that the lip service paid the geniality of Colonial days was based upon misconceptions from the mouths of waitresses dressed as great ladies of the day or of local businessmen wearing periwigs and knee britches for the occasion.

But their opinions had little in common with those democratic beliefs so firmly ingrained in the Colonel that he himself had never once thought of them, taking them for granted, just as he took for granted the sun and the moon and the stupidity of the Army. They were something to cherish and protect, all right, but as one cherished one's heart and protected one's hands. Thus it was that if the Williamsburg opinions touched him at all, they did so only now, in negative as it were, for the very firmness of his beliefs had precluded the necessity of his ever so much as thinking about them.

Thus, the Major barked about "God's Country" and what he called the "Democratic Way of Life"—by which, the Colonel understood, he most likely meant that way which, through its virtues, allowed him to go unpunished. And he became suspicious of the Colonel when he discovered that his own sentiments were not echoed, that the Colonel's lips were formed in a wry, ironic smile, and that come to think of it, the Colonel had more than once expressed the doubt that the Japanese would ever take to democracy.

The Major didn't care if they did or not. That was beside the point. The point was that it was necessary to believe that they would. And if they wouldn't, then they could always be forced to. After all, who won the war?

And so, while the Colonel was only questioning the advisability, indeed the possibility, of exporting so personal a commodity as these beliefs—just as he often wondered if Christianity, in its true state, were not a complex of emotions rather than a set of laws, and hence not too well adapted for natural growth outside those countries where, through the centuries, it had metamorphosed and hence flourished—this questioning was interpreted by the Major and all those like him only as a questioning of the concept itself. When the Colonel, in an unguarded moment, expressed the time-honored thought that America had never lost a war and never won a peace, the Major, shrewdly acute to the signs of the times, detected the heresy of un-Americanism in the Colonel.

But surely, thought the Colonel, it was just as much a sign of strength in his country that the peace should be lost as that the battle be won. Democracy was scarcely a whipping-stick for the defeated. At the most, it was an example to them. It, in its essence, defied the subtleties of diplomacy and just as rigorously disdained attempts at interpretation, for—paradoxically it is true—it was an aristocratic form of government, not an oligarchy, but a rule by that higher aristocracy which every man carries within himself.

The Colonel's beliefs put him into difficulties in yet another way. Just as he refused his support to a man who, though voicing his own—the Colonel's—opinions in any matter, managed, even though on the "right" side, to misrepresent that side, so the Colonel refused to place himself in the equally embarrassing position of seconding the opinions of a man like the Major, even though those opinions, for all the wrong reasons, happened to be right. There was, in the Colonel, perhaps foremost, pique that his own sacred beliefs should be so mishandled, and second, moral indignation that the truth in them should be so mangled that the presentation all too efficiently invalidated the belief. Granted, the Colonel's way of thinking was not practical.

His lack of practicality was, indeed, a point of no small honor with him. He fancied himself to be as impractical—that is, as visionary, as idealistic—as was Jefferson himself, who had been imbued with deistic ideas which in themselves were now entirely anachronistic and, probably, always had been, and had refused to warp his noble plan with material considerations.

Yet, wondered the Colonel, had not this very impracticality—which was the cradle of democracy—ensured its immortality? And, further, was it not the vision of Jefferson and others which, in its honest if naive belief in the application of its theory, rendered the concept of democracy valid even now—through virtue of its being a vision, an illusion, a chimera—despite its many misinterpretations, just as valid as it had been in the very hour of its formulation?

And did it not, the Colonel wondered, best suit, through this quality of genius in it (this incapability of capture, this mirage-like quality of eternal promise)—

did it not best suit the true nature of man, that nature which, eternally unsatisfied with reality, would continually strive toward that which it could not attain? And then, did not Jefferson and those others know this, perhaps? If not, why that most telling of images, that most beautiful of thoughts: "the pursuit of happiness"?

It was highly suspicious ideas like these which the Major had been quick to detect and—since they themselves, though strong, were also slender and easily twisted—had been even quicker to misinterpret to others. The Colonel's spoken query whether the Japanese had not, in their own way, won the war after all could be damaging as an admission once the Major had presented it. Worse than this, the Colonel had indulged his sense of irony a bit too often. When he had heard the plan of a high-ranking officer to solve Japan's population problem by giving them Manchuria, he had smiled and asked, then what had the war been about? Nor had the Major been long in reporting this.

The role the Major had played in the betrayal of the Colonel was not too clear to the latter, for Kean had been anything but explicit. Therefore, all of this was simply the Colonel's best surmise of what must have happened, and his surmise happened to be absolutely correct—this is precisely what had occurred.

■

An enameled clock, covered with rosebuds, struck six, and Colonel Ashcroft sat down to dinner. Years with the Army had made the early hour not only acceptable but also pleasant. He had quite forgotten there had ever been a time—long ago—when dinner (called supper) was at eight.

His wife, sitting across from him, had never forgotten. Every evening at six, not yet entirely recovered from a habitual solitary tea at four and a nap after it, she thought of the old days of her youth and of those civilized suppers at eight. Eating directly after work had been the custom of the poor whites and of the Negroes. Now she sat toying with her fruit cup, one hand feeling blindly for fugitive wisps of gray-brown hair, disarranged by the nap. Her eyes were red with sleep, and her lips were puffy. The spoon rang against the plate as she put it down.

"You're not hungry, dear?" asked the Colonel. He always asked this and had asked it for years.

"Not so very much, dear," she replied, smiling. "I had a slight headache this afternoon and took a little nap. It is quite better now, however."

"I'm pleased to hear it," he said.

The Japanese maid removed the fruit cup and brought in the soup. While his wife stirred hers, the Colonel added cream and wondered what they could talk about. Every evening his mind was furiously active during the meal, but he said very little. He was forced to be careful not to speak too much of his work nor, particularly, of the Japanese.

His wife, though she had never said so, disliked Japan very much. If he happened to mention something he had seen on the street or something a Japanese had told him, her lips became straight and she drank water or looked searchingly into her dessert. This somewhat limited their conversation.

"Did anything occur today of special interest, my dear?" he asked, as he always did, and she, as always, smiled, made an effort, and appeared to consider.

"No, I don't believe so," she said, as though she had mentally reviewed a busy day and had smilingly decided that it had been, after all, quite ordinary.

It had been ordinary, for all her days were identical. She did nothing. She seldom left the house: it was the only thing she liked in Japan. It and the huge compound of American homes of which it was one. It was quite possible for an American housewife to spend her entire time in Japan inside the high wire fences of the compound, buying in the Commissary and the local PX, seeing films at the Washington Heights Theater, and reading the *Stars and Stripes*, which was delivered daily. This was just what the Colonel's wife did. Except for the maids—and they both spoke excellent English—she might never have known she was in Japan.

More and more often now she spent her days in the house, never once glancing in the direction of the outside world. They had not been to a movie for months. Anything which drew her from her house and garden she more and more disliked. When she was forced to leave the house, she sheltered herself behind dark glasses, which she had formerly never worn. And on the few occasions when she had to leave the compound and speak with the Japanese, she was so exquisitely polite that she was often quite incomprehensible.

"No ... I can't think of anything ... except the garden, of course." She smiled again, and one maid removed the soup, while the other brought in the pork roast, which the Colonel began to carve. They often talked about the garden.

"Would a slice like this one do, my dear?"

"Oh, heavens, that's far too large—perhaps half—and no applesauce, please."

"There—is that better?"

"Yes, just right. Thank you, dear."

Yes, it would be the garden. Even in the snow she was there. And it was such a pathetic little garden, just a backyard like all the others. The others were cluttered up with bamboo lawn furniture and make-it-yourself barbecue pits, while hers was fenced in and cluttered up with a honeysuckle trellis from which hung no honeysuckle, a boxwood hedge, and a little pond in which all the fish had died.

Back home she had had a pavilion set among dwarf-magnolia trees. She wanted one here too, but the earth in which flourished rice and fir and pine and chrysanthemum would not nourish the alien plant, at least not the earth of the former parade ground on which Washington Heights had been built. He had watched the trees fade, while she, in a kind of panic, ran among the withered saplings—he had had them sent over two years before as a surprise—followed by the Japanese maid, making little cuts here and there, uttering little cries of dismay, pruning drastically.

In the same way that the one and only bloom, pale with promise, had died and turned brown, so too had she, the girl whom he remembered with a skin pale as ivory and dark Southern eyes, become a querulous matron who bit her lips when the maids slammed a door.

"This is excellent pork, my dear."

"Why, thank you very much, dear. But I really don't deserve the credit. It is the girls. They are most talented, you know."

"Yes, but it was you who taught them, if I remember rightly."

She smiled, pleased, and it saddened him to realize that this was probably the first time she had smiled with pleasure that day. He could not blame her unhappiness, for she had tried very hard to like Japan and the Japanese. She had tried—and miserably failed. From Virginia, like himself, she had been used to an affectionate disregard of servants and could not now help believing that she lived in a nation of servants, servants moreover whose insubordination was always potential. Of course, in their life in the Army she had followed him to many places besides Virginia, but to none quite so remote, quite so alien.

And still, she *had* tried. She'd given little teas for the wives of Japanese officials, those men with whom he'd found it necessary to work. She'd had little watercress sandwiches, ladyfingers, and three kinds of tea—

one Indian and two Chinese. He could imagine what those teas had been like—everyone sitting in a small circle with nothing to say to each other and no way of saying it. The wives had stayed the expected hour, and later each had invited her to her own home. She had refused all the invitations, and after that had not been invited again.

Thereafter her teas had become solitary, and she often fell asleep over her orange pekoe and ladyfingers. The girls would promise to awaken her, and she, with a smile, would lie straight in her Army bed and sleep until just before her husband returned. At first she had tried to meet the other Army wives on the post, but they soon dropped her, and she them. They were most impolite young ladies who were rude to her at the Commissary and talked behind her back. She never quite realized that it was those same unsuccessful teas for the Japanese ladies which had made her guilty in their eyes of "fraternization," nor would she have been able to understand how a word which she understood to mean "brotherhood" had come to signify a crime.

At first she had meekly refused to judge her country-women and would often say that, well, it was just that she wasn't used to Northern ways, or later, that it was just that they were so young. But when she finally condemned them, she said nothing about it to her husband. She never mentioned them again.

So she sat home alone all day and did needle point until it was time for tea. Then it was time for supper, which was invariably excellent, and if she talked at all with her husband, it was about her girlhood in Richmond or her early life with him or to reminisce about some friend long dead. Then he would forget and tell her about his work, which was all he had to talk about, and she would bite her lip and often plead one of her sick headaches, and he would not see her until the following evening. It had been this way during most of their time in Japan·

The maid removed their plates. She had not eaten her pork after all. When the salad was brought, her husband smiled at her quizzically before mixing it.

"Oh, yes, you know I love salad," she said and even attempted that old quality which, back then, had been called vivacity.

He helped her to salad, and behind him the enameled clock ticked on.

"Something occurred today," he began slowly. Then he stopped, for their eyes had met, and hers seemed to be pleading to be spared, to be left in peace. And how old those eyes looked. He could not continue. "But, actually, it was of no importance."

Her forehead became smooth and she smiled. "Oh, no, dear. What was it you were going to tell me?"

"General Kean asked me to see him."

"Oh, yes. Let me see—he's the head of your section, or division, or whatever, is he not?"

"Yes, we were in the Philippines together during the war."

"Oh, yes, I remember him well from the States—a most kind gentleman. He wears glasses, does he not, and—why, I remember perfectly now—we spoke several years ago—though just where does escape my memory. And—would you believe it?—we talked of nothing but dogs. Yes. That's right. Dogs. Imagine that. And he told me—why, I remember it as though yesterday— he told me that he owned a wolfhound that... what was it now? Oh, yes, of course—that the hound he owned was afraid of rabbits. Isn't that amusing, dear? Imagine—a Russian wolfhound, and it was afraid of rabbits." She laughed and tears of pleasure came into her eyes.

"No, dear, that was General Grady, and he died, you'll remember, about three years ago, just after that time you remember so well."

Her lower lip turned, both in pity and petulance. "Oh, of course. I don't rightly know what's the matter with me. I do so forget." She made an effort to collect her thoughts. "Of course—General Grady. Yes. And he's dead now. Yes.... Now, what about this other gentleman, dear?"

Again he lost the courage to continue. "Oh, we just talked about old times. That's all."

"Oh, that was nice. But, no—do tell me what you were going to say."

What could he tell her, he wondered, she with whom he had shared everything—or attempted to? Sorry as he was for her, he could not tolerate her having any pity for him.

"Come now," she said coaxingly. "I'm very interested in what you do—you know that, dear. Do tell me." And she smiled to show how interested she was. She blinked her eyes, and her head shook slightly. She was old—very old. Somehow older than he, though he was the elder, and her smile was that of a martyr awaiting the first blow.

"Well, he just called me, and we talked about the Service and all, you know," he began, then stopped and ate a few bites of salad. Whatever else, he must be honest with her. It was often necessary to lie, to color the truth, to exaggerate or to minimize, but he had always been as honest as possible with her, and if he erred, it was only that, rather than allow the truth to hurt her, he had shielded her from it by refusing to speak at all. But now, when the truth would so please her—that part of the truth for which she had so longed—he found himself unable rather than unwilling to speak, for with it must necessarily come the knowledge of his position, of his detractors, and the true reason they were going home.

"Well, you know, my dear, that I never asked to serve in Japan. But it became my duty—the duty of any soldier."

She nodded slightly, her head bowed. It was, he thought, as though he'd cultivated disreputable friends and insisted upon intruding them into his household. Her disapproval of his connections with the Japanese, though unspoken, was always apparent. Her father would never have asked his wife to entertain at tea the Negro wives of the plantation hands.

"Yes, dear," she said.

"But once it became my duty, then I resolved to do it as best I could. Originally the Japanese were no concern of mine, any more than of yours, but now my duty is dedicated to them."

"Yes, dear."

He started to speak again, but this was not the truth. The truth was that he wanted more than anything else to love the Japanese, those people to whom he was dedicated, just as he loved his fellow-Americans—most of them. And in that he had really failed. He had only succeeded in feeling kindly toward them, and this was wrong, because all men are worth being loved, slave or owner, Japanese or American—there is in all men an inherent nobility which loves and can be loved.

"Well, this is all actually beside the point, because when I saw Kean this afternoon, I learned ... I learned that ... "

He hesitated so long that his wife raised her head and, after waiting for the girl to remove the salad and disappear into the kitchen, said: "Dear, it's not bad news, is it?"

He forced himself to laugh. "No, no. It's good news. Good. Just the opposite."

"Well, then ... " She stopped, because the other girl had brought in the dessert and coffee.

How could he tell her, he wondered. He could say that reports had reached Kean and that he, Colonel Ashcroft, was being investigated as a possible security risk. But that would never do, for his wife knew nothing of the world in which such things as this were possible—she was of the world where a man's word was his honor. Perhaps, then, he could temper it a bit. Kean had agreed that these preposterous charges were nonsense—but, after all, that's life, isn't it, and blessings often come in black-wrapped packages, and, every cloud has the silver lining. The result was what counted—the end, not the means. This way at least he could go home.... But, no, that would worry her, for she would then never understand what the charges had been and why, if men agreed a thing was preposterous, they should act as though they knew it were not. Finally, he might augment the truth a trifle. It was true that he was but five years from retirement. The Army changed, just as did life itself, and it was natural that a younger man, a major in his own offices, would be chosen, and really it was better this way because it was keeping it in the family as it were, the man in question knew the business of the section well, and ... No, that would not do either, for that caused the Colonel himself too much pain. And his wife would understand it not at all; she would ask if the major then would become colonel, and he would answer that it probably meant a downgrading in the table of operation, and she would find that very strange.

But she would have found even stranger the truth that a major had, through circumstances partially of his own making and partially not, forced the hand of a general. And so he wondered what he could possibly tell her. All of the reasons happened to be true, and for one of the few times in his life, one of the Colonel's absolutes shone a bit less brilliantly than usual. Truth was for him a quality, like the air he breathed, almost a palpable object, like his hand before him, but now, for a second, it stood revealed as merely an opinion, or at best a series of opinions, true for one person or one set of circumstances, not true for another.

"Apple turnovers! I've not seen these for years," he said, looking into his plate.

"The Commissary got them in this morning. I waited in line for them. They'd just gotten them in."

"How thoughtful of you, my dear."

"Oh, nonsense, dear. I don't do half of what I feel I should. But, at least, they are good. I had a bite of one at tea time and found them surprisingly well made. Almost like those we had—now where was it? —oh, of course, in Williamsburg. You remember, Rand? Oh, how you disliked that place. You were so funny too. And you spilled the cream. Do you remember, Rand? Why, that must have been twenty years ago. And I wore that old organdy dress you liked so well, and after that we went to see your old professor at William and Mary, and had that lovely conversation about Shakespeare—or was it Marlowe? —I do tend to forget—and then, in the train, going home, we saw—"

"But you're not eating any, my dear."

"Oh, I'm not really very hungry." With one hand she pushed her hair into place, and with the other held the coffee cup before her mouth. "Well, and then in the train we saw— Oh, but I forgot. Your good news. Do tell me, Rand."

Perhaps he could fight. It was odd he'd not thought of that. Perhaps he could defend himself against calumny and fight just as had his father and grandfather. They had been very brave men. But, then, they had fought with swords. It had been an equal duel, and their adversaries had had no advantage. But now the weapons had changed. Telephones . . . the word of mouth to ear . . . the whisper and the innuendo. No, he could not fight as they had fought, his father and his grandfather. He could only retreat.

"Rand, tell me!" said his wife, worried.

"Well, when I saw Kean, I learned there was an op-

portunity for returning home—that was what he had
wanted to see me about."

"Oh, Rand! Is that the truth?"

He smiled sadly and nodded his head. Yes, that too
was the truth.

"He reminded me that I have but five years before
retirement and—he even mentioned you—said you might
like the change. Is that true, Lilian?"

"Oh, Rand!" she said, half between laughter and
tears. "You know that's true. Oh, could we?"

She stopped smiling and looked at him intently,
pleading: "Did you say you'd go?"

"Yes," he nodded, "I said I'd go. They're cutting
orders for me now."

"Oh, Rand, you don't know what wonderful news
this is. Why did you take so long to tell me? Oh,
I want to go so much!" She suddenly turned, one hand
before her mouth, and said: "But, Rand, do *you* want
to go?"

"Yes," he nodded again, "very much."

"Because if you didn't, why, then, you could just
tell him ..."

He shook his head. "No, it's all finished. I want
to go—very much."

She looked around the room, a bit dazed. "Oh, my,
but I have so much to do. I must pack ... and the
silver and plate. Oh, Rand, it will be so different from
last time—do you remember the last time? You know,
I don't know if you knew it or not, but I was dreadfully unhappy."

He nodded.

"But, my lands, what am I doing here? I ought to
be packing those old trunks this very minute and
getting—"

"There's plenty of time, dear."

"But, Rand—" And she suddenly stopped, remembering, then said, very softly: "Do you realize, dear,

that we'll be having Christmas at home? Just think—
Christmas at home!"

"Yes, dear, I thought of that."

She stood up and accidentally caught her sleeve on
the needlework stand. She looked down at it. "Oh,
Rand," she called out, her voice young and happy,
"just think—I'll never have to finish this." She looked
at the half-completed needlework. "Never have to
finish this," she said more softly.

The girl was removing the dessert plates, but she
was so excited she continued talking, forgetting to pat
her hair into place and look out of the window. "Oh,
Rand. Don't you just love our winters back home?"
Suddenly she could no longer talk and began to sob.
"Oh, I'm so stupid," she said through her handkerchief,
"so stupid. Here I am so happy I could sing, and yet
I'm crying like a big baby. But, Rand," she turned toward him, tears in the wrinkles around her eyes, "we
will go, won't we? We really will?"

"Yes, we really will," he said, and she, years younger
than he was, stood up straight and patted her brown
hair and smiled at him.

The maid removed the coffee cups, and the Colonel
said: "Look, dear, I still have to see about business
until I'm relieved, you know, and tonight is the opera.
I don't know if you're anxious to see it or not, but if
you are ... "

She made a girlish gesture with her hand. "Oh,
heavens, no. Why, I just couldn't sit still. I'd not be
able to hear any of the music. No. You go, because
you must. But I'll be just as busy here, believe me, Rand.
I'm going to have the girls get the trunks down, and I'll
pack away those things we won't need. Like the winter
blankets. Just think, Rand—we won't need the winter
blankets!" She laughed again and then, coming to him,
touched his cheek with her hand and said softly: "Oh,
Rand. It will be better. It will be so much better."

He nodded and closed his eyes. He had told the truth. And the clock struck seven.

■

"There goes Colonel Ashcroft," said Dottie as the sedan paused for a stoplight. She and Mrs. Schmidt were standing at the Hibiya Park intersection. "I hope you don't mind this waiting," said Dottie. "He should be along any moment now."

"Of course not," said Mrs. Schmidt. "I quite understand."

"Isn't it absurd, though," said Dottie. "Here we are, standing on a street corner in the middle of November, in the capital of the whole Orient, right in the midst of the Occupation, and yet ..."

"And yet we have no place to go," finished Mrs. Schmidt kindly. "It is singular, isn't it? Of course, we could be sitting in the lobby of the American Club —I'm allowed there—but, frankly, I'd just as soon be standing here. It is dreadful thing to say, but whenever I'm in an Occupation building I always feel as though I'm in the presence of the enemy."

"You are," said Dottie. "Look, it's awfully cold. Why don't we go to a Japanese coffee shop or something. I could stand a DR."

"It's too dangerous for you, dear. Besides, didn't you tell him you'd meet him here?"

"Yes, poor dear, it would be fairly dreadful for him to get a DR—officer and all. I guess this is the best I can do."

"I don't mind. It's like something out of a märchen. What do you call them? Like the Babes in the Woods, you know. Just look around you. Isn't it romantic— almost gothique."

Dottie looked through the trees into the park. By day it was dusty and bare, with little clumps of gray grass and groves of grayer trees. The little pond was drying up, and a pavilion built on one of the hills was in ruins. Now, at dusk, the trees seemed a blackish green, and the small knolls looked like mountains.

Here and there were fires, for the park had become home to many who had no other. The faces of the vagrants hung above the twig fires which crackled in discarded oil tins. Below them, children slept huddled next to each other. A single dog sat silently, its muzzle outlined against the fire. No one spoke, and the only sound was the softened roar of the usual evening traffic.

"Salvator Rosa might have well painted that scene," said Mrs. Schmidt, indicating the fire. "You know, a band of brigands in the mountains. Byron would have loved it. He would have called it picturesque, I believe."

"I call it disgusting," said Dottie. "Particularly those children. I don't see why we allow it."

"You can't mean allow them to use the park!"

"Of course not—I don't see why we don't feed them. Oh, I've had it explained to me a hundred times. It's not the responsibility of the Army, and all that sort of thing. The Japanese government has to take care of them. But any fool can see the government can't do a thing. They're too poor. So, even now, people starve, and since it's nobody's duty, nobody does anything about it—except let them starve."

Mrs. Schmidt turned so that her back was toward the cold wind. "That is not the worst of it, dear. These people think that America doesn't care whether they starve or not."

"But we do, really. Individually, all of us do. At any rate, I do. I don't think there is a single person in the Occupation who doesn't think about these people and wonder if, maybe, it isn't up to them to do something for them. And really, Madame Schmidt, it's terrible, living here and feeling that somehow you're to blame for what's happening. Oh, around other Americans

I always put on a big front. We all do that. It's funny—almost as though we're ashamed of showing some concern or showing that we feel sorry."

"It's too bad that the official policy of the Occupation isn't like that," said Mrs. Schmidt. "But it's not. I don't suppose any occupation anywhere has ever had such a policy, or ever will."

"God, it's cold!" said Dorothy. Then: "Funny, too—in America we wouldn't stand for it. We wouldn't sit by and let a child starve. But here everyone is so different; everyone's different."

"I think all of us—I mean all of us whom you call 'foreign nationals'—know that it isn't that you don't care...."

"Funny. This is the first time I've ever tried to say what I think about it. We just don't talk about it with each other. I don't know, but it's as though it was bad taste or something to talk about it. We always pretend to ignore it. But, believe me, we don't. We can't ignore it. Personally, I don't like the Japanese and never have and probably never will. But it's not because of what they did to us. I wouldn't like them if we'd never had a war—the men are too short and feminine, the women are too—oh, I don't know. But even if I don't like them, I still feel somehow as though I'm at fault, not them.... Oh, it's a crazy notion, I suppose, but you'd be surprised at how many people over here feel the same way. They don't say so, but I *know* they do."

Mrs. Schmidt had never heard Dorothy speak with such conviction. She felt a little embarrassed, thinking ahead to the look she'd find in Dorothy's eyes when next they met, and said: "Perhaps, it's because all of you know you aren't really individuals any more. You're—what do you call it on the Armed Forces Radio?—you're 'representatives of America.' You know that these people are looking at you every minute expecting you to behave American, and so that's what you do."

"I don't know how to behave American," said Dottie. "But I do know that Mrs. Kean once said she could never stop and give money to a beggar, no matter how much she wanted to, because she was the wife of a general and wives of generals couldn't do things like that. It's that sort of attitude that's so natural and yet so terrible. And the Swensons—you know them you said—they think they know all about Japan, but if you introduced them to any of those people by the fire over there, they'd be terrified."

"So would you," Mrs. Schmidt reminded her.

"Sure I would be," said Dottie. "I wouldn't know what to do. The only thing I *could* do would be to give them money, and that's not what I mean."

Mrs. Schmidt was going to ask her what she did mean, but then decided not to. From previous experience she realized that when she was being sincere Dottie could think in an orderly fashion for only so long. After that her reflections became more and more personal, until finally they would cease to be understandable communication at all.

"Oh, I don't know *what* I mean," said Dottie. She was tired and cold and wanted a drink.

Mrs. Schmidt looked at the distant faces, suspended above the fire, and remembered Hibiya Park as she had first known it—in bright sunshine, swarming with children and ice-cream vendors. The gravel walks had been raked every morning, and on Sunday some band or other always gave a concert in the distant bandstand. During the war it had been brilliant with bunting and army uniforms. Now it was silent and cold, the pleasure pavilion on the rise of the hill in ruins.

There was a rustle of dry leaves, and three Japanese girls, predatory in lipstick and rouge, stalked from bushes, their eyes bright in the light of the street lamps. Two soldiers were approaching. The girls stood on either side of the path and waited. The soldiers stopped and talked. Then one, carrying a paper-wrapped parcel, turned around and started back. The other came forward. It was an officer.

"Here you are finally!" said Dottie. "My god, but it's cold. You two know each other? Madame Schmidt, this is Major Calloway. He's going to help you."

The three Japanese girls returned to the bushes.

■

Michael, looking back, saw the Major talking with two women, one of whom he remembered seeing in the office that morning. The Major hadn't said anything about them except that this was the last time he was going to see "Dottie," only Michael had no idea which one was Dottie, and didn't much care. The Major, he gathered, had been having an affair. It was also the last time that he and the Major were to meet unoffi·cially. In one hand he held the package containing the military scrip—for all its looking like play-money, it had a very real value here—which he was to turn over to Mr. Ohara in the theatre that night. It was heavy and probably contained a lot.

His other hand was in his pocket. In it was the note that Haruko had left at the entrance when the MP's refused to let her in.

He decided to walk to Ginza and have a cup of coffee at the PX Snack Bar. Turning his back on the park, he walked slowly back toward the lights of Yuraku-cho. He wanted to be alone. He wanted to think. He also wanted to read the unopened note.

It was only now, late in the day, that he had begun to feel at all responsible for his actions. It was only now, walking toward the bright neon lights and distant crowds, that he began to wonder why he had done what he had. It was almost with surprise that he found him-self alone, walking among faces different from his own, hearing snatches of conversation he could barely understand, passing under signs he could almost never read.

The paper-wrapped package was heavy in his hand, and he thought about it first. He was taking part in a crime. He would be, to anyone who knew of it, a criminal. Yet he didn't think of himself as a criminal at all. He had regarded his part in all this merely as a way of making money—and not a very practical way at that. Besides the obvious danger of detection, the reward was by no means commensurate with the energy required. Every one, Japanese and American alike, took his profit, and there were so many middlemen that, as in all badly managed businesses, no one made any real profit, unless maybe it was the Major.

But he did like the feeling of freedom which carrying out the Major's plans gave him. It was like being a member of a gang. It was like knowing the password while everyone else remained in ignorance. It was like belonging to something greater than himself....

Yet, at the same time, he felt he was doing wrong. He again fingered the note that Haruko had left. It was small and just fitted into the palm of his hand, yet it was big enough to change his life. He knew it contained her real answer, and as yet, he had not been able to bring himself to read it.

At Sukiyabashi he suddenly turned around. He didn't want to go to the PX Snack Bar after all. He didn't know where he wanted to go. He raised his eyes. Smoke obscured the distance, and he smelled the autumnal odor of burning leaves, here as piercingly nostalgic as it had ever been at home.

Ahead was the Palace. He had passed it four times already that afternoon. Nearer were the taller buildings, now dark except for electric signs. A bus with "Galveston" on its side passed him, brilliantly lighted inside but empty, the back of the driver a light brown in the reflected light.

By the bridge an old man, standing behind a small table on which burned a single lantern, called to him. Michael stopped, and the old man reached for his hand. He shook his head, not wanting to have his palm read, though he knew he could have understood the old man's simple prophecies well enough. He'd often seen soldiers, though, who understood not a word of Japanese stand with palms outstretched while this old man, or others like him, traced his finger on the lines of the hand. Neither understood the other, but both were convinced, as though by magic.

As Michael passed the round theater, the marquee lights suddenly switched on, and the audience poured out. It was entirely female, and that meant that one of the all-girl shows—Takarazuka or perhaps the Shochiku Review—was just over. He was surrounded by women—baby girls in furs and schoolgirls in sailor suits, others slightly older in Western clothes or kimonos, married women with children, old ladies (now old enough to wear the bright reds and greens of their childhood) with bent backs and receding lips. Two girls, arm in arm, looked at him over their shoulders, and an old lady, her hair cut short in a shingle, smiled up at him as she pushed through the crowd, forcing her way with a knotted cane.

Under the railway bridge were girls, but these had not been to the theater. They wore short skirts and tight sweaters. Scarves were over their hair, and their lips were brightly painted. Overhead a train pulled noisily into Yuraku-cho Station. The girls stared at him, and one, wearing a garrison cap, whistled. Another, her hair frizzed away from her head in the current style, flashed a gold tooth and walked beside him, rubbing his leg with her hip. "Wan dollah," she whispered.

Money—that was all anyone wanted. Why else should this poor girl with her frizzed hair walk so industriously by his side, and why should he be carrying this large, brown-paper package around with him? He walked a bit faster, and the girl dropped behind.

The money was heavy in one hand, Haruko's carefully folded rice-paper note was wet in the other. If he opened one, then he should open the other. As yet he had never opened any of the packages entrusted to him, though he knew what each had contained. He'd always felt that if he didn't see the contents of the package, he would not be so guilty. There was a sheltering anonymity in delivering a package when he didn't know what—or at least how much—it contained. He was not really responsible for the crime so long as he didn't look. This distinction was important to him.

When he was very young he'd thought the same way. He used to steal from the large department stores or the chain groceries, but would never have tolerated any theft from an individual or even a privately-owned business. But the Army was a bit like Kroger's or Macy's: it could stand the loss. In any event, it never occurred to him that the crime itself was wrong, though he readily admitted that the context of the crime could be wrong.

He was also afraid of what he might find in Haruko's note. If the note said she would be at *Madame Butterfly*, then, despite the promise of early morning, she was lost to him, for that would mean she would officially meet her future husband. On the other hand, it might say she was not going, that she was keeping her promise. Michael really didn't know which eventuality he most dreaded. His enthusiasm of the morning had, during the day, grown considerably less now that the day of his marriage was so near, and, beyond that, he had finally begun to realize the consequences of his desires. Over and over again he kept picturing the meeting of Haruko and his parents. It would be terrible beyond belief.

This slackening of enthusiasm for the marriage—after

it had been what he had thought of and hoped for so long—troubled Michael, for he realized it was not so much that he had changed his mind as that he had never known his mind at all until now. He still believed he loved Haruko, but he no longer believed he wanted to marry her.

This indecision concerning both his crimes and his love was connected: both were forbidden, both were, in separate ways, punishable. For him, honesty, integrity, and truth had only relative meanings. And so, half-disbelieving the absolutes by which he'd been raised, he had not yet discovered others for himself. It was, however, only at times of indecision, such as this, that he felt the need of them.

Near the Sanshin Building, leaning against the Provost Marshal's window, were two soldiers. One of them carried two smudged and melted Hershey bars in one hand, and in the other he held a grimy package marked with PX tape. From time to time one whistled, and occasionally the other would howl. Neither, however, had much spirit; their faces were dirty, and around their mouths and eyes were lines of fatigue. Michael thought they looked familiar but couldn't remember where he'd seen them. Anyway, all soldiers on the make looked alike.

Further on, Greer Garson, her eyes made Japanese, the bridge of her nose painted entirely away, smiled, her paper face visible and invisible with the blinking of the neon signs around her.

He crossed the street and there was the moat and, beyond it, the medieval guard towers, dimly outlined against the sky, their white walls almost visible, the pine trees around them shining faintly in the lights from passing cars. In the distance the Diet Building was illuminated like a miniature and misshapen Fuji, and in the other direction the TWA sign of the Taisho Building blinked on and off, on and off. Michael stopped by a willow which, from time to time, caught the light of passing headlights in its remaining leaves. He stood by the moat and saw beneath him the dim shapes of great carp.

The package pulled at Michael's arm, and he rested against the tree, his eyes turned toward the darkened Palace. The passing cars, the flickering movie marquees, and the neon signs illuminated his back. He felt the damp paper in his other hand and, with no further hesitation, took it from his pocket and with his finger opened the seal—a bit of red paper, carefully cut out and pasted on.

The odor of the rice paper mingled with a perfume that was Haruko's own. It was the smell of pomade. For this reason, as well as others, the message was particularly painful:

Dear Mike-san:

O, horrid dillema of Japanese girl. O, immortal confrict of will and idea. Can I choice wise between my true Japanese way and new American way? Yes, I can wisely choice. I have painful very much but now am make up mind. I no can married American soldier (you). I marry Ohara Ichiro (student only). Please forgive me, dear Mike-san, when I say you this morning I marry. I say because I make you go so. I am so sorry. But maybe sometime you come see Haruko (soon any day Madame Ohara) because you good friend. It is horrid dillema for Japanese girl but my choose is good, I think. Please never forget you Haruko, horrid Japanese girl. I you no forget—never.

I kiss once more (for time number three in my life— and all in same day) in adieu. Please take care of your healthy. I sorry.

With sincere most cordial regards I remain yours,
Haruko.

Michael looked at the careful letters, drawn with a brush, not her usual fountain pen; looked at the jaunty red seal, so lovingly cut from paper; wondered how many times she'd recopied this note against the chance the MP's would not let her see him; and, for an instant, felt sorrier for Haruko than he had ever felt for anyone in his life. But the feeling quickly changed to an even more real sorrow for himself. He read the note over four or five times, and wanted Haruko as he had never wanted her before.

He closed his eyes and leaned his forehead against the rough bark of the willow. Now that he knew he was not to have her, all his former fears disappeared and he only somewhat vaguely realized that he was not loved and, for all he could understand, never had been. Only this morning this thought would have been impossible : he was as sure of being loved as he was certain of being fed. Love now revealed itself as being relative, too, like truth and honesty. It too could be interpreted and questioned, and as he realized this, Michael felt disillusioned and quite bitter. He had been struck in the only portion of his moral anatomy that he had neglected to defend.

He opened his eyes, his head against the willow. There, impossible to reach, was the land he had loved, the medieval Palace guarded by giant carp. There, across the moat, was his life as it should have been. Behind him blinked the distractions of life, the brilliant, transient colors, the frenetic energy wasted in a single flickering bulb, the nervous impulse of wavering neon—life as it actually was, confused, aimless, artificial.

In this land of shaking earth, of the downfall of the most splendid hopes of heroes, where the ravages of time were not measured by ruined buildings but by hearts eaten away while yet alive, he knew that nothing further could surprise him by its hopeless incongruity—in this unexpected country there was nothing further to surprise or alarm. And there he leaned against a willow tree, and nearby—he realized for the first time—sat an old and tired Japanese, carrying a sandwich board and made up as Charlie Chaplin, looking at the timeless Palace, the ageless carp.

There, across the moat, was the land he knew. It was a land beautiful in rain and fog—the only country on earth that was—yet even more beautiful when the smallest pebble was seen with a photographic clarity, a clarity that Michael's American background had never attained in his eyes. There was an abruptness of contour, a sharpness of line which was as invigorating as sea air. Against a brilliant blue sky, cloudless and enameled, Fuji stood, the single most preposterous object in this impossible landscape.

No, nothing was really incongruous in Japan. Temple boys in full costume on motor-scooters and neon signs by the Kamakura Buddha were not somehow incompatible with Fuji at sunset. The face of Greer Garson here might be that of the great Daibutsu itself. There was a cohesiveness here, a wholeness which might have been satisfying for someone other than Michael; it did not allow one to pick and choose, to like this or that. One must accept it all, for it was all necessarily both part and whole at the same time.

But this freedom from choice, this simple security fostered by the logic of inevitability, which had once so invigorated Michael, now merely depressed him. He wondered if this weren't perhaps the way the Japanese felt about their own country. Then his new depression created by his former enthusiasm, this new state of mind which so saddened him, was perhaps the perpetual outlook of, say, Haruko. Her choice meant that she was merely bowing to an inevitability which came from living in Japan. Would she have married him in Persia, in Iceland, in America?

This he would never know, just as he would never know if, indeed, he had been truly loved, as he thought himself to have loved. The thought that this knowledge was never to be his was so painful that again he bruised his forehead against the bark of the willow tree. The package was still pulling painfully at his arm. It, or at least that part of him that allowed him to carry it around, was, he decided, somehow responsible for his disillusion, his despair.

With a sudden and real disgust, and with no thought at all, he threw the package into the moat. It caused a big splash, and the shadowy carp disappeared in a flurry of suddenly white water.

The impulsiveness of his action did not relieve him so much as it horrified him. Just as, years before, he had, just as impulsively, taken a package of cookies he hadn't wanted from an A & P, he had now thrown the Major's package into the moat. He had secretly returned the cookies after almost an hour of gnawing conscience, but now his conscience, which felt relieved, was not what bothered him. Now he'd have to face the Major.

Bubbles were rising to the surface. He watched them and decided he had just made a kind of votive offering—to the Emperor, say. He had propitiated Japan, for which, as soon as it had revealed itself in its true incomprehensibility, he had begun to feel less fondness.

He had seen Occupation ladies who, thinking that the potted trees and the little houses and the charmingly well-mannered people were just darling, had been suddenly revolted by the knowledge that almost everything that grew in Japan was nurtured on untreated human excrement, that the little house was a prison for those who lived in it, and that these well-mannered people had smothered the soldiers of other nations by pressing their faces into liquid manure. Formerly he had laughed at the revolted qualms of the ladies. Now he knew just how they felt. Michael was thoroughly disillusioned with Haruko and Japan. It never occurred to him that Haruko might have been even more painfully disillusioned with him and with America had she lacked the foresight to refuse their marriage.

Bubbles no longer rose from the water; the splash had not only startled the carp but also Charlie Chaplin on the other side of the tree. Now, Michael looked at him more closely. He was very old. By the light of a passing car Michael saw his derby, little painted moustache, much-too-large shoes, and bamboo cane; saw he had a sandwich board over his shoulders, against which he now leaned. It advertised something or other —Michael could not read what. The man's eyes were closed and he sat relaxed, too tired to move. He was a good imitation, not of the funny Charlie, but of the real one, the one who faced life hopelessly but who must soon start down the road, twirling the cane, tripping over the ends of his shoes. The car moved on, and the man became a faint shadow in the dark.

Nearby the marquee lights of the Imperial Theatre went on. It was eight o'clock; the doors would soon open. Michael crossed the street intending not to see the opera but merely to see Haruko. How he would transfix her with his injured gaze! How she would tremble before the conqueror's boots, before the suddenly entrancing spectacle of what she could have had and, with a wantonness only too typically Japanese, had tossed aside. Michael didn't go so far as to consider himself a male and modern Chocho-san, but he did consider it quite apt that she would see him just before seeing *Madame Butterfly*.

Standing before the empty and lighted lobby, he saw a student coming toward him, accompanied by an older man. The man was very formally dressed. His dark kimono was nicely cut and closely fitted. His obi was beautifully tied. His feet were in tabi and low-toothed geta which clacked softly on the pavement. In one hand he held a paper fan with several large inked characters on it; in the other, a cigarette was burning in a lacquered holder. The total effect was enhanced by a derby. The only other thing Western about the gentleman was a wrist watch, but this was hidden most of the time by his graceful sleeves.

The boy was wearing the usual student's uniform. Something about the uncomfortable way he wore his uniform seemed familiar to Michael. Just then their eyes met—Michael's vaguely curious and the student's intensely hostile.

Instantly Michael remembered where he'd first seen those eyes—it was on the train this morning. And then later, in the office, they'd glared at him the second time. That's who they were—the Ohara father and son. And in a flash Michael realized—was it by instinct, or had he heard the name before from Haruko?—who the boy was. This was his successful rival, on his way to the formal meeting; this was the member of the defeated who had won the only thing this particular conqueror had coveted.

Michael's rapidly dissolving appreciation for Japan disintegrated even further under the cool disdain he discovered in Ichiro's eyes.

■

The expression of distaste which Michael saw on Ichiro's face was not directed in particular at Michael; for several hours Ichiro had been looking at everything with the same expression. Actually, he was so acutely aware that the man mincing in geta beside him was his father that he didn't even consciously recognize Michael.

Mr. Ohara, however, had immediately recognized Michael, and he cast a quick glance at Ichiro. The servant had not been slow in informing every member of the Ohara family just how things stood with Haruko, and Mr. Ohara had taken a good look at the soldier when he visited Special Services this morning. Now, when he saw that his son was oblivious to his rival, a small and secret smile appeared. He looked carefully at his son's impassive face, wondering just how much more discomfort and humiliation it might be wise to heap upon him. After all, if Haruko was going to marry the American, his poor son might lose all self-control and commit all sorts of impossible acts—say, refuse to return home.

Already he had Ichiro bursting with discomfort. This, added to the ever-present knowledge that he was facing the further shame of being publicly defeated by the American soldier, had made his face a bright red, just as though he had been drinking—another of the many pleasures in which Ichiro did not indulge. The father was fully conscious of the part he had played in bringing things to the present heat, and the thought brought a reflective smile to his lips.

He particularly relished the consternation he had created in his household by appearing, for the first time most of the family could remember, in full, formal Japanese dress. The maid had been so disturbed, and so intrigued, that she had been most reluctant to leave the spectacle and, with a look of profound awe on her face, had almost walked through the closed fusuma. His wife, a most emancipated Japanese woman who painted nudes in primary colors and had bobbed her hair, was utterly confused: should she revert to her earlier ways and bow to the tatami, or disregard this alarming change of dress altogether and merely nod as she usually did when he came into the room? She had compromised, somewhat unsuccessfully, with a most singular kind of bobbing crouch—something between a curtsy and a genuflection.

But without doubt it had been Ichiro's reaction to

the innovation which had most gratified Mr. Ohara. Although quite upset by the state of his affairs with Haruko, he had been pretending to study in his room. Around him were all the emblems of his beliefs. A scabbard hung over his desk—empty now that the Americans had forbidden Japanese to possess swords— and before him were some volumes of the more austere Chinese and Japanese poets. In the tokonoma hung a kakemono, nervous with a swift, dry-brush scrawl of calligraphy; Mr. Ohara understood this to be a Chinese aphorism on the ephemeralness of all thing—even if he could have deciphered the characters, he would have thought it much too unprogressive of him to try to do so. On the floor of the tokonoma was a single chrysanthemum, already dying.

Ichiro's room was more than a different room in the house—it was a different era—and formerly Mr. Ohara had felt a bit uncomfortable whenever he had to enter it. Now, however, he felt completely at home; it was Ichiro in his Austrian-style student's uniform who was incongruous, not he. It was with a new feeling of confidence that he had suddenly strode into the room.

Ichiro, deep in a very sad and most consoling Chinese poem, had avoided looking up at the sound of his father's footsteps. They had not spoken since morning.

"Good evening," said his father.

Ichiro carefully composed his face into what he believed a masterly combination of humility, pride, scorn, and condescension and finally raised his eyes. Suddenly his expression—to Mr. Ohara it had looked more like the beginning of a sneeze—fell away, leaving behind it nothing but a wide-eyed and alarmed schoolboy.

Ichiro's initial surprise soon changed into an almost visible horror when he realized his own position, for it was he, the son, who had forced his father into this.

"Good evening," he said finally.

Bowing very low—just as low as Ichiro had that morning—Mr. Ohara left the room with light step and triumphant grimace.

Since then they had not exchanged another word. Mr. Ohara was too amused to trust himself to speak, and Ichiro was too humiliated. Of all the many things of which he believed his father capable, this transformation was not one of them.

Now, in front of the lighted and gradually filling lobby, Ichiro swallowed and turned to his father, breaking their two-hour silence: "This is perhaps the first time one has had the honor of seeing one's father in Japanese dress."

His father nodded.

"May one ask why?"

"One may."

"Why?"

"Perhaps because my son not unwisely called my attention to the fact that I have almost never done so."

This, Ichiro realized, was doubtless a compliment, but, hidden inside, was the sharp edge of irony which, if he were to receive the compliment, he must disregard. He finally digested it. "Then, it is for myself that my father does this?"

"It is, indeed. It is because I am sorry both for my un-Japanese and undemocratic outburst of this morning."

"Oh, no, that is my responsibility," said Ichiro, seeing an opportunity of which he must not fail to take advantage. "It was my outburst and through me that it was occasioned. It was my fault."

"Not at all," said Mr. Ohara sharply. "I proclaim it to have been my own." Ichiro, he decided, was cleverer than he'd thought—there was something about his line of reasoning that was commendably like that of an American businessman.

"I must differ—" began Ichiro, seeing that his father was now aware of what he was attempting. If he could shoulder the blame, then his father would have none for himself, would look like a fool in his Japanese clothing, would find himself in utter disgrace, rather than, as it was now, the other way around.

"No, no, no!" shouted his father. "I said I was sorry, and I am. No one is sorrier than I whose complete responsibility it is. You are quite innocent, wronged, betrayed. It is I who am the more sorry."

"I cannot allow that the truth be so withheld through your own self-sacrifice," said Ichiro. "Historically, it is I who am at fault. Morally, it is I. Ethically, it is I. You must not try to shield me." Ichiro was now raising his voice also.

"History, morals, ethics!" screamed Mr. Ohara. "They have nothing to do with Japan. You are too Western-minded. It is my fault, and I am sorry!" He ended on a great shout.

Those standing nearby turned and looked, but Ichiro was too preoccupied to be self-conscious. The novelty of the charge of being Western-minded had quite stunned him, but he had the presence of mind to reach for the lobby door and insist upon his father's entering first. Then, however, his father raced ahead to the inner door and grabbed it open, thus making Ichiro enter first.

Together they ran on backstage, arguing all the time and bruising their hands on the doorhandles. There, surrounded by relatives, friends, and the entire cast of *Madame Butterfly*, they not only settled no differences, but went on to new heights of humbleness and self-abnegation.

■

Colonel Ashcroft, standing by one of the gilded pillars in the lobby, saw both the Oharas race through. He also saw Major Calloway sitting on a red-plush divan. The lobby was becoming crowded, and the

Colonel stepped a bit behind the pillar from where he could watch the Major without being noticed. The Major, however, had been watching the Colonel from the corner of his eye for some time. Each was very much aware of the other's presence.

Then the Colonel noticed that the Major was not alone. On one side of him was a very pretty though no longer young American woman and, on the other, was Mrs. Schmidt. They were talking, but from where he stood the Colonel could not hear their conversation.

"I feel I owe you a very great deal, Major," said Mrs. Schmidt.

"Pleased to be of service, ma'am," said the Major.

"But Colonel Ashcroft, who was so pleasant this morning—he's your superior I understand—shouldn't I say something to him. I'm sure he's around here some place."

"Oh, no, ma'am, that won't be necessary at all. Just paper work—that's all that's involved. No need to trouble him."

"Besides," said Dottie, "he's leaving soon. Isn't that so, Cal?"

"Yes, come to think of it, I've heard something of the kind."

"Well, really, Cal! You told me yourself. Aren't you sure?"

"Sure, Dorothy, he's leaving. That's right." As he spoke he stole another glance at the Colonel, standing slightly behind a pillar. He wished he'd go away, or at least stop standing where he could see him.

The Major was dimly aware he had done the Colonel a great wrong, but no sooner did the first nibble of conscience occur than he very successfully drove it away. In the atmosphere of freedom and security which was the Occupation, he reasoned, it was the patriotic duty of all good Americans to report an infidelity, to repeat a suspicious remark, to insure the disgrace and downfall of those unpatriotic enough to have un-American thoughts. And it was these men—men like himself, men bold in their praise of democracy, sure of its need of protection and doubtful of its ability to continue without their aid—who were in very truth the backbone of America. At least, so the Major thought.

"Oh, I'm sorry to hear that," said Mrs. Schmidt. "Is it soon? Only this morning he asked me to call on his wife and said any time would be all right. Didn't he know this morning?"

The Major looked away. It had just occurred to him that if you always found it necessary to run to the aid of democracy, then you weren't too convinced that it was particularly strong, or that it even existed. But abstract thought was difficult for the Major at the best of times, and now this was, after all, a separate issue, quite to one side. In this world it was not the side issues and moral quibblings that counted. It was results that counted.

And on top of all this, though the Colonel had lots of high-flown things to say about totalitarian governments, he'd been overheard saying he hated no individual Russians because of this. The confession had truly shocked the Major, who, on the contrary, hated all Russians simply because they existed, and who would have been tempted to refuse an invitation, had he ever received one, to any of the many parties given by the Soviet Mission in Tokyo, despite the rumored abundance of caviar and vodka.

All of which merely proved what the Major had long contended—that the Colonel was a suspicious character, if only because he refused to adapt himself to the times. As proof of how old-fashioned the Colonel really was, the Major need only recall the Colonel's quaint theory that wars were fought for possession, gaining, or protecting, scarcely ever for ideas. This opinion, though logical enough, was not only un-American but unmodern.

And so, when all these personal opinions, so unique and eccentric in the Occupation, were laid end to end, they stretched directly to the next ship leaving Japan and a disgraceful exile in America for the unfortunate Colonel.

Dorothy and Mrs. Schmidt were excitedly talking about the coming recital, and the latter was trying to decide whether to include portions of the *Schwanengesang* or the *Winterreise*, while the former was saying that the only thing which could conceivably interest their audience would be "The Beer Barrel Polka."

Continuing his reflections, the Major complimented himself upon having done a workmanlike job of weaving these opinions of the Colonel's into a pattern which anyone could understand. And from the conjunction of every two opinions in the pattern he almost invariably was able to produce yet a third. These contributions to the eventual fate of Colonel Ashcroft he called deductions. He hadn't been ungenerous in his offerings, and, before half his evidence had been placed before the proper authorities, they had become suspicious— and just the suspicions of these good men were quite enough. They were so advanced in their profession of guardians of liberty that they had quickly done away with the necessity of proof, a qualification that so often clouds the minds of smaller men.

This method, to be sure, lacked the finality that a less efficient procedure—such as the careful evaluation of any real evidence of the Colonel's guilt—might have produced, but to make up for this trifling loss, the turnover in officers might be expected to become reassuringly large and, after all, was not the real consideration the quantity rather than the quality of sin which they uprooted in this world?

The Major suddenly noticed that the two women were no longer talking about what songs to sing. They were whispering. He looked at them curiously.

Catching his glance, Mrs. Schmidt pulled her shawl tighter around her and said: "Major, you've been so very kind to me, promising to arrange for the recital. You have no idea how much it will mean to me. But I feel I must tell you something about myself—I feel you have the right to know." She stopped, and a small, hurt smile appeard.

The Major, having agreed in order to please Dorothy, began to dislike Mrs. Schmidt. He wished she'd stop looking at him as though he were going to strike her.

"You're a man of the world I know, Major—a practical man," she began.

The Colonel at any rate, thought the Major, was not a practical man. Major Calloway had never seen Ashcroft so mad as the day someone repeated to him what a noted admiral had said during the war: that if he ever saw a pregnant Jap woman, he'd kick her in the belly. The Colonel had turned white with rage, though he must have heard about it before. It just wasn't practical to act like that, not when the other person was an admiral and you were just a colonel or a major. The Colonel obviously didn't adapt well, and thus it was only right that a younger officer with more progressive, practical ideas should fill his place.

Mrs. Schmidt, seeing that the Major seemed to be paying no attention, had stopped, but his sudden glance started her again: "I mean that I—that is, my husband—was a member of the National Socialist Party in Germany."

"What?"

"I mean—I mean he was a Nazi."

"Oh, that. I already know that. Look, Mrs. Schmidt, that was almost five years ago. Don't let that trouble you. If he was a Nazi, then that means he hated the Commies, don't it?"

The Major was indeed a practical man. And he would have found further proof of the Colonel's impracticality if he could have read the Colonel's thoughts now as he watched the three from behind the pillar.

The Colonel was thinking about things which had nothing to do with his own misfortunes, had not the slightest bearing on his own particular plight. He was thinking of the youth of America—those young soldiers like that soft-spoken boy in his office. He watched them with sympathy. He saw their vacillation, their apparent poverty of absolute ideals. He saw they lived in a world sometimes meaningless and alway governed by comparative standards which, like the sands of time, shifted constantly. He found this both pathetic and destructive.

But—the Major would have continued—the Colonel was learning, for even he was not slow to realize that, given a somewhat limited choice of weapons, he was free at least to use those which had been used against him. Here again, however, there arose a childish compunction, for he hesitated to use the invaluable denouncement, that follow-up of suspicions.

Of course, the Major didn't know that the Colonel had long been clearly aware of the most vulnerable spot in the Major's defenses. He didn't know that the Colonel had noticed irregularities in payment for Japanese entertainment and had quickly—and correctly —deduced what was happening.

And still the Colonel, hovering behind his pillar, wrestled with his stubborn conscience. He realized perfectly that the means for revenge were at hand. Indeed, that marvelous instrument the telephone seemed to have been perfected for this very use. Cloaked behind the anonymity of the mouthpiece he might, with absolute safety, set into motion the machinery which would bring the Major down to the same low level.

But he was thinking of the young soldiers of his country and of his responsibility toward them. Despite their decided antipathy toward him—he knew they thought him a martinet—he might ruin all of the many examples he had attempted to illustrate if it ever became known that he had informed upon Major Calloway. Even if it were not discovered that he told, still something would have died.

Until now he had been meaning, daily, to tell the Major that he knew, to allow him to go before the proper authorities and confess what he had done. That was the only decent way to do it. But the days had become weeks, and he had done nothing: he disliked the unpleasantness that this scene would doubtless provoke. Now he wished he had—because now he could not.

Yet he still might, if he knew the Major were alone in it. But perhaps he had already involved someone else. One of these young, confused soldiers, one of these boys. Maybe even the Private in his own office. The Colonel felt he must make sure.

A tall young lady—his secretary, Gloria Wilson—had approached the three, and now Mrs. Schmidt was leaving, smiling and nodding. For a second the Colonel felt something very much like jealousy. Then he smiled and pulled his moustaches. No, there was no more room for jealousy.

He turned and saw a soldier some distance from him. It was Private Richardson.

■

The curtain was to rise at eight-thirty. "That means nine at the earliest," said Dave Ainsley as they walked down the aisle of the red and gilt auditorium, with its ornate proscenium arch at the far end.

"I know," said Mrs. Swenson. "Time is the most expendable quantity in Japan. I should know—we have a Japanese chauffeur." And her eyes twinkled while her smile prolaimed that, even though the Japanese were the Chosen Race, still she wasn't without knowledge of their little shortcomings. "They are so like children," she said fondly. "Can't you just imagine them sawing and hammering away in back of that curtain, right to the last minute, for all the world as though they were designing a Sunday-school benefit." She laughed merrily.

As they walked down the aisle they could indeed hear pounding and hammering. Occasionally there were muffled shouts and the curtain moved slightly. "Except that they take it all so seriously," said Mr. Swenson, mellowed by gin and anxious to show that he too could play the little game of locating the minor faults of the Japanese. "Just as they take seriously everything from carving those exquisite netsuke to heeding Nature's call. They are a nation which has forgotten how to play."

Dottie Ainsley had caught only a part of the sentence. "It's their toilet training, isn't it?" she asked the first four rows.

"Forgotten how to play," repeated Mr. Swenson, pleased with his observation.

"Because," continued Dottie, "I know that if I had to squat on my heels like that, I would be the most frustrated person alive. Maybe that's what's the matter with them—frustrated." She turned to her husband and used her tinkling-bell laugh. He smiled and patted her hand. "From just sitting there on their heels," said Dottie, pleased with her witticism.

Dave smiled again and guided her into a row, pushing her before him and asking pardon of those who stood.

"No, I must say that I do not subscribe to that theory," said Mrs. Swenson seriously. "Only the other day I had a letter—you remember, dear," she turned to her husband, "it was from 'Worried.' And 'Worried' said that toilet training had been overemphasized and that the Japanese ability to relieve Nature was very much akin to their ability to sleep just anywhere anytime. Now, 'Worried' said that, if anything, their toilet training relaxed them and so couldn't be held responsible for the inner tension they all seem to feel." She shook her head, half-judiciously, half-admiringly.

"Well," said Dottie hotly, "they sure crap just about any place you can name, and I know—"

"By the way, honey," interrupted her husband, "how's your inner tension?"

She sighed and patted her round stomach. "It still hurts a little."

He smiled down at her, saying: "You poor kid."

She put on her brave little smile. "Oh, it's nothing really. It sort of itches, you know, but it's not going to kill me."

A great wave of emotion swept over Dave, and he turned to Mrs. Swenson. "There's one brave little girl," he said.

"Where?" said Mrs. Swenson brilliantly, casting her eyes over the audience.

In so doing she discovered some acquaintances several rows away and, aware they were watching her, became even more brilliant. Throwing both hands in the air, she turned upon Dave Ainsley, still blinking his eyes bravely at the thought of the brave little girl's suffering.

"You know Berle was taken ill just after the party?" she asked. Her lips were composed in a joyous smile for the benefit of those several rows away, while with her eyes she attempted to communicate to Dave the terrible sorrow the news had caused her. The effect was not entirely successful.

"Yes," Mrs. Swenson's metallic voice went on, "they took her away after the party. She said she didn't feel well and then clutched herself"—Mrs. Swenson's hands went violently toward her stomach—"and so a couple of soldiers rushed her over to the Dispensary. Something female I think."

Dave was nodding diligently. He was being brilliant too. He had just seen his boss in the audience.

"Penny for your thoughts," said Major Calloway, his hand creeping forward under the outspread program.

"I'm thinking someone is going to lose a hand," said Gloria.

The fingers stopped for an instant, then retreated back to the Major's lap. "You sure know how to treat wolves like me," he said and laughed.

"You're a sheep in wolf's clothing, Major, and it doesn't become you."

He laughed timidly and then studied his program, hurt. "Feel better?" he asked softly.

"Yes," said Gloria, "it must have been something I drank."

"I should guess so. You sounded like one of our old cows taking a bath."

"Lovely simile," said Gloria.

"No offense."

"Naturally not. I just hope the old cow takes it as kindly."

"But you sure sounded sick."

"I was," shouted Gloria. "Now will you stop dwelling upon that unlovely fact?"

The Major went back to his program.

Gloria sighed. She ought to say something to him. He'd spent a lot of money on her. Perhaps she could let *her* hand creep softly over *his* thighs. The idea was so instantly repulsive that she put both hands safely out of harm's way on the other side of her.

Now that her mind was off her stomach she realized that she was bored—bored silly. The Child Cowboy at one side of her, and the Ainsleys and the Swensons—arbiters of the Occupation—in front of her. Now, who would be in back of her? The Emperor? Most likely. She turned around and then quickly turned back again. It was Private Richardson.

Well, that was just dandy. He'd doubtless had a perfect view of the Major's manual dexterity. But it actually couldn't make less difference now, because Gloria was a changed girl. She was going straight. That was what she'd thought about while vomiting up a lot of the Major's money. She quite obviously could not have her cake and eat it too, so she'd just put herself on a slimming diet, and the sight of the boyish beauty of Private Richardson, while tantalizing, was not enough to make her break her iron-clad resolve. Besides, she still had a trick or two up her sleeve. The Army wasn't the only pebble on the beach.

In front of her the Ainsleys and Swensons were talking about the Japanese. Did they ever talk of anything else she wondered. She had heard this kind of talk before. It was the same when a woman of dubious reputation moved into a respectable neighborhood back in Muncie. There was never talk of anything except her latest comings and goings, her reasons for this and that, mock admiration and scandalized surprise. But the Ainsleys and Swensons were more intelligent than that. They never talked about a person; they merely gossiped about a nation.

The Major was growing restless again. His hands were on the move. To keep him amused Gloria suddenly cried: "Look!" She pointed at random among the people in the aisle. Her pointing finger found an entire Japanese family, both the parents in formal kimonos, a lovely girl in an elaborate obi, another man more beautifully dressed even than the girl, a student in uniform, and a man in a business suit who fussily led the way.

"Well, what about it?" said the Major. "I seen gooks before."

"Oh, but these are formal gooks," said Gloria.

"Well, what about them?" asked the Major, becoming aggressive. "And who the hell let them in here anyway?"

Just as Gloria was about to admit a loss of words,

the more beautifully dressed of the men saw them and bowed, his gray hair bright in the overhead lights. "Why, it's Mr. Ohara," said Gloria quite surprised.

"So it is," said the Major, waving heartily- "Only you say O'Hara, like in Scarlett, you know. No sense mispronouncing it. Hell, you got sharp eyes. I wouldn't have recognized him in all that get-up."

"Neither would I," said Gloria.

"What do you suppose he went and did that for? He seemed like a regular guy to me."

"Went and did what?"

"Get himself up all in Jap like that. I don't think that's very friendly. Sort of rubbing our noses in it, don't you think, Miss Wilson?"

"Rubbing our noses?"

"Yeah, I mean he comes in with a suit just like everybody else when he comes to see us. Shoes and all. Civilized, you know. And now, at a formal shindig like this he runs home and puts on a costume. I don't know what that's called in your books, Miss Wilson, but—"

"Sort of like Pearl Harbor, huh?"

The Major took this for joking agreement and began reading his program again. Since his proposal, neither had looked the other squarely in the eye. He wasn't sure that she remembered his asking her, and she wasn't at all certain he had any recollection of asking. Gloria was the more uncomfortable. She realized that the Major's proposal demanded some kind of answer. Her answer was no; yet she didn't want to commit herself to it. Here she was sitting with a major who had asked to marry her. She glanced defiantly around the theater. Let them talk, she told herself; for the time being, at any rate, I'm respectable.

"No, not like Pearl Harbor," said the Major after a time, having decided it wasn't a joke after all. "But you know what I mean. Here we are, trying to give these folks a decent way of life and all. Teach them to wear proper clothes and act like white people. Then a man like O'Hara does something like this. I don't know. It sort of hurts, after you've worried about them and cared for them. It seems like they just don't understand the way we do things in the States. And if they do, they're just bound and determined they're going to be different."

"You mustn't be too hard on them, Major."

"You're just too kindhearted, Miss Wilson, that's what you are. Like with that sedan driver today. It's not good, you know. You got to teach these people to respect you, and the only thing they respect is force. You got to show them you're stronger than they are. That way you'll impress them and they'll mind better. I don't approve of this moddle-cuddling—"

"Muddle-cuddling is the word, I believe. Or is it molly-cuddling? Mully-coddling?"

"—that's going on over here," continued the Major, unperturbed. "I think we ought to be firm. Now, if you was to fraternize too much—"

"Not me, Major. Not under this Occupation. Not yet at any rate. It's still illegal to fraternize too much, you know, but there is handwriting on the wall."

"I don't know about no handwriting. I only know what's best."

"And what's best, Major?"

"Why, just what I been talking about. We're examples. We got to go around acting like examples to these people. They're going to imitate us. They imitated everything else, and now they're imitating us. And you got to hand it to them—they're pretty good at it too, unless they sort of backslide like that O'Hara fellow did tonight."

Gloria thought of herself as the glorious example followed by countless schoolgirls in their middy blouses, and felt faint. And the Major, creating the Japanese in his own likeness—or, at least, unsuccessfully trying to!

"And that's why the Army over here has to be careful about its officers. We're the ones in the—what they call it?—in the focal point or something like that. We're the ones that get stared at. We have a mission here."

"Well, you're really waxing quite eloquent this evening, Major."

"Oh, I can explain myself when I got to," said the Major modestly. "So, like I was saying, the Army's got to sort of weed out those that don't fit in. Like the Colonel over there."

"Colonel Ashcroft? Where?"

"Down in front—where else?"

She saw him stroking his moustaches. He looked small, dry, and very tired. "What about him?"

"Well, he just don't fit no more. Old-fashioned. Old Virginia method—correction by example, you know. Tries to correct me. Me! All the time. His kind won't last long in this man's army."

"He's been in it for years though."

"That's just it. Years too long. Getting a little too soft for Uncle Sammie, if you catch what I mean."

"I must confess that its significance does somewhat escape me."

"Well, this is just rumor, mind you, but one has heard that a certain colonel in Special Services is going to get relieved and returned to the ZI pretty fast. Don't know why. Maybe too many caviar and vodka parties, if you get me. After all, it's a pretty cushy job and they— the big wheels—don't see why a major couldn't fill it just as well as a colonel. Hell, it even saves the taxpayers money. Just a bit of readjusting of the old TO. And funny thing, you know, but I sort of agree with them."

"Are you suggesting you might become my boss?" asked Gloria, aghast.

"That's just what I'm saying," said Major Calloway, patting her hand.

"Oh, god!"

The Major looked around them covertly. "But not a word, you understand, to nobody. This isn't a sure thing yet. They're just working on it."

"Does Colonel Ashcroft know?"

"Hasn't the foggiest," laughed the Major, imitating Gloria.

"This is handwriting all in capitals," said Gloria.

"Thought you'd see it my way," said the Major, and again his hand touched hers.

This time she didn't stop him.

■

The curtain rose on time. There was a handsome view of the harbor, an American destroyer floating in the bay. Chocho-san welcomed Pinkerton, who entered, in the American manner, with long steps, closely followed by a Sharpless wearing white gloves. The only thing the matter with the first act was that the moon got out of control and, as the lights darkened, bobbed suddenly over the horizon, dipped several times, and after that pursued a decidedly erratic course. Otherwise the production wasn't bad.

This annoyed Dottie. During the first intermission, when most of the audience was milling in the lobby, she turned to Gloria and, with no preamble, said: "Really, when are they going to stop?"

Gloria smiled and looked baffled.

"Did you see the moon?" continued Dottie. "Wasn't it hilarious?"

"The reflection machine worked well enough. Lovely reflections."

"Oh, you're so right. And no moon over them. Reflections and no moon!—it was simply killing."

"But the singing—did you like it?"

Dottie turned vaguely away, her eyebrows near her hairline, her face a perfect mask of despair.

"Well," said Major Calloway, "if I was this Pinkerton guy I'd do just what the program says he's gonna do in the second act. I'd up and leave her too. You can have her, I don't want her, she's too fat for me."

Now that he was going to be boss, Gloria didn't quite know what attitude to take toward him. Fortunately, the first act had interested him to the extent that he was content with merely clutching her hand. One thing was obvious: she could no longer walk all over him.

"Well, she *is* sort of chubby," she finally conceded.

"Chubby like a house," the Major sniggered.

"But the singing," said Gloria, "it was rather nice."

The Major's face went blank. "Oh, well, there you're way over my head, Miss Wilson. I don't know nothing about art; I just—"

"—know what I like," finished Gloria with a weary smile.

"Oh, look, dear," said Mrs. Swenson bustling up—she always made it a point to circulate. "Here's 'Just an Observer'—or was it 'Worried'?"

"Try 'The Old Philosopher,'" said Gloria kindly.

"Oh, come now," said Mrs. Swenson archly, "*I'm* 'The Old Philosopher.'" Instantly she put one hand over her mouth. "Oh, dear, I suppose I shouldn't have said that."

"We're among friends, Mrs. Swenson."

"I suppose that's true," said Mrs. Swenson doubtfully.

"Are you enjoying the opera, ma'am?" asked the Major, ducking and bowing.

Her husband held up one slender hand. "Please, not a word," he said. "My wife's nerves are quite bad enough as it is. The poor thing still has 'Un Bel Di' to undergo. Puccini is not, after all, her precise cup of tea, as they say. I suppose you might say that my wife has advanced tastes."

Mrs. Swenson turned an astonished glance toward her husband, then obediently raised her eyebrows and said:

"Puccini, hah!" giving a hard, humorless little laugh. It was a passing imitation of Dottie Ainsley.

"But the singing?" pursued Gloria.

Mrs. Swenson turned vaguely toward her husband. "Gorgeous decor," she murmured, while her husband was drawing himself up to full height.

"I'm afraid," he began, "that the Japanese vocal equipment is not quite up to, shall we say, the—ha, ha —bel canto standards. You all know, of course, of the incidence of the White Plague in this country."

"Yes, it's another word for the Occupation," said Gloria, and Mrs. Swenson giggled until her husband silenced her with an elbow.

"I was naturally referring to tuberculosis, and if you will allow me to conclude, I might point out that the pinched chests so conducive to that disease do not seem equally conducive to the glories of song. I presume, along with those who call themselves 'anthropologists,' that this chest condition is caused by the lamentable habit indulged in by Japanese mothers of carrying their offspring on their backs, as though the infants were veritable papooses—if, indeed, the word has a correct plural—which, incidentally, is equally responsible for the stature of this race commonly known as diminutive."

"But the singing?" Gloria began, then stopped. He hadn't even heard her. She turned to smile in sweet conspiracy upon the Major but saw, to her surprise, that he was all ears and attention. He was not listening to a garrulous and effeminate old man—he had, instead, the honor of being present during the obiter dicta of a representative of the *New York Tribune*.

"You don't say so, sir," said the Major, standing stiffly at attention.

Support from the Major, whom he did not know, so surprised Mr. Swenson that he was silent a moment, long enough for his wife to say: "Shrill, nasal voices."

But that was all she said, for her husband, beaming on the Major, at once began again.

"Indeed I do, sir. Perhaps you are not aware that the Japanese torso is in every way comparable to ours. Oh, I do not mean they have, say, the fully developed pectoral muscles so invariable to the type called Nordic, but in matters of length—or height, I suppose I should say—the Japanese are not to be despised."

"Your husband's quite an authority on *things* Japanese," said Gloria.

"Isn't he just?" answered Mrs. Swenson.

"Their diminutive stature, however, is caused by this habit of binding when young upon the mother's back. Hence it quite effectively warps the lower limbs and prevents a natural growth which, ordinarily, would rival that of a straight young sapling."

"Just like they torture and pervert those little trees in buckets, eh, sir?"

"Ah, yes, the bonsai. Well, though your terms are strong, your thought is logical. Yes ... yes, I would say so ... yes. And so the Japanese is both short and bow-legged." He paused, his handsome profile limp in the overhead light, and looked about for approval.

"What barbarism!" said the Major feelingly. Then, anxious to shine in the somewhat dulled eyes of the *Tribune* representative, he drew nearer and said: "Why, would you believe it, sir, today I saw an old beggar knocked down on the street. Just happened to glance from my office, you know, and, would you believe it, no one helped him at all—just stood around in a circle and gaped. Might have been dead for all I know. And even though he was just a dirty old beggar of the kind we don't even allow in Houston—Houston, that's where I hail from, sir, the fastest growing city in the world —still, you'd think a little Christian charity wouldn't be out of place. Why, if that had happened in my home town—that's Houston, sir—you wouldn't have been able to see the body for the folks clustered around trying to help. We're friendly people out our way, and so I was real disturbed—inner-like, you know—to see that nobody cared or helped the old person. Just stood and gaped at him!" The Major relapsed into an indignant and virtuous silence.

"Was that out Shin-jew-kew way?" shouted Mrs. Swenson.

"Yes, ma'am, it were."

"But, dear, we saw that! You remember, just after we found that the celadon was only jadeite from Woolworth's—had it stamped right on the bottom. Oh, I was so furious, you can imagine. But you remember that taxi accident, don't you, dear? Only it was a priest, not a beggar. A mendicant priest."

Mr. Swenson paid no attention to his wife. During the Major's recital he had begun to smile, and as it concluded he was almost laughing. Here was just the sort of conversation he liked best. "Well," he began, still chuckling, "despite the undoubted concern of our friends in Houston, there are still many reasons for actions like those you so pertinently observed today. For one thing—"

His wife interrupted him, saying: "Well, the people really have to let off steam, as they say. And you know, dear, perhaps that's just one of the ways of doing it— by *not* helping. You know, it's sort of like not contributing to the Red Cross or something. Makes you feel all nice and evil on the inside." She giggled nervously.

Here was just the kind of interruption he liked least. And it invariably came from her. Whenever he had to handle two ideas at once he always became irritable, but this time he'd been doing so beautifully. The pleasing logic of the statement he had been about to make was now all muddied, and the charming, if elegiac, arabesque he had been about to draw before their very eyes would now seem a bit meaningless.

Exasperated, he said: "Well, naturally, my dear. That propensity which you seem bound to intrude into our discussion is time-honored. The war is a perfect example of what you apparently mean. In any civilization where the laws of behavior are so codified as they happen to be here, escape valves must be expected, indeed, encouraged. Why do you think shrine festivals with all those young men drunk and shouting and literally not caring what happens to them are so popular? You speak like a novice."

This was his most severe criticism, and his wife closed her mouth with a snap. He raised his eyebrows hopelessly, for all to see, and then, charming again and once more smiling, turned to the Major, ready again to explain the intricacies of the Japanese institution of non-interference in regard to fallen mendicant priests.

"Oh, yes," said the Major suddenly, the impact of an idea having unexpectedly struck him with full force, "like the Matsudaira murders a while back. The work of a real monster. And those women raped and the breasts cut off and all hacked up like that and all and left in the sun for a month or two. I saw a couple of the photographs—public relations, that's me." He laughed expansively; then, remembering that he was actually talking about the monstrous murders, he somewhat unsuccessfully did his best to shudder through his smiles.

Mr. Swenson always prided himself on being sane about his subject, the Japanese. He always said he neither bent too far backwards, nor forwards. Instead, he strove to teach through example. So, now, he was quite ready to forgive the rather maturely handsome major his unbelievable gaucheries. He formed his lips precisely, pursing them as he did so.

"Well, I for one should not consider the work of an admittedly pathological 'monster,' as you say, to be completely indicative of the state of any nation—whether in Tokyo or—oh, yes—in Houston."

The Major bobbed attentively, dimly aware that he was being reprimanded.

"No"—and Mr. Swenson laughed easily—"when I mentioned the need for safety valves I was merely thinking of great mass actions—the war, for example, or the many rebellions in Japanese history, or those lovely shrine festivals. That's all." He spoke sharply but smiled constantly, and the shaft struck home. The Major didn't say a word.

Contented, Mr. Swenson prepared to pick up that first part of the conversation which his wife had knocked flat. "And so, regarding the lower limbs of the Japanese—for that *is* what we were discussing—I must admit they do have one uncivilized attribute, and that is the binding of those thighs and calves, the result of which is, as you know, the single flaw in the beauty of the race."

"They sure got some cute numbers," said the Major, agreeably. "But they're not really barbaric like I said. I was sort of joking."

Mr. Swenson instantly warmed to the Major. "Oh, no, nothing like that." He laughed lightly. "Nothing like that—just short-sighted or what have you. But I must warn you that, much as I disapprove of the mind militant at work, I am contemplating a rash action and must at once admit to the intention of firing a small campaign—which you might with reason stigmatize as barbarous—the results of which would be the abolition of back-carried babies and back-carrying mothers. But, then, is it not equally barbarous to tamper with nature to the extent that strong calves, straight thighs—those adjuncts to perfect beauty—are completely absent from the race?"

"Yeah," said the Major, anxious to please. "And then they put on silk stockings. Wow!"

Mr. Swenson's smiling face froze. "Silk stockings? Silk stockings? Not at all. The Japanese is not an effeminate race. It never has been. What you so tastelessly refer to as 'silk stockings' might perhaps be the court garb of the Heian Era, or it might be any number of other articles of clothing—manly, virile, and quite above your slanders."

"Huh?" said the stunned Major, and Gloria decided it was time they moved away. Old Swenson was likely as not to make a fine scene before very long.

"Come, I'm thirsty," said Gloria, drawing the Major away by an oak leaf.

"Yes, yes," said Mrs. Swenson, bird-like, pecking at her husband's flannel sleeve, nodding busily. "Next intermission, next intermission."

"Never did find what anyone thought of the singing," said Gloria.

"What's the idea dragging me away like that?" said the Major. "That's Swenson of the *Tribune*—a good man to know."

"And that's just what you'll do—in the Biblical sense —if you're not careful."

"I don't follow you."

"You'd better not—I'm going to the powder room."

She left him standing by the big marble staircase. Near him was Private Richardson, smoking a cigarette. Whenever the Major and the Private met outside the office, which was rarely, they never talked, always pretending not to know each other. This suited both of them. Now, however, the Major turned and, with an extraordinarily conspiratorial air, spoke from one corner of his mouth.

"Got the package?" he said.

"Yes, sir," said Michael, after a pause.

The Major relaxed his mouth a bit and laughed. "Don't want anything to happen to that baby. Safe, eh?"

"Safe as the Emperor's carp, sir."

"Huh?"

"Yes, sir, real safe."

"Good work, boy. See you tomorrow." He turned rapidly and bolted in the direction of the drinking fountain.

Michael was rather pleased. Now that the package was gone, the less he saw of the Major the better. Except that now he wondered what the Major would do when he discovered the loss. He doubted if even the Major could have the moat drained. And one consoling thought was that you couldn't bust a buck private.

He looked up and saw the only officer he didn't dislike coming toward him. It was Colonel Ashcroft, looking sadder than ever.

"Good evening, Richardson," said the Colonel.

"Good evening, sir."

"Are you enjoying the opera?"

"Not particularly, sir."

"Well, that makes two of us." The Colonel continued standing before Michael, thought it soon became apparent that they had no more to say to each other than the good-mornings and good-nights they exchanged every day. The Colonel, however, obviously had something on his mind.

"I really wonder," he said, "why we ever sponsor a thing like this—not that it's a bad performance, but that it's opera."

"Well, it amuses the civilians, sir."

"Yes, that's true—I don't see many of your friends here."

That was one of the things Michael liked about the Colonel: he would never have used the word buddies. "No, sir, they're sure not here."

"To be frank, I'm a bit surprised to see you here, Private Richardson."

Michael colored slightly. "I came with someone else."

"A lovely young Japanese, if I interpret office gossip rightly."

Michael smiled in spite of himself. He suddenly hoped that nothing bad ever happened to the Colonel—that he would always be happy. "Yes, sir," he said.

"Well, that's nice," said the Colonel, pulling his moustaches. He was plainly preoccupied. "Speaking of office gossip, there is one thing I wanted to ask you."

Michael nodded and hoped it would not be concerning the rumor of the Colonel's own change of command. It would be unlikely he would ask a private, however, even under the Occupation. But he was still more disturbed when he heard what the Colonel was saying:

"Do you know anything about Major Calloway? I saw him talking with you just now."

Michael colored and said: "How do you mean, sir?"

"Oh, I mean irregular activities—black market and the like."

This chance of getting the Major was even better than dropping the package in the moat. At the same time he could both do the Colonel a favor and insure the Major's downfall. He was certain that, until the Major actually knew what had happened to the package, he wouldn't involve him, Private Richardson, preferring rather that Michael, as he hoped, would see the business through for him—that is, unless he got cornered. But, at the same time, Michael didn't want to inform on the Major. There were no real reasons not to, he realized, yet he still believed it wrong to tell on anyone.

"Oh, I don't quite know what you mean, sir," he finally said. "I'm sure it's just rumor—that's all. I've never seen anything."

The Colonel smiled, apparently pleased. "I thought as much. Just checking, you understand. That's the disgraceful job we all must do, I suppose.... Well, enjoy yourself ... Michael. Good evening."

He turned and walked through the lobby, content

in his belief that Michael knew nothing. The last obstacle was overcome. One must certainly check. He'd been right. One never knew when one of these confused young men might lend themselves to someone like the Major, not even realizing they were doing wrong.

But the Private—Michael—was made of finer stuff. The Colonel suddenly realized, with some emotion, that this soldier, to whom he had never before spoken a personal word, would be the only person in Japan whom he would miss. He passed Miss Wilson and nodded pleasantly.

Gloria smiled briefly at the Colonel and walked directly toward Michael. Before she reached him, he said: "Well, where're the furs?"

"Checked—and, Mike, let's just for a second not joke. I want to ask you something, and it's deadly serious. In fact, I'm deadly serious. Take a good look, for you won't often find me like this."

"Well, I've got the time—if you've got the place."

"Will you be serious! I'm with the Major, but I'll dodge him. Will you wait for me after it's over?"

"Well . . ."

"Oh, I know, you've got a dozen faithful Japanese maidens on the string—" Then she noticed his face. "I'm sorry Mike, but I'm all upset too. Wait, will you?"

The Major had found her and was tugging at her arm.

"Stop that," said Gloria. Then hopelessly shrugging her shoulders, she waved good-by to Michael. "Stop pulling me, I said!"

"We'll be late. Buzzer sounded," said the Major.

"I didn't know you were enjoying yourself so much."

"Love it."

"Oh, yes—'Jap Girl Gets Long-Due Come-Uppance' by Puccini," said Gloria.

The lobby was rapidly becoming empty. Near the corner phone stood the Colonel. He was waiting to use it. A woman had been ahead of him. He seemed undecided whether to phone or not. Just then the woman finished talking. She hung up and turned around. The Colonel saw it was one of the two women he'd seen talking with the Major, the smartly dressed one who was so well preserved.

The phone was free at last. The lobby was empty. The Colonel lifted the receiver and heard the answering buzz. Then he put it down. He could not make the call.

■

Haruko didn't see much of the second act. She was crying too hard. Poor Chocho-san sat before her paper windows and sang her heart out. One fine day he would return—and Kate would be with him, and Butterfly would have to kill herself. Chocho-san to be sure did not yet know all this herself, but Haruko already knew the work very well and was in agonies of anticipation. She was privately of the opinion that the play was of a much finer quality than the one about Macbeth which she had been forced to read in school: Butterfly made her cry much more.

It was so beautiful . . . so sad . . . so true. Between almost inaudible sniffles, Haruko raised her eyes to the stage, waiting for the next revealing comment by Suzuki, the next innocent but, oh, so telling phrase from Chocho-san. Then she would bury her nose in her hand-kerchief and silently sob. Comprehending the revealing comments and telling phrases, however, demanded a concentration which somewhat detracted from the flavor of her sorrows: all the arias were in Italian, while all the rest was in Japanese, except that Sharpless and Pink-erton sang in an approximation of English.

Her father and mother, apparently unmoved, sat on either side of her. Mr. Ohara kept glancing at her, smiling, indicating the stage, the orchestra, the singers, the brilliant audience—the new Japan. Next to him sat his son, his face red, his collar too tight, his back too straight. He didn't seem to be enjoying himself at all. No one paid any attention to Haruko's private sorrows, and that was the way it should be.

Through tear-filled eyes, with her handkerchief before her mouth, Haruko gazed at the stage. Suzuki shook her powdered head knowingly, and Butterfly flitted around touching the flowers. It was all that a real tragedy should be—so terrible it was lovely. Tears ran down over Haruko's quivering lips. She was enjoying herself enormously.

Then came the celebrated night scene. It was beautifully done, with Butterfly kneeling before the shoji, waiting for the faithless Pinkerton. The music sobbed softly, but no one came, and no one was going to come. Then, little by little, the sun rose, its light shining through the paper door. Fragile Chocho-san, exhausted from her long vigil, had fallen asleep kneeling. He had not come.

It was here that Haruko most clearly saw herself on the stage, waiting for she knew not what. Was it only the night before that her very own Pinkerton had come, scratching like a cat at her shoji? Yes, it was. And it might have been she who, like Butterfly, would kneel for a lifetime—waiting, waiting. This made her think of the lovely final scene with Butterfly, the Knife, Little Trouble, and the American Flag. She could no longer contain her anticipatory sobs.

Her father turned and looked at her once with a glance he might have given a misbehaving animal. Like the animal, Haruko became instantly quiet and closed her eyes tight. In so doing she missed the rather spectacular effect occasioned by the man in the flies controlling the sun; at that moment he kicked off a bucket of bolts, which fell heavily to the stage, narrowly missing the sleeping but vigilant Chocho-san.

Suzuki, with commendable presence of mind, calmly gathered up the spilled bolts, put them back into the bucket, and trotted off stage with them, just as though they always had their bolts delivered to the house that way. Butterfly alone appeared slightly shaken.

Most of the audience, however, were wet-eyed by this time, and there were only a few who laughed. Haruko didn't quite remember this being in the libretto, but she had to admit it made a fine effect and showed real imagination on the part of the producers. Having a bucket of bolts dropped on her was just one more welcome indignity for the poor, faithful Chocho-san. On this final, touching scene the curtain slowly descended to great applause.

Haruko quickly dried her eyes, and when Mr. Ohara waved his fan at her, she stood up and preceded him and his son toward the lobby.

"Are you enjoying this famous classic of song?" asked Mr. Ohara in English.

"Very like," she replied.

"And my son?" he asked conversationally in Japanese.

"Yes," said Ichiro. He was in a difficult position because, for the first time within memory, he was forced to approve of his father. He realized what an enormous sacrifice it must be for him to appear among the Americans in Japanese clothes, and yet he was forced to admit that his father was behaving beautifully. Even Haruko, for all her American infatuations, apparently felt no desire to sneer at the kimono, the obi, the geta.

"May one compliment Mr. Ohara's most elegant clothing?" asked Haruko.

"If one is Mr. Ohara's future daughter-in-law," said Mr. Ohara slyly.

Ichiro blushed. Things had not gone well for him today. First his father, then Haruko. Both were central supports in his life, and his father's absurd Americanism had been just as expected as had Haruko's devotion to Japanese method. The day had reversed everything— Haruko had betrayed him with an American and, worse, had shown a shocking and most Western indiscretion in talking openly of the fact to him that afternoon; his father had betrayed him also by making himself unobjectionable. Ichiro felt his world tottering.

But Mr. Ohara's implied question was still hanging in the air. For an answer Haruko turned and smiled at the confused and suspicious Ichiro. Suddenly her smile became a bit less bright: she had just caught sight of Michael moving through the crowded lobby. For a terrible moment she felt sure that her one fear was about to be realized, that Michael was going to come to them and make a scene. He was now so firmly identified with Pinkerton in her mind that she was convinced he was capable of anything, and with only a bit more persuasion she could have been convinced that it was he who had betrayed *her*. But when she saw he was not coming to them, her smile grew bright again.

Michael saw them smiling in a closed little circle, and for a second he thought of going over and wishing them happiness. But he fought resolutely against his better nature, and instead, he looked past them to where Gloria was talking with the Major, the Ainsleys, and the Swensons. Though he made as much fun of Gloria as everyone else did behind her back, it had always privately pleased him that she should be so constantly available to him. The potentiality had been such a pleasure that he had never before seriously considered taking advantage of this obliging quality of Miss Wilson's. Now that Haruko was gone for good, however, he thought he might lower his sights as well as his morals; if he could not love, he could at least enjoy. Besides, he doubted very much that love animated Miss Wilson's advances—she was just a good-time kid.

"Well," said Gloria, interrupting both Mr. Swenson and Mr. Ainsley, who had been talking to each other simultaneously, "you'll remember that famous captain who was so caught up in the night life—and the day life—of the Occupation that he never took time to see his five-year-old son. (His mother was in the States and wouldn't come over but had sent the kid.) One day he finally decided to spend an evening with him for a man-to-man talk—you know, 'not father and son, but buddies.' Well, the captain discovered that the poor child had spent so much time with the neighborhood children and the servants that he'd forgotten every word of English he'd ever known and could only speak Japanese."

The rest chuckled agreeably at this. "It *is* catching," remarked the Major. "Why, I heard that there was this officer who was walking down Ginza or someplace and this GI comes along and doesn't salute him. So just to shame him this officer salutes the private. And you know what the dope does, without thinking apparently —he bows to the officer!"

The others merely smiled at this, while the Major slapped his thigh. Then there was a silence.

"I wonder if Lady Briton will 'show,' as the dear woman puts it, presumably meaning show up," said Mr. Swenson. Then, seeing the baffled looks of the others, he added: "In other words, I mean, will she appear this evening?"

"Don't you remember?" said his wife. "She's having a little dinner tonight. Colonel and Mrs. Butternut, General and Mrs. Hughes, and Major General Custard. He's a fine catch, so she tells me, for he 'never goes anywhere,' though as a matter of fact I've met him on three separate and distinct occasions at three altogether different parties. It's what she called an 'intimate gathering.' Can you imagine her being intimate?—ugh, horrid thought." The Britons had never once invited the Swensons any place to anything, and Mrs. Swenson was not unmindful of the fact.

"Well," said Dave, his mouth already curling in a smile, "that gathering is probably quite intimate by this time, and I don't think Lady Briton is going to 'show' for quite a while."

"Well—that's a cryptic remark!" said Mrs. Swenson, intrigued.

"Then you didn't hear what happened?" asked Dave, quite certain she had not.

"No. Do tell!"

"You'll just die with laughter," said Dottie, unsmiling.

"What, what, what?" asked Mrs. Swenson.

"Well," said Dave, "it appears the Lady Briton went home after Berle's cocktail party and was preparing for her big soiree tonight. She really wanted to impress her guests, you know, particularly big-wigs like Custard."

Mrs. Swenson clucked her tongue appreciatively: the tone he was adopting exactly suited her.

"So," continued Dave, "Lady Briton was out in her garden cutting chrysanthemums around five or so, and—"

"How do you know all this?" asked Mrs. Swenson, anxious to learn his authorities in case her own version of the story was ever questioned.

"Mrs. General Hughes, her hand all bandaged up from the horse the other day, with added details courtesy of Mrs. Colonel Butternut, her thigh doubtless inflamed. The Briton's friends all get chawed up, it seems. We met them on our way here. Apparently they'd just come from the Dispensary."

"Oh, so amusing! Do go on."

"Well, so she was cutting flowers and making with the house beautiful, when all of a sudden she looked over the garden wall—they live way out in the country, you know—and what do you think she saw? You're right—a mistreated animal. It was one of those surly oxen, and it was pulling a honey cart."

"Oh, no!" said Mrs. Swenson in raptures, anticipating the end of the story, her eyes shining with delight.

"So Lady Briton rushed out to the side of the road. Apparently the night-soil man had finished for the day and had quite a load." Here Dave's voice went into a raucous falsetto somewhat reminiscent of Lady Briton's.

"He was simply unutterable. Worse, he had piled his cart so high that the poor dumb friend was simply killing itself trying to get up the jolly old hill. And there he was in his silly costume, pulling at the rope, using that vicious switch, and simply shouting, my dears, shouting at the top of his voice."

"Oh, really, stop. Stop!" said Mrs. Swenson, her breasts swaying slightly, helpless with laughter.

"Stop camping," muttered Dorothy, who had already heard the story twice.

But Dave had often been told that he told stories well, and there was now no stopping him. "Naturally, it just made her blood boil, but she retained possession of herself and kept that upper lip stiff as a board and marched straight toward him and asked him what he thought he was doing. Of course these people don't understand a *word* of English, and so eventually she had to call one of the maids, a pleasant though dull girl, who was to 'interpolate' for her."

"Oh, no—mercy!" cried Mrs. Swenson.

"Well, the man had the temerity to appear amazed. And all the time he kept right on beating the poor animal. So she, with a swift gesture of command, summoned all the kitchen help, and while she watched to make sure none disobeyed, they began unloading the wagon of all those heavy and doubtless dripping buckets."

"Oh, ugh! Ha-ha. Stop!" said Mrs. Swenson, shaking.

"So, when she thought a sufficient number had been removed," continued Dave in his natural voice, "she dismissed the young man. He was naturally stunned and just looked at her and backed away. And despite the fact that one usually backs from royalty's presence, it didn't this time impress la Briton, because the boy stared so. Mrs. General Hughes told me she said: 'So impolite these people. Where on earth did they ever get their reputation for common civility? Oh, they bow and scrape a great deal but it's different, don't you think?

The quality of the really well-bred simply does not exist here—not as it does among us Aussies, you know.' "

"Most interesting, that comment, began Mr. Swenson, "for the Japanese, in actuality, never—"

"But *that*," continued Dave, "was only after the finale had occurred. A couple of hours later, on the telephone. So, after this unfortunate overloading incident was happily over, she went back to the 'mums,' hurrying because dear Randolph would soon return bringing all the illustrious guests. Then she heard the car turn into the drive. You know—'Oh, that native driver of ours, he simply races all the time. What if he should hit a cat, or worse, a *dog*?' Well, he was racing again. Then, suddenly, she heard the brakes (so like the cries of some poor dumb thing) only the noise went on for so long and the tires continued screeching and sliding so, that she realized the car was skidding. Then it fetched up with a great thump beside the house and she and all the servants ran around to the front to see what had happened."

Mrs. Swenson was so taken with the story that she forgot to laugh. "Not really," she whispered.

"You can just imagine the sight that met her eyes. They were all poised in the open doors, throughly shaken, and Mrs. Butternut had her hat over her eyes, and Major-General Custard had buried his swagger stick in poor Mrs. General Hughes, and dear Randolph was sort of sitting on the radiator, and all about them was this perfect sea."

"Can't you just see them now, like a modern Ark, holding hankies to their noses, screaming and bellowing—surrounded, absolutely surrounded," screamed Mrs. Swenson.

"Well," continued Dave, "Randolph, as host, realized that something would have to be done. Since he fancies himself still something of the athlete—shoots golf, things like that—he made a sprightly leap from the radiator, intended to carry him over this impromptu moat and to the safety of the lawn. Only he missed. And, worse, he hit the pavement at a slight angle and consequently emerged looking somewhat like the shingle in that favorite Army recipe."

Mrs. Swenson was quite weak with merriment by this time and could only hold up a hand in protest. Dottie was chuckling too. Her risibilities were prone to this sort of thing.

"Well, Lady Briton was standing there, horrified, when Randolph, furious, engulfed her and 'he really surprised me, because you know how unemotional Randolph usually is.' Well, the last their guests saw of them they were disappearing, rolling violently down the hall."

"And the guests?" pursued Mrs. Swenson, already busy on her own version of it.

"Well, there was a lot of the stuff, you know (she'd really relieved that poor ox) and so the servants tried putting out planks to those marooned and so forth but it simply wouldn't work and none were foolish enough to try. Finally the driver simply backed the car out and they all called sedans and left, having never once glimpsed their hosts again."

Dave stopped and took a deep breath. A brave job well done.

"Isn't that priceless?" screamed Mrs. Swenson. "My, but how I wish one could print it."

"It would not be the better part of valor," said her husband who had curled the corners of his fleshy lips to show that he was not above such simple amusements as this one had been.

Gloria was trying to decide which was the more revolting, Lady Briton rehashed at breakfast by Dottie Ainsley or after supper by her husband.

At that moment Gloria saw two men in overcoats walking through the lobby. "I'll bet anything those two are CID," she said.

The Major started nervously. "What?" he said.

"Those men—I was simply remarking they must be CID. No one manages to look more casually inconspicuous than the CID—or the FBI, its big brother, for that matter. And that's why they're so easy to spot. They look so ordinary they practically scream at you."

"You sure got a funny sense of humor," said the Major, a bit shaken.

"Oh, maybe they just like opera."

Gloria glanced at Michael. He was standing by one of the pillars, looking at Mr. Ohara. Mr. Ohara in turn was glancing at Michael from time to time out of the corners of his eyes. They didn't speak, however. Then Gloria noticed that the Major was looking at both the soldier and Mr. Ohara. She had the uncomfortable feeling that she didn't understand what was going on.

"Why don't we go over and say hello to Mr. Ohara," she said helpfully.

The Major shook his head.

"Now, now, Major," said Gloria, "remember our purpose in being in Japan at all. We are supposed to be kind to the natives and to—"

"Please stop, would you, Miss Wilson?"

Gloria looked at the Major in surprise. His face was whiter than usual, and the freckles appeared bright orange. He looked a little ill, or else a little frightened. She privately decided that the drinks were taking their toll, and rejoiced.

At the same time she felt sorry for him. It was a novel experience, feeling sorry for a man. She undeniably felt warmly protective toward him. He looked exactly like a little boy who had done something he oughtn't and was now going to be punished. The thought of the Major as a little boy appealed to her, and while he was bleakly looking about for the two men she'd mentioned, she smiled at him.

But it was Michael, standing by a far pillar, who caught her smile and smiled back. The smile was wry, however. He could have Gloria any time he wanted. He could never have Haruko.

There she was, standing next to the tall student who was going to marry her. Michael stared at them both. Another culture, another race—they might have come from the other side of the moon. Yet Haruko was all he had ever wanted, and the student beside her was an alien—strange, a bit forbidding, always incomprehensible. He wondered how he could think of them each so differently. Or was it that Haruko was just as alien, just as strange, just as fantastically different from him? And was it then that Haruko and others like her would always prefer other Japanese? and that Michael and others like him would always have—what?—others like Gloria?

Michael looked at the floor and then at his own white hands. For the first time he realized that he never would be able to understand what he loved, and that that might well be the reason he loved it so. His earlier disillusion fell from him. Again he loved Haruko, and he loved her because he would never understand her, nor the student by whom she stood, nor the fatuous Mr. Ohara, nor those other Japanese near them.

He turned away and, from the pillar, could see, through the doors of the theater, the sidewalk, the street, the moat, and the outer fortifications of the Palace. A single man on a bicycle passed, slowly pedaling, illuminated for a second by the lights of a passing car, and Michael closed his eyes, slowly crushing the tears that had formed.

■

The third act was short, but that didn't save it from being disastrous. If the Americans had cried before— and there were many who had, Mr. Swenson among them —there were now a great many who howled with laughter all during the touching finale.

It all began with the entrance of Pinkerton and Kate. "Oh, god!" said Gloria when she saw Kate. Pinkerton's

American wife, being American, wore a great wig—bright red—to emphasize that fact. And, since American women were known to be highly developed, the young Japanese girl playing the role had stuffed what appeared to be grapefruit in her bosom. Whenever she turned—which was often, for she was the vivacious type of American lady—the grapefruit, undecided, would pause a moment before turning with her, and then roll comfortably back and forth until they finally settled, hanging straight down in the folds of her dress. This somewhat mitigated the pitiful quality of Butterfly's entreaties, which could scarcely be heard over the laughter of the audience. And the whole improbable effect was still further heightened by the fact that in this act, for some reason, Pinkerton sang only in English and Kate spoke only in Italian, while Butterfly contented herself with Japanese.

Even the death scene didn't come off too well. Little Trouble refused to wave the American flag, and Butterfly's urgings grew stronger and stronger, while the hushed but scandalized voice of Mrs. Swenson proclaimed: "Japanese children are ordinarily so well-behaved on the stage." Eventually the child began to cry. This might have aided the pathetic effect somewhat had not Butterfly, after retiring to die behind a large screen, kept popping out to give the flag a few suggestive pushes. The child grew furious and finally tore the flag from its stick, thus intruding a somewhat suspicious note into the morass of symbolism which is Butterfly's death.

Even so, things might have straightened themselves out. Butterfly had skilfully draped her scarf over the screen, and when the knife entered her breast she was to catch at the scarf. The long piece of silk disappearing over the screen as she fell was to have spoken volumes. Instead, however, she succeeded only in knocking the screen over, not only burying the flag-tearing Little Trouble, but also revealing herself, squatting on the stage in perfect composure, her hand still grasping the end of the long scarf, a very prosaic face turned toward the audience. She had the instantaneous presence of mind to fall forward—unfortunately onto the screen, setting Little Trouble kicking and screaming with terror.

Thus, when Suzuki entered, on cue, it appeared more as though she had merely been called by the wailing infant. What was frankly meant to be a sentimentally tragic scene—the infant waving the flag, the scarf beside the screen, and Butterfly's hand outstretched—became truly cathartic. Suzuki's discovery of the corpse, was scarcely the poignant thing it should have been : first she had to shift the body of Chocho-san, put up the screen, replace the scarf, pick up the howling child, and then, quite suddenly, discover the little outstretched petal-like hand—which, incidentally, she had forgotten to put into view.

The audience howled louder than the child, and Mr. Ohara, his face fiery, sank deep into his seat as the curtain fell on this scene of carnage. The applause was both indulgent and genuine. Little Trouble got a bigger hand than anyone.

Both of Haruko's parents sat impassive. They neither smiled nor sobbed, laughed nor applauded. Mr. Ohara had almost disappeared from view, his head sunk down in the collar of his kimono.

Haruko, somewhat bewildered by the conclusion of the beautiful tragedy, turned toward Ichiro. He had the oddest expression on his face. His mouth was set tight but apparently wanted to turn up at the corners, and he was looking at his folded hands. As she looked at him, he turned slightly and, from the corners of his eyes, saw her. He blinked manfully, but his mouth curled still wider. She suddenly saw he was trying to keep from smiling, and the expression on his face—so like that when he had been the little boy she had known so well—made her forget all about the sad fate of Chocho-san. It was so infectious that she smiled a little herself. Blinking with effort he tried to compose his face, but couldn't. He looked so ludicrous that Haruko laughed out loud. Her mother cast a single piercing glance at her, but it had no effect, because Ichiro was now laughing too.

They looked into each other's eyes—across the heads of the three bewildered adults—and laughed like children.

■

As the audience slowly moved out of the auditorium, the Major pulled Gloria into a corner of the lobby.

"Now, you and me are going to do some talking," he said.

She looked wildly about for Michael, couldn't see him, and was forcibly pushed into one of the chairs. She began to like the Major more. He could be rough.

"Now . . . I asked you to marry me—" he began.

"I was wondering when you were going to admit it. I thought you'd forgotten."

"I haven't thought of nothing else but."

"Well, this is flattering, I must say, but—"

"I'll put it right on the line, Miss Wilson. I'm going to be worth a lot of money."

Gloria looked at him curiously. "Oh?" she said.

"I mean—you could do worse maybe."

"Well, I don't know," said Gloria. "At least you are a man of few words. But you're not buying a horse, you know; you're asking a lovely young lady to—"

"I'm just putting my cards on the table, that's all I'm doing."

"O. K., I'm game. Why is you going to be worth lots of money, Mr. Bones?"

"Because I'm honest and dependable and save my pay."

"Well, that's an anti-climax, I must say," said Gloria. "I'd have thought you were up to your ears in the black market to hear you talk."

The Major laughed easily. "You'd laugh out of the other side of your mouth if you knew how much I made this evening.... Yes, this evening, while we was here listening to the pretty music."

"If I had another side to my mouth, I should be pleased to use it, but I think I should inform you that during proposals you don't need to sell the girl on you. All you need to do is ask her, and then receive your yes or no like a man."

She suddenly noticed that the Major was embarrassed. He sat beside her and looked at the floor.

"Aw..." he began. "I know that the money don't matter, but, you see, Miss Wilson, I know too that you don't really much like me and that you're only being kind to me now—and I hate it. But still I got to ask you. But first I ought to tell you something about me."

"Where the money comes from?" she asked brightly. "But you've already told enough so I can imagine the rest."

He was silent for a moment, and then said: "No. I had another girl."

"That makes us even, Major. It so happens I've had another boy."

"I mean...I sort of still got her. I won't have for long. Already I'm getting away. Like just this afternoon, you remember, after I took you home to lie down for a bit, why, right after that I rushed right over to meet her because she wanted a favor done and I told her right then and there that that's the last favor I was ever going to do her and it was sort of a going-away present from me. That way, you see, I was able to let her down without hurting her. My, but she got mad though, but I went right on telling her. 'Cause I'd already made up my mind and asked you to marry me and I just wanted to end this other as soon as I possibly could." The Major was silent, and he looked both self-righteous and noble.

"And what is the name of this forlorn female?" asked Gloria curiously.

"Guess I can tell you since we shouldn't have no secrets from each other... It's Mrs. Ainsley—Dorothy Ainsley."

Gloria stared at him in surprise, and then said: "And then, last night... after you left me, you..."

The Major turned red. "How'd you know?" he whispered.

Gloria remembered her breakfast with Dottie—her saying that Gloria should be married. And here was the chance, all gift-wrapped. So amused she could hardly keep her mouth straight, Gloria also realized that this was the way to get rid of the embarrassing Major once and for all and yet still stay in good graces at the office. She was wondering which pose to take—perhaps maidenhood threatened, a protective gesture with both hands, somewhat reminiscent of nymphs in flight, that sort of thing—when the Major suddenly caught sight of two men standing in the almost-empty lobby.

"Those them?" he asked.

"Those who?" said Gloria.

"Those men you saw before."

"Yes, I think so. Their faces are familiar, as all CID faces should be. In fact, the face of every man in the CID is as familiar to me as the palm of my mother's hand. Actually, one of the qualifications for their being chosen, I hear, is that they must betray a striking resemblance to the palm of Gloria Wilson's mother's hand."

The Major turned to her and grinned sickly. Just then the two men moved away from the wall and walked toward them.

Stopping beside the Major, one of the men said: "Major Calloway?"

The Major looked up, his face white, and nodded.

"Might we speak with you for a second?... Excuse us, ma'am."

The Major, his face a dead white, stood up with them, and all three marched around the corner.

Gloria sat alone on the chair and tried to decide exactly what she would do with the Major. His proposal seemed quite touching, a declaration of faith rather than of love, and the very fact that she had received it made her think less frequently of what she had overheard about herself that afternoon.

As she idly examined her stockings for runs, she wondered if she would be the same if she were still in America. She finally decided that she would want to be, but wouldn't have the opportunity. There she'd have to be reasonably good. But here she didn't have to be. Suddenly she understood why people in the Occupation were the way they were. Like her, they were intrinsically rather nice, but simply being here had been enough to demoralize them. If they fibbed at home, they lied here; if they only occasionally picked up little items in the five-and-ten at home, they robbed the Army—and the Japanese—blind here; if they liked the opposite sex at home, well, then...just look at Miss Gloria Wilson.

These thoughts somewhat reassured her. It was the environment, or something, she decided. Perhaps it was just part of being a conqueror. At any rate it was quite demoralizing. She slipped her feet from her shoes and curled up in the chair. And it was such fun being demoralized.

She noticed someone standing near her. Looking up, she discovered it was Michael. "Oh, heavens," she said, "you've discovered me thinking—and with a straight face. This will never do. Come, sit down and get warm."

Michael sat down heavily.

"You don't look too well."

"I don't feel too well," said Michael, turning to look at her for the first time. His eyes were red, as though he had a cold.

"Well, I'm glad you waited for me," said Gloria.

"I won't be very good company," he began, turning slightly toward her. "But couldn't we go someplace together, just you and me?"

"I've wanted to hear those very words for a long time, Michael, but I more than a little suspect I wouldn't be hearing them now unless something fairly unpleasant had happened to you recently. Come on, instead of going out and boring each other with fun and games, why don't you just sit here and tell Aunt Gloria all about it. They won't dare try to close this place up as long as we conquerors choose to stay here."

"I wish you'd be serious."

"And how does one be serious?" asked Gloria seriously. As she looked at Michael she felt that, even now, she was playing some kind of part, had cast herself into yet a new role, this time that of the defender of the wrong and injured. Gloria, mother of the world; Gloria, the picture of warm, compassionate womanhood. It was such a strain not being oneself.

As she continued looking at Michael she realized that she didn't know which was her true self anyway. Was it the way she had been with Sonoko that morning, the warm, protective, school-chum type; or was it, perhaps, the palpitating female with Michael later on; or, maybe, the devastating cynic with the Major? Or was she really just a loud-mouthed, lecherous female with pretensions to kindness, love, and culture?

Suddenly she realized her steady gaze was embarrassing the soldier. Looking down at her knees, she said: "I wanted to see you to ask you something about the Colonel. I've been given to understand that he's leaving. And that means we'll both be at the tender mercies, for a time at least, of the Major. Now, do you think maybe—"

At that moment the Major appeared around the corner, flanked by the two men. One of the men stayed behind with the Major, and the other one walked over to Gloria and Michael.

He smiled an apology at Gloria and said: "Private Richardson?"

Michael nodded and stood up.

"May we see you for a minute?" asked the man. He begged Gloria's pardon again, and all four men marched back around the corner.

Gloria waited and waited, but they never came back.

■

In another part of the lobby a few more of the audience still lingered on, also confident that none of the Japanese staff of the theatre would dare tell them it was time to leave. Dottie and Dave were holding court with a few others near the closed soft-drink bar.

"But," said Dottie for the fifteenth time, "did you see Kate?" And, for the fifth time, she bent her delicate face into her hands and shook her shoulders. "Those breasts!" she gasped.

"Well," said her husband—he had gallantly attempted a new rejoinder each time Kate was brought up—"seeing as how the Japanese girls have so little, they overcompensate by giving the Americans credit for too much. You know, like us white American males with Negroes —and I don't mean breasts."

Usually this would have brought an appreciative giggle from Dottie, but at present she already had more than enough to laugh at. "And that fright-wig!" she screamed and again put her face in her hands.

Mr. Swenson smiled tolerantly: "Well, it is a well-known fact that the Westerners have always been known as the 'red-haired barbarians,' but never in all Japanese art have I ever seen the fact so graphically portrayed."

"And the bucket of bolts!" screamed Dottie, searching now back through her memory for even the less spectacular events of this spectacular evening.

"That, in a way, was too bad," said Mrs. Swenson, cautious lest she cast a pall over the little gathering by reminding them of the beauties of the performance. "For, in its way, that second act—the night passage, you know—was quite charming. The set, for example, was utterly darling. I shall doubtless write a little note of appreciation for it."

"More—more than that," said her husband gently. "Far more than just the second act was fine in this performance. In fact, everything *Japanese* in it was fine. But, as always, no matter how exquisite the effect in their own milieu, whenever they attempt ours the effect is often as tragic and, I'm the first to admit, as comic as the spectacle tonight. The approach is different for them. You will have noticed that mistakes of this nature are almost an impossibility in the Noh, the Kabuki, the Bunraku, and even in the popular theatre—like the Takarazuka, though I am the first to execrate it. They literally don't occur. And it's more, I believe and maintain, than sheer technique." He paused a moment, trying to decide what it was, and then finished lamely: "More, much more."

"Why, when I was at the Met," said Dottie suddenly, "they would have laughed this off the stage."

"But this isn't the Met," said her husband gently. "And, anyway, what about the time you told me about when Mélisande got her hair caught in the ivy on the tower, and Pelléas couldn't get it loose—for the whole scene. And the time the donkeys in *Aïda*—misbehaved."

"That's not the point," snapped Dottie, and her husband took a few steps backward. An ugly mood was coming on, and Dottie's eyebrows thundered darkly. He attributed it to the hysteria of the performance and to the fact that the liquor before it was wearing off. She was tired, and her china-doll face was pinched and wrinkled-looking under the crystal chandelier.

"Now, now, now," said Mr. Swenson easily. He'd

had enough liquor that it hadn't worn off so quickly, and besides, any time the Japanese made a mistake—like tonight—it somehow reassured him. "After all, they are children. We would not laugh at a childrens' performance. We could, indeed, commiserate, we could sympathize. That poor soprano must be suffering agonies—maybe she'll even lose her contract. And I imagine that Little Trouble is being put straight to bed—for he won't be harshly whipped the way one of our own children might be in these circumstances. They *do* take their failures so seriously, especially when it's a question of face. So, my dear, we must not judge too quickly."

Mr. Swenson had not intended so personally rebuking a tone. He was simply being expansive and was feeling sure of his audience. He smiled benignly and turned his profile to where it showed to best advantage.

"Don't you my-dear me! I'll judge as quickly as I damn well please," said Dottie suddenly.

Her husband put up one ineffectual hand, as though to clap it over the beloved little mouth. Instead, he put it over his own.

Mr. Swenson was feeling good. He took no offense. Instead he would simply use this petty remark to climb to even greater heights—one must not spurn the lowly foothold. "I assure you that the use of 'my dear' in which I so unhappily indulged was purely rhetorical, and so far as swift judgment goes—which is far indeed—I presume you will continue to outdistance us all, no matter what we say."

He was both gallant and offhand, and his twisted compliment reached nowhere near Dottie, who sat stiffly furious on the plush and understood only that she was being patronized.

"Darling," said Mrs. Swenson urgently, "the car will be waiting, and I'm sure they want to close the theater. We really ought to go."

"Good-by, good-by," said Dave suddenly. He even began waving, trying to shield Dottie behind his back.

She pushed him roughly to one side and said, in a clipped and metallic little voice : "Well, at least I don't judge the Japs like you do."

"Of that, my dear, I am fully aware," began Mr. Swenson, still smiling, self-assured, handsome, and dignified under the chandelier. "As," he continued, "your constant use of that most unpleasant abbreviation of a nationality would seem to indicate." It would be well, he decided, to let this little fool have her say. After all, it was people like her whom he most disliked. They were all the same—let them say enough and one could crush them—one could fight her with her own weapons. One's native learning and genius would come to the fore.

His wife pulled his sleeve frantically, but he gently removed her hand.

Mrs. Swenson and Dave looked at each other, their mouths open. Both were aware of what was doubtless going to happen, though they never dreamed it would go so far, and both were helpless.

"But," concluded Mr. Swenson easily, as though talking to a child, "I do think it would be most amusing to discover your idea of the criterion I employ in judging the Japanese people."

"Their baskets, you old fairy !" screamed Dottie.

Mr. Swenson turned pale. Dottie did too, terrified by what she had just said. Mr. Swenson and Dave went on standing helplessly by. They stood in complete silence, and the old man, too shocked to answer, slowly bowed his head. His hands shook, and when his wife caught one of them and drew him away, he allowed her to lead him by the hand, his shoulders sagging, his profile wrinkled.

The silence continued after they had disappeared down the staircase. The lobby was empty and the janitors were waiting patiently for the last Americans to leave. A workman in straw sandals stood by the light switches; an electrician stood some distance off and examined an ashtray; two carpenters waited in the doorway.

"Oh, Dottie," said Dave softly, "you shouldn't have done that. I have to work with him. He's important."

The color had returned to Dottie's face, and her cheeks were growing red. "Oh, Dave," she cried softly, her voice shaking, whimpering, "I didn't mean that to come out. I was just mad, and upset, terribly upset, that's all, and..." Two large tears rolled down her cheeks, and her eyes, bright blue, glistened. Dottie was never more beautiful than when she was contrite. It was not often she was this beautiful.

"Poor little lamb," said Dave and put his arms around her.

She buried her face in his coat. "I'm so wicked, so wicked..." she sobbed.

"Poor little ... lamb," said Dave again, unable to think of anything else quite so appealing as that.

"Oh, but Dave," she said, raising her eyes, "it isn't only that. Oh, I've been so wicked. I ... I called the CID."

"You what?" shouted Dave. While he believed that the way he obtained beautiful art objects in exchange for occasional cartons of cigarettes was rather worldly and dashing, he didn't like to think of it as being illegal.

"I called the CID and turned someone in. Oh, Dave —I informed!" She burst into fresh sobs, while the electricians and the carpenters stood silent.

"There, there," said Dave. "You come on home and tell me all about it. It can't be so very bad."

"But I did it all to help poor Madame Schmidt. I got him to make out a requisition blank for her and sign it; then I knew he wouldn't go through with it if he could help it, so I did this—I turned him in."

"Honey, who is this person?"

She didn't answer, but sobbed all the harder.

"There, there," said her husband. "We'll just go on home now. Poor little...little kitten."

"Well," gasped Dottie, "at least poor Madame Schmidt will get her recital now. At least I could do that. That's the only reason I turned him in. Really it is, Dave."

"Don't think about it, honey," said Dave. "And about Swenson—well, he won't hold it against us. We really don't mind about that sort of thing, and it's his own business. At least now he won't go around believing that no one but his wife knows about it. That's it! You really did him a kind of favor, you know. Sort of like in the advertisements. Like telling your best friend he ought to see a dentist." He laughed weakly, but Dorothy still sobbed, disconsolate.

"Look at it this way, honey," he said. "You didn't do any harm at all this evening. You only did people favors. I bet all of them would thank you for it later on. Think of it that way, honey."

Dottie tried and eventually succeeded. Together they walked down the wide steps and into the outer lobby. Behind them the electricians began turning off lights.

Through the glass doors Dave saw the Swensons waiting at the curb for their car. Swenson was white in the glare of headlights, and his wife supported him; his shoulders were bent.

Their sedan pulled up. Mrs. Swenson sat in the rear seat and pulled the door closed after her. Her husband sat in front, as was his habit, beside the young Japanese chauffeur.

In the darkened lobby, Dave held his wife close to him, and she, completely submissive, leaned against him, her chest still rising with sobs, her face a bright pink. Really, thought Dave, it was old Swenson who had, inadvertantly, done *him* a favor. Now they could go home and, eventually, with laughter and a few tears, Dave could enjoy his wife. He smiled in anticipation, his face half in the light, for Dottie only allowed his attentions when she felt herself to have been naughty, when she was contrite and longing for punishment.

The Swenson's car was slowly pulling from the curb. Mr. Swenson, talking earnestly to the chauffeur, seemed to have recovered some of his animation.

■

The Ohara party had left the theatre some time before, and even then the streets were almost deserted except for the small crowd waiting under the marquee. The street lights, brilliant in the dry cool air, shone like the stars overhead. American jeeps and sedans and a few Japanese limousines of mixed vintages were at the curb, their motors purring. There was the smell of exhaust and of burning leaves.

With some ostentation, Mr. Ohara insinuated his way through the thinning crowd and led his party to a waiting Rolls Royce—ancient enough to have escaped requisitioning—which he had rented for the evening, along with the tight-collared chauffeur.

"Here we is," he said in English and assisted Haruko, her mother, and Ichiro into the back seat.

Haruko's father sat on one of the folding seats, and Mr. Ohara himself sat in front with the chauffeur. The bowing and smiling middleman stood on the curb and waved the car off, smiling to himself. The meeting of the young people had been a great success.

In the car Mr. Ohara found much to praise in the performance, despite the few imperfections, and resolved to scold no one. He would just release the soprano and the child, and that would be the end of it. No use being old-fashioned about it. Sitting beside the driver and feeling himself the personification of magnanimity, he laughed gaily to himself. All had really gone well, and everything was going to be all right.

Actually, the main reason for Mr. Ohara's euphoria

was that he had worn Japanese clothes; though he had long realized that, indeed, clothes do make the man, he had never before extended this truth to Japanese clothes. But until this evening he had never been treated with more respect, had never received so many bows, hand shakes, and subtly deferent nods. It had not taken long for his agile mind to discover the reason. But Mr. Ohara's mind was modern, as well as agile; thus he was able to think of his use of the national dress as a positive virtue. He now sat beside the chauffeur and felt almost holy because it was, after all, in deference to his son that he had struggled into the clothes in the first place, and now, lo, the bread he had cast upon the waters was returning and he was all the richer. First thing when he got home he would tell his wife she should henceforth wear only kimono, let her hair grow longer, and take up the Noh or something.

The chariot of Elija—Mr. Ohara often thought in Biblical metaphors remembered from the days of his impressionable Christianity—surely the chariot of Elija was no less glorious that this limousine. Except for one thing: he hadn't received his dollars. Still, one couldn't expect to understand big business all in one evening. Now that things looked so bright, however, he did hope nothing would go wrong.

From the back seat Ichiro saw a group of students standing half-hidden by the shadow of the marquee. One of them was Yamaguchi. He turned quickly away so the student would not see him, but at the same time he hoped with some amusement that he was looking, for Yamaguchi's seeing him in a chauffeured limousine would seem to justify every one of his former suspicions and accusations.

But Yamaguchi, looking unusually glum, was apparently seeing nothing. He was staring at the pavement and looked very much like a dirty little bird caught in the rain.

As the car pulled away from the curb Ichiro felt Haruko beside him. She had touched his hand, as she had when they were children; feeling very proud, he slyly put his other hand on top of hers.

Both her parents studiously ignored them and looked out of the windows.

As the limousine moved away, Comrade Yamaguchi looked up. He had seen Ichiro all along, but now one more capitalist made little difference to him. He was a miserable failure, and more than that, he was not alone in this opinion. The other students, all former comrades, looked at him suspiciously, and the girl with the cannibal-frizzed hair was whispering in shrill syllables. The Japanese, he began to realize, did not make good communists.

And he had been one of the worst. His first command had been an utter failure. And when it should have been so glorious—stench bombs, a false fire-alarm, and he would have been making a small speech over the shambles of *Madame Butterfly* scenery. But it was all ruined now: at the last minute the demonstration had been canceled, and this hardy little group had stood in the cold outside the theatre all during the performance waiting for further orders. It was the frizzed young lady who had brought them, and by overhearing her whispers, Yamaguchi was at last able to piece together what had happened.

He had been denounced and reported to the Committee as having ideas inimical to the aims of his student organization. And tonight there was to be a disciplinary meeting. He didn't yet know what the precise charges would be, but he did overhear that he had been seen talking with Ohara, a most suspicious character, and that, on the whole, Yamaguchi's character was regarded as "controversial"—a damning description within his organization.

But, worse than anything else, they had discovered

his books. They had gone through the tiny room in the boarding house where he lived and had confiscated his Emerson and O. Henry, his Longfellow and his Melville. They had taken them all away, and soon he would have to account for his possession of them. And he didn't know what to say other than that he liked them. The Committee was, he realized, quite stupid, but even they weren't stupid enough to believe any "know the enemy" explanation.

Now, for the first time, he really began to wonder about what had happened to him. Standing in the cold, the wind at his neck, he realized that until now no enthusiasm of his had ever been questioned, none of his interests had been called to account. He had never had to apologize for himself. And he realized that he could not do it, that he wasn't all black and white, and that what he could say in his defense would seem the most damaging of admissions.

He wanted to run away, but his ex-comrades were regarding him with veiled suspicion and would probably run after him. They were waiting for the truck which was to carry them to the meeting, which would carry him to his judgment. He thought with sudden affection of Michéle Morgan and a really nice pre-War German airmail stamp, in mint condition.

He looked in either direction. The street lights faded endlessly into the distance. There was no escape for him.

■

"Special call for Tadashi's number," said the blond lieutenant on night duty at the Motor Pool as he turned from the routing chart.

The Nisei sergeant raised his eyebrows. "What gives?" he asked.

The lieutenant looked at the trip ticket. "A Mrs. Dorothy Ainsley, to be precise."

"Probably forgot her glasses or something and will expect to find 'em," said the sergeant. "These DAC's kill me—go around taking the driver's number, checking license plates. That all they got to do?"

"Probably," said the lieutenant, giving the ticket to the sergeant.

The sergeant went into the next room, where the drivers were warming their hands around a stove. "One more, Tadashi," said the sergeant. Although he knew Japanese well enough, he never used it if he could help it. "O. K., one more, you go, yes? You hubba-hubba one more, O. K.? Be careful. You go Mrs. Ainsley. Understand. Bad Mrs. Ainsley. This morning—remember? DR. One more DR, and you go right out of Motor Pool. Understand? O. K. Mrs. Ainsley pretty, no?"

The sergeant laughed, and Tadashi, smiling weakly, stood up. "O. K. Hayaku!" said the sergeant.

Tadashi buttoned his collar and went out to his sedan. It was cold, and he shivered, the trip ticket in his hand.

Again the ticket said Naka Hotel. He hoped Mrs. Ainsley would be more punctual than she had been that morning. As he drove through the empty streets, he told himself that if she wasn't in the lobby, he would turn right around and go back and she'd have to get herself another driver. The sergeant hadn't told him he'd been requested by number.

He was pleasantly surprised to find his passenger outside waiting for him—at least he presumed the tall woman in the fur coat who walked to the car as though expecting him was his passenger, the Mrs. Ainsley who had failed to show up that morning. There was something vaguely familiar about her, but he didn't bother to try and recollect—after all, all Americans look rather alike.

He opened the back door, and with a gracious smile she seated herself inside. Behind the wheel, Tadashi awaited instructions. The lady in the back seat said

nothing, so he turned slightly, took off his cap, and said:
"Where, please?"

"Oh, you speak English," said the lady.

"I no speak English," said Tadashi, making a small negative sign with his hand before his face.

"Nonsense. You're doing very well."

"Where, please?"

"Oh, heavens, I don't know. Why not go to . . . to Ueno? Yes, that's it."

"Ueno?" asked Tadashi, a bit surprised. No Americans lived near there.

"Yes, Ueno," said the lady more positively.

Perhaps she wanted to go to the railway station there, thought Tadashi. He started the sedan.

Behind him the lady tried to light a cigarette, but her hand trembled. "Oh, really!" she said.

Tadashi turned his profile. "What, please?"

"Nothing, nothing," she said, and looked at the line of his neck, black against the approaching lights. She leaned back in the seat and smelled his clean rice smell which mingled with her perfume and the dusty odor of the cushions, his hair pomade and the gritty odor of oil and grease. She bit her lips and closed her eyes. . . .

Gloria had waited in the empty, darkening lobby until they actually closed the theater. But neither the Major nor Michael came back. Lonely and baffled, feeling completely left out, she marched back to the hotel. She wanted a bath: it seemed she had been wearing these same clothes for a week instead of a day. But she didn't want to go to her empty room. As her eyes grew accustomed to the dark she saw that a couple was kissing in one corner. She looked away, tried to feel virtuously disgusted, and only succeeded in feeling envious. This was no longer for her. Nevertheless, she quietly took a seat in the lobby from which she could secretly watch the couple.

No, not tonight, nor any other night, she remembered.

She was going to have to watch herself closely. The only trouble with her was that she wanted her cake, and then tried to eat it too. Well, if she were still stupid enough to want to be virginal Miss Dew Blossom from Muncie—and she apparently did want just that— then she'd just have to watch her step. No more casual officers, and no more Private Richardsons either.

Watching the man and the girl on the sofa, she again felt that familiar sensation of abandoned despair. Her father, during one of the few times he ever talked with her, and on one of the even rarer occasions when he tried to tell her a little about the more intimate relations between the sexes, had informed her that although men often looked at women and wanted them, women never looked at men that way. With women love—that kind of love—was all highly intellectualized, and they never thought with their bodies the way men did. Thus, for women, a handsome male form meant nothing—it was only their other qualities, mainly their souls, that counted. Really, Father, thought Gloria, her eyes caressing the recumbent male, you should see me now.

With sudden irritation she ground out her cigarette and stood up. Now was the time for bed she decided —a nice, cold, empty bed, to be nice and fresh for that damn party tomorrow morning. But as she walked toward the elevator she knew she would have to pass the telephone booth, knew too that, despite all her good intentions, she would not go past it. She would stop there.

It was almost midnight, and she would do what she had been thinking of doing for almost twelve hours— perhaps longer. At seven that morning the thought would have been impossibly cruel, insanely wicked. But it wasn't seven now. It was the mysterious, Oriental hour of midnight.

She had picked up the phone and called the Motor Pool.

Later, waiting in front of the billet, she'd had time to think the whole thing over and regret it. But, still, it was a lark of sorts and, though doomed to failure—she was sure of that—it would still be worth the kicks.

She got no kicks standing in the cold outside the door, watching a group of girls return to the billet, laughing on the arms of civilians, sergeants, lieutenants, majors. She wrapped her fur coat around her and tried to ignore them, but that was difficult. How, she wondered, had she so successfully remained unaware of their glances up to now, of their sarcastic smiles, their half-pointed fingers and swiftly whispered words?

Now she looked straight ahead and ran the gauntlet of their derision. "Go on—cast the first stone!" she said under her breath, and tried to be the great lady, lovely, unapproachable, on business of her own at midnight in a fur coat, leaning against a brick wall.

The slamming of the billet door cut off their laughter, and Gloria shivered with the cold. Well, at least she had been right all along. These people were fools—like her parents. And since they were so foolish they could be led to believe her especially virtuous. They could be made to think twice before so much as swearing in her presence. And they would too! She would make her plans later—tomorrow.

Right now she was engaged in more practical thoughts. She would simply *have* to be more circumspect, or else she could cut herself off completely from the world of laughter and mockery. After all, she'd been limiting herself rather severely, rather artificially, in entertaining only the Occupation personnel. There was the entire Japanese nation at her feet, as it were. A whole new world existed just pleading to be taken advantage of. And there was no liaison between Japanese and American, no channel for rumors, at least not on the level at which she intended working. Little Miss Ambassador —that's what she'd be.

She had never been one of those who found Japanese males unattractive. To be sure, there was a high percentage of short little men with glasses and bad teeth. But she'd been around—she'd seen students who looked like Genghis Khan, lumber workers built like Greek statuary, bus boys as beautiful as Polynesians, pedicab men with the straight, hard faces of extraordinarily handsome prize fighters. Yes, she'd been around all right.

"There, see!" she said to herself, "life is just beginning." At once she felt much better.

And, beside all this, adventure too. She now admitted she'd never been particularly excited by the prospect of a lieutenant or a major. The outcome was always known. But this would be different. She felt so entirely the aggressor and knew that the outcome was so entirely in her own hands that her palms became wet with anticipation.

Just then the sedan appeared. She worried for fear the driver might have gone off duty, but, no, it was the same driver she and the Major had had that afternoon. As she stepped into the car she remembered having seen him someplace else and then remembered that he was Dottie Ainsley's driver after all. She'd seen him that morning. Perhaps it had been this subconscious memory which had led her to give Dottie's name when ordering the sedan to which she herself was not entitled. Well, well, wasn't it a small world after all . . . and the car door slammed, separating her still further from the girls inside the billet.

After deciding that Ueno sounded as unlikely a spot as any, she sat back on the cushions and tried to light a cigarette, but her hand trembled. "Oh, really!" said Gloria. She had cramps—pure fear she guessed. It was too absurd. . . .

She opened her eyes. They were at Ueno.

"Turn right—right," said Gloria. Ueno was as brilliantly lighted as a Christmas tree. Oddly so, she thought, for the name had always sounded dark and mysterious.

"Asakusa?" said the driver in some surprise.

"Yes, wherever that is," said Gloria.

Tadashi nodded. He was becoming suspicious. It was very irregular for an American lady to be in these districts even in the daytime, much more so at midnight. Also, this drive was taking time and he didn't dare get another delinquency report.

He slowed down to turn toward Asakusa, but Gloria leaned forward, her face almost touching the back of his neck, and said: "Straight."

"Straight?" asked Tadashi, now more frightened than suspicious. But he followed her directions.

They drove across the Sumida River into Honjo. There the streets went in all directions.

Completely lost, Gloria said: "Right."

He began driving faster. If the lady simply wanted a ride, what would he put on his trip ticket? He decided that before long he would pretend to misunderstand a direction and get them back across the river. Fukagawa lay directly before them.

"Left," said the lady, her mouth at the back of his neck.

She had seen an enormous expanse of unlighted field, a road running white and dim down the middle of it.

He stopped the car.

"Left," she said again.

He started the car and turned to the left. The headlights illuminated a blackened stretch of ruin, covered with weeds. The road stretched into the darkness toward distant lights on the opposite side of the open stretch.

When they were in the middle of the charred and blackened expanse, Gloria called "Stop!" more loudly than she'd intended.

Certain that the American lady was either sick or drunk—or both—Tadashi stopped the car with a jerk.

"Yes, please?" he said quickly, turning around.

The poor boy is frightened, thought Gloria, and it made her feel better that they should both be frightened, for she was too—quite frightened.

She quickly opened the door and climbed into the front seat. That back seat was at least one obstacle she could get around. Quite suddenly she wished for a drink, a drink for both of them. Drunk it would be easier. It was going to be difficult with both of them sober.

"Cigarette?" she said, holding out her pack and smiling.

It was then that he recognized her. He pointed a finger at her, his mouth half-open and his eyes black in the flare of the match.

"Yes, it's me," said Gloria, both touched and pleased.

Tadashi started putting the automobile into gear, but Gloria reached over and turned the ignition switch.

"Now, you don't want to run away," she said evenly. She didn't really care what she said as long as her tone was reassuring. The tone she used to Tadashi was the same she used for talking to animals.

"What you want to run away for? Heavens, it's only little me, and I wouldn't hurt a fly. You know that. We'll just sit here, real comfortable, and smoke our cigarettes and be friends."

"Friends?" said Tadashi, that being one of the few English words he knew. He sat very straight in his seat and puffed his cigarette swiftly. Americans were certainly friendly. Almost never had he had this so spectacularly proved as now. Apparently all she wanted was to be friends. Still, though he would like to be her friend, he had to think about the Motor Pool and about returning to it. He must not lose his job.

"Yes, friends—tomodachi," said Gloria.

"Tomodachi," said Tadashi.

Gloria had never run into the language barrier with

such force before. It both intrigued and infuriated her. Really, conversation did have its place after all. It would be just too much if she, like Major Calloway, let her hand slide across the sedan seat to his, to the fist he was holding by his side. The poor boy was doubtless terrified.

To reassure him, she turned her head away and looked around them. This was the most extensive ruin she had seen since coming to Tokyo, and they seemed to be in the very middle of it. In the distance, on all sides, were the lights of the city, distant as stars. Between them and the car there was nothing but blackness. The sedan was an illuminated island on the black field, and the white road led away from them into the darkness. The odor of burning leaves was blown by the cold wind. It smelled as though the earth were smoking, scorching.

Her studied inattention may have reassured *him*, but the surroundings certainly didn't reassure *her*. She decided they should play a game. After saying "What's that?" and pointing in several directions, she got her idea across.

"What's that?" she said and pointed west.

"Sumida-gawa," said Tadashi soberly.

"What's that?" She pointed north.

"Honjo."

"And that?" She pointed south.

"Fukagawa."

"What a delightful name!" said Gloria, laughing in her throat.

Tadashi said nothing.

"And right here?" She pointed all around them.

"Susaki."

"Lovely place, no?" said Gloria and looked around. The wind blew dead leaves across the road.

"New game, new game," said Gloria and wrinkled her nose. "My—name—is—Gloria."

"Guroria," he repeated.

"Yes, Gloria Wilson. It's perfectly all right, darling —we'll never see each other again." She smiled briefly. "And what's yours?"

"Guroria Wiruson—you," said Tadashi. The American lady was lying. Her name was Mrs. Ainsley—a married lady. It said so on his trip ticket.

"Yes, dear—me, Tarzan; you, Jane."

"Missu Wiruson," said Tadashi. If the woman was demented, as he had begun to suspect, he should probably agree with her as much as possible.

She looked at his profile and felt sorry for him. He was just too good looking. At the same time she felt sorry for herself. They were no longer Myrna Loy and an Indian prince in disguise. They were merely Gloria Wilson from Muncie, Indiana, and a poor, frightened, and—unfortunately for him—roaringly handsome sedan driver who, for all she knew, had a wife and kids at home, all hungry and waiting. The whole thing had begun to seem a bit sordid.

She remembered dark tales she'd heard of other American women who had stolen across the color line. How on earth had they gone about it she wondered.

"Where?" asked Tadashi helplessly.

"Oh, you bad boy," said Gloria, laughing. "Why, right here I suppose. Do you know a better place?"

As soon as she'd said this she looked out the window, irritated with herself. This really was too much! How self-indulgent could you get anyway? Why didn't the fool boy start the car and just get them out of here. He was the man. He was supposed to do things like that.

Yet, if he did, she knew she'd do everything she could to stop the car again. It was always the same. The only thing different was that this time it was Gloria who made the advances, directly rather than indirectly. Besides, she told herself, if I don't, I'll be an even bigger fool than I am now. I'll lie sleepless in that damn bed and think about what *could* have happened. I'll really kick myself if I don't go through with this. Beside, what does it matter? Come on in, the water's fine....

She grimaced with a sudden cramp, closed her eyes briefly, reached over and took Tadashi's hand in her own, and opened her eyes. Well, that was easy. Tadashi hadn't moved.

He was terrified. It had just occurred to him what it was this Mrs. Ainsley was after. The responsibility would have frightened him in any event, for such an occurrence was without parallel in his experience. But now it frightened him all the more because, through it, a pattern of his life was revealing itself to him.

All day the pattern had been forming; now it was revealed. Mrs. Ainsley had been with him three times that day, for now he remembered having seen her that morning too. This was too often for coincidence. But it also seemed he had seen her once before, long ago, in Shimbashi, the night of the fire, when his sisters and parents and friends had been killed. Was she not perhaps the unknown lady in Shimbashi, the lady in Western clothes? She was very like her. And now they were sitting in the ruins of that fire, he and the lady who had kept him from his duty, the duty of being burned with his parents and sisters. They were sitting in Susaki—the section devoted to the pleasures of the flesh, where his father had been burned to death almost five years before. The destruction of Tokyo rose before Tadashi's eyes, and the dark plain burned fiercely. He was a very superstitious young man.

Gloria leaned forward, and as he turned his head, her mouth, its fleshy lips like little arms, caught his and held him.

He smelled her perfume, the odor of her lipstick and of tobacco. He closed his eyes and held his breath.

"Ardor—that's what I like," said Gloria as she pulled away.

She lighted another cigarette, and he refused one. She still held his hand, and as her match flared out she saw the palm of his hand, wet, like her own.

"Let's look at it this way," she said, "this is democracy in action,"

"Democracy," said Tadashi.

"Sure, honey. And now you see—democracy *can* be fun! Now I'll give you one of the finer points—this is the Monroe Doctrine."

She held the cigarette in one hand and bent over him. This time her lips very gently pried his open. His were cool and yielding.

It was actually a bit clinical, like being at the dentist's, thought Gloria, for the child didn't know how to kiss. Well, she would teach him!

She slipped one arm around his waist, thinking, goodness, how masculine can you get. The wool of his Army uniform scratched her wrist softly. She could see herself, spreading democracy and good cheer all over these lovely islands. And one nice thing—there was no shortage of material for democratization. She'd really been limiting her talent by confining her attentions to white males—these little people were delightful. They made one feel so masterful. Before long General MacArthur himself would have to be awarding her a medal.

And the dear boy's heart was like a triphammer. Probably just as appreciative as he was reluctant. She had a pleasing vision of her future—her reputation reestablished with those whose opinion counted, and the entire male Japanese population stretched at her feet like that platoon the Major had mentioned—all stretched out and not caring what happened. If only the good Major could see her now—what a shock he'd be in for!

Really, how predatory can you get, thought Gloria;

then—oh, well, the hell with it—she slipped her tongue between Tadashi's half-opened lips.

Frightened, he pushed her away.

"Did I frighten my little lamb?" asked Gloria, looking at him closely. His lips were still partly open, and in the reflected light it looked as though he were smiling.

"Well, you're a sly one," she said. "Lookie, dear, just wait until I get out of this fur job I've got on. See, you're almost democratized already. To say nothing of myself.

Finding she couldn't get her coat off in the car without mussing herself all up, she opened the door. There'd still be plenty of time later for mussing.

"Missu Wiruson," said Tadashi.

"That's the name," said Gloria, and backed out of the car, enjoying the cool air on her calves. "Just wait until I take off this coat and we can..." She stood outside, still struggling with the fur coat her mother had sent her. "And then we can—"

The car door suddenly disappeared, and with it the car.

Tadashi drove so fast that he had only a fleeting image in the rear-view mirror of the lady struggling with her coat before she became a small, dim figure in the distance, and then disappeared in the complete darkness.

He drove away from the Susaki district as fast as he could, and at last found the bridge leading over the Sumida River from Fukagawa to Nihombashi. He drove across the bridge, where years before he had found the bicycle; and passed the corner of the Shirokiya Department Store, where he had bought his mother the bolt of cloth. A lone pedicab driver nearly fell off his bicycle before he succeeded in escaping the sedan. The tears in Tadashi's eyes blinded him, and finally he slowed down.

His tears were not caused by his fear of the inevitable deliquency report and its consequences, nor by his fear of the friendly lady. The day had another pattern: it was the pattern of his own failure to himself. Twice today he had been given the opportunity to become himself, to act upon his own convictions. He could have taken the soldier to Shinjuku. He could have satisfied the lady.

Ordinarily he would have had little compunction concerning either. Both were essentially friendly, human acts. To be sure, he would have been enormously in the lady's debt, but the situation was so unusual that he need not worry about obligations. And yet he had satisfied neither the soldier nor the lady, and, more important, he had not satisfied himself. He, who scorned the military, all militaries, who hated discipline, who wanted more than anything to become a real individual. In that he had failed, yet again.

Ahead were the lights of the Motor Pool, brilliant in the surrounding darkness. Individuality, Tadashi decided, was a luxury. Could one be an individual when there were mouths to be fed at home, when his job and not his soul was the most important thing there was? His own feelings seemed so unimportant by comparison that he was ashamed to think of them. He must think of others' feelings.

One of the first of whom he must think was Mrs. Ainsley, alone in the dark. In the middle of the ruins, she was miles from anything American. It would be hours before she could find her way back. He pitied her, out there alone with the ghosts of the dead, and he hoped nothing happened to her. And one more reason he should help her was that she was insane— he was sure of that. Why else should an American woman want what she had wanted from him?

The humiliation of telling what had occurred would be extreme, but he must do it. First, they could rescue the lady. Second, if they knew the truth, perhaps the final delinquency report would be withheld. Then he must go home. His wife would be very worried.

He parked the sedan. The guard at the door took the unsigned trip ticket in to the blond lieutenant. Tadashi followed him in, cap in hand.

The lieutenant looked at the trip ticket. "This is just your hard-luck day, isn't it, Tadashi?" he asked. "I don't know how you're going to get out of this."

Tadashi bowed, then turned to the Nisei sergeant and bashfully held his hat with both hands. He talked for a long time, and finally the sergeant understood.

The sergeant turned to the lieutenant. "Boy, he's gotta wild one! Says some dame made a pass at him."

"Geisha or what? What was he lugging around in that sedan anyway?"

"No, sir. An American girl."

"No kidding!" said the lieutenant and smiled. "Is he lying?"

"I don't think so, sir," said the sergeant. "He's all upset. He's too embarrassed to be lying."

"In that case," said the lieutenant, "the CID ought to be interested in this."

"Boy, they had a busy night, eh, Lieutenant?" said the sergeant.

"You can say that again."

"Yeah, like that major in Special Services. They're out dredging the Palace moat right now. Seems he was a real big operator. Them MP's in the jeep a while ago was telling me. Dollars, you know, and one of his boys got flighty and tossed a big hunk of scrip smack in the Emperor's front moat. They got a boat out there now and are fishing around for it. That's one fish I wouldn't mind hooking myself."

The lieutenant was filling out a form. "That's the truth," he said, then looked up. "Well, it takes all kinds—this is a good Saturday-night average for any man's army." He looked down at the report. "Here's another little job for the boys. He let her out at her house?"

"Hell no, she's out in that old ex-whore-district out near Fukagawa."

"How appropriate."

"If the little lady wanted fixing up, how come she started on the nationals I wonder," said the Nisei sergeant. "Hell, the whole Motor Pool is just ready and willing."

"You can count me out," said the lieutenant. "I don't think I'd be interested. By the way, did he get in?"

"Says not,"

"Probably didn't. He looks awful upset."

Tadashi turned to the sergeant and asked a quick question.

"Wants to know about his job," explained the sergeant. "If he gets a DR, it'll be his third, and you know the commander."

"Well, it's up to the Major actually, but if we get this dame and if she corroborates his story, he probably won't get the ax. So far it's just his word, but if she admits it, then he won't get anything except possibly the Silver Star for gallantry in action."

The Nisei soldier snickered. "Boy, I'd like to see the dame that would own up to a thing like that. Had it all planned too, looks like. Liked the looks of our boy here, called him up, and they had a little date. Some fun."

The lieutenant looked at Tadashi. "Well, he can always join the militarized police force. They're looking for ex-servicemen. Particularly officers. You know, he used to be a lieutenant once." He smiled at Tadashi, who smiled back; then he sighed, saying: "Well, there but for the grace of god go I."

He closed the paper folder. "We'd better call the

boys and get a search party out for our little lady in distress."

"Boy, what a bitch!" said the sergeant. "I can't understand how anyone can do anything like that—and a married woman too." He shook his head wisely. "She's just plain nuts."

"Oh, I don't know," said the lieutenant. "It's funny but she probably had good reasons for what she did. They all do. All these Saturday-night folks. They think about whatever they do beforehand, all of them."

The sergeant snickered and shrugged his shoulders.

"Anyway," said the lieutenant, smiling, "after something like this I like to remember that these folks are only a small percentage. I like to think about all the thousands of others we didn't hear anything about this evening. The peaceful citizens, you know. But these others—what do you suppose makes them like this over here? If they'd stayed back home, it wouldn't have happened probably. I don't think it's being American. I think it's winning the war that did it.... Well, we'd better inform our MP friends—and Mr. Ainsley too I suppose."

They both looked at Tadashi. He was looking at the floor, his cap still in his hands.

"These poor Japs!" the lieutenant said, shook his head, and picked up the phone.

The Nisei soldier looked at him warily, then smiled and showed his white teeth. "Yes, sir," he said, "that's what we used to say back in Seattle." He laughed. "These Japs!"

■

"How you spell that?" asked the corporal on night duty. "A - I - N, yeah, I got it, S - L, oh, Ainsley? Whyn't you say so." His white helmet was too big for him, and he kept pushing it up to get the phone next to his ear. "CID? Oh, won't have to call them. They're all here, really cluttering up the place. We got the Big Rowboat Mystery under way across the street, in the moat. You hear about it? Yeah, big deal. Everyone comes in here to warm his hands after paddling around out there. All the brass, you know." He lowered his voice discreetly, and continued. "Yeah, all big boys and more shavetails than you can shake a stick at, more goddamned lieutenants—What's that?" There was a long pause. "Yes, sir. Yes, sir. Yes, Lieutenant. Yes siree! Oh, no, sir. No. Thank you, sir."

He hung up the phone, his face red, then importantly beckoned two MP's over to him and began explaining.

In the other corner of the room stood a number of officers, some civilians, and one private. One of the civilians was talking to a colonel.

"I know, sir, but this man has already confessed. There is no mistake about it. I know he was your PIO, sir, but this has ceased to be the affair of Special Services, if you'll excuse my saying so. It belongs to us now."

"He is still under my command, sir," said the colonel, "and I intend to see that he and this soldier here have proper defense. It may be no longer an affair of Special Services—but it is certainly an affair of mine."

"I know how you must feel, sir, finding something like this in your command. But at the same time you're making it very difficult for us. Your actions, if I may say so, are quite unprecedented."

The colonel pulled his moustaches, then said: "I can well believe that they are. Still, do you think that I am wrong in demanding a fair trial for my men, in helping them in their difficulties."

"But they are guilty, sir," said the civilian.

"That remains to be proved," said the colonel.

"Look at it this way, sir. Don't you yourself believe them to be guilty?"

The colonel looked first at the major, then at the private, then at the civilian.

"No," he said slowly. "I believe them to be innocent."

"But the evidence—" began the civilian.

"Evidence be damned!" shouted the colonel and all the others looked at him. Then the civilian sighed, shrugged his shoulders, and moved away.

"Sir," said the private, "you oughtn't involve yourself like this."

The colonel looked at him, smiled, and put his hand on his shoulder. "Michael," he said, still smiling, "what else have I left to involve myself in? But I do wish you'd told me the truth, back in the theater."

"Why don't you just go home, sir?" asked the major. "I got myself into this, and I got him into it too. O'Hara's in on it too. I guess I got it coming."

"Oh, I'll go home," said the colonel, and the major looked at the floor. "But, first, you see, I've got to help my men. That is what an officer is for."

A lieutenant-colonel looked out of the window and said: "Well, shall we go back to the moat? Really, soldier, you might have picked a more convenient place to throw it."

Slowly they all went outside, and the MP behind the desk said: "So you go get her husband and then go out and pick her up, OK?"

"Us boys get the juiciest assignments," said one MP.

"Yeah, like our loco friend a while back."

"Who was that?" asked the MP behind the desk.

"He's in the guardhouse now. Got a big red nose. Funny as hell to look at. Charge was molesting the nationals. Got looped and then got into some kind of fight. Says he was just trying to be friendly and got a real crying jag on, tears running all over that big raspberry nose of his. They'll probably section-eight him out fast I bet."

"They'll stockade him even faster. Mac doesn't like the boys beating up his Gooks any more."

◼

It was near morning when Gloria reached her hotel. She was so tired she could scarcely walk. Her fur coat was heavier than sin. There had been not so much as a pedicab until she reached Ginza. By that time she had walked for hours. She'd walked in great circles over the burned rubble, terrified by the sound of the wind and dead leaves. When she reached the deserted streets, she'd taken wrong turnings, endless alleys which led only away from where she wanted to go. Finally she'd found a bridge, and then a pedicab. She told the startled driver the name of her hotel, and then fell asleep. He woke her at the hotel. She had no yen, so gave him all her cigarettes.

"No yen," she repeated to herself, but it wasn't so funny. She was too tired to laugh, and she was still frightened. An MP jeep had wailed behind her in the dark. One of her endless circles had taken her back to the spot where the sedan had left her, and she saw their lights in the ruins. Squatting down behind some rubble, she heard them calling: "Mrs. Ainsley! Mrs. Ainsley!" Well, at least the driver hadn't told her real name; maybe he didn't even remember it.

Another jeep drove up, and she heard Dave Ainsley's voice speaking in a rather dazed way to another occupant of the vehicle: "But I really don't understand it at all. What could she have been doing here? We were just ready to go to bed when she suddenly remembered something she'd forgotten to tell Madame Schmidt. Has anyone gone there to try to find her? I kept telling you, you know. What would she be doing here? Why won't any of you tell me?"

Well, thought Gloria, I guess I'm not the only one who'll have some explaining to do. Because Dottie's no more at Mrs. Schmidt's than I am—as Dave will discover soon enough. But she didn't feel at all guilty at having gotten Dottie into a mess of her own. It had to come sooner or later. Davie-boy couldn't go on forever living in a private heaven.

Then when the jeeps moved on, she'd run so fast in the opposite direction that she'd broken one of her heels. It was only now as she started into the hotel and thought of her appearance that she realized it.

The night clerk looked startled when she pushed open the door.

She smiled wanly and waved a hand. The boy bowed. He'd remember her, Gloria was sure of that. It was as though she had committed a murder and thought everyone knew about it. Still, she didn't stand much chance of being caught. That cute little driver just couldn't be that nasty to her. After all, what had she done to him anyway? Nothing. Besides, not all Japanese drivers got kissed by lovely American ladies—at least she hoped not.

But this time flippancy didn't work. The elevator boy, startled out of his sleep, looked at her curiously and bowed. There's another one who will remember me, thought Gloria, I must look a perfect mess. She hobbled off the elevator on her broken shoe.

She unlocked the door and turned on the light. It seemed ages since this morning. As she crossed over to the mirror she saw a note on the bed. It was from Sonoko:

"I think you please no forget pahti tomorrow in honor of best friend Miss Wirson." It was signed: "Very truly yours, Roomgirl."

No, she certainly wouldn't forget the "pahti," nor the day that had preceded it. Not for a long time. She looked at herself in the mirror. Yes, she was a perfect mess. Her lipstick was smeared, her hair mussed, her dress torn.

She looked at her face and, very slowly, said: "You whore!" Then she began to cry.

The tears ran slowly down her reflected face, and she, too tired to move, stood and watched them. She cried for a while, then washed her face with cold water. Seven in the morning was never like this, she thought; then she realized that it would soon be seven. Well, come seven and the great daily accounting for her sins, she'd be fast asleep and well protected.

Not for long though—the party. Well, at least it wouldn't be like a Muncie party, than which nothing could be worse. And, even though it was Sunday, it wouldn't be like those endless Muncie Sunday mornings. If she heard the name of Jesus Christ, she felt certain she would scream.

She was too tired to hang up her clothes, so she put her coat on the chair and patted its fur, as though it were a faithful animal. She flung her dress over the end of the bed, tossed her slip over the big doll with the broken wisteria and the "Off Limits" sign, and threw her brassiere and panties in the direction of the stalking tiger.

She stood, naked, in the center of the room, her arms around herself. It was cold, and she opened the window wider, standing in the autumn breeze. She felt like taking a bath, but decided not to. I wonder, she said to herself as she leaned out of the window, what it would be like to go straight—just for the kicks? I'm not the only pebble on the beach, and I could take up flower arranging or something like that. I'm actually a good kid, just a trifle impetuous, just a bit on the neurotic side. Better still—what if this good, virtuous kid went home to Muncie?

The idea hurt her so much that she positively enjoyed it. "Go home, go home," she repeated to herself, still leaning, naked, out of the window and looking at Tokyo sleeping beneath her.

After a while she sneezed and decided that if she were going to live and make good her resolves, she had better go to bed. She looked at the flag. It was tacked against the opposite wall, a Japanese flag, made of silk, the red ball hanging stark against the white. She didn't remember where she'd gotten it. Perhaps some officer had given it to her. Perhaps it had been in the room when she'd moved in, left behind by some former occupant.

The white field was covered with brush stokes. They were names—the names of a platoon, or a regiment, Gloria had no idea which. Hundreds of ink characters lay black upon the white silk, forming the names of men long dead.

Gloria stared at the names. Some were delicately drawn, with the finest of strokes; others were broadly painted, and the ink had run. She thought of these men who, perhaps only five years before, had gathered around this flag and carefully written their names. They had knelt ceremoniously, surrounding the flag, and each one, bending carefully forward, had left behind on the white silk his name. Then each had disappeared.

The flag made her feel sad, but not personally, painfully sad. It filled her with an enveloping sorrow very much like memory, very much like the sorrow she felt when looking at old photographs, or seeing old newsreels.

Naked, still hugging her shoulders, she looked at the flag, and a tear ran down her cheek. She was not feeling sorry for herself, nor for the dead soldiers. She didn't know why, but she felt sorry. She also felt cold.

She remembered the candy bars and, forgetting the flag, put a pile of them on her night stand so she'd be sure to remember them in the morning. For a moment she considered prayers on her knees—like a dear little child, all naked and chastened beside its bed. Then she decided against it. Probably would end up with pneumonia, and after all, one must be moderate in all things—even in virtue.

She climbed under the covers and decided she wouldn't compile that little list she'd been thinking of that morning after all. Instead she'd write a real book, maybe even about the Japanese. Everyone else had, so why shouldn't she—she who was on the verge of being an Authority? Maybe she and Swenson could compare notes or something. She'd call it *Live Better and Be Longer*, or something of this sort which was so popular nowadays.

Oh, well, tomorrow was another day, and the sun—in a sinfully short space of time—would dawn upon the new Gloria—Gloria, lady bountiful; Gloria, friend to the oppressed. Come to me, you homeless, starving, etc. That lovely, innocent party was just the note on which to start all over again—purest strawberry festival. Then it would be Monday—a new week, and she'd be back with her own little family: the dear Colonel; that good Joe, the Major; and, finally—for he had seemed most appreciative that evening—Private Richardson. She could hardly wait to get to the office—what a surprise!

She fell asleep very quickly.

■

Outside the window, the east was faintly pink, and the stars overhead were growing dim. Below, the street lights were extinguished, and the fires in the alleys cast the shadows of the waiting drivers behind them. Behind the paper windows of the houses were the lights of early risers.

The smoke of household fires and of waiting charcoal-burning taxis rose into the air. In the houses the bedding was folded into closets, and the mats were swept. Beneath the hanging pillars of the early rising smoke was the morning sound of night shutters thrust back into the houses' narrow walls; the sound of geta clicking on the pavement, the geisha hurrying home.

The rising sun cast the shadows of the buildings far behind them. The distant rails shone silver in the sun, and Greer Garson luxuriated, her paper face half in the shadow.

■

The morning train left Yokohama at precisely six-thirty, but it was Sunday and the train was not crowded. Sonoko had her choice of any of a dozen seats. Even the veteran with the double amputation and the sweetly pomaded hair found a seat.

Three times she had opened her *GI English*, and three times she had closed it again. Today was the day of the Party, and she simply could not concentrate. In just a few hours she would be again on the train, and beside her would be her beloved Miss Wilson.

At home the whole family had been up and ready for hours. The lunch was finished already—real Japanese home-cooking, which would certainly delight Miss Wilson. All cold and very good. Tender squid and nice raw fish and some lovely marinated sea-urchins which her father had been saving. And, in addition, "mother and child." The house was clean too, and they had all put on their best clothes.

In the tokonoma, the picture of Christ had proved to be an excellent likeness. He looked even more handsome than the hanging scroll he had supplanted. When Sonoko left, Mrs. Odawara had already arrived and was bustling about being very cheerful as she arranged the cushions for prayer meeting.

As Sonoko looked from the window, she was particularly pleased that nothing had gone wrong. Even Mrs. Odawara's suggestions of the day before now seemed just the thing with which to flatter and enchant the infinitely obliging Miss Wilson. She would be their guest!

Sonoko was so proud that she smiled at everyone on the train.

She felt in her pocket. There was the aspirin wrapped in a bit of tissue paper. Miss Wilson had asked for it yesterday, and then Sonoko had ungraciously forgotten all about it. She put the aspirin back in her pocket. The chances were that Miss Wilson would not need it this morning. Still, Miss Wilson was not nearly so healthy as she looked. She often had headaches when she first got up, and Sonoko was carrying the aspirin just in case. She wanted nothing to go wrong today.

And it really didn't seem in the least likely that anything would. Mrs. Odawara had taken care of everything, had even arranged for that intelligent nephew of hers who probably spoke English so well, the one who was so important in Transportation, to come and spend the day with them. Sonoko had seen his picture. He was very handsome, and Miss Wilson seemed to love beauty in almost everything, even in men.

He would doubtless be there when they returned, and he and Miss Wilson would be friends forever, and she would love them both, and Mrs. Odawara would stand over them, blessing them like the Christ Himself.

Sonoko smiled and looked out of the window. She could hardly wait for the moment when Miss Wilson—Gloria—saw Mrs. Odawara's nice nephew, Tadashi, the poor, but handsome boy from Fukagawa. She could just see Miss Wilson's face now!

Everything was going to be all right, but, still, life did have its responsibilities. With a happy grimace, Sonoko turned from the autumn landscape and opened *GI English*.

■ ■ ■